through

eyes

of

grace

by
Dave Payton

Illustrated by: Krissy K. Morse
Model: Kelsey Borth

Is God willing to prevent evil, but not able?
Then he is not omnipotent.

Is he able, but not willing?
Then he is malevolent.

Is he both able and willing?
Then whence cometh evil?

Is he neither able nor willing?
Then why call him God?

– Epicurus

Here's what readers have to say…

"You think you know, but you don't…"

"Each chapter gives you another twist!"

"Any advocate of the Prosperity Gospel
needs to read this…
and do some serious thinking."

"A great plot full of twists and turns that keep
you guessing while compelling you to examine
your own beliefs. Is life fair? Is God good? Is
God sovereign? It helped me see the world
through eyes of grace."

1.

SO THE BOOK SAYS...

Did God create a perfect world?

It may be hard to fathom that the Almighty Father would build great beauty in such a small amount of time. In six days, God created the sun, the stars, the moon, the waters, the planets, the animals, and the humans.

There was beauty all around. The plants were pleasing to the eye. The water was cool and clean. The sun was warm.

The male was created first, so the book says, and the Lord named him Adam. The book doesn't tell what the man looked like; only that the man was created in God's image. One can pontificate that the man was smart and handsome, but we really do not know. Adam was the firstborn of the Almighty Father, and Adam was loved, so the book says.

But Adam, the man, was lonely. And so the Father created a sister, a partner, a lover. The man decided that she would be called Eve, the mother of all beings.

She was beautiful. She was naked, as was the man, and they both felt no shame. The two frolicked in their beautiful space without a care in the world. They loved the Father, and in return the Father loved them, so the book says.

They were happy day-in and day-out. They hung and took care of the garden with no worry in the world. The two praised their Father, and the Father was pleased, so the book says.

Everything was perfect.

But was it?

No. Life was not perfect, because God created a talking snake waiting to devour them.

In perfection, there would be no temptation.

In perfection, there would be no talking snake to tempt them.

In perfection, there would be strength to counter the temptation.

No, it was *not* perfect.

A perfect father created an imperfect world.

Why?

That's the toughest question men and women of all walks have been asking since the onset of time:

Did humanity betray God—
or did God betray humanity?

Slowly suffocating, the two females trembled with fear, huddling in an upstairs bedroom as the hot flames crept closer and closer. All alone this night, the older sister hugged the younger and tucked her under her wing. By now, this fire engulfed the wood stairs, and at that juncture, the only way to safety was by jumping out of the second-story window. They could have thrown that soft mattress out the window, but neither girl was thinking, and even if they had been, the girls would not have been strong enough after the first few minutes of inhaling the intoxicating smoke.

The poor girls never knew what hit them or how it even started. They were close to dreamland when the whole nightmare began, and by the time they knew it, it was too late.

The older girl was the first to realize it as she had not yet succumbed to that tranquility of nighttime bliss. The youth flew downstairs as the smoke dashed furiously upstairs. Now standing safely outside, the older sister didn't know in that brief moment, she was choosing between her life and her death.

The girl could have run over to her neighbor's to call, but thinking a neighbor was already calling, that child ran back in the house to save her little sister.

It was only minutes after nine in the evening.

Surely someone was coming to get them.

Bravely through misty smoke and flames she drove, elbowing into her sister's bedroom. That younger sister was ceaselessly coughing and crying under her bed.

Older sister went under the bed, not knowing what to do. The paralyzed children cried under the bed, each pleading to her apparently merciful and loving heavenly father as he was on a prolonged cigarette break.

The girls waited for a hope that never came.

Not twenty minutes later, three strong firemen burst into the house and brought them out of the burning, collapsing building.

But it was too late. They were already sleeping.

The children never had a chance.

7

Seth Adams is the pastor at Oostburg Community Church in Oostburg, Wisconsin. Oostburg? Oh, yes, it's a real small town with real small people in it. Oostburg is the type of town where everyone knows your name. And they know your mother's name, and so they know her mother's name, too. Approximately 1,000 people stayed in Oostburg, married in Oostburg, and reproduced in Oostburg. Life started in Oostburg and it ended here, too. Dreams were achievable and easy: two people get married, raise their two children, and spoil four grandkids.

His dreams were no different. Pastor Seth always had the nudge to be a preacher. From a very early age, Seth knew he had the desire to tell others about Christ and His love for people, His plan for people.

His parents were church-going, Lord-fearing folks who brought Seth and his younger sister to church. Seth's dad worked in a cheese factory—the family loved to joke that he was paid to cut the cheese—for forty-three years before having an unexpected heart attack at sixty-three. The sudden death of Seth's father—and six months later his mother—were the first challenges of his faith.

The first of many.

His beautiful bride Evelyn is forty-three, almost two years behind Seth. They met in high school when she transferred from Kiel. Her dad's small factory position relocated thirty minutes south and, thankfully for Seth, dad brought his sweet daughter along. Seth knew the moment his eyes set on her that he would be asking her out one day. Seth did not realize it would take several attempts to get the date, but he was not going to give up.

It was her large blue eyes that first caught his attention. Eyes are important; they are the windows to the soul as many people attest. One eye could see pessimism while the other might glance at optimism. It really all depends on what chapter of your life you see those things. Could you be bitter? Or… will you see the world "through eyes of grace" and forgive, as scripture calls for each of us to pursue?

Evelyn Wick was a hard candle to light. It took a year of asking and patience. Seth's faith and devotion toward Christ didn't help as the gal didn't attend church. Her father was an atheist until a second before he died. Then he gave his life to Christ; it was either genuine or a get-out-of-Hell-free card, as Seth will one day find out.

In his senior year of high school, Seth asked Evelyn to a church evening and finally got the date. Her father's response was: "Why can't you kids be normal and just have sex in a car?" A year later, when Evelyn told him this, they both got a huge, hearty laugh. After the laughs died, Evelyn looked at him in the eyes and he thought for sure they were going to wrestle for the first time. Thankfully, Seth—ok, she—was able to resist and they ended up saving their bodies for marriage. Yeah, it was hard—pardon the pun—but they achieved what every Christian aimed for: purity until their wedding night.

Though Evelyn Wick was not a full, true Christian at the time, Seth encouraged his gal daily to see the blinding light and make that life-long commitment to Christ. It was wearying and tough, but she eventually gave her life to Christ as Seth started attending Moody Bible College in Chicago. When he left, she still had two years of high school, and so it was their faith in Christ and in their relationship that got them through these two years of distance. During that painful separation, she got a part-time waitressing job at this local restaurant, Knotty Pine, and was able to put away a nice spot of money to pay for part of his tuition—much to the angry displeasure of Mr. Wick. Even before they were married, Seth Adams and Evelyn Wick were partners. Friends.

Nothing could tear them apart.

Nothing...

2.

THIS IS HIS STORY

Seth Isaiah Adams and Evelyn Anne Wick became Mr. and Mrs. Adams on Saturday, October 12, 1996. They were happily married by Garry Britton—the man Seth would replace at the only pulpit in Oostburg.

Their congregation had saved up enough to purchase them a surprise honeymoon cruising on the Caribbean. Seth's dream was to just simply go north to Door County and spend a weekend in a log cabin not watching television, but some plans people make don't follow through. It made Seth contemplate never making plans at all: winging sermons, eating whatever he found in the refrigerator, and not worrying so much about the higher calories. He tried to plan, and whenever he did, it usually didn't go according to schedule.

It was on this free honeymoon that Seth developed quite the desire for gambling. Seth sat hours and hours just playing bingo, roulette, and poker. They spent about two hundred dollars on bingo cards and didn't see a dime in return. Evelyn did not understand, but she supported her husband as any dutiful wife would do. Didn't want to have their first battle be over how much they spent at bingo.

After all, the cruise was free anyway.

One evening on their way back to their stateroom, they "unexpectedly" passed by the casinos. Glancing in, the pastor asked his gal if they could stop in for just a minute. The woman submitted even though she was tired, and if they were going to get their sixth tackle of sex in, they better do it now.

Seth chose the casino that moment, and thus began a long line of sad disappointments for Evelyn. They went in at eleven o'clock at night, and Seth left at three in the morning. Evelyn quit at one and ended up going to bed on her own for the first time in their three-day marriage.

Even though Seth won twenty-thousand dollars that night, Seth lost big.

Pastor Seth returned to the stateroom and quickly noticed Evelyn's green down pillows were slightly damp, apparently from tears. Her black mascara had fallen below her soft cheek staining the pillows. Seth thought about waking her for the apology and their first make-up sex but he didn't. Seth decided to snuggle into bed and lay next to her, gently caressing her hands with his. Evelyn did not wake; or pretended not to, the pastor wasn't sure. But one thing he was sure of: for the first night in their short marriage, they weren't going to be intimate. He waited until morning to tell her about the winnings. She didn't seem as excited as he was. Seth and Evelyn's free honeymoon ended up costing them more than quite a bit.

After that evening, Seth Adams was hooked. He began playing the lottery, too. In addition, the pastor found a bookie so he could place a bet on many sporting events. He won a lot and he lost a lot.

Of course, being a minister, Adams kept this from everyone; his wife, his sister, his congregation, and when you keep a secret from people, it is oftentimes wrong. Seth continued to justify his tiny addiction by telling himself that it wasn't a sin. After all, he was using the money for God's Kingdom... and scripture does say to use your money for the holy glorification of His purposes. Seth's winnings jumped to various places like church renovations; other winnings went to the mission. He spent his winnings wisely, even if Adams was getting them sometimes illegally. With this logic, Seth could justify robbing a bank, too.

Well, dang. Suppose it is a sin...

That is the tricky thing about the scriptures.

Men and women alike use scriptures to build their own opinions; murder anybody if there is a right reason behind it. The death penalty, wars, abortions. Adam and Eve got the death penalty, and all they did was steal a piece of fruit. Yes, they stole; they were guilty. But let's be honest: their punishment did not fit their crime. If somebody went to Walmart and stole an orange, surely they would not get the death penalty.

And you know what? No one is perfect; including pastors. Adams sinned like everyone else. It was tiring when everyone in the town saw him be this triumph of Christian morality. Sometimes Seth couldn't bear it. He should've turned to the Lord, but Seth usually ended up turning to his computer bookie instead, whom he had yet to meet.

And this secret online bookie called himself: 1timothy610@aol.com.

Seth did not know any "Timothy".

Ok, so here we commence. What is so special about a middle-aged man who occasionally rolls the dice? He's a hypocrite, for sure, but so are many others: pastors, kids, cops, authors. What's so important about Seth Isaiah Adams? Did Seth cure cancer? Surely not. Is Seth the first minister ever to battle with temptation? Also, surely not. But here, Seth Adams is about to meet something so horrendous, that it's worth bringing forth to light.

This is his story.

Pastor Adams enjoyed watching home movies they had filmed across the years. Birthdays, Christmas, firsts—first time in the snow; first BBQ, etc. One particular video was watched frequently to remind himself how imperfect he was—how in one small, significant second you can relinquish everything you hold close. Life really does just happen second-to-second, not year-to-year.

In this particular DVD, he watched as his daughter, Grace Bela almost got killed by a car.

Oh yes, before we move on: Seth and Evelyn were blessed over time with two daughters. Grace Bela Adams, whom Seth and many others—not Evelyn— call Gracie, came into their easy lives on April 17, 1999. Gracie was not planned— at least not by them—for the parents yearned to be financially stable before they brought a kid into this world. Nonetheless, Seth and Evelyn were surprised and thrilled when they found out she was carrying their first child.

This child was as perfect as humanly possible. Of course, her dad was biased, but she really was a decent young gal. Last year, 2015, she raised two thousand dollars all by herself. Babysitting, doing odd jobs and other people's chores, walking dogs. She wanted to earn the money, not just take it. The trip didn't cost as much as she raised, so Gracie ended up buying things for the poor citizens of Mexico—items like toothpaste, shoes, and other items Americans take for granted.

Every February, Seth and his Gracie attended this daddy-daughter ball held by Campus Life, a ministry that helps teens and younger kids get in touch with the Lord: an organization that Oostburg Community Church was proud to support any chance they could. The daddy-daughter dance was a special, once-a-year date night that gives fathers that opportunity to show their daughters how a boy is supposed to treat them. This was Seth's favorite moment as a father, taking his special girl to the daddy-daughter dance. He stopped to wonder—he couldn't think of one moment where Gracie ever had a date. There was a teen in their congregation, Matt, whom Seth liked quite a bit. Matt was a good student, and the pastor was sure he would wait till marriage.

Unlike Gracie, Seth and Evelyn's second daughter, Lainey Michele, was planned because her parents felt it was time for Gracie to be a sister. Lainey joined the family on June 6, 2003. Lainey was a tiny, fierce spitfire—ok she still is—but they curbed her somewhat. There is always that cold fear that when parents curb a spitfire that perhaps they are taking away aspects that God bestowed upon them, but both folks felt their second girl Lainey needed to learn how to be a tad more, shall we say, pleasant. The youth did not even want to attend the daddy-daughter dance, which broke Seth's heart. For one, Lainey did not enjoy socializing, and second, she did not like to dance. In time, he got over it, as Seth and Lainey became more and more distant.

Anyway, back to the video. In addition to filming, Seth Adams was also barbequing. Adams was not much of a handyman, but he could work a cell phone camera and upload videos. God gives every man and woman different gifts, and modern technology wasn't one of the "gifts" of Seth.

As Seth was grilling, he noticed in the corner of his eye the girls throwing a ball around as they dodged their two smaller cousins. Lainey tossed this ball past Gracie, and Gracie ran into the street to catch it. She was more focused on the blue ball than on the speeding car squealing down their slender road. Gracie ran into that road and before Seth could react, his brother-in-law swooped in and saved Gracie, almost killing them both.

The video goes haywire here, but Seth remembered what happened:

He dropped the phone on the ground and ran to his little girl. He took her out of his brother-in-law's arms and held his girl as tight as he could.

"Please Gracie, forgive me! Forgive me... for not being there!"

To which the gracious eleven-year-old replied:

"Of course, daddy. I forgive you. Now *you* forgive you!"

Seth hugged his daughter tight as he saw the car speed away, not even to stop and see if they were safe nor were they even bothered that they might have just committed manslaughter.

That one guy who almost ran over his princess. He can—

Stop, Seth. Forgive... forgive...

How could Adams forgive someone who almost killed his baby? One of these days pastor would hopefully meet him and punch him in the—

Forgiveness.

Punch him in the forgiveness?

That doesn't make sense.

Forgiveness.

Isn't that what you preach, Seth Isaiah?

"Yes, it is Lord. And she is still in my arms, in one piece. I... can forgive. I can forgive..."

And he felt the Lord almighty preach down to him, as clear as the sunset:

"One day, Seth Adams—PASTOR Seth Adams—
you will have to forgive the unthinkable..."

3.

NEW YORK CITY

Vicki Weathers walked up the stuffy corridor with a knot in her belly, smelling the puke mound that tried to hide by the wall. Not very well hidden, for the ugly, pungent stench rose above the sad padding of a days-old newspaper that pretended to act as a broom. Perhaps not ironically, Hillary and Trump were on the cover.

Entering the lobby area of her police department, she approached the desk. Her good ally, Patty Dole, was there and on the phone, passing on a potentially secret tip. Vicki couldn't help but eavesdrop. Apparently, the stolen car was found on Greene Street: a silver four-door Honda that had been missing for a few days.

She missed the hustle, her final case being two years past. Longing for one more chance, she knew deep down that she would probably never return to the dark streets of New York.

Vicki continued to wait as Patty jotted down a secret juicy tip. Vicki was removed from the department after her mental breakdown but desperately wished fate was different.

She loved her beat, perhaps caring a bit too much. Oftentimes, when you care too much about anything, that is when you get in trouble.

And Vicki got in trouble, and pretty bad. She had found the murderer of Gabrielle Adjami. Unfortunately, her boss believed she had made a tiny mistake. Sam had an ironclad alibi, and so the police did not deem him a suspect anymore.

But Vicki could not let it go.

Sam Fogarty did kill Gabrielle Adjami on a cold March night in 2014, but Vicki couldn't prove it.

It was not fair. It was not fair how an innocent, carefree teenager could just vanish... and then one day turn up in pieces.

Life wasn't fair.

Vicki had attended church for quite a bit of time before giving up those thoughts of a "loving Father." A loving father would not let all these things happen to the children he created. No, there couldn't be a loving god. He was either uncaring or not real at all.

This newfound questioning of faith broke the sick heart of Vicki's mother—yes, literally—for on the day Vicki questioned the almighty ruler, the almighty ruler gave Vicki's mother a fatal heart attack.

How nice, mr. god.

Vicki had been a cop for some time; her baptism by fire week on the force was... September 2001. On the eighth day of her career, Vicki faced the cruelest enemy of all as two low-flying planes smashed into the World Trade Center.

And Vicki ended up at the scene of terrorism. She did get seven scared workers out of North Tower but lost three others, as well as her first partner. Officer Jay Miller and Vicki had powered up through several flights of stairs when they found ten people scared to wits end in an office. Vicki led the team downstairs with Miller book-ending the back of the line. Just as the group was about to exit the unstable, burning building, the whole ceiling collapsed, killing Miller and three of the ten. Vicki got out, with the seven, but it didn't matter how many she saved.

Vicki only kept track of how many she lost.

Gabrielle was the twenty-first loss.

Gabrielle was seventeen and gorgeous, with brown, stringy hair and sparkling green windows. She attracted attention, and there was a long line of boyfriends.

Sam Fogarty slashed Gabrielle into thirteen parts and got away with it, parading the streets of New York, waiting to strike again.

And the god sat back; sitting on his golden, cold throne, popping hot popcorn into his big mouth, perhaps even laughing at the tiny puppet show called Earth that he created. Laughing and smiling at humanity.

Vicki nodded to the heavens and raised her skinny appendage as Patty looked over.

"Hi, Vicki. Here to see the Chief?"

"Yes, four o'clock."

Patty picked up the phone, speaking to the Chief:

"Yes, Weathers is here. Will do."

Patty hung up and smiled.

"You know where he is. And Vicki, I miss you."

Vicki smiled. Patty was a good friend, but a good friend that had very little power in helping poor Vicki change her current dilemma.

"Thanks, Patty."

"Coffee sometime?"

"Sure."

She walked about the collection of cubicles until she caught the last door on the right: Gagliano's.

Vicki Weathers knocked before entering; being one who followed the protocol even if she was being cruelly treated.

"Come in."

Slowly entering, she could tell that not much had changed in her four-month absence. Gagliano, though committed to losing weight, had seemingly gained twenty pounds. Captain Tony Gagliano was a large guy and loved his cannolis. Lucky for Vicki's metabolism or she would have weighed a solid two bills, too. Standing at five-foot-six, two-hundred on Vicki's scale would have been fifty miles over the speed limit.

The room smelled of mint cigarettes, another vice Tony Gagliano had promised to defeat by her return. His wife had left him because she couldn't stand kissing an ashtray anymore. That and she found the sexy new mailman delivered a nice package.

Rough combination for Gags.

"Have a seat, Vicki."

Gagliano closed the silver door and Vicki's heart shrunk. She hated shut door meetings; usually, they were not a good sign.

Weathers had been doing better. The woman skipped less therapy and picked up yoga. In her spare time, she also enjoyed smoking cancer sticks, but she wasn't going to let that camel out of the pack.

"How's Kim?" Vicki asked.

"She's a bitch."

Vicki paused for a second to see the distance her humor could go.

"Always was," Vicki joked.

Weathers and her chief shared a small laugh. They had a great camaraderie, which made the situation a tad harder on both ends.

They looked at each other for ten seconds before Gagliano split the air.

"How you doing, Vicki?"

Small talk. Vicki didn't love it so much, but she could improvise when necessary. After all, she began it by asking about his failing marriage.

"Fine. Ready to get back on the streets."

She was too and tired of staring at those stupid inspirational cat posters as well as chilling with cats who looked like said posters.

"I am glad to hear that."

Vicki smiled. She passed and was going to get her badge back! All her work and counseling paid off. Thank ... um, well. Herself. Thank herself.

"I wish your statement were true, though."

The warm bubble inside Vicki decreased. Vicki was going to be stuck in that overly priced apartment that she could barely maintain when she was working. She was on medical leave, but it was getting harder financially as well as psychologically.

"Are you saying I'm not fine?"

Please... Please, coach. I hate the sidelines.

"I don't see it, Vic. I wish I did. Believe me."

Vicki did believe Gags. At that moment she hated him, but she believed him.

"I just don't think it's gonna happen."

Gagliano searched.

"At least not here in New York."

Vicki felt liquid clouding both eyes, but she was not going to lose them, not in front of Gagliano. Vicki rarely cried. She punched things and destroyed pillows, cussed a little—okay, a lot—but rarely... cried. She doubted that punching a wall would help her case, especially after what she learned in anger management. And she hated anger management; it made her so... angry. Maybe she should show the feminine tears...

"Chief—"

Gagliano cut her off quickly:

"Victoria. Take a couple of months. Continue your therapy. Try... please, for the love of God try to forget about Gabrielle."

Gagliano went to his coffee bar and began to make his cup of joe. A tactic he used when he wanted to pass off a difficult conversation.

"Forget? She's just a child!" Vicki pled.

"You haven't gotten over it—"

Vicki stood up.

"Chief, I did everything by the book! Everything! And still nothing!"

Vicki could feel the bitchy growing inside of her and see her arms develop and her breasts burst from her shirt. She felt like tossing his coffee bar, but then she recalled that was what got her in hot crap the first time.

"I'm sorry Weathers. You are off for now. I need cops—"

"Who apparently care less!" argued Vicki.

"No! I need—*New York* needs cops who can handle the mental stressors of this job. You... have lost some steps, Victoria. Right now I can't even let you sharpen pencils."

Vicki left Gagliano's office without saying good-bye, returning three seconds later to toss his coffee bar.

Vicki walked down the dark, grey corridor knowing she would never return. At least not as part of the force. Maybe in cuffs as a prisoner, but certainly not as a cop.

She turned the corner to see an adult roughing up a teenage girl. Vicki knew the cop, Will Diaz, and also knew that Diaz enjoyed roughing up prisoners. Apparently, Diaz was a better cop than she, since she was now taking the walk of shame.

She went back to her corner of the city to gather her belongings. She didn't have much remaining, for the force had been slowly handing her crap back to her one-by-one. The only things that remained were a few sketchbooks in a drawer—and a photo of her old Aunt Coralee, who lived about twenty-something hours away in a little podunk town in Wisconsin.

Vicki couldn't lay in New York anymore. She could not inhale the streets, the trash, and the citizens without being able to protect them. She knew as a cop she could help, but without the badge, there was little Vicki could do, unless she became Batman.

So, for the first time in her thirty-seven years, she was at a complete loss. Vicki picked up the photo and left.

She walked the three and a half miles back to her small, depraved apartment in Harlem. Harlem was a rough crowd, but Vicki had gotten used to it. If someone could deal with 9/11, you could deal with anything.

She opened her dirty refrigerator and cracked a beer. It overflowed a little, dripping on the hardwood floor. Lucky for Vicki, her four cats were alcoholics who liked to lick up the beer stains.

After ordering a pizza, Vicki plopped down on the couch. Staring at the three corners of her tiny studio, Vicki began to feel dizzy. It wasn't the beer... it was simply the truth that she had nothing to do, nowhere to go. For the first time, she was without any direction. A total end, or as some people see it, a new beginning.

She had to leave New York.

But first, she needed to vomit all over the floor.

The pizza guy arrived twenty-seven minutes later. Standing by the fire escape, Vicki knew a large pie for one average-sized woman and four cats was going to last at least a day.

At least she had that to look forward to.

Vicki spent the next three hours flipping through channels. A silly infomercial on a shiny knife that was strong enough to cut through shoe had garnered her att—

What the hell am I doing?

Vicki had few options. She had friends, but most were married with brat kids, and she didn't want to be a setback for them. Nor did she even like kids: they were incredibly annoying, even the obedient ones, and she did not want to end up a glorified babysitter.

No, Vicki was pretty much alone. And mom died the year before, 2015.

She never met her father.

She did have that aunt: the crazy old Coralee who lived in Wisconsin.

Coralee was her mother's sister; couldn't recall if she were older or younger. She lived in a spot with a population of about a thousand. She could not recall the name of the place, for she had never been there. She did have a fun cousin in Green Bay, Jessica, whom she hadn't seen in quite some time.

Maybe a road trip was in order.

She picked up the phone and dialed.

"Hello?" said the voice on the other line.

"Jessica, it's Vicki."

"Vicki! Long time no hear! How are you?"

"Um, well do you want the truth or a lie?"

"A lie, of course."

Vicki could see Jessica smiling on the other end.

"Well... I just gave an old dude some crack right before he left for a campaign rally."

"Exciting. What did it taste like?"

"The blood, sweat, and tears of Mexico."

The ladies burst into laughter.

"And the truth?"

Vicki sighed and gave Jessica the truth:

"I lost my job. I doubt I ever get it back."

"Sorry, cuz. I know how much being a cop means to you."

"Yeah. I hate it when the bad guys get away."

"I know." Jessica paused. "So what's your next chapter?"

"Just sitting in my apartment eating a pizza."

"Exciting. I wish I could run to NYC and help you finish."

Vicki smiled.

"I love you, Vicki."

"Love you too, Jess."

There was a pause on the other end before Jessica had the courage to muster up the new information.

"Mom's not really doing so hot."

"Sorry, Jess."

"Yeah. She's slipping fast. Dementia... sometimes does that. One day she'll be fine, and the next day, she won't even remember my name."

"Sorry."

"Yeah. So... I guess there is no chance you would return, huh? How long have you been in NYC anyway?"

"Um, mom brought me to NYC in... eighty-eight. So I've been here... twenty-eight years."

"Yeah. Wisconsin is quite different."

"Maybe I need different."

"You could just give it a try, maybe come out for a few months or so. Give her a call."

"I certainly don't have anything to achieve these final fifty years of my life. The only thing left on my bucket list is death."

"Oh stop being so morbid, Vicks. Give her a call. She misses you. She's not the only one."

"Can I move in with you?"

"Sorry, cuz."

"A couch?"

"We have a couch, but you know Dave thinks you're a bitch."

"Tell your husband I am a bitch."

"But, seriously, mom really needs you. Please cuz, call her. For me."

"Okay. I will."

"Promise?"

"Yes... I promise."

It was a tad of a chore to call Aunt Coralee. She was dear and witty... but there was something different about her.

She had *Jesus*.

A couple of days later, Vicki fulfilled that tough promise.

Aunt Coralee loved the idea of Vicki's moving west. Since Coralee's dementia had gotten worse, she lost her driving license—not that old Coralee minded getting rides from the handsome men of Oostburg. Coralee bragged about how she gave some teenage girl piano lessons three times a week, but other than her church activities, Coralee really had not much going on.

Coralee needed Vicki as much as Vicki needed Aunt Coralee.

So Vicki decided that she was going to accept her aunt's contract of free room and board in exchange for Vicki driving her around and attending church activities. She didn't love the deal, but free rent is free rent; and given that she had had only disability the previous months, she had no choice, and she could surely use the change of scenery. Besides, Aunt Coralee had promised Vicki an interview with the local sheriff's office since one of the older deputies recently retired. Maybe things were looking positive for little podunk Oostburg.

The hardest thing was leaving her cats. Her aunt was allergic to felines, and a twenty-hour car ride with four cats would be hell on wheels.

She could not find anyone who wanted four, so she ended up splitting the cats. The super of her apartment building took the two males, Bert and Ernie.

A former friend took the two females, Sexy Thelma and Slutty Louise.

Vicki chose not to tell her former friend and current enemy that old Sexy Thelma was pregnant.

Oops.

It didn't take Vicki long to pack her belongings.

She had very few clothes as she was not the average, stereotypical female. And since she was moving into her aunt's home, Vicki had no use for any of her crappy old furniture; so she sold it all for three hundred dollars and a pack of mint cigarettes. Vicki had not decided if she would fill her sweet aunt in on that little secret.

Perhaps she'll quit smoking on the way.

And on Tuesday, a colder day in October, Victoria Weathers started the next chapter of her life.

Vicki typed into her cell: "Oostburg, Wisconsin", on her Google Map.

It was a solid fourteen hours from Harlem.

4.

MY NAME IS DOROTHY

Since Vicki was not in any hurry to get to chilly Wisconsin, she decided she was going to make a joyride of it. The interview was on Friday, but the sheriff told her "whenever" was fine as well. Did not seem like they stuck to much of a schedule out there in the boondocks. The sheriff was also quite clear that he did not really need another body, but he was content to have one more. Apparently, there were only two other officers on their force.

She decided to stay in Pennsylvania on Tuesday night. She stopped at a silent bed and breakfast in the middle of Bloomsburg. Two lesbians owned the joint, and they each seemed to use Vicki to make the other jealous. One gal would fluff Vicki's pillow while the other made a pie from scratch. The pillow fluffing lesbian won as the pie had some pecan in it. A little awkward, but again this was the new life brave Vicki was carving for herself. Things were going to change. Things were going to be slower and easier. Vicki was going to go with the flow, be calm, and have less rage.

Vicki left Sally and the other Sally early Wednesday morning, hoping to hit Cleveland by lunchtime. Vicki was not used to driving long distances; she did drive in New York City, but she was frequently in the passenger's seat as her partners were usually older males. On her days off, Vicki did not use her car much either, since New York City boasted one of the greatest public transportation systems in the world. *You were an idiot to use your car for anything*, she thought.

The country was idyllic. It wasn't anything Vicki was used to, but she enjoyed the peacefulness.

Cleveland came around noon, and she wanted to get a tour of the Rock'n Roll Hall of Fame. She stopped for a break from the travel to stretch those appendages and enjoy hardcore rock'n roll. She had never been to Ohio, other than a drive-by when she was a teenager.

She got to Fort Wayne, Indiana, by Wednesday night and stayed with a friend from college who relocated after she married. The friend, Kari, had two and a half kids that were very excited to meet Vicki. The two noisy kids were bothering each other and pulling each other's hairs, screaming for some seventy hours straight before going to bed where they continued to bitch for another two hours. Vicki decided today was not going to be that moment she stopped her cancer sticks, and she lit one up by the swing set.

Saying good-bye to Kari, her husband, and the brats, she got into her crummy car and headed for windy Chicago.

Vicki sighed with huge relief as she could see the grey buildings. Glancing up the giant skyscrapers, one could hardly notice the differences between the cities. Vicki had been gone for two days, and she was already missing the big city. She hoped this was not an inkling that she had made the wrong decision, but then again, it was not like Vicki was marrying dear Coralee and promising to be her caretaker for all of eternity.

Vicki drove past a homeless person and decided to stop, planting the car at a meter.

Walking around the corner, she was content to see the homeless woman still there.

"Can I buy you lunch?"

The homeless woman grinned and spoke: "Praise the Lord! Another blessing!" which almost made sullen Vicki lose her breakfast.

Vicki took the woman to a nearby restaurant where they were able to talk about their lives and histories. Vicki guessed that her new friend had not showered this week, but Vicki wasn't going to let that deter this new friendship. Being from New York, Vicki had had many special encounters with the homeless population, and she didn't desire to stop now. Vicki predicted that by moving to small Oostburg she probably would not bump into another homeless person again, so she reveled in this potentially final opportunity.

"My name is Dorothy."

At the restaurant, Dorothy spoke of her life as if she hadn't talked in a week.

"I lost my husband in eighty-one. Reginald had... some, um, financial setbacks if you will, and found that the death clause in his insurance policy would help his wife and son. Unfortunately, this death clause was also invalid due to suicide, so we didn't receive one nickel."

"Sorry to hear." Vicki took one sip of her drink. "Where's your son?" she asked.

"RJ died in Iraq in ninety-one."

The sad story enraged Vicki with more anger for the king of kings. Here was a perfectly happy young family, ripped to nothing because they could not even afford to live. Living was so horrendous that the husband thought death was the better solution.

Vicki held back her opinion as she didn't want to inform Dorothy that it was silly to believe a heavenly being could love her. She sat and smiled quite a bit during that lunch. Crying on the inside. Covering the hurt. Faking smiles. She had gotten used to it.

"Listen, Dorothy. I don't need to be in Wisconsin until tomorrow afternoon. Would you like to be my guest tonight? Hotel for two?"

Dorothy beamed.

Hours later, after the tasty meal and the shower, Vicki and Dorothy laid side-by-side. Vicki was happy to do her good deed for the day.

She could not sleep, due to Dorothy's snoring and her own rambling thoughts.

Vicki's interview wasn't for another twenty or so hours, and Oostburg was now only three hours from here. Sweet Dorothy was so excited to receive the burger, and now a shower, that she was incredibly giddy. An elderly black woman preaching about how good God was to her.

Father, Lord Almighty. Vicki just did not get it. There was so much suffering in this world; all over the planet and god just seemed to be zoning at the wheel. The Father is so powerful, right?

Why doesn't God do something about the homeless people? Why doesn't he do something about cancer? Why doesn't god do something about terrorism? Does god hate homosexuals? Well, then perhaps god should stop creating them.

Oh god.

She was about to enter old Aunt Coralee's den of Jesus. Probably the guest room had pictures of Jesus Christ too, maybe the cross. Maybe, for the rest of her life, she would have to sleep at the foot of the cross.

And it hit Vicki.

Perhaps this was not going to be simple. Perhaps this was all a mistake.

Vicki zoned out on her roommate Dorothy and began internalizing everything. She was no longer confident of her decision.

Aunt Coralee was going to make her go to church. Probably prayers and maybe even have a one-on-one Bible study. And there was nothing she could do if she wanted to live rent-free. But it was not even the free rent; she had promised her cousin that she would look after her dear mother, and she was a woman of her word. Vicki needed to take care of her Aunt Coralee, and then she would have to go to church to do it. And then... she was going to bump into the pastor. And he would want to talk, too. Talk about how Christ loves Vicki even though her pops ran away before she was hatched and her mother struggled to make ends meet years as a single mother in New York City. And then...

Crap.

She made a mistake.

Vicki left Dorothy a hundred dollar bill and made the dreaded drive north to the frozen tundra. Every thought in her brain was negative now. It was too late, she reasoned, as Aunt Coralee and Jessica were counting on her. If it wasn't for Jessica, she probably could've made a U-turn, for Aunt Coralee may have forgotten she was coming.

She remembered some advice her mother gave her:

"Everyone, at some point in their life,
comes to the proverbial fork.
It doesn't matter if you're old or young.
It doesn't matter if you're right or wrong.
The right choice for one
may be the wrong choice for another.
You may have regrets one day;
but today is not the day for regrets.
Life is a game of chances.
You win some; you lose some.
I have loved; and I have been loved.
I have sought; and I have found.
I have lived, and I have—"

Vicki's mother said this minutes before she died.

It was true though. Everyone has a path to take. Those paths may be different for others but we all have to follow that inner nudge that guides us down the next alley. We don't know where it will lead, but we do know—or at least think—that it's the right step.

Christians like using the phrase: "He doesn't give you the total journey; he gives one step at a time."

She recalled that from her childhood when she did believe.

Having your mom pass away from a heart attack can change an outlook on whether or not god loves his people.

Vicki wondered who she would meet in little ol' Oostburg...

5.

MEET THE OOSTBURGERS

Coralee Mentink was a sixty-five-year-old gal and getting ready for that next chapter of life. As she rearranged the room, Coralee got goosebumps like a schoolgirl giddy for a sleepover.

The food was all set up. It had been a long while since Aunt Coralee bought for two. The eggs went in the dryer—next to the toothpaste, of course—and the seven boxes of saltine crackers were placed in the freezer. The cabinets had room for the three gallons of milk she had bought, and the shovel looked nice under her sofa.

Coralee checked the cold room to make certain her adult niece would have all the amenities the lady would need. One toothbrush, two pillows, a small stuffed bear, and a baby doll.

"I hope Veronica still loves baby dolls," Coralee wondered as she prepared Victoria's new bedroom.

There was a knock on the door. Coralee started to cry and quickly grabbed her shovel...

It fucking sucks being short, the man thought to himself.

At sixty-three inches, he was not going to gather his large dreams. They were too sky high for his little body, and everyone knew it.

Most painfully, Wesley knew it.

It is a taller man's planet. No one says this out loud, but most everyone knows it. If you are a male and under five-nine, you might as well stab yourself in the neck. It is okay for a lady to be short. They can wear heels.

Being short costs men lots of things; females for sure prefer a tall guy. If a man is shorter than a gal, he should not waste his time talking to her. He is just going to get his heart broken. Sports? Forget it. Don't even try. Others will make fun of you and beat the hell out of you.

What hurts men most over the lack of height is it robs them of chances in life... but even something more than girls and jobs.

It robs men of their *confidence.*

Smaller males usually do not reach—pun intended—their dreams. The men dream and eventually fade away; fading into the background while working at some little nothing store.

Wesley Demko was bored as Hades at the counter of the lone local video store. It was close to lunch when he could be by himself and write the intricate chapters of his first novel. One never knows when one will come up with that great idea. Sometimes good ideas would flow, like an angry fight with a Mexican infusion of diarrhea; other times he would need that laxative. This was one of the latter.

Wesley yawned as a teenage boy threw DVDs on the counter.

"Hey D. B.! Pay attention!" scolded the teenager.

Wesley could not believe the youth of today. *What a pile of dicks.* Wesley couldn't live another second in this hell-hole of employment. He hoped for his novel to take off but he kept getting writer's block. At the pace he was going, it would never be finished. He would always be this sad video store clerk with a little name tag and bigger dreams.

There had to be some way out; a path where no one could tell him what to do... where he could be...

Wesley.

Wesley checked the jerk out, and the loser went on his splendid way. He looked out the window and saw that bratty kid flip him the bird as he biked off.

"*I hope that kid gets hit by a garbage truck. I'm tired of taking everyone's crap.*"

The man quickly walked over to the front door and flipped the sign to "closed". Wesley did this sometimes when he was alone at the store and needed a time out. He went to the back office and shut down the surveillance.

Looking directly into the surveillance camera, "I am going to see the world pay."

Robert Zimmermann closed his Bible.

Opening his eyes, Bob looked around this smaller, not in the corner office. He couldn't get over the fact that he had been passed over by the stupid congregation for Senior Pastor at Oostburg Community Church. Bob was mad as hell; even his mother voted against him.

It seemed he was destined to be the Head Elder, an Ass. Pastor for all of his eternity. But that wasn't what he wanted for his life. At fifty-five, he was running out of time and well aware of it as the receding hairline was a small ticking reminder of his futility. Gals weren't the only ones who can feel their clock ticking.

Women...

Damn, he missed his wife.

Bob contemplated many paths how he could get past Adams, who in his very humble opinion, did not deserve the title of Senior Pastor anyway. Seth had never been a Senior Pastor, whereas Bob had led two congregations, excluding here as an interim. There just had to be some way of getting past the hump. Something... perhaps he could quietly convince Pastor Seth to get out of the way... maybe there was something that could be done to distract... what if Adams couldn't go on... what if there was something to hold him back... what if smug Seth had something that could be revealed...

A little blackmail never hurt anyone...

How desperately Bob Zimmermann desired to be that man in charge.

Perhaps, the Lord would let him in on some way to get to the top of the food chain.

He closed his eyes and prayed.

Brooke sat on their toilet and saw her clock tick away as she cried tears over the last negative test. It had been negative every month for the last eleven, and she was about ready to give up. She did not even notify her husband about the last seven tests. Not that he wanted the kids anyway.

Without her husband realizing, cunning Brooke was doing everything right: seducing her man on the correct nights, not swallowing pills that she said she was, and poking unnoticeable holes in the condoms. And yet, lady luck had no result. The stress had really gotten to her since the incident.

Brooke just could not get pregnant, no matter how hard she tried.

Was this the rest of her poor life? Being a nurse in a senior care facility just did not fulfill her soul anymore. Their marriage was failing and if she couldn't have a baby, then what was the point of going on?

Oftentimes she felt as if her husband didn't want her anymore as she was always initiating the sex. There is a problem when the male doesn't initiate the sex.

Perhaps he didn't find her attractive any longer, now that she couldn't walk...

Matt shot a few hoops as he noticed an older dude watching him back. *Who is that guy?* Matt asked himself. In a town as tiny as Oostburg, everyone knew everyone.

Except this guy.

Matt skipped up the court for a layup and decided enough. He was going to find out who this guy was.

As he walked over, the old gent slowly got up and moved to another space. The man dropped his binoculars, quickly retrieving them as he left the sweat-fumed gymnasium of Oostburg High.

"Probably someone's out-of-town relative," gangly Matt said to himself.

The youth continued to shoot two after two as he practiced for this coming Saturday afternoon's game. Matt was Oostburg's finest player, even though they had not been victorious yet this season. Alas, fifth time's the charm, as his dad would always say whenever he felt like jabbing his son, which was quite often these days.

The high school senior lined up for one more shot but could not get that old dude off his brain. For some reason he was fixated on him; like a dirty relative you know you should not have anything to do with, but he is so flippant and naughty you just yearn to be around him anyway.

Matt looked to the cheerleaders, quickly noticing that small Gracie wasn't among them. It didn't surprise Matt, since she was absent from school that day. Wonder what happened to her? She rarely misses school...

Who was that guy...?

He wondered what would happen tonight. The church was holding a fundraiser and Gracie was singing. Gracie had a wonderful voice and one could easily connect with the good God simply by closing their eyes and listening to her sing. It was funny since her father, Pastor Adams, had no singing ability whatsoever. Talents don't always get passed down. Matt understood this as his father did not have any basketball ability.

This annual fundraising event was to increase the missions program at Oostburg Community Church. The bold teens would be sent out once a year by the church to go to less fortunate places of the world. Matt was sure to go on this upcoming summer event as they were headed to the Dominican Republic. The teen had never been out of this country, rarely ever been out of Oostburg for that matter, and he was feeling pent up. You can only keep a bird caged for so long. Matt was ready to fly.

Now tired, he hit the locker room for a breather, checking his lonely voicemail. It was from Joe, his bud from school. Joe's message said he was going to come to the fundraiser that evening.

Matt shut down his cell and went back to the gym.

It was going to be a great evening, Matt promised himself.

But where was Gracie...?

"Come in."

Gracie turned around to see her pops peek through the door.

His girl was everything a father could ask for in a teen. She was smart, caring, and responsible. She did not hop from one boy to the next. Seth loved his little girl very much.

"Hey sweetie, you ready?" he asked.

She was ready now, as her diary was hidden in the locked red box under her bed, and the key was in a very small crack in the wall behind her bed.

Even good girls have secrets.

The pair treaded downstairs, passing where Lainey had been planted for the last few hours in their living room. Lainey had a half-day for teacher in-service and so most of that afternoon was spent lazily wasting away flipping through channels.

The younger gal watched her daddy and sister walk past, laughing and not even seeing her, as if they were the only two people in the damn world.

Lainey picked up on this.

She *always* picked up on this.

"I tell you, Matt talks about you all the time," Seth slipped.

"Stop, he does not—"

Lainey finally got up from their couch and peeked around the corner to see her mom conversing with her father and sister. Young Lainey went back to the TV and turned it on again, this time lowering the volume.

Lainey started the DVD where Gracie almost got hit by a car.

Lainey smiled at Gracie almost getting hit by a car.

And she rewound—and watched it again.

Evelyn quickly put down the landline.

"Where are you two going?" the mother hen asked.

"Gracie has a cheerleading practice, and I need to get some work done at the office."

Good save, Pastor Seth, he thought.

"You feeling better, Grace?" asked the mother.

"Yes, much better."

"Ok. See you at six," reminded Evelyn.

"Six," Seth agreed.

"Did you pack?"

"I will tonight," Seth smiled and kissed his wife; gently patting her butt cheek. It was a benefit that he enjoyed as a married man.

Gracie smiled at the butt pat; it represented the fun and healthy marriage. The type of marriage that she hoped to enjoy someday with her own husband.

Seth and his little princess left as his wife stealthily picked up the phone.

The wife paused for a second and asked:

"You were saying?"

Seth and Gracie drove the streets of Oostburg, which were not too many streets to drive.

Seth playfully teased his daughter:

"He has mentioned you."

"Matt?"

"Yup."

"Well, it doesn't matter. I'm not interested."

Pastor really did not understand what her problem was. According to Seth, a male in his mid-forties, Matt was everything that a young teenager would yearn for in a boy. Matt was amiable. He enjoyed church and seemed to be walking in his faith.

Yeah, Seth just did not get his girl's flippancy towards this catch of a future son-in-law.

"Ok, fine."

Gracie smiled.

"I appreciate that you're trying to set me up—as weird as that sounds. Yeah, he is a nice guy, handsome, kind, but... everyone has different taste buds so... it makes sense that everyone has different love buds."

Seth chuckled.

"You would think most fathers would be happy that their daughter is not interested in a boy," Gracie added.

Seth continued to drive.

"I'm just surprised, that's all. He's a good kid, nice looking—"

Gracie looked out the window.

"Maybe I'm looking for something different."

Seth worried that there might be some slick kid in the picture; a boy who mowed the lawn on Sundays. In some ways Seth wished they lived in the olden days, where the decision would be his; Gracie would marry Matt and live happily ever after next door. Pastor acknowledged under those stipulations, he never would have married Evelyn.

"Like what? Prince Charming?"

Seth waited for his girl to say there was another guy in her life, a companion not as worthy as Matt, but she sat there silent. This empty silence cued him to know it was time to change the subject. He wasn't going to convince her to date Matt today.

"How's *Twelve Angry Men* going?" he asked.

"Very well. Last week of rehearsals next week."

The gal received the most complicated role in *Twelve Angry Men*, the play at the school. She got the part of Juror Number 8, who defends a kid accused of murdering his father. The play opened in a week, and she was ready for opening night. It was a lot of memorizing but Gracie had a great memory.

"Looking forward to seeing it, for sure. It's one of my favorite courtroom dramas. A terrific concept. An in-depth study of talking things through and doing your research. Phenomenal story."

"I'm having trouble with just a line: *Does anyone think there still is not a reasonable doubt?* It is just too wordy. I hate that line."

"Eh. Just keep saying it over and over again. The line will stick."

Seth smiled at his princess. He was incredibly proud of the woman she had become.

Seth was now one block from the school. Daddy was thankful that his Gracie was not embarrassed yet by him enough to make him drop her off a city away, as some of her friends did.

"Ah! There's Michelle," said Gracie as her friend entered the school.

"Oh... if coach has a problem with you practicing after missing school, just tell her to call me."

"A tough guy, huh?" Gracie teased sarcastically.

Seth smiled.

"Yeah. Real tough. You okay now? You seem fine."

"Well, I'm fine now. Been fine since lunch."

"Just threw up a little?"

"Yeah, breakfast was weird."

Seth pulled up and Gracie looked out the window.

Gracie got out of the car and looked into her father's eyes.

"Bye, dad."

She blew her dad a kiss that was reciprocated and appreciated.

"Bye, sweetie."

All Pastor Adams could do was stare as his Gracie innocently walked away. He knew six months from now, in April, she would be an adult. Free to make her own bed, her own choices, free to leave, free to...

Time was running out.

Gracie walked across the dirt school quad to find it empty. It was later Friday afternoon, and most people were either home salivating over their upcoming weekend or they were inside practicing for the game.

Gracie was coming to terms with her final year of high school. She looked at the quad and grinned.

Eight more months.

For now, she had to get through this year. It was still only October. Only eight tiny months till June... summer would be the start of a whole new life for young Gracie Adams.

She walked through the black double doors to find two of her gals awaiting her arrival.

Gracie had known Michelle Fenwick since the first day of kindergarten and even one time saved Michelle's life. One cold winter, their fourth grade, Michelle and Gracie had gone ice skating at the nearby pond—Michelle's dad had given her permission but her mom had been a little more cautious.

Well, Murphy's Law and all, Michelle was not as experienced as Gracie was, but she bravely went skating where she shouldn't have and fell in. Gracie had to pull her up with all her strength. Good thing Michelle was a little girl or Gracie might not have been strong enough to get her out. Since then, eight years ago, Michelle had been Gracie's sidekick and best friend.

Stacy Reinbold was a little rougher around the edges. Kicked out of North High in Sheboygan, Stacy had stolen some essay answers for a test her sophomore year and was more street-smart than little Michelle. The three females were quite tight, with Gracie getting most of the attention. The other two didn't mind, since Stacy was usually up to something and Michelle was just happy to have a friend to rely on.

"Why won't you tell us his name?" asked Michelle.

They knew Gracie had a crush on some dude but did not know who that lucky male was. Everyone assumed it to be Matt, but no one knew for sure. Outside her diary, Gracie was never one to flaunt her thoughts.

At that moment, handsome Matt walked past the two staring does. Matt was wearing a basketball uniform and girls liked watching Matt dribble his ball as they dribbled over him. As he passed them by, he winked at Gracie. The gal barely acknowledged him in return, much to the surprise of the others.

Stacy smiled.

"You don't need to tell us his name."

Oostburg did not have a great team. Matt was good but after him, it was country miles before anyone could compare to the leading scorer. It was alright; Oostburg never had a good team in all their years of playing, so they were not letting anybody down. Oostburg was not as competitive as most towns. People accepted the poor results; while the other towns practiced on Sundays, Oostburgers had family time.

One particular old gent was smiling regardless of the screwed layups, crap two-pointers, spilled dribbles, and sad chaos. Amongst the many teenagers gathered this Friday afternoon was a sightseer. The teenagers did not even realize the man was there, as with usual teenagers they are oftentimes too caught up in their own drama to survey their surroundings.

With his large binoculars, this particular sneaky gentleman zeroed in on the ladies practicing their cute tumbles, pratfalls, high kicks, and fun pyramids. He had a notebook, a little out of place.

Matt turned to his teammate, Erik. "Ever see that guy before?"

"Nope. He must be a scout. Look, guy's got a book and a pen. Time to show off!" Erik ran to miss his next shot.

The mysterious man was a scout, of sorts.

However, he was not the type of scout these girls wanted to be scouted by.

He liked their bodies wearing their short tight skirts with their even smaller waistlines that had not yet born children.

Charles Raile made some notes, closed the report, and quietly left the building.

Getting into his inconspicuous car, Charles Raile dialed his pre-paid cell phone.

"I have another job for you."

Vicki crossed the border from windy Illinois into even colder Wisconsin. It was about two o'clock, and she realized she had not eaten lunch. She stopped at McDonald's for that weekly craving fix, a Big Mac and fries. She loved those things.

Chomping away at the burger, she was annoyed that her cell rang. It was her aunt, checking on her for the two-hundredth time during this drive. She thought about letting the call go to voicemail before finally picking it up with her greasy fingers.

"Victoria?" she heard on the other end.

"Yes, Aunt Coralee?"

"Where are you now?"

The Wisconsin newcomer peeked out the windows and eyed a highway sign that read:

"Kenosha. Eating lunch at McDonald's."

This pleased Coralee as she thought her niece was getting closer.

"Very good. Now you eat safe and drive fast. Love you, nephew."

Officer Vicki's red flags soared. Eat safe. Drive fast. Nephew. Maybe dear Coralee was planning on having a boy. Coralee's tone definitely sounded as if it had a double meaning.

"Why are you so excited?" Vicki interrogated.

Coralee couldn't contain her excitement.

"I just... miss you!"

Vicki turned her head to see an employee slip and rip their pants as she took another huge delicious bite of her Big Mac.

"You better not be setting me up."

Coralee didn't realize how perceptive her niece was.

"I'm not. Love you!"

Coralee hung up the phone and turned to her left. Sitting next to her was a tall, handsome gentleman. The man may have been romantically attractive if it weren't for the fact that his disposition matched Barney Fife.

Sheriff Ellis Kirkbride was a man whose looks and personality simply did not match. He was, well, a dork; but he was also, well, quite lovely.

Being the sheriff of Oostburg, his job was fairly simple as Oostburg wasn't known for its drug dealers or rapists, murderers, or well, anything. The sheriff spent most of his days reading the newspaper and sleeping; or occasionally playing Uno and Monopoly with his two subordinates, Momma and David Penny.

Sheriff Ellis needed a fourth because old Patrick McConnors retired. McConners had been with the Oostburg force since he formed it in 1809. Ok, that's hyperbole, but you get the picture.

Fortunately for Vicki, the old gent retired, flew south to Florida, and left the fourth chair just waiting to be slept in. He knew he would probably hire the gal, if not just for her appearance in the photo, but he did contact Gagliano back in New York City. The job was hers.

In addition to Vicki being attractive—he saw a photo—Ellis felt a sense of care towards Coralee. Coralee was old enough to be his mom and in many ways, she was, as his mother passed away shortly after he graduated high school. The sheriff justified by hiring the gal he was bringing her to old Coralee, and that made him feel good as well.

"She knew," Coralee spoke.

Ellis smiled.

"She sounded cute."

"You are going to love her. Or shoot her. Four of the three."

Ellis smiled and cocked his gun.

"Sounds like my type of woman."

The woman sat on her bed. Gazing into her wedding photo on the nightstand, she pondered the happy moment that had been a long memory. A nice looking couple when fixed up. She loved how her hair looked back then, with the three strands of red down the left side of her soft cheek. Each long strand represented the three kids they were planning to have, but the woman didn't let her man in on that tiny secret. On their first date, her future husband had remarked how he loved flowing red hair, and really being a blonde, the woman dyed some of her hairs auburn. Brooke cried as the good memories came back. It was a beautiful time.

Amazingly, the wedding was perfect.

Unfortunately, it was all downhill from there.

Brooke and her hubby grew distant over the years. Fifteen years is a long time to be with a male that you barely knew, a person you barely loved, or a person you barely even like. Most of their sad evenings consisted of viewing *Jeopardy, Wheel of Fortune,* and the news when they were together. Some nights she worked; some evenings he did. Two passing ships in the ocean. Brooke wanted to save their marriage but did not know where to go next.

But in their defense, life had not been comfy for them. The two had been through downs and further downs, including her car crash some months prior that led her to this position. Brooke had finally gotten used to the wheelchair. Her therapy was going well. The woman could feel her hard forearms getting stronger by the day.

Downstairs, Brooke could hear the noise of small footsteps slowly making their way up. Closer and closer they grew as she placed their wedding album back in the drawer. Little point letting him know the wife had been daydreaming again about their loveless marriage.

Wesley Demko opened the door.

"Thought you worked today."

Brooke picked up on Wesley's disappointed tone.

"I do. This evening."

"Ah."

And that was around the extent of their talks for the last few months. Years, actually.

Wesley began to change out of his work attire and into his sweats. As he changed from covered to mostly nude, Brooke tried to remember the last time she was excited to view him nude.

It had been a while.

"How was your day?"

"Usual."

Brooke made the attempts. It was quite painful to carry on verbal ping-pong with him when he was not willing or interested in oscillating back. The marriage was a failure, and in Brooke's opinion, it was entirely Wesley's fault.

"Well, if you talked more maybe I would know what *usual* meant."

Now dressed and ready for absolutely nothing, the man headed on to the bathroom.

"Probably."

Brooke raised her voice:

"One-word answers don't make a marriage, Wesley."

The man took a loud, relaxing piss that drowned out the beginnings of Brooke's pleas. *Take that woman.*

"Yes, dear."

The famous words of a husband that doesn't care a bit to get into another forty-minute fight on what kind of butter can go with a piece of toast. *Females can get so annoying sometimes. Can't women understand that most guys just do not care about ninety percent of what goes on?*

Wesley returned to the bedroom after not cleaning either hand. He did put on deodorant.

He continued:

"See."

"See what?"

Wesley was starting to get smart-alecky:

"*Yes, dear* is two words."

He stopped caring about the relationship. Then he stopped caring about the woman's pleas for help. He did the worst thing a man can do to a woman emotionally:

He gave up.

The wife shook her head with disapproval. The man walked over and offered his hand. Brooke took and held his hand, leaning on her husband. Gently lifting her, he helped Brooke to the wheelchair. She looked up towards Wesley; kissing him on his pink lips. Brooke still loved the guy, even if he treated her like crap.

A lot had happened to them but she wanted to rebuild.

Wesley didn't kiss back, but rather slowly walked away.

Getting the message, she sighed and wheeled away. Noticing the woman was gone—finally—Wesley slid over to his computer and clicked it on. Looking out the door and seeing that Brooke's eyes were not looking at their screen, he checked his phone.

There was a text that made him smile.

Wesley wasn't content much these days, especially not at home. He put his phone down and began to do what he was born to do.

He wrote.

Evelyn Adams was a better driver than her husband. She took fewer chances and gambled less with the people on the roads. And this particular trip had her going to the bank to investigate a transaction that she couldn't figure out.

Oostburg State Bank—Oostburg's only bank—was about a five-minute drive. Everything was a five minute drive in Oostburg.

Evelyn entered, nervous because she had no idea where the money was. It was not the first time this had happened and knowing her husband, it probably would not be the last. Nonetheless, she wanted to see if the bank teller knew anything about it.

The teller was Evelyn's friend from church. Margie was one of eleven ladies in the women's ministry, and they had done some baking to support various events including this evening's fundraiser.

Margie was an older lady who guided Evelyn from time to time.

"Hello, Mrs. Adams. What can I do for you?"

Even though Margie Stromsvold was much older than Evelyn, she called her "Mrs. Adams". Evelyn didn't like it, because it made her feel older, but she did not say anything anyway.

Evelyn was not good at being real. She was pretty decent at being fake, though.

"Hi, Margie. How are you?"

"Well besides my mother's two kidney stones, life is going well."

"I'm sorry."

"Praying round the clock these days."

Evelyn gave a fake smile. Even as a pastor's wife she knew prayers were meaningless. Please god, cure her of those kidney stones that you blessed her with. And yes, sometimes god does heal but sometimes god doesn't. God is very random. And moody. Perhaps he just flips a coin.

"Can I help you, Mrs. Adams?"

Yes, you can stop calling me Mrs. Adams.

Evelyn got to the matter at hand.

"Hopefully. I saw a transaction on my account. No idea what it is. A withdrawal for two hundred dollars?"

Margie looked through her computer.

"Ok, let me get your account up."

The teller retrieved the account quickly.

"Yeah, two hundred dollars was withdrawn on September 30th."

"Yes, I saw that."

"I'm sure it was just your husband—are you ok?"

Evelyn had become quite well at wearing a façade.

"I am fine. Just wanted to make sure. And I will pray for your mom."

"Thank you."

Evelyn fake smiled and left the bank.

Furiously, she stormed back to her car. The woman crawled inside and hit her head on the ceiling.

"Damn it, Seth. Not our anniversary weekend."

6.

CAT AND MOUSE

The man drove his old car through the stop sign a little too fast; catching the eyes of Oostburg's newest resident, Victoria Weathers, and in the process, nearly dinged her car.

If it wasn't for her New York City reflexes there would have been major damage. She turned swiftly to the left just as the man's ride was coming close. He veered right at the last second, narrowly missing her.

Vicki got out to survey the damage and walked up to his car.

"Hey! You ran that stop sign."

He rolled down his window.

"Completely my fault. Forgive me?"

Vicki took a second. "If I were in charge, I would nail your ass to the ground. Two hundred, easy. But I don't have a badge, so I'll settle for a sorry."

The man smiled smugly.

"Sorry, miss. Glad you're not a cop."

He looked over and saw her license plate.

"You lost, young lady?"

Vicki was angry. This guy clearly did not respect females as equals and in addition to his blatant disrespect for the laws of common driving, this made her double mad.

"I'm never lost."

He smiled.

"Well, in any case, welcome to Oostburg!"

The man waved and carefully drove away.

The former cop stood and watched him. She quickly took mental note of his plate and hopped in her car. Vicki currently wasn't a cop, but she would be in a few hours and this would make a nice impression if she could bag a criminal on her way to the interview.

She got in her car and trailed him.

He drove to the interstate and headed south with Vicki trailing him by eight seconds. She had great eyesight so this was easy; easier than New York. In New York, she had to deal with dodging traffic.

Vicki's cell phone rang to which she answered it, a clear driving violation. Two months ago, she wouldn't dare answer her phone and break the law but the next months had changed Vicki and now she was willing to do anything to stop a criminal—even if it meant becoming one herself.

It was her aunt, worrying for the hundredth time:

"Sorry, Aunt Coralee—I can't talk right now."

"But you're going to be late for the interview."

"I'll be fine."

Vicki picked up speed as the man was gaining ground and getting off at the next exit. He put on his blinker way too early, but Vicki was not being safe either, so who was she to judge?

"Alright. I'll leave your lunch in the microwave. So it's nice and warmer. We have the concert tonight as well—starts at seven."

Damn, she forgot about that church concert she promised to take Aunt Coralee to.

"Don't worry, I'll be there. Love you."

The guy jumped off at exit 113, not very far from where they got on. Guy turned right off the interstate and drove for about a mile.

Vicki turned off her speaker and continued the pursuit; still only about five seconds behind.

Vicki's mouse pulled into a dirty gas station and slowly walked his way to the pumps. Vicki parked across the street, watching.

As the mouse fed his car, Vicki began to feel a small bit of doubt creeping in. Maybe the guy was not doing anything wrong. Maybe he was just a poor driver.

You know gut, sometimes I hate you, she thought.

After a few minutes at the pay pump, Vicki's hunt returned to his car and continued down the road.

The game of cat and mouse stopped when the mouse pulled into this parking lot of a bar called Jesus Take The Wheel. Guy got out of his car and stealthily put on his sunglasses.

This did make Vicki feel better. Why would he put on his sunglasses and go inside after he had just driven down the highway for about ten minutes? She smiled—she was right. This stranger was up to no good.

Jesus Take The Wheel was a crummy little establishment about three minutes into Cedar Grove. It smelled like cheese; brie, perhaps. Vicki's first time in a bar in Wisconsin and it smelled like cheese, go figure. Not many customers, but then again it was Friday afternoon, not even 7PM. This stranger must have been getting that head start to his weekend.

Vicki saw her mouse sitting in a dark corner with another male. The other male was pretty attractive; Vicki did think so herself.

Vicki walked up to the overweight bartender.

"Well, hi pretty lady. Haven't seen you before."

Vicki hated being hit on, especially in a bar.

"And you probably won't see me again. I'll take a soda."

"Frankie's the name."

"Coke with no ice."

He realized she wasn't interested so he went back to his job.

"Coke and no rocks coming up."

Frankie left to go get the drink and Vicki turned her head in time to see Mouse and Handsome shake hands. *Damn it*, she already missed something because she spoke briefly with Jabba the Bartender.

Jabba handed her the drink. She gulped as she inched closer to the little Mouse's corner. From there, she was able to sniff out pieces of their conversation. Jesus Take The Wheel loved blasting that fierce country music. *I hate bars*, she thought.

Stealthily, Vicki walked to the booth just across the joint. Through the corner of her eye, she saw Mouse pass a grey envelope to Handsome. Handsome peered in it and appeared to be counting. Money, probably.

A slutty-looking waitress of thirteen steered her way to their table. Handsome grinned as she laid down a large burger in front of him. He tipped her by pinching her ass, to which she smiled and walked away.

Vicki couldn't hear anything, and it was really getting her quite a bit annoyed. Screeching that Kelsea Ballerini on the radio wasn't helping.

Jailbait the waitress dropped her plates; sending many pieces of cutlery and plates airborne in several directions and she grabbed the opportunity to walk over and help the waitress clean up the silverware. This got her within ear distance of hearing the remainder of the conversation, at least whenever Jailbait shut up.

Handsome definitely seemed to be in charge of the meeting.

"Look, sir—"

"Cody."

Jailbait thanked her for the third time as sneaky Vicki continued to ignore her.

"Cody," Mouse repeated.

Handsome smiled.

"Not my real name—so don't even try to search me down."

Mouse appeared nervous.

"I need this to... work out. Make it happen."

"I can't do that. Pass the ketchup."
Jailbait continued:
"Thank you, really—I know it's silly to wear the heels…"
You're still here, Jailbait?
"Look, I have no more—"
Mouse was cut off as another man entered the bar, an older man of about fifty.
"Well, hello. Fancy seeing you here."
"Bob—umm, hi," the mouse fumbled for words, fidgeting a little. "Funny seeing you here."
Bob smiled.
"Getting my son's paycheck. That boy, I tell ya."
"And my boyfriend, he told me that—" the waitress continued.
SHUT UP JAILBAIT!
"I'm sorry, Bob, this is Cody."
"Cody."
The guys shook hands. Cody did not bother to wipe the ketchup off of his hand with a napkin so instead, he used Bob's palm.
"Bob."
Bob shook his head in disapproval.
"I guess I will see you in a couple of hours."
Mouse smiled.
"You will."
"And perhaps you as well. Take care."
Bob walked past her, just as Jailbait finally got the hint that Vicki was not talking back to her or even really listening. *Now, why would Bob attempt to have Cody see them in a couple of hours? Why was Bob attempting to invite Cody somewhere but never really saying where or when?*
"No thanks. You wouldn't find me dead there."
Where? Stop talking in code!
Mouse spoke up:
"Well, I disagree. Now, where were we?"
Your dinero, perhaps? Vicki felt like whispering. That mouse. She hoped he was not a doctor or a lawyer or someone important.
"The money," Cody reminded the mouse.
"Ah yes. And remember—I need a positive result."
A positive result? Vicki was definitely perked.
"It's out of my hands."
At that point, the mouse looked at his watch.

"Crap—I have to get going. Going to a concert tonight. I have to go. You should come."

"Not interested."

The mouse stood up.

"Well. You may find something you didn't know you needed."

To cover up spying, Vicki began to clean a nearby table with her sleeve as the mouse walked away. She quit her momentary chore and followed him out the door.

The mouse returned to his car and put his hands on the wheel. For the first time, he noticed the pretty lady he almost collided with about forty minutes ago.

Vicki looked at her watch and finally remembering her interview, she sprinted back to her car. It was not far to Oostburg, but she better haul ass if she was going to be Oostburg's newest deputy.

Evelyn walked past bored Lainey, who continued to channel surf and mold into her parents' comfy couch.

"Lainey, wear something nicer."

Evelyn made her way upstairs and went through the second door on her right, which was her bedroom. It was a very nice room, especially on a pastor's salary. They were struggling, them and the church, but she was still able to have a walk-in closet and that was important to her.

The wife entered her walk-in and quickly shut the door. Kneeling, she quietly went through mounds of shoe boxes, sixteen in all. In the bottom-most box, her jogging shoes, she grabbed a fist full of cash.

At the bank, Mrs. Stromsvold was enjoying the last hour of her week. Margie did not have to work this Saturday, so she was doubly content. She liked the job but nobody wanted to work Saturday. Or Sunday. Or Monday through Friday, for that matter.

Margie was surprised to find her friend return so quickly.

"Evelyn—again?"

Evelyn fake smiled again and lied.

"Sorry about earlier... I found the money that we were missing."

"Oh super. Just in the wrong place, I suppose."

44

Evelyn handed over the cash.
"Yes, something like that..."

A pot began to boil over.
Quickly, Wesley tramped into the kitchen. Nervous for his house, his novel, and his general well-being, the man yanked the kettle from the stove just as it was about to boil over.
The kettle was safe from the boiling point... but Wesley Demko was not.
"BROOKE!" Wesley screamed furiously.
Waiting for the female, he turned on the overhead fan for the stove just as she wheeled herself in.
"Brooke!" Wesley yelled: "Brooke! That kettle was on too long!"
"Sorry—I've been looking for my—"
Wesley interrupted:
"I don't care what the hell you're looking for!"
"Don't raise your voice to me!" Now Brooke boiled over, having enough of Wesley's verbal attacks.
Wesley pouted:
"I'm off."
The man made his path to the hallway as that lost puppy dog of a woman followed.
Brooke asked:
"How are you getting there?"
"Walking."
The concert was that night, and Brooke planned to be in attendance.
"Did you see my pu—"
Wesley couldn't believe his roommate was not more careful nor was she even the slightest bit moved by the fire hazard.
"I don't give a damn what you are looking for."
Picking up his keys, Wesley stormed out.

Wesley got about two blocks before his cell began to buzz. *Brooke.* She was always first to apologize when they fought. She could have burnt down the house.

45

He let it go to voicemail.

After waiting a minute, he checked the message.

It was not Brooke. It was that bitchy secretary from the Aurora Health Clinic.

"Hello, Wesley. This is Karin from Aurora Health. You missed your appointment with Dr. Malachi at 3PM. To re-schedule, please call us back at—"

Wesley hung up the phone. He didn't want to go to his appointment. He was sick of those voicemails. Every week they were harassing his voicemail. Demko wanted to quit therapy altogether, but the woman would have found out, and then there would be hell to pay.

He deleted the message and began his jog.

Every other Friday after school, Gracie Adams led a Bible Study for high school girls. On this particular Friday it was different—in a very special way— because in addition to her gaggle of Stacy and Michelle, Gracie was blessed to have Ivy Watson in attendance.

Ivy Watson was the toughest female in the school, even tougher than Stacy. Ivy had been let go from a few schools across the United States, a truth that she wore proudly on her chest. Her sins ranged from beating up a teacher to theft to urinating on a teacher's desk.

Ivy transferred to Oostburg a month ago, back in September. She was staying with her uncle, a pillar of strength at the church. Nearing twenty, this was her first and final year at Oostburg High.

Gracie prayed to end the study. All of the gals had their eyes shut, except for Ivy, who was quite cynical about the whole fiasco.

"Lead us not into temptation, but deliver us from evil, for thine is the Kingdom, the power and the Glory forever, Amen."

"Amen."

Stacy confessed:

"I don't get the temptation part."

"How so?" asked Gracie.

"Jesus gives us the feelings, right? And if those feelings are from Jesus… why would He want us to resist them?"

Gracie was startled by Stacy's question because she did not know the answer. Gracie had temptations all the time, temptations that one time might cause her harm. Her parents were fairly protective of their little teen princess, to the point where she was the only seventeen-year-old not to be allowed to wear lipstick.

She did anyway, sneaking lipstick to school, then putting it on in the ladies' room, and then cleaning it off good before the day ended.

"Good, Stacy. I think, um, well.... I think it is good to control urges when they try to—get the best of you. It's what He would want—"

"Like He's testing us?" asked Michelle.

"Yeah, yeah, Michelle. Testing us to make sure we truly love Him."

Ivy snorted.

"So that he can love us back?"

Gracie smiled. Perhaps God was using her to reach Ivy. Gracie loved helping others.

"Right."

Ivy shook her head in disgust.

"That's bull. What kind of god lord creates people not to love him and… then punishes them for not loving them? Screw you, god."

Gracie bit her lip, not sure of how to answer.

"Well, He doesn't want to create robots."

Ivy shook her head. "Typical, crappy, Christianese response. That and "God has a plan". Bull. You're stupid, G."

Gracie had been called stupid before, mostly by her little sister Lainey. She had never been called stupid before in Bible Study, though. Gracie was determined to pass and take the high road.

"Well, you are entitled to your opinions," Gracie said.

Michelle chuckled, much to Ivy's chagrin.

"Oh, so that's funny?" Ivy asked Michelle.

Gracie defended Michelle, who Ivy would've easily handled.

"We don't mean to laugh—sorry if we offended—"

Ivy got in Gracie's face.

"It's cause I'm black, G. I'm one of the few blacks in this damn—"

Gracie reassured Ivy:

"We don't care that you're black—"

"Shut up, white chick! I have thoughts too and it is not to love a lord who tortures me! G, why are you stupid enough to believe in a god that doesn't give a crap about you!?"

"Ok, just settle down," Gracie said.

"What about those kids in the fire? Where was he then, G?" Ivy asked.

Gracie took a breather. She did know the two kids who died in the fire.

Ivy got in Gracie's face.

"You want to fight, white girl?"

"No, I don't—I just—"

And then, in front of all the girls, Ivy walloped Gracie right on the face, leaving a red mark.

Again, Gracie could feel the Lord testing her.

And again, she was determined to pass.

"Want to turn the other cheek?"

Ivy knew her scripture.

Wesley peacefully jogged past the hectic Oostburg High. He was making pretty good time. He was not really training for anything; he just enjoyed the solitude, cause he got away from the carping female once a day.

The jogger continued, viewing the sheriff hanging outside with a mug. It appeared as if Ellis was waiting for something or someone. *Ellis had the easiest job in the world*, Wesley thought.

"Hey, Wesley."

He didn't want to chat, but Wesley paused anyway.

"Hey."

Ellis walked up to him.

"Training for a marathon?"

"Just clearing my head," Wesley said.

"Nice day to do that."

Ellis took a swig of his steaming coffee.

Ellis must have nothing to do if he drinks coffee at this time of day, Wesley surmised.

"Looks like you have another simple day," Wesley zinged, a diss that went over the sheriff's head.

"Yeah, not much trouble in Oostburg."

Ivy had Gracie in a headlock as the other females failed to break it up. Miss Watson was strong and tall—six foot one—the three of them combined could not take her down. Stacy quit and decided if she could not fight Ivy physically, she could at least film the battle with her cell phone for evidence.

Tough Ivy ripped one of Gracie's earrings out and threw it on the ground, making their Bible study leader bleed. Crying in pain, Gracie dropped to the ground.

"Guess god was not here to protect you, Christian white girl!"

Ivy spit on her and quickly left the room.

Michelle walked over to Gracie and helped her up.

Stacy picked up the earring from the ground, giving it back to Gracie.

"Gracie, you okay?" asked Michelle.

"I'll live."

"Boy, she really had it in for you, Gracie," said Michelle.

"No, not me. She had it out for God."

Michelle gave her a tissue to wipe the blood off her ear.

"She thinks God does not care about us," Michelle said.

"God does care. And He loves you. All you have to do is let Him in your heart. Let Him take care of you."

Stacy proudly showed her cell phone.

"I got it all on camera if you ever want to sue."

Gracie smiled and shook her head. Sue. That's not what Jesus wanted from Gracie Adams. God wanted to show love and tolerance, mercy, and yes, *grace*. Not persecution, even if Ivy deserved it.

Ivy dashed out and left the school, positive that Gracie was calling her uncle or the sheriff.

Unfortunately for Ivy, there was a different car waiting outside the school. The old man rolled down his window.

"Need a ride?"

Ivy glanced around. Knowing the sheriff's station was only a block away, she was thankful this older guy had a cab.

Ivy got in the car.

It was a nice car, clean with black leather seats and an intoxicating smell. A Toyota. *That peppermint air freshener in the front was really a nice touch,* the gal thought.

The car began to roll as the driver asked:

"Where to?"

"205 Lincoln St."

The car started driving. It was going pretty fast in Ivy's opinion.

Ivy looked about. The car didn't look like a cab.

Ivy's street smarts were five seconds too late.

"Are you a cab driver?"

"Do you like turkey?"

Crap. He avoided the question. Not a good sign.
"Are you a cab driver?"
The pretend cabbie smiled.
"I usually prefer white meat." He paused and then turned around. "But, occasionally I go dark."
Ivy's ears perked up but it was moments too late. The cabbie was quick—he locked the doors. The car was going too fast now for young Ivy to break a window and jump.
Her only chance was if the sheriff caught the cab driver on a speeding ticket.
The cat snatched his mouse as Charles Raile ate his first Oostburger.

7.

THE MAN WITH THE RED TIE

    If Sheriff Ellis Kirkbride were surveying around his simple little town, perhaps Ivy Watson would still be present. However, from his experience, nothing ever happened in Oostburg, making it the perfect target for something very wrong to happen.

    Vicki Weathers found Oostburg just when this town needed to be located. Coincidence? Yes, people may say. Others would say it was an act of God.

    Vicki walked up to the secretary, on time for her interview. She was an older African-American, about sixty, who had the gentle momma feeling to her. She was a tad overweight and had bifocals. She appeared to be someone you could immediately speak to, someone who may bake you banana bread for no reason. And for that matter, the place did smell of fresh baked goods, come to think of it.

    Vicki walked up to the heavy-set woman.

    "Hello. I am here to see Sheriff Kirkbride."

    The desk lady smiled warmly.

    "Ah yes, you must be the new female deputy. Just one moment."

    Why would the lady note "female", Vicki wondered. *Had they never had a female deputy before?*

    She picked up the phone.

    "Ellis, your appointment is here." The woman paused; smiling again. "Oh yes, she's very pretty."

    Vicki instantly rolled her eyes. *Oh, Christ*, Vicki thought. There is going to be some misogyny or a sexual harassment suit here for sure.

    She put down the phone and looked up at Vicki.

    "One moment. And please, call me Momma."

    Vicki looked around the department. It was little and empty, unlike her previous place of employment. For here, there were only three desks: Momma's being one of them. The other desk was a mess, with a pizza box on it. Two slices. The third desk was naked, presumably hoping to be clothed.

    Sheriff Kirkbride entered from his back office.

    He grinned wildly when he saw Vicki, as a child in the candy store.

    "Well hello there, Miss Weathers."

    Vicki's smile was not as excited.

They entered his office. Again, not too much here either. Almost looked like a hangout rather than a room of serious government employment. Vicki was confused... were all police departments across the US like this? It might take some getting used to the small-town life.

"Have a seat. Can I get you anything?"

"No thank you," Vicki said as she sat down.

Ellis continued to small talk. The sheriff made himself a coffee and by the appearance of his dirty cup, this wasn't his only today.

"So... the Big Apple? All the ways to this little town? What are you hoping for—early retirement?"

Wow. The sheriff's not just some hick cop after all. He has a bit of perception.

"Um, no—"

Ellis continued.

"Cause you know we get all kinds of crimes here."

This surprised Vicki.

"You do?"

Ellis smiled.

"Oh sure. Littering and Sunday lawn-mowing. Real bad jay-walking. All of them hardcore criminals. I even saved a cat last year."

"I'm sorry, I don't know you well enough to tell if you're being serious."

"So these past one hundred seconds have not meant anything to you?"

Was he flirting in some poor country boy way?

The sheriff got closer to her... he was coming onto her in some dorky manner!

"No, but sexual harassment does, Sheriff Kirkb—"

"Call me Ellis—"

Vicki stood up.

"Look, I came from New York City because I want a change. Where I do not get hit on by every cold-blooded man—"

Ellis smiled and tried to crack a joke.

"Now we know who shot the sheriff."

"Besides, my aunt needs help."

"So... you just told your potential boss that you want an easier life where you don't have to do—"

"That's not what—"

"Well, Miss Weathers, our life may be slower here than New York City, but that doesn't mean we just read newspapers and eat donuts all day—"

A deputy shaped like a bowling-ball came bursting through the door in excitement as if they just snatched the town jaywalker.

"Donuts are here!"

And he was gone, presumably to eat said donuts.

"That's... just bad timing."

Vicki was sick of this nonsense.

"Look, do you have a job for me or not?"

"Yeah. I need someone to sharpen those pencils."

Dumbfounded, Vicki left the room in a huff. *Where was she?*

New Deputy Vicki Weathers was in Oostburg, Wisconsin. A quiet, small populated town of a thousand or so where everyone knew everyone.

At least they thought.

Oostburg thought they knew their simple minister, Seth Adams, as they thought he was a decent, upstanding citizen. Little did they know that he was a cheat; some gambler who played around with their money. The cash in the collection basket wasn't always used for ministry.

Seth sat at his desk as his colleague, Pastor Bob Zimmermann entered.

"Knock-knock."

Seth looked up, so he didn't need to ask.

"Who's there?"

"Mind if I shut the door?"

Seth played along.

"Mind if I shut the door who?" asked Seth.

Zimmermann shut the door and walked over.

"Eh, I got nothing."

Zimmermann sat down.

"You doing okay, Seth?"

Seth put down his pen. He didn't really desire to go on about his marriage or the casinos.

"Yeah, sure I'm fine."

"Evelyn alright?"

Seth smiled. *Why did you want to take her out?* Pastor Adams thought.

"Yes, we're fine."

"You know I'm here for you Seth if you ever need to talk. Please, use me. The people need you too, Seth. We need you in tip-top condition to lead us."

Seth knew that his associate was feeding him lies because Robert Zimmermann did not care about anyone other than Robert Zimmermann. The congregation also figured this out just before they voted Seth as their pastor, even though Bob was ten years older and a little more experienced.

"I got it, Bob. I got it."

"Yes, you still got it. Hello, Bob."

Zimmermann turned around. It was Evelyn. His plan to get Adams to step down would have to wait.

"Evelyn," Zimmermann said.

Seth grinned. He bet the wife was there to bother him about packing for the weekend again.

"And no, I haven't packed yet."

Zimmermann stood up, prepared to exit.

"Twenty years married. It's hard to be married to the same person," Bob stated.

Seth smiled.

Zimmermann fixed his collar.

"Time for her to trade me in for a younger model, huh?" Seth joked.

"Or maybe an antique."

Bob smiled, knowing it was time to go.

"I will leave you two. And Seth, if you ever want to chat, please do."

"Thanks, Bob."

"Alright. Well, I'll see you out there."

"Bye, Bob."

Zimmermann left Seth's office, bumping into young Lainey outside, sitting on the floor.

Zimmermann closed the door as Lainey never looked up.

"You so want my dad's job. It's pathetic."

Bob Zimmermann looked at the little girl. How old is she, Twelve? Thirteen? *What a snot!*

The man also knew she was right, so he pouted and walked away.

Back in the office, Evelyn had her own plan.

"Bob's right you know—you can't just keep silent all of the time," Evelyn said.

"Evelyn. I talk to people."

The wife sat on the chair previously occupied and crossed her long, lithe legs. He briefly lost focus as he stared at his wife. Those legs. She still had it.

"Seth... we have been married for twenty years on Wednesday. Dating for eight more. I have known you for more than half my life. I know... I know something is... the matter. You're... distant."

Evelyn got up from the chair and sat on his desk.

"Evelyn, I'm just..."

"What?"

Seth sat back. He really didn't want to be having any conversation right now... especially when they were hours away from a romantic trip sans kids.

"I'm just under a lot of stress, that's all. It's just a phase."

She leaned in over to her husband's face and gave him a sweet, reassuring kiss.

"It's been a long phase."

Seth touched her knee.

"It'll be alright."

Evelyn stood up, removing his hand from her knee, the tease.

"Maybe Bob's right. Maybe you should see Ben or someone."

"A therapist? Evelyn."

"Well... you're not talking to your wife or your closest colleague."

Evelyn paused.

"Why not?"

"Cause I'm not..."

"Crazy?"

Young Gracie Adams knelt at the second pew in the sanctuary of Oostburg Community Church. It was really a beautiful sanctuary, full of pews and a pretty organ in the front, right behind the baptismal tub and her dad's pulpit. Hanging on the back wall, lived the painting of *The Last Supper*. Miss Adams always found it interesting that of the twelve disciples, Judas was the only one not looking at Jesus.

Gracie headed the Bible study and prayed, reading her Bible regularly. But there was some disconnect: she was not perfect. She yearned to be perfect and sinless. But she couldn't achieve that. Not with what was on her mind. Not with those sins that were clouding her heart. And she was not going to give up these sins, which would be far too difficult.

And Gracie felt like such a hypocrite because...

Well, she was a hypocrite.

Gracie's eyes closed as she began to pray.

"Forgive me, Father, for I have sinned."

Gracie opened both eyes, and the very first thing she saw was that painting. She loved Jesus, but her eyes rested on Judas.

"Forgive me, Father, for I am about to sin again."

Spying on Gracie up on their church balcony, were Matt and his good friend Joe, also a member of the teen ministries at Oostburg.

"Pretty girl," said Joe, stating the obvious.

"Yup."

"You sure?"

"Yup."

Joe took a look at Matt and baiting him, said:

"She could be everything you ever wanted."

The males watched Gracie come out of the pews and go on the stage. She began to gently sing the first few notes of *Amazing Grace*. Miss Gracie Adams really was close to perfect. So perfect that guys do not dare touch her; for the fear you will break her, much like one of those dainty *Precious Moment* dolls or a glass figurine. Not a lot, actually not any, guys had asked her out. The girl was on the market but way too expensive.

Joe said:

"I bet her father would approve. So would yours."

"You don't know my dad," Matt said.

"Well, then you can run away from this town, just you and Gracie. It would be perfect."

"Life would be perfect, I suppose."

Joe looked at Matt again.

"But it wouldn't," Joe finished.

Vicki knocked on her aunt's door. She had no options other than the one in front of her, which she thought was a joke. The sheriff was a joke. The whole department was a joke and this was the next chapter of her life.

Aunt Coralee was holding a pot of coffee.

"Yes? May I help you?"

Vicki stared briefly and then realized dear Aunt Coralee forgot she was coming.

"Aunt Coralee, it's me, Victoria."

"Victoria? No, she died many years ago."

"No, I did not. I'm right here. I'm moving in, and I just had a job interview at the police station."

Snapping back, Coralee remembered again where and who she was.

"Yes, come on in. So how did it go, Victoria?" asked the aunt as she watched her niece enter her home.

"Surprisingly... as expected," replied Vicki in a smart-aleck way.

"Interesting way of putting it," observed Coralee as she poured a mug of black coffee for her niece.

"For once, I would like to live in a city where I didn't have to worry—"

Coralee interrupted.

"Worry? About what? You know, my sweet nephew, the Good God has it over control."

Vicki rolled her eyes.

"I know what you're doing," reassured Coralee. "I see that you are trying to run away from Satan."

The quirky old aunt made a point but Vicki didn't want any part of her religious interpretations.

"Can you stop with the religious propaganda?"

Coralee smiled.

"Well. I need a ride to church."

Time to pay the rent.

Vicki waited patiently for Coralee to fasten her seat belt, which she didn't do. Vicki thought how weird it was that someone can be there in one second and gone the next.

Eventually, Vicki buckled up her aunt and began to drive the five minutes to Oostburg Community Church.

Vicki took a left.

"I followed this guy around town today. Went down to Cedarberg... or ville, something like that."

Coralee laughed.

"Oh, you may not need me to set you up. You are a stalker!"

Vicki sighed and shook her head.

"Is that all you think about?"

"Once you're married I can get married too."

At sixty-something, it was unlikely Aunty Coralee would ever slither down that blessed aisle of matrimony again. Even at thirty-seven, it was very unlikely Vicki would either.

"Aunt Coralee."

"So what's his name?"

Vicki took a right.

"Not a clue, auntie," Vicki said. "I'm convinced he was discussing some illegal activity. I'd love to keep eyes on him. Anyway, he's not marriage material."

Vicki pulled up to the dilapidated looking church and took a breath. She didn't want to go to church. She had a twenty-something year streak of absence, and this was going to break it.

Like a first grader, Vicki asked:

"Do I have to?"

Coralee tried to get out of the seat belt but after a few seconds of not succeeding, Vicki helped her.

"Not many people eat broccoli, but they know they should, right? Besides, it is part of the deal we made. You go to church when I go to church, and you can live with me rent-free."

She remembered that.

Vicki looked at the building again. What a dump.

"This may be the most expensive rent I have paid. And I'm a New Yorker."

"Not anymore."

Zinged.

"You will like it… I'm very sure. I know at least fourteen single males in your age range."

"My age range? And what is my age range, Coralee-Harmony?"

"Over 30."

"And under...?"

Coralee pointed out the window. "Ah, there is one now."

Vicki turned to see the oldest gent in the galaxy attempting to walk up the stairs at a deathly pace. The man was too old for Aunt Coralee.

"Oh my god."

"You're going to like it here."

Vicki got out of the car and walked around it to help her aunt.

"Let's get this over with."

Vicki and Coralee took the lengthy, painful steps into the detention office. Halfway up the steps, Aunt Coralee grabbed her niece's arm.

"I love you, Victoria."

Vicki, unable to reciprocate, looked away.

They entered the building, which appeared just as regular and old school as the outside. That poor stench of immorality and hypocrisy took over Vicki's nostrils. She had been to church before but it had been years. It was rarely about God or Jesus. It was more about the tithe, the sin, the judgment, and the glaring looks.

She entered the lion's home once again and looked around; fixating on a man whose presence shot red flags in the air.

"My gut says this guy is up to no good."

"You have to stop listening to your gut," advised Coralee.

"Your gut will change once you settle in. We will kick that New Yorking out of you. I told your mama not to move to New York."

Now moving into their sanctuary, Coralee took her niece by the elbow, attempting to guide her down to her favorite seat in the church.

"My gut is rarely wrong," Vicki defended.

"Any proof?"

For a lady with dementia, she was sure putting up a battle.

"No."

"Then stop thinking about this man. Unless he was single...?"

"He had a ring."

Coralee turned a one-eighty:

"Then just wash this man right out of your hair. Just clean him out completely."

"I can't."

"Why not?"

"Cause he is standing ten feet away from me."

The man who Vicki was chasing all over Wisconsin, was now standing right there. In this very church.

"Who?"

Vicki could see a little man pushing a woman in a wheelchair.

But she was not referring to him.

Vicki saw another man taking a breath mint from a basket.

But she was not referring to him.

It was the third person she was referring to, the grinning male with the red tie.

"The man with the red tie."

The man with the red tie smiled as he walked slowly towards the ladies. Aunt Coralee smiled back.

"That is the man who is doing criminal activities in Oostburg?"

"That's him."

The man got closer. Vicki was surer than ever this was the male she had been trailing this afternoon, from that close accident at the stop sign to that weird conversation in Jesus Take The Wheel, to now.

"Victoria, you're crazy. That's our shepherd, Pastor Seth Adams."

8.

THE MAN
CHALLENGES HIS SHEEP

Pastor Seth walked up to Coralee Mentink and took her hands between his; a sure sign of friendship. Vicki looked back at her aunt and could not believe her eyes; her old aunt was on friendly terms with this suspicious pastor, and to top it off, there was no way Coralee was going to buy anything that Vicki was selling.

Based on Seth's gaze, Vicki could notice that the pastor recognized her but was attempting to put the one final piece in the puzzle.

"Good evening, Pastor Seth. Are you excited about Brooklyn?" asked Coralee.

"Chicago. We leave after the concert."

"Pastor Seth, let me introduce you to my, umm, my daughter—I meant niece, I'm getting so forgetful! This is Victoria."

Seth offered his handshake which Vicki cautiously accepted.

"Hello," said Seth genuinely.

"Hi."

"Have we met before?"

She wasn't sure if Seth was lying or really daft. They had just met about three hours past when he almost ran into her car.

"Well—"

"You look familiar."

Yeah, you almost cost me thousands of dollars in repairs, jackass.

"Guess I have one of those faces."

The three shared an innocent, awkward chuckle.

"Well, we are about to begin. Nice meeting you...Victoria. I'm sure we'll meet again."

The pastor stood at the pulpit. Vicki could smell that arrogance from the middle of the sanctuary, as she had smelled the stench before in various other churches of so-called worship. Like the pastor's body language, this room was stuffy; Vicki felt as if she were suffocating. Vicki had to get out of here but she also had to pay her rent. Perhaps in a few months, she could get on her feet and leave, but right now her aunt needed her, more than Vicki needed Coralee and she couldn't leave her.

Aunt Coralee was fading.

Vicki looked around this congregation. Sitting to the right of the pastor was a young lady. One that from some distance looked oddly familiar. She could see that wheelchair woman sitting at the end of the aisle, right next to the short male. Presumably, they were a couple. Makes sense that the short dude would be with the wheelchair. Short males can't be picky. In the front row, there was a pretty female in her forties; Vicki guessed she was the pastor's wife. The blonde lady had the same vibe as Seth did but Vicki could tell right off the old bible that she was fake as hell. A teenager was next to her; successfully sneaking something without her mother knowing. In the back, her new boss—ugh—Ellis, sat by himself. Vicki was glad Sheriff Kirkbride didn't have a woman with him this evening. It would have been awkward to tell the lady that her boyfriend had been borderline flirting with her at the job interview.

Pastor Windbag began.

"So what do you do? When someone hurts you so bad? Makes you cry at night wondering why God—why God did You—let this happen? Most of us know that our Lord can do anything. The Almighty. He can change hearts; change lives. Can end pain and suffering. But sometimes He doesn't. Sometimes, He lets us go through that pain; that suffering so we can see Him on the other side. How do you rise up during moments of hurt? Do you punch and scream? Do you turn to God for that very first time? Or do you delete it all and start fresh? Do you... ask for forgiveness? Do you continue to question Lord Almighty? Or do you repent? Do you *forgive*? Heavenly Father, heal the wounds. Let us praise You in the storm. We pray for those out here who are listening to Your word, oh Lord. May we hear You—may we have eyes to view. May we see the world—

—through eyes of grace."

Vicki cheated and opened her eyes. Looking around the scene, she was dumbfounded by the sheep. During the sermon, Vicki could see a subtle uneasiness amongst the parishioners. That wheelchair woman glared at the short guy several times. Ellis, her new boss, dozed off for a second. A fat kid dug his canal, wiping the gold wad on a hymnal. Vicki briefly grinned. She was probably on her way to Hell but she didn't care. She didn't want to be in Heaven, anyway. *Why would anybody desire to spend eternity with the almighty healer who sometimes chooses not to heal? What good is the physician if he is not going to hand out the cure?*

"In Jesus Name, Amen," Seth finished his sermon.

"Amen," chanted the sheep.

Vicki looked around again. Surprised—and happy!—that this may indeed be the shortest church service she ever attended, the new deputy continued to be in awe of the robotic response—a cult-like atmosphere of sad Kool-Aid drinkers who had nothing better to do on their Friday night.

What was his deal? Vicki wondered. *Why was the pastor meeting a man in that shady old bar? Why did the pastor hand the guy quite a pile of money?* There was something fishy about this pastor; as he certainly was not fishing for men, Vicki was sure of that.

The preacher continued:

"Amen. Thank you for coming to Oostburg Community Church's annual fundraiser event. And lastly, for those of you that do profess O.C.C. as your church, please if you see a new face, say hi. And remember—"

Pastor paused and stared at a male in the back of the church. Vicki turned around and noticed it was that man she saw steal a mint.

Seth cleared his throat.

"You know what? I don't normally do this—well in truth, I have never done this. But I'm going to take my own advice and welcome a stranger. Not to put you on the spot, sir. Yes, sir in the back—I've never seen you before—"

The entire congregation turned around to stare at this specimen of a heathen, obviously not comfortable with all the attention. The man looked about and smiled sheepishly. Man, that preacher put him on the spot!

"My apologies for the unwanted spotlight... but I also want to welcome you to Oostburg Community Church."

Vicki could tell that the outsider was not happy. She was content he didn't call on her. *What a jerk!*

"How are you, friend?" Seth asked.

Nevertheless, the stranger spoke:

"I'm fine. Just fine."

Vicki recognized another male, the man who caught Seth in the bar with the other suspicious guy. Now, what was his name—ah, Bob. Oh boy, Bob looked embarrassed. Vicki also saw even the pastor's wife slouch a little.

"Very glad to hear. And what's the name, friend?" pursued Seth.

This man looked around like he was being unfairly interrogated by the mob of sheep.

"Bernard," said the man in the spotlight.

"Bernard, nice to meet you. We wish you very much happiness."

"Bernard" nodded quickly and sat down in the last pew, thankful that his fifteen minutes were up.

"Now where... oh yes, all the proceeds from this evening go to the church outreach fund. Um, many of our members have made items or baked items to sell, including my wife Evelyn's delicious brownies."

The fake woman in the front, whom Vicki predicted was the equally fake pastor's wife, turned around and smiled.

Vicki had a coarse time with the Christian atmosphere. It was all fake; ever since she went to Catholic school back in New York. The Jesus kids were supposedly believers, Christians, whatever. They lied and gossiped and hurt just as bad as these non-religious kids. There just did not seem to be much difference between the two worlds.

Pastor continued:

"And now, I will have my beautiful princess grace us with her wonderful voice."

The pretty, familiar teenager lowered her head in embarrassment. Yup. Typical daddy embarrassment time.

"My princess has always been the glee of my life; always striving to be a better gal than she was before—seeking truth, seeking love. Ha, funny story... when she was... Gracie, may I embarrass you once?"

The teenager giggled. She apparently enjoyed this attention, but yet at the same time did not want people to know she liked it.

"When she was eight, Gracie once told me I had to brew the coffee. Then I asked why? And she said: "Daddy! Because... "*he brews*"... get it? Hebrews—Hebrews?""

The congregation laughed like it was the funniest thing since the Lord smote whoever the Lord smoted. Vicki didn't think it was that funny.

The teenage beauty leaned forward to her clueless dad.

"Dad—that was Lainey."

Now Seth was embarrassed, but he continued:

"Ah, my mistake. My beautiful young princess, Miss Gracie Adams."

The sheep clapped. Gracie—now she knew her name—tramped over to the microphone and said something silly that went over Vicki's realm of experience.

Something about loving and forgiving one another.

She started to sing.

The girl did have a nice voice.

"She sure has the talents," declared Joe, leaning up against a wall in an obscure corridor. "So... what's wrong with her?"

"Nothing..." Matt scanned into the door window as he dreamed of the life that could be with Gracie. Maybe the perfect life, a life that maybe his Heavenly Father would approve of. A life so perfectly happy, that it was not really what he wanted.

"Nothing. She is the perfect girl."

Inside the room, a room in which countless teenage ministry activities were planned and put to bed, sat Gracie and her young Christian entourage.

"So tomorrow night—we invite all the guys on the basketball team and have a sleepover—"

Bianca interrupted Michelle. She was another girl in Gracie's tiny circle, just as feminine and boy-crazy as the next girl.

"We're going to be really naughty. R-rated movies and gluten."

"I don't know..." Gracie said.

"Adams, your rents are going away for a three-day weekend. This is that perfect opportunity for a party," Bianca said.

Gracie was hesitant.

"But my parents trust me. And plus there's Lainey."

"Please, Lainey's a nothing. Just give her twenty bucks, and she will shut up," said Bianca.

Michelle continued Bianca's pleas:

"Tomorrow is Saturday. You know Saturday night is when the bar lets teens have discount beer."

Gracie's eyes bulged.

"Michelle!"

"I... heard."

Gracie apparently did not want to go out.

"There's church the next day."

"Fine, tonight then," Michelle suggested.

"No, tonight's not... good."

"Already got plans?" asked Bianca.

"No, it's just the rents aren't leaving till like nine o'clock—"

The friends just did not get where Gracie was coming from. It was Friday; they could pass for twenty-one and get some liquor and call it communion.

"You're getting lame, Gracie," stated Bianca.

"Fine, tomorrow night—one party—but not the whole basketball team." They won.

"And that's how peer pressure works, my friends!" Bianca stated.

Matt wandered his way outside. Gracie was beautiful and kind and everything a man could want in a partner. Smart and held faith. Fun. She wasn't going to get arrested anytime soon. She was probably going to go to college and do some mission ministry.

The teen walked over to a man, who was staring at the moon.

"You were that guy in the back... Pastor Seth pointed out. Bernard, right?"

Charles Raile nodded.

"Ah, yeah, kid." He paused to change the subject: "Lonely night, huh?"

Lonely yes, but it was nice at least for October. Matt didn't even need a jacket. It was peaceful. Almost too peaceful...

"Yeah."

"You into all this stuff?" Charles asked Matt.

"What stuff?"

"Religion, faith, Jesus."

"Oh, I don't know. My dad is the Assistant Pastor here," Matt replied.

"Ah. The *Ass Pastor*."

"Yeah, I guess so," Matt chuckled.

"And your mom?"

"Mom died last year."

Charles Raile connected.

"My mom died last year too."

They both looked up at the sky.

Matt was unsure about his future. He was going to graduate eight months from now and had no clue where he would end up. The teen certainly didn't want to be a bar janitor the rest of his life.

"So you believe all this?"

Matt paused, but went on:

"I have my doubts."

Raile nodded.

"Me too kid. Me too."

If it were possible to be comfortable and uncomfortable at the same time, Matt was feeling it. The teen had no idea what to say to this older man but the night was so calming that he had no reason to leave either.

"Looks like a storm's coming."

Raile smiled as deep in his head screams of Ivy were penetrating.

"You have no idea."

Pastor Seth Adams counted the cold money from the collection plate. There was a sweet fifteen hundred and forty dollars, not too bad for an eve of a few songs, a couple of testimonies, and a very short message. Fifteen hundred dollars would go a long way at a casino in Milwaukee. Pastor briefly wrestled with the idea and would've toyed with it longer if it hadn't been for the forceful knock on his office door.

"Who is it?" Pastor Adams asked full-knowing who was on the other end.

"Bob."

Seth started to put the cash in an envelope.

Unfortunately, those casinos would have to wait.

"Come in."

Bob Zimmermann entered and shut the door.

"Uh-oh. Shut-door conversation."

Confidently, Bob walked over to the pastor's desk and plopped heavily in the empty chair. Not wanting to get into it with Bob this late at night, he put his head in his hands. Zimmermann smiled. Seth felt Bob liked scolding him; as a mentor enjoys belittling his teenage prodigy when they have made a poor choice.

"Bold move... um, putting that spotlight on a total stranger."

Ah. So this was about the stranger in the church. He guessed incorrectly that it would be about the cash.

"I know. Bob, I know. Have you ever just had a... feeling, where you know it may not be kosher but you do it anyway?"

"Yes. It's called temptation," Bob smart-assed.

"Did I go too far?"

Bob grinned smugly. The second banana massaged in the mistakes as if he would perhaps get Seth to one day quit. Mind manipulations were a favorite tactic of Bob.

"Oh... I doubt we ever see that gentleman again."

Bob continued:

"Temptation is tough, much like, say, speeding."

Seth stared at him; unsure if his old nemesis was baiting him.

"You might want to get somewhere quicker, but you know you should not cross the lines of society."

"Was I wrong to do that?"

"Oh... you had the right heart. You certainly had the right heart."

"Well, it's in His hands."

"It always is," Bob one-upped.

The pastors stood up and walked to the door.

Seth buttoned his suit jacket and patted the trusted rival on the shoulder and gave a smart-ass grin.

"How is it that I got this job instead of you?"

Bob Zimmermann patted Seth on the back and smiled; a false grin that contradicted the steam in his ears.

"Oh, Seth... I ask myself the same question," Bob said sarcastically.

On his route to the sanctuary, Seth walked past his younger kid. He almost forgot about her. There were so many items on his mind, the money, Gracie, the money from the concert, and the money. This girl was simply an afterthought. She usually was, actually.

"Can I have another cookie?" Lainey asked.

"Did you have one already?"

Lainey was busted, and she knew it.

"Didn't mom say only one?" continued Seth.

Lainey smiled. She was cute when she wanted to be sneaky. Seth could not resist and gave the girl another gingerbread person cookie.

"Don't tell your mom," Seth said as he left his daughter all alone.

"I never do."

Lainey bit the head off the cookie.

About half the congregation petered out, but Aunt Coralee was the type of woman that needed to say hi and bye to everyone; and since she had dementia that could be more than once per person. Vicki tallied this as she watched her aunt.

Vicki made plans with her cousin, Jessica, Aunt Coralee's daughter, up in Green Bay.

Coralee filled her tea with a little creamer. Vicki let it slide.

"Still think our pastor's a crook?"

Vicki sighed.

"I don't know. Maybe I'm stressing too much."

Looking around aimlessly, she stole a look at the pretty young lady. It was the teenager who sang just a half hour ago... *what the hell was her name...* and the youth looked exactly like—

"Gabrielle," Vicki whispered to herself.

Gabrielle walked up the hallway, toward Vicki and old Coralee, without a care in the world. Gabrielle was beautiful; looking the exact opposite of how Vicki last saw her... the only minor difference was the hair color. Gabrielle was a brunette. This girl was a redhead.

She walked over and hugged Coralee tight.

"Gracie, you were wonderful," Coralee spoke as she glowed with pride.

"Thank you, Aunt Coralee."

Vicki continued to stare at this Gracie/Gabrielle combination with disbelief. Had Vicki been a crier, she would have been bursting out both windows. Vicki wasn't a weeper though; she just swore a lot.

"Gracie, this is my sister's girl... yes, Victoria. And this is Gracie, Pastor Seth's daughter."

Gracie smiled—a pure, innocent grin:

"Hi, nice to meet you."

All Vicki could do was stare, which Gracie surely picked up on even if she did not know the reason for Vicki's lapse of speaking ability.

Finally, Vicki said:

"Nice to meet you."

"Gracie has adopted me over the last couple of... years. I am her, um, piano teacher. Every Monday and... Tuesday."

"Hello, your aunt means so much to me. We have been playing the piano together for an hour on Tuesdays and Thursdays, Aunt Coralee, for the last two or so years."

Coralee leaped a little.

"Oh, that's so exciting!"

What the hell do you mean? Vicki thought. The kid just smiled. Gracie knew Coralee's quirks more than Vicki; in many ways, she was more family than Vicki. The kid even called her "aunt".

"So are you excited about being the only adult in your house this weekend?"

And at that point, Gracie waved to another young girl and shouted:

"Hi, gorgeous! Excuse me."

And she was gone, to run away in all her innocent perfection, politeness, and life.

How unfair it was that this youth, this practical doppelganger for Gabrielle, same looks, height, weight, eye color, age, could be so vibrant and the other so... dead. It was just unfair. How did Gabrielle get the bad cards she was dealt and Gracie get these cards?

Because God is in control.

And he favors some people, that's how.

Vicki continued to watch the teens walk away as a nosey photographer stopped her to take a picture.

Gracie even smiled like Gabrielle.

"Cute kid."

"Just beautiful inside and out. She went Mexicano once for a mission trip, raised all the money herself," said Coralee.

Vicki stared and corrected her aunt.

"She went *to* Mexico once."

"That's what I said."

Vicki nodded her head and was about to speak when Coralee went on:

"You are going to like it here. There are so fewer worries and even lesser worries. More men."

"Oh, stop. I'm not interested anymore. At my—"

And then, much to her chagrin, Sheriff Kirkbride came into her tunnel. She just wanted to be off to Green Bay and hang with her cousin.

"Aunt Coralee," Ellis said.

Ellis kissed Coralee on the cheek and old Coralee walked off. Coralee turned around to wink at her niece, as if "here's your set up!"

"Aunt Coralee!"

He smiled and offered his arm.

"May I give you the tour?"

Walking into the comfy fellowship hall one minute later, Vicki began to ease up ever-so-slightly. The new deputy of Oostburg thought perhaps Ellis spiked the tea he had handed her but slowly realized Sheriff Kit-Kat probably did not have the brains nor the fortitude for such an elaborate scheme.

"So... how are the first seven hours living as an Oostburger?" Ellis asked Oostburg's newest resident.

"An Oostburger? With cheese, apparently."

Two could play at this game.

"Nice."

"Good Lord, I've entered the sticks."

"These sticks have been very kind to me. A lot of friends and not a lot of worries." The man reminisced. "I have lived here all of my life. Born in Oostburg, and I will probably die in Oostburg. I went to school here, wasn't a great student but not a bad one, either. I was quarterback for the junior and senior varsity. I wasn't horrible but not good enough to be drafted. A real true Oostburger."

"That is attractive, Oostburger."

Ellis smiled. He was working his easy charm. *"Why was he single?"* she thought.

"See you're getting the hang of it."

They made their way from the fellowship hall over into the lobby.

"What kind of name is "Oostburg" anyway?"

"I think it's Dutch."

Vicki had heard of some weird rules people abided by. This gossip came from Aunt Coralee, who either made it up or didn't remember correctly.

"Can't even mow your lawn on Sunday?"

Ellis confirmed:

"It's frowned upon."

"Can I burp?"

"Not on Sunday."

"I can tell you this; I am quite looking forward to semi-retirement in Oostburg."

"How old are you, forty-two?"

Vicki's draw dropped. Ah—that's why he's single. Two can play at this game.

"Jackass."

Ellis's eyebrows rose as Vicki gave a quick, sassy smile. He looked around to see if anyone had caught an ear of Vicki's mouth.

"I'm not a prude, but in church?"

Vicki justified.

"Jesus rode on one."

Vicki playfully grinned.

"So, deputy. You are looking for a simpler life. How come?"

Vicki looked at Ellis. From the juncture of their acquaintance, she did not really yearn to dive into her past. He was now her superior, and Vicki felt this was a question that would be more suited for a man who was in pursuit of her.

"Miss Weathers will pass on this conversation."

Sensing her tone, Ellis relented and went back to the banter:

"With a cool last name like weathers, I think you missed your calling: you should be a weather girl."

Vicki almost laughed at the corny comment.

"The 90s called, they'd like their joke back."

Ellis touched his heart.

"Ouch."

The two cops made their return back to the lobby, where Vicki noticed the pastor chatting with three other guys. She was probably mistaken about his actions but she hated to give up on such a suspicious person.

Pessimism was listed on her resume.

"So those two are my best friends—Seth—"

"The Pope guy."

"Yeah... and that other guy is Wesley, that guy standing next to the punch bowls. Wesley works at a video store. Wes and his wife, Brooke, have been trying to get pregnant, but they haven't been..." Ellis paused, and Vicki sensed he was about to tell something that he shouldn't—and then he switched gears. "Well. It's, uh, taken a toll on their marriage."

She smiled; full-knowing he kept part of the story to himself.

"You gossip like a woman."

The little guy left the picture just as his wife, that female in the wheelchair, rolled in. Vicki assumed the man left because he saw his female and was avoiding her. Vicki always thought the worst of someone.

The handicapped lady wheeled over to them.

She asked:

"Hey, have you seen Wesley?"

Ellis turned around. "He's by the punch bowls—oh, he was a second ago," stated Ellis.

Wesley left without Ellis even noticing. For a sheriff, Ellis was not very observant. Vicki noticed that the guy had left seconds after that woman entered. Maybe there's trouble in the marriage.

Brooke sighed as she looked around.

"Okay. Tell him I have to go to work."

"You need a ride?" asked Ellis.

Brooke smiled.

"Asking a woman in a wheelchair if she needs a ride?"

Vicki was impressed. It seemed people in Oostburg had an intelligent sense of humor. Maybe she would like it here after all.

Brooke continued:

"I am driving our car to work, so it's Wesley who'll need a ride."

"Not a problem, Vicki can give him a ride," Ellis said.

Vicki wasn't sure if he was pulling her leg.

"As you said, I'm your boss now."

The three walked their path to the church parking lot. Vicki could see her breath blow in the air. It was beginning to get a little chilly as the sun had dropped for the night. In the cold, there was peace and beauty.

Ellis helped Brooke get into the driver's seat by slowly picking up the lady and gently putting her in the ride. Vicki was impressed with Ellis's down-to-earth happy personality and his desire to help others. Vicki helped as well by folding up the wheelchair and placing it in the trunk. The car was handicapped accessible.

"Thanks," said Brooke.

"Someone at work will help you out?" asked Vicki.

"Yeah, they always do. Thank you. And nice meeting you, Vicki."

"You too."

Brooke shut the door and drove away.

"Car accident; nine months ago. The winters stink here. They say she will walk again."

Thanks be to that lord. Another horrible accident that should have been prevented by the almighty healer.

Another coffee break, she guessed.

Back in the church lobby, the small Wesley walked right past Pastor Seth.

"Hey, Wesley. Glad to see you here tonight."

"Yeah."

Seth pressed a bit but could tell Wesley did not want to talk.

"It has been a little while. I'd love to do lunch with you sometime. See how you and Brooke are doing. Is anything new?"

Ellis and Vicki walked over.

"And here are your three stooges. Ellis, Seth, and Wesley. We used to have some fun times, right guys?"

Ellis turned to Vicki.

"And this is my new deputy, Vicki Weathers."

"New deputy?"

"Yes, Pastor Stop Sign," Vicki sarcastically teased.

Vicki smiled; hoping it would cue Seth's memory.

"Listen, I need to leave," stated Wesley, staring out a window. "Headache."

"Need a ride?" asked Ellis, remembering that his wife had the one car in the Demko family.

"Nah."

"You sure?"

"Yeah, I'll walk."

"Lunch," stated Seth.

"Lunch."

Odd Wesley was off. He appeared to be... late for something or maybe just uncomfortable with the company. Maybe he didn't like women. *What a drab little man. Not much for conversation*, Vicki thought.

"And this is the town pastor?"

Seth smiled proudly.

"Yeah, there's only one in this town."

Ellis piggybacked:

"Not a lot of sinning going on in Oostburg."

Vicki grinned and turned her head. Through her peripheral vision and the open window, she could see the wind blow the curtains open as a cool October breeze came through. Outside, she could see small Wesley get into a ride. That Wesley Demko, who had not two minutes prior said he was going to walk home...

Vicki mentally went back to the two males she was conversing with.

Seth began the interrogation:

"So, where did you go to church in—"

She wasn't going to let him start interrogating. She had a few questions of her own, church be damned.

"Where'd you get your license?" Vicki pressed.

"Pastor's or driving?" Seth smiled.

"Driving."

Seth nodded.

"I asked you first."

Vicki submitted.

"New York City. And no, I did not go to church there. Actually, I haven't been to worship in... a long time. I came here to move in with my aunt."

"Miss Mentink, I sure will appreciate your assistance. Dementia is hard. I always pray for her."

"Oh, you don't have to."

She shook the ark. She knew prayer was useless. Vicki didn't care that Seth was a pastor; she was going to crap on his god, his daft religion right on his home turf. Perhaps a few people will even pay attention and listen.

It was her turn to preach:

"The way I see it, pastor, prayer cures people of the responsibility to do something useful."

Seth coughed a little as Vicki continued:

"The god can stop suffering, so why doesn't it?"

"You tell me."

"Jesus loves the little children, then why does he let them suffer? Kids do not deserve to die of cancer."

"Life and death are all in His hands. We all must die," Seth responded.

"And yet, theoretically speaking, of course... if it is all in "His hands", whatever the circumstance is, then you should be optimistic that the positive outcome will prevail. But, if it is in His hands, then how come the positive outcome doesn't always prevail? I say, the question is: "Is He, God, in control?" If the answer is no, then—humanity sucks. If the answer is yes, then it is god who sucks."

Seth stood patiently listening. He could handle whatever the cop was going to tell him. Knowing an angry seeker when he saw one, the pastor silently prayed for clarity on how to handle this attack on his God. He asked God for strength and patience.

Vicki continued:

"Either god is too weak to solve the problems, or it doesn't care, or it doesn't exist."

Vicki remembered that day in New York. March. The day they found the first piece of Gabrielle. Covered in blood. God did not fix that. God didn't care. Maybe it couldn't. Or maybe, just maybe... it is all a hoax. One of the three.

"So pastor, either the god is powerless, uncaring, or imaginary."

He nodded with the years of counseling experience he had. Adams did care about her. She was sad like all lost are. Seth did not agree with Vicki's surmising but he cared for her. Christ cared for this deputy too, she just didn't know it. He was saddened by the hardness of her heart but this was no time to attack the poor girl. This was the moment to lend an ear.

She continued:

"And I got to thinking... that is so true. If god did love us, it would not let us suffer." Vicki began to notice her blood pressure build as she defended teenage Gabrielle's circumstance. "Pastor Adams. There are many people out there who do a lot of suffering. Take a hurricane. People build up their account and pay off their mortgages, just to see Jesus blow a storm their way, and bam! They lose everything. Everything. And yet, god can prevent that."

Damn it, lord... Why did you let Gabrielle suffer? Why did she die so young? This stupid pastor is nodding but he does not know what it is like to suffer. One day maybe he will...

She paused, and Seth took the opportunity to step in.

"So God's... cruel?" Seth asked.

Vicki stared at Adams for a good second. "Yes. It is cruel." Vicki took a step closer. "I believe, Pastor Seth. Yes, I believe in god. But it doesn't love us. No, it doesn't. It's out to destroy us. Kill us. Every day, someone perishes... because it decides "enough"."

Vicki looked directly into his eyes. She could tell he was a decent guy. Just stupid.

"You do not know reality, pastor. You are a Jacob amongst Esaus."

Vicki's phone rang. She looked at the caller ID.

"I believe. And I'm terrified. Good night."

Vicki left the gentlemen to fend for themselves.

"Miss Weathers is a rare breed," Seth analyzed.

Ellis grinned.

"Eh, she's a solid eight."

"That's not what I'm talking about. She is not an atheist. She is a dysthiest."

"What's that?"

"Someone who believes in our God, but thinks He's evil..."

Furiously, Vicki stormed into the parking lot.

"Damn it," she said to herself. She would have to return to the sad, lie-fest known as Oostburg Community Church every Sunday morning and evening. Vicki promised Aunt Coralee she would take care of her; and that meant driving her to this hellhole.

Vicki looked about and saw a homeless man sitting against the church wall, right under a giant crack that seemed to almost end up in the guy's skull.

Three happy churchgoers walked right by him; oblivious to the cold dude's presence. It bothered Vicki to see these church-goers bouncing out of service could simply pass by this man. This is why she didn't follow Christianity. It was all too much about the Lord God and little about taking care of others.

Vicki walked up to the man and gave him a twenty-dollar bill. The homeless man spoke:

"Thanks, pretty woman. Name's Homeless Jay. I'll be sure to return the favor!"

Vicki smiled and wished she had more time to talk to this brave gent, who based on his pins and looks had served in Vietnam forty-plus years ago. Vicki could not stay; she had to find Aunt Coralee.

"Excuse me," she said to the man.

"Yes, Aunt Coralee? Where are you?"

Vicki stomped over to the ride and found her aunt there. Why did she call sounding so scared? Oh my Lord, this was going to be a bad few pages in Vicki's life if she was going to essentially be her aunt's baby-sitter.

Coralee smiled. She was relieved that Vicki found her.

"It's nice to have my own personal chauffeur."

Vicki shut the door.

"Glad to be of service," Vicki stated. "Didn't we lock the doors?"

"I'm pretty good with a bobby pin."

"Oh my God, Aunt. That's breaking and entering."

At least Vicki was going to get to see her cousin soon. She pulled out of the parking lot. She was mad as hell but she couldn't let that affect her driving.

Vicki split open:

"I just... can't believe you buy that church crap Aunt Coralee."

Coralee was of full faculties now.

"You changed, Victoria. You used to be so... umm, positive."

Vicki turned a corner. She wished there were some street lights. Yeah, Wisconsin sucked.

"I'm positive. Positive that it's junk."

"I just wish—"

Vicki cut her off.

"Look, I'm glad you have some higher god being to turn to. But it's... not for me. Please respect my beliefs, and I will respect yours."

Coralee reasoned with her final strands of common sense that was an inch away from being tangled.

"How do you think the moon was created, Victoria? Just a cloud of gases that exploded? You're crazy."

"With all due respect, I'm not battling dementia."

Damn it, Vicki! She briefly shut her eyes knowing she had crossed a line.

Coralee swallowed; not knowing what to say or how to respond. She stared for two moments at her niece and then turned her head slowly to the side.

The man touched the freshly painted bookcase. The stench of fine oak could still permeate through the air. "A good smell," said the man. The special bookcase weighed about a hundred pounds, not much for a man of his size. He moved back the bookcase, covering the very secret door behind it...

After his job behind the bookcase, the man walked back to his 2008 Buick, as inconspicuous as possible, for he was carrying a heavy black body bag. It was a little earlier than normal for this type of operation but this eager client wanted the baggage as soon as possible.

The calm man moved the body bag to the back seat, picking it up rather quickly. The man shoved the bag in the rear of the car, but in a very gentle manner.

That black bag slowly began to move and groan.

Staring at the bag, the male closed the back door and got in the front.

He took out his cell and dialed.

A man, taking a dump, picked up the phone.

"Where to, boss?"

"Chicago," said the boss.

The employee, Cody was the name, hung up his cell phone and looked in his rearview mirror.

The bag moved a little more vigorously...

Charles Raile left the warm men's room and looked around.

Peering through the large oak double doors of the sanctuary, Charles saw the pretty blonde laughing with a few older women.

Three laughing women were interrupted by that pastor and another guy. The pastor came from behind and goosed his wife. Raile went back and hid behind a large plant.

The three women giggled as Pastor Adams and his red-faced wife were playfully inappropriate in church. No one really cared; it was nice to see the pastor show public displays of affection once in the while. It also created tightness with the congregation; the minister who was transparent with his feelings was probably more likely to be honest, they felt.

"You're all packed?" Evelyn asked her husband.

"Hun, we are leaving for a three-day weekend. How much do I need to pack?"

Ellis turned to the ladies.

"Three days? Seth doesn't even need multiple underwear."

Seth and the ladies laughed. Only Evelyn seemed a little embarrassed.

"Go Pack!" Evelyn said as she smacked the pastor with her handbag.

Pastor Adams spiked a pretend football and made a little touchdown dance.

"Go Pack Go!" Pastor yelled as he danced down the hallway and through the double doors.

"What a dork!" Evelyn smiled as she giggled.

"And he's all yours," confirmed Ellis.

Sheriff Ellis walked away as the gossiping ladies followed.

Now all alone, Evelyn left the sanctuary through the large double doors and bumped into the gent. Evelyn looked around hoping no one had seen this encounter. By now, there were only a small handful of people mingling and they didn't seem to notice.

"I told you not to come here," Evelyn whispered.

Raile smiled.

"Ironic, no? That the pastor's wife tells a small humble seeker not to come to church."

Evelyn continued to glance around; making sure no one was hearing this exchange.

"You are not humble."

Raile cut to the point.

"Going to Chicago this weekend?"

She began to walk away but Raile stopped her.

"I have a friend that I want you to meet." Raile persisted. He took out an envelope and pressed it against Evelyn's shapely torso.

"I need you to deliver this envelope."

Evelyn began to leave again but the man grabbed her wrist tightly.

"Your church still needs the money so you will do as I—"

Evelyn attempted to stand her ground.

"I draw the line. This is the last delivery."

"Oh, I don't think so, Evelyn. I would hate for something very horrible to happen."

She took the simple envelope and hid it in her purse.

"Good little sheep."

9.

AFTER CHURCH FRIDAY NIGHT

"I'm such a bitch sometimes," Vicki said to the empty chair. The new roommate hurt her aunt and now she needed to maul some humble pie. Walking up to Coralee's room, Vicki found her aunt turning down the sheets for the evening. The old lady was in her pajamas, a great contrast to the evening attire Vicki was dressed in as she was still going out for a nightcap.

Vicki walked to the door frame and knocked.

Coralee was startled, perhaps forgetting that she had invited Vicki to live with her.

"Hey," Vicki began.

Coralee continued to make up the bed. Perhaps she did not hear Vicki. Maybe she did and was ignoring her. Wonderful way to start this odd couple living arrangement on night one.

"I wanted to apologize for earlier."

Coralee smiled and stopped her chore.

"For what?"

Vicki went on anyway:

"For being an insensitive bitch."

Coralee shook her head and went on with her comfy pillows.

"Oh don't cuss like that, Victoria. It's not ladylike."

"No, I was. I was horribly mean to you. You don't deserve that."

Coralee finished and walked over to Vicki.

"Victoria? Whatever are you talking about?"

Holy crap. She forgot.

Vicki tilted her head. Was this how the next chapter was going to be? She could basically get away with anything she said or did. If Vicki wanted a twenty, she could go into old Coralee's purse and remove it without anyone the wiser. If she were a criminal, of course.

"Aunt Coralee, I completely insulted you."

"When?"

"I—"

Vicki realized it was useless to continue the discussion. Coralee was going to forget it; she already had so there was no need to beat a dead horse.

They walked downstairs and into the kitchen. This was a nice little home, great for two, too vast for one. As they walked downstairs, Vicki wondered how long they would actually be there. Stairs aren't friends of the elderly. They may have to sell and find a one-floor arrangement.

"I love you." Vicki meant it too. Her heart was steely and bitter, but there was still a soft place for her aunt. Probably the only reason Vicki moved here in the first place.

"I love you too. So, I was thinking we could play poker or solitaire together—"

Vicki chuckled.

"I'll take a rain check. I'm going to visit—"

Coralee smiled.

"Your cousin?"

"Yes. How far is the drive to Green Bay?"

"Oh, about three hours. Give or takes. Okay, well you two have an excellent visit. I have a date with Ben and... um... Her."

"Jerry."

At peace that dear Aunt Coralee forgot her severe transgression, she began to exit.

"One of these days I'll need a key."

"Oh, the door is always open so don't worry about a key. And please, don't stay out too late. And tell my Jennifer I said hi!"

She entered her car and plugged in her phone GPS. It was already about 9PM, so if Coralee were right, she was looking at an ETA of midnight or so. No way was she driving home tonight if that were the case. She looked at the phone and was tempted to cancel her date but she hated canceling so she went anyway. She typed in Green Bay and discovered it was only a bit more than an hour.

"Three hours? Not even close."

Downing a scotch, Bob Zimmermann was particularly bitchy this horrible evening. He was not going to win "Father-Of-The-Year" anytime soon. He hated when Seth wise-mouthed him. Bob hated the church that mostly went against him. And he despised that little rascal who called him out a couple of hours ago. What a sucky night for Bob!

His son walked in; his hair a hot mess.

"Where have you been?"

Matt walked towards his room.

"Out."

Bob took a gulp.

"Obviously. A little more specific, boy. Where have you been?"

Matt stopped.

"I hung out with my friends. I don't have to tell you everything."

Being the final straw tonight for Zimmermann, the dad got out of his chair. Bob took leftovers everywhere he went but he was not going to receive them from his own flesh and blood. Getting a tad too near his old man, Matt could smell the alcohol on his father's breath; so he stepped away a little as his dad got closer.

"Oh yeah, tough guy?"

"I am eighteen; I don't have to tell you my every chess move."

Bob steamed.

"Yes you do, you punk. I am your father. You live under my roof—so you live under my orders. Understand? Now, where were you?"

Bob was correct. It was his roof, and therefore he was technically Matt's landlord. Bob had married into money, and his father-in-law purchased the couple a home as a wedding present. He did not really like his father-in-law and was content when he died eleven years ago.

"Maybe I'll just leave," declared Matt.

Bob hurled his glass across the room, scaring the son. Matt was about four inches taller than his dad but when his dad got the crankies, the son knew it was time to back off.

"Go. Go ahead, Matt. Let's see what kind of joint you can afford on a janitor's salary."

Matt left his father to pick up the broken glass.

Bob glared down the hall towards his son's room.

"Arrogant little bastard."

Seconds later, the phone buzzed, and Bob picked it up.

"Hello? Margie. How are you? Oh, I am so sorry to hear. Of course I will pray for your mother—"

Matt heard the hypocritical conversation from his bedroom door.

The door and walls weren't that thick. Matt frequently heard his old folks having sex, unfortunately.

His phone beeped as he plopped on the bed to read it. The message made him giddy as a schoolgirl.

At 9PM and bored watching her mother pack again, Gracie received a message on her phone that gave her an excited smile.

"And remember, Lainey is down by ten the latest," the momma hen said to her elder chick.

"Yes, mother. I got this. I've babysat before."

Evelyn zipped her suitcase.

"I know you have. But never a three-day weekend."

Gracie tucked her cell phone into her pocket.

"I'll be ok, don't worry."

Grabbing her shoulders and pressing hard, the mom kissed her face. Evelyn peered into her young girl's eyes and Gracie returned the stare with strong eye contact.

The daughter knew this eye contact would be a comfort for her mother, full-knowing that deceptive persons are usually not capable of eye contact... unless they were incredible liars.

"You are a beautiful young woman, Miss Grace. I am really proud of the lady you've become. I trust you."

Gracie smiled.

The two ladies tramped downstairs into the foyer. The mom carried two suitcases as did Gracie even though it was only a two-night getaway and the couple would be home Sunday for dinner. Seth held his lonely duffle bag and waited patiently for his bride. He was used to this as most men with twenty years of marital experience are.

"And remember; call us if anything—I mean anything—goes wrong. You burn dinner; anything. Right, Grace?" demanded Evelyn.

Seth coughed.

"I mean, call Sheriff Kirkbride."

"I got it, mom."

"Honey, remember your favorite line," Seth teased before he continued:

"Does anyone think there still is not a reasonable doubt?"

"Thanks, dad."

Evelyn squeezed her little girl tight once again. Mother grabbed the purse on the corner table, the purse that contained whatever Raile wanted her to deliver.

"Love you. Bye Lainey!"

Gracie smiled as Lainey mentally flipped them the bird.

They walked down their driveway with Seth opening the passenger's door for his bride. He hadn't done that in a while. Looking at her, she was as beautiful as the first time they met, even more now almost thirty years later. Seth thanked the Lord for everything he had—and he had everything. A beautiful partner, his girls, a cozy home, and a steady job. Not only that, Seth had Christ in his heart. This made his world easier, knowing the Savior had his back. The couple knew twenty years of being married to the exact person was quite an achievement. After just a few short months of dating, lovers can see the flaws. No one is perfect and yet, numerous people end up spending the rest of their moments holding hands with that same person. It's like saying: "I commit to eating only fish every eve for the rest of my life." It—marriage—really is an amazing feat.

Seth and Evelyn Adams accomplished this wonderful achievement, and Jesus willing, they would have another good forty or fifty years together. Of course, it wasn't easy. Most marriages thrive or die for only one reason: commitment. They knew entering in that if they stuck to this marriage, it probably would remain. They also knew that if they were going to leave at the first sign of trouble, then probably it would fail.

Seth started the car and looked at his wife. She smiled.

"Yes, Mrs. Adams?"

"Nothing."

"Right, nothing. Peace and quiet. Me and you. Two days. And... two nights."

"It's just that, I don't know. Ever feel like, it is just all... going to end?"

"We're going to make it, babe."

"It isn't the finances, Seth. I just—don't know. My stomach is upset."

Seth pulled out of the driveway.

"Well, Chicago's two hours, so if you want to go, do it now."

"It's not that." Evelyn stopped. "Do you ever get the feeling that something bad is going to happen? It's odd. Like, gut or a mother's intuition."

"I'm not a mother," joked Seth as he continued to drive the speed limit.

"Marriages. They come and go so fast these days."

Evelyn thought of Brooke, probably sitting at her desk this evening, perhaps even crying that her husband wasn't showing the affection she deserved. The Demkos had a real abysmal marriage, but in their defense, they had been challenged quite harder than Seth and Evelyn.

Seth began to worry as they entered I-43.

"You okay?"

Evelyn sat forward.

"Is there anything you haven't been telling me?"

She was aware of a weird money flow leaving their savings but she didn't know anything about where the money was going to or coming from.

"You know everything I do," Seth spoke nervously, not knowing what Evelyn knew.

Evelyn smiled but she knew he was lying.

The pastor pulled the ride over, a somewhat dangerous thing to do on the highway, and gave his wife a warm, passionate kiss.

"Our marriage is fine."

The wife felt bad for asking this question. After all, Evelyn wasn't being completely open either, as she clenched her purse.

On the opposite end of the highway, Vicki was not having quite as smooth a transition. She killed her passenger's side rear tire.

Probably on a sharp cheese curd, she thought.

She got out to examine the damage.

"Damn it. Now would be nice to have a man."

Suddenly and without warning, a male entered the scene. He was an older man, about sixty-ish, and he had something huge in his right hand. Vicki was caught off-guard and took a few steps back. She reached her hip to grab her taser, which of course, was no longer there.

This old gent got closer. In his hand appeared to be a sturdy jack.

"Need a hand?"

Vicki sighed in relief. *Praise the Lo*—she caught herself. The dysthiest was not going to praise Jesus in the storm when nine times out of six he was the one who caused the damn storm in the first place.

"Where ya from?" the old man asked her.

"Uh, Oostburg," replied Vicki.

"Heard of it."

Vicki chuckled.

"At least about four hours."

"Ah."

"Oostburg, Wisconsin. A tiny thousand-person town where nothing ever happens."

The old man knelt to work on the tire.

"Isn't that what you wanted?"

What? she thought. How did this man know? Vicki looked around... so weird, there were no cars. Where did this old man come from...?

Gracie Adams came downstairs in a nice and rather conservative outfit. She filled it out quite lovely, and it was in no way inappropriate.

She entered the kitchen to find her little sister sitting at the island counter eating a hot dog.

Gracie went through her purse and took out her keys.

"Where you going?"

Gracie smiled.

"You're cute."

"Evasion," Lainey said, wise beyond her years.

Gracie walked over to her little sister.

"Watch a movie and go to bed. Don't wait up."

Gracie kissed Lainey's head and said:

"Good night, little sister."

Charles Raile stared in his living room, admiring his beautiful bookcase.

Staring at him was an old worn Bible, quite dusty from years of inactivity. He plucked this Bible out and blew on it, coughing a little.

Raile knew the old stories, not that he believed, but he did have the "head knowledge" as most Christians say. He just didn't have the heart knowledge. Returning the Bible to its rightful spot on the shelf, he spoke:

"Time to add another book to the collection."

The Friday evening traffic had been blissfully in their favor. They crossed the Wisconsin-Illinois border and made it to Chicago not too long after.

Seth and Evelyn checked into their hotel and made it downstairs just in time for the last round of reservations, which was late for dinner. Seth and Evelyn had skipped out of dinner earlier so they were starving.

The restaurant, Devin's, was a nice and decorated joint they could not afford on the regular basis. About everything on the menu was close to three digits, their waiters and waitresses were all in black and dressed to the nines. The bathrooms had attendants. Yeah, this was definitely out of their budget.

The host of Devin's, Kristoff, led the hungry duo to their table. Evelyn was impressed by how much effort her man made to make this a special evening. She didn't even care about the blemish it would do to their credit card. They both felt some occasions were worth breaking for.

Their friendly waiter left them with the menu and promised to return in a brief moment.

"Reservations at 11:30PM?" the wife flirtatiously asked her husband.

Evelyn raised her glass of the grape and the pastor followed. She was so beautiful in her purple gown. Even after twenty years and two kids she still had a body that drove Seth crazy. Apparently, it drove a few other guys crazy too, as heads turned in the restaurant.

"Thank you for twenty wonderful years and the kids," Seth cheered.

"Here's to twenty more," Evelyn returned.

"Years, not kids."

They clinked glasses.

Remembering she was still a mommy, Evelyn glanced beyond the window even though they both promised not to discuss the kids this weekend.

"Grace is just... amazing. Isn't she?"

Little did they know that their amazing Grace had put a condom in her glove compartment "just in case."

Sheriff Kirkbride chilled on his porch petting Conrad, his golden retriever, and massaging a drink. His life was quite simple, not too much work to do as a sheriff and since he didn't have a wife or kids nagging him at home, he was a cool cat. Ellis didn't understand marriage and certainly didn't want to get in that mess. Just like many women, Vicki was sweet. And he certainly would not mind a dinner, maybe sex if she was worth it, but no way marriage.

Ellis could hear someone approaching his sidewalk and stood up to see. He looked at his watch—it was now 11:35PM, way past Oostburg's strict curfew.

"A little late to be jogging, huh, Matt?"

The teenage boy stopped at the man's voice.

Matt looked around. The teen knew he was taking a risk jogging past the sheriff's house on his route to a booty-call.

"Curfew is ten, buddy."

Matt shook his head.

"Sorry, Sheriff Kirkbride. I'll head on home."

Good thing for Matt, this sheriff was more like a cool big brother.

"Eh, don't worry about it. Have fun, bud."

Matt gave the sheriff a high-five from a distance and jogged away. Kirkbride took his last swig and threw his beer can in the recycling bin. Slapping his healthy thigh, he went in and Conrad obediently followed.

"I love you, Evelyn Adams."

"I love you too, Seth Adams."

The two kissed briefly. Evelyn looked around. The waiter was a bit late; they had been waiting for a good thirty minutes. Adams ordered the ribs and Evelyn had a well-done steak. Now they both were quite hungry having saved their appetites for this restaurant. Antsy Evelyn glanced around, blown away by the architecture. But she did have other reasons for glancing around, as she knew Raile's lackey would be in the vicinity.

"This place is breathtaking."

"Someone must love you real hard."

"Pastor Seth, are you trying to flirt?"

"Trying? I guess I need to be quite a bit more obvious."

Evelyn's eyes widened embarrassingly. She smirked and giggled quietly. Seth had lowered his body slightly to place his foot on hers.

Evelyn whispered:

"Pastor Seth! No footsie in public." She couldn't believe he was doing that.

Seth tried a little harder.

Evelyn quietly laughed as she glanced around. The wife always found it quirky when her man put his foot in her crotch beneath her dress. They took one look at each other and left.

They stormed past Kristoff, who sweated like a whore in confession watching his patrons leaving.

"Is something the matter—"

As they were about to leave, Evelyn spotted a man standing in the corner. She grabbed her husband's elbow and said: "Bathroom."

Evelyn walked around the corner and seconds later the man followed. Seth was so horny he did not notice.

She waited until a black lady entered the ladies' restroom and right after she was gone Evelyn passed the envelope over to the man and left.

.

Charles Raile paused at the gas station patiently waiting for Gracie to finish filling up. The gal pulled away; unaware that she was being followed.

Gracie and Raile drove around five minutes to the outskirts of Oostburg, where Gracie picked up a passenger. He couldn't catch a glimpse of this passenger with his naked eyes, so he took out his grey binoculars just in time to see the passenger enter Gracie's car.

He quickly grabbed his phone and snapped a photo, snatching a picture of her passenger entering. It was blurry but good enough.

Looking through his big binoculars and being a lip reader, Raile could read that she reassured her pal it was going to be just fine, that no one knew their secret...

Bob Zimmermann stormed into his son's bedroom and switched on the light. He scoped the bedroom and to his chagrin found it completely naked. It was a little cold because the window, Matt's obvious point of escape, was left open.

"Damn it, boy!"

10.

A NIGHTMARE OR A REALITY?

It took a while to heal the tire and the old dude sort of bothered her, so the deputy did call Jessica to reschedule. It was way after midnight when she returned home.

Aunt Coralee's bedroom door was open so she could spy on her aunt sound asleep, snoring only a little. At peace with the view, Vicki smiled.

Vicki walked downstairs and cracked a Sprite. After a guzzle, she smiled and said to herself:

"Maybe I will like the simple life."

Tired Vicki made her way into the living room and plopped on the couch. Flipping channels, Vicki caught a great film noir on TV that she had seen a few years ago called *Double Indemnity*. Barbara Stanwyck and Fred MacMurray play partners tied up in the killing of her hubby. Edward G. Robinson was in it too, so that was a major plus. It was twenty minutes into it, so she settled in, tucked a pillow under her head, and enjoyed the movie, before...

Vicki and three other cops raced quickly upstairs with their guns ready. Four-story buildings without an elevator were uncommon, but this apartment building was one of those old-fashioned ones.

"Clear!" yelled one of the cops.

They got to the door at the top of the stairs.

After stopping for a quick second, the biggest of the four, Alf O'Malley, kicked the door open. Without care for themselves, the four cops swarmed in, each one taking a section of the hostile apartment. This was the place they were going to find her, and they needed every second. There was no time to strategize. The teenager's life was paramount.

"If anyone is out there, come out with your hands up," warned Officer Ristow.

She glanced slowly into one of the rooms and then gently opened the door wider.

Her face grew with intensity.

"Guys."

After a second, the officers reunited as they entered the room.

She walked over to the bed, which had not a thing on it but a pair of bloody, pink underwear.

"We're too late."

Vicki woke up drenched in cold sweats. She looked about hoping to see Gabrielle, but instead, she only saw the dial strike 2:30AM. It was now Saturday morning and in a few hours, Vicki Weathers would begin the next chapter of her life. The TV was still on as Fred MacMurray was delivering his final speech. Hearing a car driving fast past her house, she got up to look out the window but by the time she opened the curtain, the quick car was gone.

She turned about and much to her surprise saw the teenager who looked so much like Gabrielle. Gracie, but now Gracie was wearing a brunette wig, odd looking even more like Gabrielle Adjami.

This had become the norm for Vicki. Daydreaming, nightmares. Vicki did not always know what was real and what was fantasy. Another damn nightmare. The newest deputy had seen a shrink twice in New York about it but nothing really helped. Nothing helped...

Sitting in the side chair Gracie was beautiful... except for the big bloody gash on her left temple...

"You're too late, Officer Weathers," Gracie proclaimed.

Vicki walked to that chair but as she got closer, Gracie disappeared into thin air.

"Yeah, Jesus," Vicki whispered to herself, not desiring to wake up her aunt. "You can stop with the damn nightmares now!"

Around 3AM, Wesley Demko finally made his path to his front door. Hoping the woman was asleep, tired Wesley bumbled with the keys, taking some time getting the correct keys in their correct holes. Holes were not his specialty. The Demkos were the only people in Oostburg who locked their doors.

He entered his home and put his keys on the white kitchen counter. He opened the refrigerator and drained the carton of orange juice. She hated when Wesley did this but he really didn't care about impressing her any longer. The little gent was his own man these years; a real bad-ass drinker from the carton. He did not care about anything other than finishing his novel.

The man left the kitchen and tried to walk up the stairs but was interrupted by the sound of noisy wheels. Unfortunately for him, those wheels weren't in his head. Wesley clicked on his cell phone light to get a better glimpse of where it was coming from.

The woman wheeled closer and closer until the two wheels were almost at Wesley's shoes. The flashlight in his cell engulfed Brooke; decked out in a beautiful red nightgown with some lace around her chest.

Even with the wheelchair, Brooke was still quite tempting, but looks weren't everything.

Unfortunately for Brooke, Wesley did not love the woman anymore.

"Hello," Brooke seduced.

She grabbed his thin waist and climbed his little torso, making sure to get eye contact with Wesley. Being almost the same height, their noses touched.

Brooke gently began kissing his neck.

"Tonight might be a good night for..."

"I thought you worked tonight."

"I left early."

"Where were you?" Brooke asked as she nuzzled his neck.

"Just out. Went for a walk."

"This late?"

"Why not? You were working."

Uncomfortable with the foreplay, the male fumbled for an excuse not to have sex with the woman.

"I'm... tired."

Brooke was persistent and kissed his neck again.

"That has never stopped you before," said Brooke, although she was mistaken. He had used that excuse many times. Many of those moments, the man was lying. Wesley had become accustomed to lying to the woman.

Actually, the man learned how to deceive everyone, and he was quite good at it.

Attempting to cockblock himself, Wesley grabbed her bicep with his left hand. She kissed his ear and Wesley needed to make a second excuse.

"I'm... not feeling well."

She pulled back, seeking to look through his eyes in the dimly lit living room. Her suspicion was aroused as much as her libido.

"What's wrong?"

Wesley looked right in her eyes.

"Nothing... I just..."

The woman played hardball. She was not taking no for an answer, not this evening. Caressing his arm, she worked her route down his arms and took the right hand out of his pocket. She could notice an odd substance on his middle and pointer fingers. Being a nurse for quite a few years, she could recognize blood even in the dark.

"Wesley, you're bleeding."

"Yes, I just—stupid box cutter at work. I'll get cleaned up."

Wesley gently placed the little woman back in the wheelchair like a dolly returning on a shelf after a playtime rejection. Wesley left the woman and tramped upstairs. Brooke could do nothing but longingly watch.

Quickly and quietly shutting the door, he entered his bathroom. He turned on the faucet and began washing his hands vigorously. After a really good cleansing, he dried them with a towel and wiped his face.

He glanced in the mirror.

Wesley did not like the reflection.

"My god. What have I done...?"

11.

SLIDING ROCKS

Lainey Adams began Saturday a little before 8AM.

Turning on her right, she saw the clock and realized she awoke an hour before she longed to. Staring up at the ceiling, she punched her blankets. *No point just lying here.* After going to the bathroom, she went downstairs to the kitchen. Opening their fridge, she took the orange juice—*where is breakfast,* she thought. Then she remembered her parents were goners. It wasn't often that there was no adult in the house; actually, this was the first opportunity her rents had entrusted Gracie to watch after her long term. *Stupid parents.* She didn't need Gracie to watch over her. She could take care of herself.

After finishing her orange juice, Lainey made her way over to the oven. Being a mature thirteen-year-old, she was able to create herself a scrambled egg sandwich with ketchup and buttered toast. Not very tiring. Maybe tonight she would try something more difficult, perhaps ordering Chinese from Sheboygan.

Now with her tummy satisfied, the girl plopped on the living room couch to surf for some Saturday morning cartoons. Flipping from pointless cartoons to pointless politics, the youth realized she had no aspirations for the day or tomorrow and by then the two would be back. It was a shame to waste all this freedom and not have a damn thing to do.

Tired of the TV, Lainey made her path upstairs to look in Gracie's room. The room was empty.

"Even her bed is perfect," she whined.

She went back downstairs to the landline in their kitchen. "Sucks that I don't have a cell phone," Lainey carped. Most of her classmates did have a cell but her parents didn't want to get her one. Her parents said it was all about the bills but Gracie received her cell at eleven, so clearly their parents loved Gracie more, *the bitch.*

Lainey picked up the landline and dialed Gracie's cell number. "Hey, this is Gracie. I'll get back to you as soon as I can, have a blessed—"

She clicked the phone off; as she did not want to hear any more of Gracie's fortune cookies.

It was peaceful not having anybody there. She was going to enjoy it when she moved out. Lainey would live all alone and never get married. She may even work from home so she didn't have to meet people. Maybe she could have her groceries delivered to her and she would never even have to leave the house for anything.

But being an adult led to more than just personal freedoms. It also led to responsibility.

The more young Lainey thought of it, the more she realized she should let someone know that Gracie wasn't home.

Lainey did not want to call her parents. She knew if she did call, they would be home in an hour and she didn't want to see them, so she decided to call Sheriff Kirkbride.

"You tried calling her?" he asked.

Lainey felt dumbfounded that Ellis was Oostburg's sheriff. *What an imbecile, of course, I called her.*

"Of course," Lainey said as politely as possible. She was glad nobody could hear her thoughts.

Within fifteen minutes, Ellis drove over to check on Lainey.

Sheriff Kirkbride sat down to finish the cold egg sandwich that Lainey could not finish.

"And you made this all by yourself?" asked Ellis, quite impressed with the culinary skills of a thirteen-year-old.

"I'm thirteen, not a retard."

Ellis took another bite.

"Shouldn't use that word, Miss Lainey."

"Why are they made?"

"Who?"

"Retards. What purpose do they serve?"

Sheriff Kirkbride was beginning to feel a tad bit uncomfortable with this little lady. The sheriff stole another swig of coffee that Lainey also made.

"Oh, they serve a purpose. And remember, the good book says there is a reason for everything and I assume that includes them. You believe the good book?"

"Not all the time, no. So why were they made?"

Ellis was amazed by her. She was... unique. Ellis knew Lainey all her life. He had driven Evelyn and Seth to the hospital when Evelyn was in labor with Lainey.

"Maybe... that's something for the pastor to talk about. Know any pastors?" Ellis smiled and continued, trying to change this subject. "And you can make coffee, too?"

"Yes."

"You don't need Gracie to watch you."

Lainey happily agreed:

"No, I don't."

Ellis wiped his lips and stood up, finishing that egg sandwich and coffee. He looked around the kitchen.

"So, Gracie's not home."

"No, and her car isn't here either."

"Well, she is probably just enjoying her freedom. Your mom and dad have a short leash with you girls. Um, I tell you... if she is still not here by noon, call me again, okay?"

"Sure."

Ellis got in his car, glad he was away from young Lainey. That was the first moment he and the girl had a heart-to-heart. He even briefly debated telling Seth the rather harsh opinion his daughter had spewed but having his reputation as a carefree sheriff to uphold, Ellis decided not to.

Ellis dialed his cell phone, hoping to reach Seth or Evelyn. The cool sheriff did need to tell them about Gracie even though it was probably nothing.

They were snoring, naked as Adam and Eve. This was the first Saturday in quite a long spell they could sleep late, and they took advantage of it.

Seth's phone rang twice, waking up the pastor and his wife. Evelyn turned around and looked at the phone. Seth sat up and took it from her without checking it.

"Remember what we said: no phones."

Again without glancing, Seth clicked his cell off and put it under his pillows. Seth clocked out from the world, and nothing was going to convince him to tune back in. The pastor finally felt mature enough to clock out and recharge his batteries. He knew Evelyn had a harder time—women usually do—but she went with the flow.

He lunged in for a kiss.

The first-day veteran yawned as she walked in the kitchen wearing her newly-pressed deputy uniform. The deputy was incredibly happy to put this new uniform on. Deputy Victoria Weathers was back on the case and feeling very... cold, she looked at the temperature out the window—it was thirty-two degrees.

"Holy *Frozen*! It's not even winter," she spoke to herself. "Am I going to need gloves in October? Ugly. I hate Wisconsin already."

Coralee was sipping coffee.

"Oh, don't you look pretty."

Deputy Weathers walked over to the coffee pot and poured herself a cup.

"Pretty is not the look I am going for."

"Nervous?"

Vicki took a sip. *Boy, I need this.*

"No. I am at peace, I think. Thanks."

Coralee smiled.

"Old people have wisdom sometimes."

Vicki smiled back.

"Sometimes."

She walked over to Coralee and kissed her aunt on the top of her head. Vicki began to head out but turned around.

"Thanks."

"Break a leg."

"That's a theater term."

"Knock em' dead."

Vicki shook her head.

"Also, not a desirable term."

Coralee shrugged her shoulders.

"Love you," said Coralee.

Vicki smiled. *Perhaps, Gags and Aunt Coralee were right. Maybe the tranquil country is just what I need.*

Vicki pulled into the station parking lot two minutes after nine.

Two minutes late in New York would've made her paranoid but here, in Oostburg, times were different. Vicki did not mind anymore. It was only two minutes.

She looked out the car window.

"It's going to be a good day."

Vicki walked into the station with her one box of items to find the secretary playing darts with that big deputy, the one who ran in with donuts yesterday during her interview. Glancing at the location of the darts on the board, both were quite good, too, but that was beside the point. Where was the structure; the hustle; the law and the order?

"You're getting good, Momma," the fat guy said.

"Always was!" Momma bragged.

She was gentle, Vicki could tell. So was the huge deputy. Vicki was in for something quite different. She took another step in just as the huge guy threw a dart, which landed right at her feet.

He walked over.

"Ah, you must be Nicki."

Vicki picked up the dart and gave it to the round deputy.

"A little off the mark. It's Vicki."

The round guy offered to take her box, which made Vicki pause, and then she accepted his help.

"I'm David. David Penny. And this is Momma."

Momma walked over and presented Vicki with a big, warm hug, which at first made Vicki feel uncomfortable, but Vicki eventually embraced it, especially beyond the thirty-second mark.

"Welcome to the family, Vicki. What kind of bagel can I get you?"

"Oh, I just ate, thanks," she lied, but she didn't want to waste time eating. Vicki was anxious to get put on the streets and help in any way she could.

"Where can I put my things?"

"Oh, just over there in the corner."

Momma ushered Vicki over to the naked desk in the corner. The grey desk was small, as was the corner, but it would suffice. No computer on the desk, though.

"Is Ellis—I mean—Sheriff Kirkbride around?"

Momma smiled and nodded.

"Oh yes, Ellis is in his office."

"Great," Vicki said. "I'll put these down and see him."

Momma raised her hand like she was praising God.

"Oh, honey—we don't disturb Ellis right now."

Vicki backed off a little.

"Oh, he's on a call."

"No, it's his nap time."

What.

"Darts?" asked Penny.

Matt Zimmermann arrived at his house to find the front door locked. His father, no doubt, had discovered he was gone and locked it in spite.

Dad never locked the door.

He dug through his coat but didn't find his keys. He must have left them on his dresser, since who brings keys when you're sneaking out of a window and your pops never locks the door?

He knocked.

Bob opened the door a minute later.

"Yes?"

Not acknowledging him, Matt walked past his dad.

Slamming the front door, the man asked the son:

"Don't you think I have the right to an… explanation? Why were you out all night? Where were you?"

Matt began his trek to his room.

"I don't have to tell you."

In his bedroom, he laid down on his bed, smiling. It was quite a happy evening for Matt.

"I'm leaving to finish my sermon," the teen could hear his father yelling behind the door.

"Not that you care."

A text came through on his cell. Matt read it.

"Come and find you? Like hide-and-seek? We're not twelve anymore..."

He liked hide-and-seek.

Wesley Demko was taking a nice steamy shower. The man had a hard evening that only a flaming shower would suffice, at least for a few minutes. He was in over his head, and it was only a matter of time before life as he knew it would change forever. Maybe for the better, but he wasn't so sure.

Through the steam, he could hear the woman enter the bathroom. He turned on the hot faucet a little louder.

Brooke wheeled up to the shower and yanked on the curtain.

"Dr. Malachi called again."

Wesley rolled his eyes.

Brooke persisted:

"He says you've missed a few appointments."

Banging his head gently on the wall, he hoped the woman would go away. Alas, it didn't work. He was going to have to answer her.

"Three. I've missed three."

Brooke paused and then went on:

"So, you're just not going to see him anymore?"

Wesley shook his head. *Every damn time.* He wanted to give up the marriage, but she wouldn't let him.

"Wesley, you're not willing to go to any marriage counseling or couple's therapy or even see Seth but the least you can do is fix yourself! I'm sick of being the only one fixing this marriage. A real man would fight for his wife!"

Wesley was silent.

"Really? Ok. You know Wesley if you're not going to talk to me the least you can do is talk to someone." Brooke paused to verbally strike him harder, attempting to hit a cord:

"Or perhaps you are already talking to someone."

Brooke paused.

"Oh, and I checked your pills. You haven't been taking them."

Brooke waited for a response, but knowing that he was also waiting for her to leave, she gave up.

Wesley heard the door shut.

"Bitch," he mumbled under his breath.

He leaned his soaked head against the wall. After knocking it thrice, the man turned his head and saw her razor. He picked up the thin razor and slowly placed it to his wrist. He could very easily end it all today and not have to face the world after.

"I have to finish the book. Then...?"

He thought back to his silent jog the day before. He couldn't kill himself. He had to tell their story.

He finished the shower and got in his uniform. Going downstairs, he found a pile of stacked bills on the table. He shifted through the envelopes and tossed them aside. *I wasn't made to pay bills and die.* He checked his cell phone. No text message. Putting his cell in his pocket, he entered the kitchen.

She was there and handed him a cup.

"I made you coffee."

Great. Now the woman was being nice to him, which meant he had to at least attempt civility.

"Thanks." It was still hot as Hell, with lots of cream and sugar, just the way he liked it.

"You work today?" she asked.

Wesley took his keys from the counter and started to leave.

"Yeah."

She interrupted his departure.

"You're not going to kiss me?"

Wesley paused. He was handcuffed into kissing her, and he knew it. He stopped kissing the woman quite some time ago and did not really miss it. When a spouse does something so... horrible to you... you do not feel like being affectionate towards them. They did have sex occasionally, and while that was very good, in those brief moments of intimacy they were one. But other than that, they were separate. Wesley turned around and went back to her and gently kissed her forehead.

"Am I that repulsive? Is it because I've gained a hundred pounds and these wheels? Huh? In sickness and health?"

Wesley stared at the woman. This, their discord, had *NOTHING* to do with her looks or condition. Yes, she was paralyzed but he would've loved Brooke with no legs had she—it didn't matter. He looked down and shook his head, trying to avoid an unpleasant conversation before an unpleasant day at work.

"You think I want this? Your life is not the only one inconvenienced because of this accident. Damn it... Wesley. Love your wife. You said you would. I know we've been through some rough times—"

He turned around in anger, and almost yelling:

"Rough times? Is that what you call it?"

"Maybe I should just die, Wesley. Would that make your world easier? Then you can just sit and write that stupid god damn book of yours. All you do is write and—"

"The pen is mightier than the sword."

The wife slammed a banana down on the counter and began to cry.

Wesley paused briefly and left.

Seth woke up and stretched across to put his left arm around Evelyn, surprised to see that he and his wife had slept-in naked for the first time in he didn't remember. It was pretty cool to breathe that way again; to have the burdens of responsibility lifted from them. It felt so good to clock out. The couple didn't get to do that very often.

"Do we ever have to leave?"

Evelyn snuggled the pillow tighter.

"Eventually. A very comfy mattress. Organic," the wife admired.

"Organic. Just in case we want to eat it."

Seth kissed her as he played with her hair.

"Round two?"

Evelyn smiled and chuckled.

"Round two? I'm forty-three, not twenty-three! I think it is time to start the day."

"Ok..." Seth said sadly.

Evelyn got out of bed and put on a medium t-shirt and sweats from one of her suitcases. Now modest again, she walked over to the kitchen area. After all, neither of them had eaten since they ditched the restaurant the previous evening. Both were quite starving, having only eaten a tiny bite at church. Evelyn searched around for the breakfast menu.

Seth walked to their bathroom, and from the shower, he bellowed temptingly:

"I'm showering if you care to join me."

She continued to poke around for the menu. As she looked, she could hear the showerhead turn on almost as loud as her stomach. It was a little chilly and a nice, warm shower sounded great at the moment but so did that cheese omelet on the menu. *Ah, first-world problems.*

"Just a minute," Evelyn yelled as Seth started to sing one of their favorite songs: *Shine Jesus Shine*. He had a wonderful sound, at least she thought, especially in the shower. Showers usually had good acoustics. That was where Grace got her ability. Evelyn could not carry a tune in her purse but she was pretty so she had other skills. Under his singing, Evelyn thought she heard the door knock.

"Hun, did you order room service?" she grinned in pleasure.

She opened the door.

To her surprise, of all places, old Charles Raile stood there.

"What are you doing here?" she whispered angrily.

Raile smiled from side-to-side, like a wolf about to eat a heavenly sheep.

"Oh, I just enjoy checking on my friends. Did you deliver?"

She glanced back at the bathroom. The singing and the shower were still going.

"Yes, I did. Now leave!"

Raile peeked in, looking around for the mate, but only hearing the shower he made an assumption:

"I don't see the good reverend. Showering?"

"Yes, he's in the shower—"

Raile smiled.

Seth yelled from the shower:

"Hun, who is that?"

Evelyn hoped her husband would remain in the bath long enough for her to get rid of Raile. Whatever Raile was doing, she was a part of, even if she was not privy to what was going on.

Evelyn whispered again, with force:

"Get out, now!"

Evelyn shut the door on Raile's face and blew the hair out of hers.

Damn it! How dare he try to ruin their anniversary weekend?!

Seth popped his head out of the bathroom door.

"Who was it?"

"Nobody, don't worry about it."

Seth didn't completely buy it.

"We leave our worries in Oostburg, hun."

Evelyn gave a half-smile and a nod.

"Oostburg."

Removing her clothes, she followed him into the shower.

Vicki Weathers unpacked all her belongings and made herself at home with her desk in the corner. There was a lovable picture of her Aunt Coralee and a picture of the dead ringer of Gracie from New York: Gabrielle.

Tapping her toes, Vicki monitored Momma and Penny jump from game to game. She checked the clock, wishing she could muscle into the sheriff's office and demand a barrage of responsibilities or at the least, paperwork. The clock struck 11AM, and she had been there for about two hours, and organizing her desk took ten minutes.

"Checkmate," Momma said humbly.

Penny sat back in defeat to study the board. Momma had won again. She was a smart cookie, that secretary.

"You're good, Momma."

Vicki considered how to express some concerns and frustrations. She didn't want to get sent back to anger management.

"I'm sorry... is this all that happens here?" she asked as politely as she could be.

Momma just looked at Penny, seemingly confused by the question.

"Well, we do have lunch coming up."

Vicki stared at the ineptitude.

Penny was excited:

"Saturday is Ellis's day to buy!" he said.

Vicki asked:

"You don't patrol, you don't scan the perimeter?"

She wasn't sure they understood the question.

"When we get called," Penny explained.

No, we are supposed to be out anyway. That's what we did in New York City—and then she remembered—Vicki was not there anymore. A different town and a different protocol. Still, it frustrated her.

"When was your last call?"

The dynamic duo thought over the topic for a few seconds; looking at one another to see if the other had remembered.

"Tuesday," declared Momma confidently.

Penny disagreed:

"May have been Wednesday. Remember the cat?"

"Ah, that Richard."

Vicki lost her patience:

"Look, I'm sorry but I need to speak with Sheriff Kirkbride right—"

And that lanky sheriff entered; his hair a little tussled.

"Yes, Deputy Weathers?" asked Ellis.

"Can I speak to you in private?"

They made their way back into his office. A paper was on his desk but it didn't appear to have been read.

"You okay?" Ellis asked as he sat back down. "The job stressing you out too much?"

Vicki could not tell if he was being sarcastic or serious.

"Well, no, quite frankly. I'm not stressed, and I'm not ok. See, there just seems to be a flippant attitude to this department."

Ellis smiled.

"Flippant? Well, that's a fifty-cent word."

Vicki folded her arms; feeling like a mother with three kids.

"How would you describe your department?"

"We work hard—"

"They just finished a game of chess."

"I missed chess?!"

Ellis looked through his door window, like a mutt who lost his bone.

"Look, I don't mean to be insubordinate—"

"They played chess without me."

"We really need to be out in the community."

Ellis downplayed her suggestion:

"Vicki, nothing ever happens here in Oostburg. Bad things happen in big cities, like Milwaukee or Chicago. Not Oostburg."

"Have you even left your office today?"

Ellis smiled again. *Handsome, but what a lunk.*

"Of course, I went to Seth's house."

Vicki shook her head.

"Having coffee with the pastor doesn't count."

Ellis bragged:

"I didn't. His daughter called me."

"Why?" Vicki asked. It was odd for the youth to be calling the sheriff.

"Her older sister, that girl who sang last night, Gracie, is missing."

What.

Vicki exploded:

"Missing!? And you're not looking around?"

"It hasn't been twenty-four hours."

Vicki pointed to his coffee and newspaper.

"Oh, and you're so busy!"

"Hey, I haven't even read my paper yet!"

"It's hard to read the paper when you nap! Ellis, if you aren't going to search, then I am."

Vicki could not believe what was going on at this station. He was not cute anymore, either. He was a dip.

She left the office and headed for her desk, with Ellis quickly trailing her.

"I will tell you what happened. She hung out with her friends and came back home after Lainey was asleep. Then, Gracie left in the morning. Her phone is probably dead."

Vicki put on her jacket.

"Did you check? You called her?"

"Of course."

Vicki grabbed her keys.

"What's Lainey's address?"

Ellis sighed.

"Fine. I'll go look around."

Ellis snatched his jacket from the coat rack.

Momma and Penny sat there not knowing what to do. Momma spoke:

"Ellis, are you getting lunch? Subs maybe?"

"Yeah, we are starving. Uno will do that to you," Penny added.

"Momma, hold down the fort," Ellis ordered.

"He should be out too," Vicki scolded the department.

"Draw two," Momma demanded.

Penny's smile disappeared.

The three officers split the station and bounced to their respective cars. Vicki took charge of her boss.

"What's the address?"

"108 North 9ₜₕ street," responded Ellis.

Vicki got in her car and shut the door.

"I'm off to see Lainey. You drive around."

Vicki buckled her seatbelt, she asked herself: "Where am I?"

She drove away as Ellis and Penny watched.

Down their main street, which was in fact called Main Street, Vicki spotted a big black guy depositing some trash cans into a dump truck. After she noticed the big guy following her, she parked her car.

She was concerned anyway, but for no real good reason.

"Damn it, Vicki. That's racial profiling."

The black man appeared at her window. He was very large, bald, and imposing.

"Hello, miss."

His deep voice reminded her of that kind giant in *The Green Mile* with Tom Hanks. She loved that movie.

"Hello, sir. Nice day today."

"Yes, nice. Are you new?"

It was probably the phone in her hand looking for directions in little Oostburg that tipped the dude off. Perhaps he should be the sheriff. He was more observant than Ellis.

"I am. First day. On the job, that is. I moved in yesterday."

The large man grinned. He had a playful, warm, and comforting smile. It made her feel horrible for that initial reaction.

He handed her a dangling earring.

"Well, I will make your first day easy. Here's an earring I found on the sidewalk—just yonder. You could fill out a missing report if you like."

He grinned. Vicki smiled back.

"My first case. Thank you, sir."

Vicki took the jewelry and briefly studied it. Quite an ordinary earring.

"Welcome to Oostburg. Name's Big Mack."

He offered his hand and she reciprocated.

"Big Mack. I'm Vicki." She continued. "Thank you. I'll keep this at the station."

Big Mack stood up straight again. Looking up from her car, she could have sworn he was seven feet tall.

"Nice meeting you. Safe travels."

Vicki smiled and pulled away. He was a nice gent. She kept glancing in her rearview mirror, seeing Big Mack wave at her. As Vicki drove down the street, he didn't seem to get smaller.

She despised the fact that she was a bit racist. Deputy Weathers guessed that most people were racist, at least a little bit, but that didn't make it right.

Big Mack waved and said to himself:

"She's pretty, for a skinny white girl."

12.

A TIME TO SEEK

Sheriff Ellis Kirkbride drove to the South Street Parlor, an ice cream joint on the beautiful Lake Michigan. The parlor was Gracie's place of employment, and he felt this was likely a good place to find her. Besides, he had a craving for the ice cream and the parlor would be closed down next weekend for the winter. It was some time of travel since the parlor was in Sheboygan, but Ellis wanted to drive right now to kill the clock. The weather was almost freezing, but Ellis didn't care, the ice cream was that good.

Ellis walked up to the counter and met Mr. Thomas Packard, the proprietor of the parlor. Packard only had it open six months a year, which sucked because Ellis liked the treats twelve months a year. Packard employed just a few teenagers, typically high school juniors and seniors, which was Gracie's demographic. She had worked there since last May. It was her first job.

Mr. Packard grinned as Kirkbride walked up to the counter. The sheriff knew that the old gent appreciated his dedication to law enforcement, and since Mr. Packard served in Vietnam, the two shared a "protect and serve" connection.

"Sheriff! To what do I owe the pleasure?"

Ellis grinned and sat on the barstool. He looked around at the neat trains circling the upper portion of the room. He loved trains.

"Hello, Mr. Packard."

"What can I get you, the usual?"

Even though Ellis liked all the flavors, he had a "usual".

"Two scoops mint chocolate chip."

Mr. Packard made quick work on the order.

"Well, for all you do for this community, it's on the house."

"I don't even work much in Sheboygan," Ellis said humbly.

Mr. Packard reminded him:

"You saved Oreo last month."

Ellis smiled.

"I did do that."

The fat cat was always getting into trouble. Thinking he was a bird and trying to get a canary from Mr. Packard's tree, Oreo got trapped, so Ellis climbed that tree and saved him. He did it without a ladder, too.

"Two scoops, coming up."

Ellis said playfully:

"If it's free, make it three." Ellis was a charmer, not only with the ladies but also with the old war vets too.

The gents smiled as Mr. Packard began to make the ice cream.

"Anything new?" asked Packard.

The sheriff sighed as he didn't want to have this conversation. For one, he really did not sense anything was wrong and two, Ellis was lazy. He did manage to see that Gracie wasn't on the frontline. Hopefully, she was in the back.

"Well, Mr. Packard... I was wondering if you have seen Gracie Adams today."

Packard shook his head as he continued making the ice cream.

"No, I haven't. I did see her at the concert last night. Spoke to her a little. Something wrong?"

The sheriff was distracted by the mint ice cream. Ellis was hungry, and it was almost lunchtime—ah, that reminded him—it was his turn to buy lunch.

"Don't know. She wasn't home when her sister woke up."

"Ehh. Kids. I wouldn't worry," offered Packard.

Ellis asked:

"Do you know when she works next?"

Packard thought about it.

"One second. My seventy-year-old brain can barely remember Oreo's name, let alone a kid's schedule. The wife writes out their schedules."

Mr. Tom Packard finished making the ice cream and served it to Ellis, who dug into it ravenously.

"Thank you."

"Your new deputy is cute."

Ellis took another bite.

"Thanks, I made her myself."

"Gracie's schedule."

Packard put on his glasses and got the scheduling book. Flipping through a few pages, Tom put his finger on the spot that stated "Gracie Adams". It was a quick look since she was the first employee alphabetically.

"Ah. Gracie works today at one o'clock—in forty-five minutes she should be walking through that door."

Ellis looked at the clock. 12:15PM. He felt content now knowing that in forty-five minutes, Gracie would be accounted for.

"Ok. Great. If you could, give me a call when she arrives."

Packard closed his notebook.

"Will do," Packard smiled.

"Thanks."

"Take care, sheriff," Packard waved as Ellis left the parlor.

Driving back to Oostburg, he was content that his belly had something in it, and his head had knowledge in it.

Now, time for lunch.

Vicki searched the perimeter of the Adams' house. The porch was completely normal: a few steps, a nice, old swing. Pretty, actually. Vicki wondered how the pastor of a small church could afford something this nice. Man was probably ripping the church off somehow, that's how. Pastors are usually doing something at the expense of their sheep, in her experience.

She looked at the driveway and could see new tire tracks. Vicki did not see any cars so she presumed this could've been Gracie's tracks after she left her little sister last night.

As she poked around, she could see a mailman walk up the drive. From the side of the porch, she saw him place some letters in the mailbox. He was forty-ish and overweight which surprised Vicki because mailmen get so much exercise.

"Good afternoon, deputy," he said cheerfully.

First morning on the job, and she was meeting some friendly men of Oostburg. Some brave ones, too, he must have been a true Oostburger—he didn't even wear gloves on this frigid day.

"Good afternoon," Vicki replied.

"Hi, can I help you?" asked the mailman.

"Maybe. Are you familiar with the family?"

The mailman smiled.

"This has been my route for fifteen years. Yeah, I know Pastor Seth and Evelyn very well. My family goes to church. I thought I recognized you."

Small town.

"By any chance, have you seen Gracie lately?"

"I saw her at the concert last night. Gracie has the loveliest voice. She's been singing in the choir for years. Did you hear her?"

She really didn't want to get into chit-chat with the mailman, but she was on a mission.

"Yes, I was there, too. If you see her, ask her to call the sheriff's department."

"Will do. Take care!"

It was so peaceful here in quaint Oostburg. Vicki felt at ease even though she was unofficially investigating the missing teenager. Though it had not been made official, she felt the exact way she did when Gabrielle first went missing in New York. She hoped the situation would not mimic the last one.

But this search was different, in one feel—tone. It seemed as if there was not a worry on the planet, and that tone came strictly from the head of the department itself. The sheriff was carefree—a tad bit too carefree for her taste. Everything in New York City was go-go-go. Here, it was quite laid back. They could have a serial killer on the loose but it's okay, 'cause it's Taco Tuesday! She wondered how many cases Ellis actually cracked, or even been a part of. He couldn't have been much older than her; perhaps younger. There probably weren't many chances for sleuthing here in Oostburg. Vicki then wondered where Ellis was. Was he even looking or was he grabbing a pizza? She guessed the latter.

Vicki turned around the old porch and walked down the side of the house. It was very pretty. Their garden was all neat, packed for the upcoming winter that Vicki was not looking forward to. She hated the winter in New York and based on the bit she heard, Vicki knew winters here would be even worse.

Vicki shook her head thinking of her life and how it had taken this turn. Never in a trillion years would she have guessed she would be living in this place. She was a city gal. She wondered if she had made the right choice, but it was her only option. At least, for now. Maybe in three months, when she grew bored of this country life, she could move up north to Jessica in Green Bay or the dangers of Milwaukee. Both cities must have more crime.

But no, as many Christians say, God planted her here in Oostburg for a reason. Vicki went to church most of her life and knew that phrase "everything happens for a reason". Vicki really didn't like the expression; cause it meant that even the Holocaust in Germany had purpose and slavery and viruses and all those other horrendous, gut-wrenching things that happen all over the place.

Car accidents, stillborn babies, missing teena—

Then it clicked. Vicki was working; not the time to pontificate the deep meanings of life right now. She was here to find a girl that had been gone about twelve or so hours. A youth that everyone loved and cared for yet no one had seen since the concert.

The deputy walked around to their backyard. There was nothing out of the ordinary here: a metal swing set that probably hadn't been used in some time, along with a hula hoop and a pink jump rope, both mostly buried in dirt. Vicki grabbed a breath and stared at these items, hoping that they were not the last relics of innocence.

Please. Don't let this happen again.

Vicki wanted to think positive but she could not. Not after what Vicki had been through with Gabrielle in New York long ago. She thought that most people, if not everyone, want to be positive. Nobody really wants to be negative. Life got to her, ate her, swallowed her, and vomited her out. After all that it was hard for her to be positive; she couldn't help thinking negatively. And it hurt. Yeah, it hurt badly. Vicki felt those thorns and had been feeling them for a long time now. It is simply a block, where you can't think positively no matter how hard you try.

It sucks.

She picked up the jump rope. Vicki remembered her jump rope days; the days long gone now and how innocent they were recalled. The crowded streets of New York were arduous but being a child of the eighties and nineties, there were still many times of innocence. Playing catch with her good friends on the street.

Before the innocence had been robbed...

Looking around some more, she found a spot in the garden that had a fairly large divot. Perhaps a stone had once lived there. Out of sheer curiosity, Vicki started to dig.

"You really don't have a warrant," she spoke-sung to herself.

"People who speak to themselves are usually quite smart," stated a young voice from behind.

She smiled at the sassiness; it was something she might have said when she was the kid's age. Vicki stood up and turned around to view the owner of that innocent little jump rope. The girl couldn't have been more than thirteen or so. It sliced Vicki's heart to see her. She hoped she wouldn't need to give this girl the same grim report she had given Gabrielle's sister. She remembered holding that little girl in her arms as the youth broke down, crying for a solid hour. That was the final straw for Vicki's connection to the god. It broke her in ways no scripture verse would ever repair.

"You caught me." Vicki smiled guiltily.

Vicki offered her hand to shake.

"Are you Lainey?" asked Vicki, full-knowing the answer. She did remember her from that concert even though they didn't talk.

"I am Lainey."

Vicki cut to the point.

"Sheriff tells me Gracie is missing? Is she still gone?"

Lainey began to play with her hair.

"Yeah. I haven't seen her all day."

Deputy Weathers tried to block the negativity out of her thoughts. If not for her sake, for Lainey's.

"When was the last time you saw her?"

Lainey paused.

"Um, about nine o'clock last night, I think. A little after."

"Ok. I want you to know we are looking around. In about eight hours we can file a report. Lainey, have you called your parents?"

"I tried, but no one answered." Lainey continued: "Texted too. I think they shut their phones off."

Vicki nodded.

"Do you know Coralee Mentink?"

"Sure. She's Gracie's piano teacher. She's nice and funny."

Vicki smiled.

"Lainey, if you don't mind, I'd like to bring you to our home. She is my aunt."

"She's your aunt?"

"Yes. Would that be fine? Would you like to go to our home; just for now?"

"Should I pack a bag?"

Vicki wasn't in the habit of inviting children to spend the evening over other people's houses, but under the circumstances:

"Sure."

"Where do you think Gracie is?" Vicki asked carefully as she drove through the streets of Oostburg. She wasn't familiar with Lainey and didn't know if she were a crier or not. She couldn't handle another little girl tearing on her shoulder. It hurt too much to not really be able to do anything.

"Probably with her friends," replied Lainey.

Vicki made a left turn.

"Wouldn't she call?"

Lainey looked straight ahead.

"She doesn't always call."

"It's a girl," Vicki said, being cute.

Coralee entered the living room with an apron on.

"Why hello, Lainey. What are you doing here?"

Vicki couldn't let her aunt in on what was really going on, so she was vague.

"Aunt Coralee, would you mind watching Lainey for a little while, I'm going back to work."

Coralee was having a good moment.

"Sure, is something wrong?"

Vicki widened both eyes, trying to get Coralee to not go with this line of interrogation.

Coralee nodded to indicate she got the hint.

"Lainey, why don't you help me bake cookies? They were going to be a surprise, but my niece had to arrive early!"

Vicki mouthed "thank you" and left.

Back in Chicago, Seth and Evelyn decided to grant Devin's another chance, since they got caught up in bigger matters the night prior.

They waited for their meal and started in prayer. Seth and Evelyn were not perfect, not by any stretch of the imagination, but they did pray before each meal and with the girls before bed. They were holding hands, and the public display of affection caught the eye of their young waitress. The girl was respectful and stood there waiting to take their order.

Seth led the prayer.

"And Lord, protect our family. May our girls grow to love You, follow You, and follow You always. May they marry gentlemen who love You, and them. Please bring us safely together again tomorrow. In Jesus Name, Amen."

"Amen."

They raised their heads to find a waitress hovering over them.

The three shared a smile.

"Hi," the waitress began. "Welcome to Devin's."

Seth let go of his wife's hand.

"Hello, miss. What can we get you?"

The three chuckled.

"I just want to say how sweet it was to hear your prayers. Wish my dad would do that," informed the young waitress.

The pastor felt the conversation drifting towards spiritual matters. It was something that he was always thankful for; when the Holy Ghost was so clearly evident in a gospel moment. Although here he could feel that she wasn't a seeker. The young gal was a believer; yearning for her Earthly father to have that same relationship she had with her Heavenly Father. He could understand the circumstance after having to banter with Evelyn's father for many years.

"The Heavenly Father is protecting you, young lady, no matter what your Earthly father is doing. God is watching. God is all-powerful, all-knowing, and everywhere."

The waitress sniffed a little.

"Thanks, I really needed that. Your daughters are very blessed."

Seth and Evelyn shared a smile. Apparently, their waitress had been listening to the prayer.

"Can I pray for you? I am a pastor," he paused and looked at her name tag. "Kelsey?"

Kelsey glanced around to make sure her supervisor wasn't checking on her. It didn't appear to be too busy so Kelsey nodded and agreed to a one-minute prayer vigil.

"I don't normally get a prayer break."

She smiled before continuing:

"My father beats me."

"Sorry to hear that," replied Seth.

"Sometimes, not a lot, once in a while. There was one time he hid my medication. I'm diabetic. He hid the medication for a few hours and then I found it." Kelsey forced the tears to stay inside. "He hurts me so much, but I know he is my father and I need to love him, so I stay."

"But it's abuse, Kelsey."

"I know."

"Have you forgiven him?"

"I need to forgive him," said Kelsey.

Seth prayed: "Heavenly Father, take watch of this young lady. Keep her safe and let her be able to witness for You in any circumstance. In Jesus Name, Amen."

Seth gave teary Kelsey a napkin.

"Thanks. I really needed that. I love my dad, but it's hard to respect him. My dad does not go to church; he feels that it's just a money-making scheme by pastors."

That hit Seth a little.

"I will get your drinks and bring your menus. Oh, I'm sorry—what would you like to drink?"

"Ice Tea," ordered Seth.

"I'll have a Sprite," Evelyn added.

"Great. I'll get your drinks and the menus. Thank you, pastor."

"Thanks, Kelsey," said Seth.

Evelyn smiled and touched Seth's hand as the teen waitress returned to her life.

"I love you, Mr. Pastor. The girls really hit the jackpot with you as their father."

Pastor grinned at the word "jackpot" and wondered where he could get a little action. Maybe place a bet with the waiter over who would get the biggest tip or something silly like that. Seth loved to gamble; and it didn't really matter what the gamble was... the pastor just liked the thrills. And he did win—not often— but often enough to make Seth continue. Once, he won thirty grand in Vegas. That was the biggest jackpot; six years ago.

"Love you, babe," Seth said.

"Oh, honey—that reminds me—we haven't spoken to them at all today!"

Evelyn took out her cell to turn it on.

Seth quickly scolded her:

"Evelyn our phones are off for a reason. No kids. This weekend is only for building into one another—not be mom and dad but be Seth and Evelyn. If couples went away, paid a little less attention to the kids, maybe divorce rates would decrease," Seth reasoned.

Seth took the phone.

"Evie, our rule—no phone calls this weekend."

Evelyn attempted to retrieve it, but he would not give it back.

"Seth, they're not adults."

"No, but they're old enough to handle themselves for a weekend." Seth looked around for Kelsey. "We need this. To re-connect. They'll be fine. Nothing ever happens in Oostburg."

Unfortunately, on this particular noon... too many things were happening in Oostburg.

Seth was wrong.

Big Mack opened the door.

He clicked on the light to find the room peaceful and empty. As normal, the bed wasn't made. Clothes were all about the room. Everything was normal.

Except it was empty.

A young teen's pad... with no young lady there. Big Mack furled his big, black eyebrows. This girl had left so many times before, so it wasn't uncommon.

But for some weird reason, this day felt slightly different...

Oostburg continued to be quiet at the end of the afternoon. Ellis and Vicki pursued and questioned but no one had seen or heard from Gracie Adams since the sister saw her leave home Friday night.

And while she was chasing down earrings and older sisters, Ellis felt like renting a video.

His phone rang. It was Vicki checking in.

"Any luck?" she asked.

"No, nothing. You?"

"I went to the Adams' home and nothing was out of the norm. So, I took Lainey to my house so Aunt Coralee can watch her."

Ellis grinned, feeling sorry. He couldn't imagine an elderly woman like Coralee in the beginning stage of dementia watching over spitfire Lainey Adams.

"Or perhaps Lainey can watch Aunt Coralee," Ellis put all his bones in his mouth as he chuckled.

"Jerk. She's got dementia."

Sitting in the video store parking lot, Ellis did feel bad but it was still comical. He didn't want Vicki to quit on her first day, either.

"Sorry, that was not polite... I am sorry," Ellis apologized as he stifled a grin. *You get away with that when you're on the phone.*

"Find Gracie and we'll call it square."

Click.

He looked at his cell and realizing his side-chick hung up on him, he put his phone away and headed into the video store.

He walked in to find his friend Wesley behind the counter, staring into space. It was slower than normal since Green Bay had a home game tomorrow and the Mecca demanded worship.

"Hello, Wesley."

Wesley yawned.

"Sheriff. Looking for a video date tonight?"

"Maybe. Anything new?"

Wesley turned around to point out a poster.

"Yes, we have this new thriller called *Behind The Veile*—just came out. About a detective on drugs. Heard it was really good," Wesley said. "The three-dollar sale would pay my rent."

"Eh. Wesley, you haven't seen Gracie today, huh?"

"No, why?"

Ellis looked around.

"Just asking. Nobody has seen her."

Wesley began to clean some DVDs.

Ellis saw two teenage females walking around, and trying to avoid them, he turned around to Wesley again.

"She left home a little past 9PM last night. That's what Lainey said."

Wesley zoned out briefly.

"I... hope everything is alright."

"The Man In The Empty Chair? That's lame. If the chair is empty, how can anyone be in it?"

Stacy was intrigued.

"That's pretty dope, like a moron-oxy. We should get it," she said.

Bianca kept the DVD.

"I hope she can toss that sister tonight," continued Stacy.

"Hopefully. Have you heard from her?"

Noticing the handsome sheriff at the counter, the shallow teenagers wandered over in an attempt to lure Oostburg's most eligible bachelor in a round of pin the badge on the sheriff. Stacy gave him a wink.

"Hello sheriff," she said seductively.

Ellis smiled.

"Still under eighteen, Stacy."

The young lady was persistent. "Actually I really want to be a sheriff's wife. Some women like older men, like me. Two more years, sheriff. Keep waiting."

Bored Wesley fidgeted at the counter, raising the volume on the TV behind him.

"Girls, have you talked with Gracie today?" Ellis asked.

Stacy looked at Bianca and spoke:

"No, I haven't. Funny, we were just talking about that."

"We both left voicemails this afternoon."

Bianca placed the DVDs on the counter and Wesley began his job.

"We're hanging out tonight," Bianca continued.

"Still need to get the ice cream," Stacy reminded.

"Oh, good—ahh! Ice cream. Mr. Packard! I forgot to call. Hey, girls, can you do me a favor, have Gracie call me, ok?"

"Is she in trouble?" Bianca asked.

Ellis stood up tall and began to make his exit.

"No, just have her call me. Wesley. Ladies."

Bianca grew worried, unlike Stacy.

"Man, I would love to take that pistol out of his holster."

Stacy smiled as she checked out the butt of their sheriff strolling out the door.

Wesley rolled his eyes.

"That will be nine-fifty," he declared.

"His ass is nine-fifty?" Stacy asked.

Ellis walked to his car and stopped when his cell phone rang.

"Hello?"

It was Mr. Packard.

"Sheriff! I'm sorry. I got tied up here and I forgot to call."

Ellis wasn't the only one who forgot.

Mr. Packard continued:

"Gracie did *not* show, nor did she call in either, which is very odd."

He looked around the parking lot.

"She didn't?"

"She did not. She's never done that before. She's only called in sick once in the time she's worked here. Very odd, since next weekend is closing weekend for the year."

The sheriff took a breath.

"Thank you, Mr. Packard."

He hung up. Now 5PM, he had dilly-dallied all day long, farting about.

For the first time, in a very long while, Sheriff Ellis Kirkbride… began to worry…

Getting back in his car, he dialed his cell.

"Hello, this is Pastor Seth at Oostburg Community Church. Thank you for calling. Sorry, I'm not able to take your call, but if this is an urgent matter, please call the church office at 456-9234. Thank you and Jesus loves you."

Beep.

"Seth, it's me. Call me back."

Ellis hung up and sent a text message to Seth. He sat there for a couple of minutes waiting for an answer but alas, no luck.

He couldn't wait anymore.

Vicki arrived to find Momma and Penny reading the papers. There were Subway wrappers all over; apparently, Ellis had treated them. She realized she had not eaten since breakfast and was briefly tempted by the unopened sandwich on her desk.

"Is sheriff back yet?" she asked the other two.

Momma spoke:

"No. He said he was running an errand."

"Was he here before?"

"Oh, yes. He brought us Subway for lunch and left again."

"Any luck?" asked Penny. The man still had tomato sauce on his chin. Maybe he was saving it for later.

"No. It's almost time to call this official."

"Official?" Penny asked. "Like—paperwork?"

Vicki looked at him for a brief second to determine if Penny was joking. He wasn't.

Vicki's hand ruffled in her pocket, bringing out the earring.

"Oh, do you have a lost and found?"

"Of course we do," confirmed Momma.

Vicki gave the earring to Momma.

"A sanitation worker passed this off to me."

"Sure, I'll take it back there. One of my biggest responsibilities is taking care of the lost and found."

She seemed quite proud of her chore as if it were her only chore.

Momma placed the earring in a treasure box. In it contained a notebook, moldy dentures, and some change, a dollar forty-five, to be exact.

Ellis stormed in with one empty glass Coke bottle and went straight to his office. The three subordinates noticed the change of pace.

Vicki entered Ellis's office.

He sat on his chair and placed the empty Coke bottle on top of his newspaper. Vicki shut the door.

It was silent for a moment.

"Nothing?"

Ellis looked up at his new deputy.

"Nada. I talked to her friends, Lainey, her boss. Nobody has seen or heard from her."

Vicki leaned on his desk. She would not have done that to Gags in New York, but here the rules were quite casual. Plus, even though he was the chief, Vicki already felt she could barrel Ellis over.

"Sheriff, with all due respect... we need to take action."

Vicki saw a change in Ellis, not psychically, but emotionally. Vicki wondered if the sheriff had ever had this type of case. She also wondered if she was about to have to take over the case.

Pausing for a tiny moment, she looked down at the desk. Vicki's eyes zeroed in on the newspaper, and she picked it up. Vicki grabbed the empty soda bottle and used it as a magnifying glass.

"Sheriff, look at this."

Ellis looked at the paper.

"What?"

She pointed to the cover picture. The picture was taken from the charity event at the church. Gracie full-blown smiling. She could even see herself photobombing; her giant head gracefully emerging from Gracie's right shoulder like an alien. First night in Oostburg and she was already on the front page.

Ellis looked again.

"Yeah, it's Gracie. What's the big deal?"

Vicki pointed to the girl's head.

"Look at her ears."

Ellis looked again, this time with an emphasis in that area.

"Her ears? I don't see—"

"Follow me."

A minute later they were in the lost and found.

Vicki got the box and pulled out the earring.

Vicki gave the earring to the sheriff; who looked at it and matched it to the picture in the paper.

"It's the same earring."

"This sanitation worker handed the earring to me today. The man found it on his sanitation route."

"Where was he? What street?"

Vicki tried to remember.

"Damn it. I didn't take note."

"What did the sanitation worker look like?"

That Vicki remembered. How could she forget a guy like Big Mack?

"Big black guy—named Big Mack."

"Big Mack?"

Vicki's ears perked up. She hoped she was correct about Big Mack. Even though she only met him once, Mack didn't give off a criminal vibe, once she spoke to him.

"You know him?"

"Yeah. I am going to try reaching Seth again—you notify the press."

Vicki left.

Ellis once again attempted to text and call Seth, to no avail. Ellis tried Evelyn as well; that yielded the same result.

Ellis sighed.

If Seth and Evelyn weren't answering their cells, there was only one thing left to do.

13.

SCATTERED TO THE WINDS

Job was a blameless man who desired the Lord. His life was as perfect as could be. He had a wife and many children. Many livestock, riches, and crops. Life was great.

One day, God decided to have a moment with Satan. And Satan, ever the trickster, decided to bait the Lord by offering: "I bet you that I can tempt any of your loved ones against you."

The Good Lord sat back to ponder over this little proposition. After a bit of thinkage, the Lord Almighty informs Satan: "Sure, what the hell. Satan, you may have my servant, Job. You may wrench him over as much as you desire, murder all his loved ones, burn his toast and I guarantee he will not say anything bad about me."

So, Satan did just that. Job's wife, children, and cattle pass. His companions betray him, proclaiming Job must have been a bad gent because God let so many horrific things happen.

Job sat back and swallowed everything his friends proclaimed, and instead of cursing the Lord, Job of the Kool-Aid continued to praise the Lord, even in this perfect storm that God allowed in the first place.

In the end, God won his bet with Satan. Why?

So that his name could be praised.

Well, that is just so loving of you, Mr. God. You screw over one of your children, this one who loves you more than many of the others so that your name could be praised.

So the book says...

Pastor Zimmermann was asleep at his desk when the telephone loudly rang. Bob answered; and it was another prayer request to place into their bulletin. Aw shucks, darn it, that bulletin was already printed for the next day's service, and cousin Sammie's gall bladder whatever would have to wait a week.

Zimmermann looked down to see his pillow: the old Bible. Book: Job. After all, his sermon was going to be on Job tomorrow. He was incredibly excited to preach for the first time in God knows how long.

If only Seth were out of the picture forever...

Seth and his wife cuddled on their cozy red sofa in their too-lavish-for-their-paycheck hotel room. It was past 7PM and they were waiting for their evening reservations three blocks away.

"Life is a gamble, you win some," Seth smiled and then he continued: "You win some more!"

They chuckled and playfully kissed.

Evelyn sat back.

"Oh, I wish I had the strength... that everything will get together. It's almost as if you don't worry at all."

Seth looked at her with intent.

"I worry all the time."

"Well, you certainly don't show it."

Seth smiled.

"I'm made of iron."

"You're Iron Man."

Evelyn felt comforted. Seth could always do that; ever since high school, he could calm her down when she was "overreacting" or just being a female. She lovingly looked at him and nuzzled his soft cheek as they closed their eyes.

Seth squeezed her tightly and brought her in.

"You and the kids rely on me. Our family is my joy, and I would never, ever, allow any dangers to come your way. I don't know what I would do without you or Gracie or Lainey—"

"Even Lainey?" Evelyn joked.

Seth sighed and smiled.

"Even Lainey." He went on: "I would lose myself."

He kissed the top of her head.

Three quite impatient ladies got ready to co-host a party at a certain vacant house. Unfortunately for these ladies, the fourth co-host, the girl who actually lived there, was conspicuously absent.

This trio of friends—Bianca, Stacy, and Michelle—rang the doorbell a few times. They expected a big bang tonight; cute boys were coming in a couple of hours but they couldn't have a party without the owner.

Michelle looked through the window.

"No lights."

Bianca stomped her foot.

"Where is Gracie?"

"Where is Lainey?" asked Michelle.

"Nobody's home!" pouted Stacy.

"What do we do now?" asked Michelle.

At the police station, Vicki was about to call it a night, at least take a two-hour break. This small new development had made her restless. She couldn't believe the circumstance from New York was now seemingly repeating. Vicki stared at that lonely earring. The beginning of leaking tears was quickly stopped at the sight of Penny and Momma. She did what she was told and notified the press. The hot potato was passed along and now she had to eat. She wasn't thinking clearly, and it wouldn't be good for Gracie anyway.

"I am going home to grab some dinner," Vicki told the others. "I'll be back soon. Let me know if anything happens."

"Will do—oh, take your sandwich," Momma said.

Vicki smiled and took the Subway sandwich.

She drove the short distance to her house. It was not too late, about seven, but Vicki was exhausted from having the horrid nightmares of Gabrielle Adjami, followed by the reality of Gracie Adams and now the lack of nutrition.

Deputy Vicki got home and looked for her aunt and Lainey. She found them upstairs as Aunt Coralee was now putting young Lainey to rest. It was pretty early for a thirteen-year-old to go to bed.

Vicki saw that Lainey was staring at the ceiling.

"How you doing?" Vicki asked the teen.

"Did you find her?"

Vicki paused. She hated that she was reliving the last four years of her life.

"Not yet."

"I just... want to rest," Lainey said.

Vicki and Coralee went downstairs as Vicki heated up her sub.

"How'd she do?" asked Vicki.

"She's fine. You?"

Vicki shoved a hot bite in her mouth to avoid the question but realized that it wouldn't last forever.

She finally swallowed and said:

"It's happening all over again, Aunt. There is... nothing worse than losing a child."

Big Mack hung in his simple living room, watching television.

Nothing was on.

The Oostburg garbage man was not paying too much attention anyway—

He was too busy cleaning his rifle...

Looking for a guinea pig to preach to, Zimmermann opened the door to his son's bedroom. He was gone again, and Bob had no idea where he was or who he was meeting. Bob hated preaching in front of the mirror as it didn't return much feedback.

But he couldn't be there, as the teen was playing hide-and-seek with his friend in the forest...

"Marco?" Matt called about gleefully. The sun had set, and Matt was walking around the woods in the night; searching for his friend in the frigid night.

"Come on, where are you, my sexy playmate?"

The man walked over to his bookcase and grinned. Oh, how he loved literature. The man dialed a number on his private, unlisted landline.

A few seconds later, the other phone picked up on the receiving end, and Raile didn't beat around the bush with his message:

"Greetings. And don't worry about who I am. Worry about what you were doing last night and who saw you. I will be in touch."

Not very far from the Demko residence, Wesley was walking home. It was getting a little chillier, and tiny Wesley blew down on his hands. Looking at his hands, he noticed his naked wedding finger...

Wesley nervously looked around.

"Where the hell is my ring?" he asked himself.

But it was no use. He quickly remembered where it was.

With all his fingers in his pockets, Wesley walked into his home. He saw the woman aimlessly watching TV and assumed he would be able to bypass her. Wesley quietly made his way up the first two steps when the cold woman called out:

"Dr. Malachi's office called, and I made you an appointment for 3PM."

Wesley stopped in his tracks.

"I work on Monday."

Brooke stared at the TV.

"Not at three."

Wesley was miffed. Woman had checked his schedule and made an appointment without his permission. She was always doing crap like this, and it pissed Wesley off to no end.

Somewhat concerned, Sheriff Kirkbride shot down I-43 toward Chicago. He made it to I-94 East and crossed into Illinois when he heard an obnoxious siren getting close. The sheriff decided it would be best to pull over. Ellis was a sheriff after all and this matter was quite serious. Ellis was confident with his badge, his story, and his charms, he could get out of this infraction. Although, he did regret not taking his sheriff's car instead of his own. Even without boobs, he was going to get out of this ticket.

"Hello officer," Ellis said in an overly-friendly tone.

"You know how fast you were going?"

"Yes, officer. I am in a hurry."

"Obviously."

"Let me explain."

"They always do."

"I am Sheriff Ellis Kirkbride of the Oostburg—"

"Oostburg? Where the hell is that?"

"It's—"

"Sounds made up."

"It's not. Listen here, there's a missing teenage girl, and I need to tell her parents—"

"Why don't you call?"

"I tried—"

"Text?"

"Yes, I did that too, their phone must be—"

"You could Facebook, that always—"

"Look, just give me the damn ticket."

After a fulfilling dinner of ribs for him and the steak for her, Seth and Evelyn strolled along the Cherry Avenue Bridge. They each had one adult beverage. One, and only one. Being equally yoked when it came to the debate on whether or not Christians should drink alcohol, they interpreted that the good book was pretty clear: getting drunk was sin, and so they didn't drink in excess. Although they did disagree with a few believers who felt consuming alcohol of all types was a sin; if that were the case then Jesus never would have turned the water into wine.

"This was nice. No distractions, just us talking. Simple. Life has gotten... so difficult these past years," Evelyn said.

Evelyn snuggled next to her husband. Seth removed his jacket and gave it to his wife.

"Well, that's life. People change and priorities change. Money... becomes... difficult."

Seth sensed a little tension.

"We're doing ok, right Seth?"

Some two hours and two hundred bucks later, Ellis Kirkbride made it to the hotel a little quicker than he expected. Walking up to the front desk, he was happy he called Lainey Adams to ask what hotel they were staying at and equally glad the phone number was on their refrigerator.

"Hi, may I speak to Seth and Evelyn Adams?"

"I'm sorry; we can't give out guest information—"

Ellis pulled out his badge.

The concierge coughed.

"Very well."

The concierge picked up the phone and dialed.

After a few moments of waiting, he hung up.

"I'm sorry, Officer. They are not in their room."

Ellis tapped on the marble counter.

"Do you know where they went?"

A bellboy in his early twenties walked over.

The kid had a slight Russian accent.

"Da."

Seth took a few steps.

"Um, we're ok. The Lord won't let us starve, that is for sure."

"We did just drop two hundred dollars on dinner," Evelyn reminded him.

Seth laughed.

"Well, once a year we can afford it. It's back to the dollar menu on Monday."

Evelyn smiled.

"I'd rather be eating dollar menu with you than fancy menus with anybody else. Unless it's Matthew McConaughey. Then you're screwed."

Seth played along:

"Well, you tell McConaughey to throw along Nicole Kidman's number, and we have a deal."

Seth kissed his lady tenderly as the round pretty moon gazed above them.

"Seth, the last couple of years... we have been a little distant. I know life gets in the way, but please let's commit to making each other a priority."

"Yes," agreed Seth.

"Please, let's not be like Brooke and Wesley."

Seth and Evelyn made their way across the bridge. They hoped they weren't going too far out of their way. Neither was very great with directions, and they did not have their phones on.

"And please, Seth... let's always tell each other everything... even if it's not pretty," Evelyn stated.

Seth nodded.

He had been a jerk lately, well, really the whole marriage. He felt bad, but at the same time didn't want to repent.

"Will do."

Evelyn began:

"Seth, I'm—"

And at that exact moment, Sheriff Ellis Kirkbride pulled up and called out from his car:

"Seth!"

Seth thought it sounded like his friend but could not fathom why he would be in Chicago at the moment. He knelt and peered into the car window.

"Ellis?"

An impatient cabbie honked loud at Ellis, who was momentarily blocking traffic.

Ellis turned around; showing his badge.

"Police!"

Evelyn knew this couldn't be good.

"What's going on?" she asked.

Ellis looked at them.

"Come home."

Seth turned to Evelyn.

"It's Gracie."

And they swallowed their hearts.

14.

DON'T TAKE MY GRACE

Minutes were hours and hours were years as Seth and Evelyn paused hopelessly. The couple didn't desire to ask the obvious next question.

What did Ellis mean: "*It's Gracie*?"

Who knows? Perhaps she just broke an arm or a leg. Please let it be minor... legs and arms heal.

"Where's your car?" Ellis asked quickly.

"At the hotel."

Ellis opened the passenger door.

"Get in."

Seth and Evelyn quickly obeyed.

Sheriff Ellis drove with haste as they made their way back to the hotel parking lot. Seth sat silently in the front holding on to the armrest. Evelyn was in the back dialing her phone. Thankfully, Seth and Evelyn had not wandered far from their hotel.

"No one knows where she is," Ellis spoke. "Lainey saw her a little after 9PM last night, but Gracie never came back."

Evelyn spoke to the message on the phone.

"Grace, this is your mother. Call me ASAP. I love you."

Evelyn looked out the window.

"Gracie has not answered calls from Lainey or her friends. She missed work as well."

Seth bit his lip.

"That's not like her."

Evelyn began to cry.

"Oh my God. Oh my God... oh my god... my god no."

In a few minutes, they were back at the hotel parking lot hopping out of Ellis's car and into their own.

"Follow me," Ellis said.

Ditching their luggage, Seth and Evelyn sprinted for their car.

Within seconds, they were in their car and out of the parking lot heading up to Oostburg. Ellis led well, and even the speeding did not deter him. Seth was ready to follow.

Evelyn went back to her phone and dialed into the silence.

"Grace pick up. Please."

She hung up. Looking out the window, she couldn't help but think if things may have been different... had their phones been on. *Why didn't they have their phones on?* she thought to herself. And then... she remembered:

It was her husband who banned them from this excursion. Her husband. Seth Isaiah Adams.

She turned to him and glared.

This was *his* fault.

Evelyn held her phone tight and continued to cry. She stared out the window pleading to view her Grace... walking along the highway... *as long as she was safe... as long as she was alive.* That's all that mattered. Her safety. Everything else could go to Hades in a Mercedes as long as Grace was safe. Please, God. Protect her.

"My God. Seth, what are we going to do?"

Pastor did not respond to Evelyn's question other than grabbing his wife's hand.

At that very moment, and for the first time in their marriage, she did not want to hold his hand.

But she did anyway.

"She's ok. She's ok. We're going to find her."

He put his foot to the pedal harder.

Pastor held back the tears. He couldn't weep. Not now. He's driving. Not now. She will lose it even more. Seth had to be strong. *It sucks being a man sometimes.* Seth wanted to cry like hell especially if it meant she would be home, safe. Safe. Oh, Jesus. Please. Not this. Anything but this. She is his heart... his first child. The daughter he attended that daddy-daughter dance with every February. The tickets go on sale the first Monday in December. He had just put a reminder to purchase the tickets on his calendar last Tuesday. Please God Jesus. Anything else. Burn the house, take the money. Any—

Unknowingly, he spoke out loud:

"DON'T TAKE MY GRACE."

The two cars got back to Oostburg in record time, one hour and thirty-nine minutes. They were only pulled over once—Racine—but Ellis was able to debate his way out of this ticket.

Pulling up to the Oostburg Police Department a little before 11PM, they were greeted outside by a massive stampede waiting, most all of Oostburg. People had heard those reports on the Sheboygan Scanner as well as the news. Little Oostburg was hitting the spotlight and getting their fifteen minutes of shame whether they liked it or not.

Ellis got out of his car and blasted his route to the doors, ignoring everybody. Seth and Evelyn followed Ellis; dodging reporters' insensitive questions such as: "Where were you guys?" and "Pastor, why was there not a babysitter?" Seth stared down that reporter briefly, as if she were going to get punched. It probably wouldn't look great for the pastor to punch a female, even if she was being a bitch and deserved it.

At the front door, Momma was there to greet them.

"It's been a madhouse since the press was told."

"Good. More people looking," Ellis deduced.

The four entered the main lobby to greet Vicki.

"Can I get you something to drink?" Momma asked a down-trodden Evelyn, ever living up to her name.

"Water," said Evelyn.

Momma was back in seconds with the cup of water.

"Sheriff, the press was notified and Deputy Penny is out organizing a search party," Vicki spoke. "Ellis, you only have four officers?"

"Three. Momma's technically the secretary."

Vicki looked carefully at the Adams' couple. That husband was cool as he consoled his wife. The wife kept nervously tapping her feet.

"We're going to need a lot more people."

Evelyn looked up.

"Where's Lainey?"

Vicki walked over.

"Lainey is ok, Mrs. Adams. My aunt has her at our home."

"Who is "our"?" asked Evelyn.

Vicki forgot that she was new around town.

"Coralee Mentink is my aunt. Lainey is with her."

Ellis took charge.

"Seth, Evelyn, here is what we know: Gracie and Lainey were home. Lainey told us Gracie left after 9PM, maybe a little later. Lainey called me around 8AM, when she realized Gracie wasn't home. We also know that some of her friends phoned Gracie. No one has talked to her since Lainey saw her leave somewhat after 9PM."

Evelyn sobbed.

"My God..."

About 11:30PM, Seth and Evelyn finally made their return back home; roughly twenty hours sooner than they had planned.

A pesky reporter was standing off to the right of their home. Seth recognized her from television... the Milwaukee news station.

That reporter spoke clearly as a sturdy cameraman filmed.

"...Oostburg High School senior Gracie Adams has been gone for approximately twenty-four hours. The teenager was last seen by her sister Friday night as she was leaving their home. Local authorities have been searching the area but so far have been unsuccessful."

Seth and Evelyn Adams pushed through the vultures blocking their home's entrance. Unfortunately for them, these reporters smelled blood as they shoved their cold microphones in the faces of the grieving parents. A few photographers stole moments from their tragedy as well.

Evelyn conceded as she stood on the top step. She turned around and spoke into a microphone, although she had no idea who was holding it.

"Please, if anyone out there knows where my Grace is please contact me. We love you, Grace."

A car pulled up. Evelyn's eyes widened, demanding it to be Grace, who had simply gotten lost, perhaps her phone just died. Everything... innocent. *Please, lord. Fix this...*

It wasn't Grace. It was Vicki driving their other daughter, Lainey. Vicki got out and opened the door for Lainey and Coralee.

The group of reporters stormed over as Vicki held and protected Lainey; barging onto the Adams' porch.

The hounds were fierce:

"Do you have a minute?" asked one.

Lainey shut them down, huddled in that protective cloud of the tough Deputy Weathers.

"Lainey, where did your sister go?" asked another reporter.

Vicki stormed up the stairs.

"She's not answering any questions, thank you."

Evelyn grabbed Lainey and dragged her inside.

Inside the Adams' living room, everyone was silent, almost as if they were already at her funeral.

Taking the opportunity to check around, Vicki saw quite a few photos on the walls. A brief history of the girls' progression into near adulthood. They were pretty; both of them. This family looked content in the photos, sans Lainey. Vicki realized that Lainey was not smiling in any of them. Studying all of the photos, she could not see one smile. She looked over to Lainey. She wasn't a happy gal tonight, either. But in her defense, according to the photos at least, she was rarely a very happy girl anyway.

"The good news is that most members of the church are running around. Deputies probably doubled in number tonight," miscalculated Ellis.

Deputy Weathers continued to look at the walls of photography.

"Is it possible Gracie ran away?" asked Vicki. By looking at the show of pictures, you would think Lainey would be the child to run away, not Gracie.

"I don't know," Seth replied hastily. "I feel we should be out in—"

Ellis interrupted:

"Seth, there's about a hundred people looking for her—"

Seth broke:

"Except the ones who care the most!"

Seth stood up and started to leave before Sheriff Ellis stopped him:

"Look, we need some answers from all of you. That will help us locate Gracie. I promise."

Vicki added:

"We searched her room thoroughly. We did not find anything out of the ordinary. Did she keep a diary?"

Evelyn looked at Seth, who returned the look.

"I'm not sure. Not that I know of."

Vicki looked at the past photos, particularly the most recent one: Evelyn sitting on a chair, pretty blue gown, with the daughters on the sides and Seth standing proudly behind his ladies. The family cleaned up nice, that is for sure. Gracie really looked like Gabrielle.

Deputy Weathers walked over to Lainey and kneeled beside her. Lainey was no longer the upset little girl. She stared into space.

Ellis spoke:

"Lainey. How are you doing? I know this has to be hard for you. You looked up to Gracie. She was—"

Vicki spoke to Ellis.

"Is."

Ellis looked up at Vicki.

"Is," Vicki quietly repeated.

The sheriff nodded; indicating silently that he fully understood the importance of word choice.

Ellis turned back to Lainey.

"Is a wonderful lady. Okay, Lainey. Me and Deputy Vicki need you to think real hard. Please, tell us everything you remember."

Vicki added:

"And remember, even if it's the tiniest thing, it could be very important."

"We played cards. We didn't play for long."

"How long?"

"I don't know. Fifteen, twenty minutes."

"During your card game, did either of you... make a phone call; even answer the door?"

Lainey nodded.

"She was texting. Laughing and texting."

Vicki's ears perked up.

"Who was she texting?"

Lainey shrugged her shoulders.

"She wouldn't tell me."

Deputy Vicki half-smiled, knowing the smile might give away that she thought the youth could seriously be in trouble.

"You know what, Lainey?"

Lainey did not answer.

"She may have saved your life."

"May I go now? I... can't remember anything else. I'm really tired."

Coralee took Lainey's shoulder.

"Mind if I tuck her in?" Coralee asked.

Evelyn nodded.

Lainey glanced at her parents, waiting for a hug, a wave, a blink, anything. The young teenager left with nothing but pain as she and Coralee went up the stairs.

Coralee tucked Lainey into bed and kissed her forehead.

The lady smiled at the young teenager.

"So what really happened?" asked Coralee, waiting for the little girl to finish her bedtime story.

Lainey smiled.

"You don't remember anything, huh?"

Coralee smiled. A second later, Lainey produced a small key from underneath her pillow...

"Seth, Evelyn. Is there anything else... anything at all? Does she have a boyfriend or any enemies?" Ellis asked.

Evelyn stood forward.

"There is one boy who likes her. Matt—"

Ellis interrupted, informing Vicki of the boy.

"Matt Zimmermann. Nice kid from the church."

"Are there any bad feelings between them?" Vicki asked.

"Not that I know of. I don't think they are dating but they are friends," replied Evelyn.

Vicki changed the subject:

"What about her finances? Does she have an account or a credit card?"

Evelyn nodded as Seth continued to pace about. He was losing his patience talking and not doing.

"Yes, she has both. The credit card is only to be used in extreme emergencies," Evelyn explained.

Vicki nodded.

"Okay, that is good. If Gracie has used it, we'll be able to track wherever she has been. And if you can get me her bank statements that would be great."

Evelyn walked over to the computer and clicked it on.

"Yes, of course."

Evelyn sat down and began typing. "I know Grace's passwords."

The pastor glanced out the window, trying his best to block the tears. He knew there were many eyes out there looking for her; knocking down doors and searching all over. But it was now midnight and things slowed down... people were tired and were not going anywhere. No phone calls had come in, good or bad. Pastor desired to be out there, wherever she was, not in here, talking to these two officers, his best friend, and the new deputy.

"She was so perfect..." Seth caught himself before his wife pounded on the keyboard, startling everyone in the room.

"Stop! Stop! Stop talking like that! She is alive somewhere! Just stop it, Seth!"

Seth walked over to his woman, knowing it was his words, his great pessimism that led to her slamming the keyboard.

"I want my baby back!" Evelyn shouted.

"She will come back, I promise you, Evelyn. We... will find her," consoled Seth.

Evelyn ignored her husband's promises and pointed to her computer monitor. The three went over and looked over her shoulder, quickly searching for any suspicious activity.

"Gracie has... nine hundred and twelve dollars," stated Evelyn.

Vicki scrutinized the information.

"She hasn't made any big transactions. Thank you, Mrs. Adams."

"Did you have any enemies?" asked Ellis.

There was a noticeable, golden silence in the air for longer than was desired.

Evelyn looked at Seth.

Vicki pressed further.

"Money issues?"

Seth glanced back at Evelyn, who remained silent. Then he turned to the side where the windows were. In a very brief instant, he would swear on a thousand Bibles that he saw his daughter. Gracie was present and within his reach... although he couldn't touch her. He quickly glanced around to see if anyone else noticed her but no one moved. Seth wanted to call out to her; just to tell her that he loved her. He couldn't believe no one else saw her.

Gracie spoke, short and sweet and to the point:

"Don't risk your pulpit, dad. Trust me."

And before the pastor could take one step toward her, she was gone.

What did she mean?! "Don't risk your pulpit?" How did Gracie know what I was going to say? Was she—gone? Was she alive? Innumerable thoughts flew through Seth's head. *I saw my girl though, so she must be okay, right? Maybe she was able to speak from her captor's lair. She must be alive... she must be alive...*

"She must be alive!" Seth yelled the last one out loud. Everyone looked at him.

Seth looked around to see three pairs of eyes staring at him questioningly. "Um. I just heard her voice in my head. Sorry."

Ellis continued:

"Seth, you don't have any debts, do you?"

Seth swallowed.

"No," he lied.

"Your finances?"

"We're doing fine."

Evelyn looked away.

"And you, Mrs. Adams? Anything unusual going on?" Vicki asked the pastor's wife.

"I've been... doing some work. Delivering mail."

Seth turned to his wife.

"Evelyn?"

"What kind of mail?" asked Ellis.

Evelyn got up from the computer chair and glanced out the window.

"Oh, Lord! I don't know what he has me doing! Just the other night, he wanted me to deliver an envelope to a man in Chicago. A man named—umm—Mike Pool. I had to pass him an envelope or he was going to—oh Lord—and the guy—oh my Lord—said he would: *"hate for something horrible to happen"*. Oh my Lord! My God! He has her! He kidnapped our baby!"

Vicki stepped forward.

"Who?"

"His name is Charles! Charles Raile! The guy who said he was "Bernard" at church last night when you called him out! I have two phone numbers."

"Can you describe him?" asked Vicki.

"About sixty or so, a little overweight and around six feet. White hair. Blue eyes. I know where he lives!"

"You have his address?"

"No, I don't—oh! But one time when we were speaking, Raile spoke about living around the block from the bank; cause he was complaining about the bell ringing so loud. He lives around the bank!"

They opened the front door to find a huge congregation of soul-thirsty reporters. Ellis, with his deputy and Aunt Coralee right behind, broke through the masses. The selfish reporters shouted callous, uncaring questions, to which Ellis quickly replied:

"We're doing the best we can—please no more questions."

The sheriff took Vicki and Coralee to his car. In the frenzy, Vicki forgot she drove her car to bring the sister home but Oostburg was so little she could sprint back and get it later.

Now she just wanted to get her aunt back home.

Coralee joked:

"So, this is what it feels like to be in the back seat of a police car."

Vicki turned around.

"Don't get used to it."

Returning to their kitchen, Seth and Evelyn Adams questioned every decision they made that weekend; maybe even their whole lives. They had no idea what was going on. For sure, Charles Raile sent Evelyn on a crazy list of mail deliveries. When she bucked up to him, it could have sent him over the ledge... and perhaps that is why Grace Adams might be in danger, but he also may not have had anything to do with her disappearance. The couple secretly prayed their Gracie had all of a sudden become irresponsible and not returned phone calls.

Something was wrong. This wasn't like Gracie. Not one bit.

He poured himself a coffee and grabbed his keys.

"I'm not staying here."

Evelyn wanted to leave home too, but she was very confident that Grace was coming home. Evelyn dialed her phone. She heard Grace's perky voice.

"Hey, this is Gracie—"

Evelyn hung up and dialed again.

"Hey, this—"

The frantic momma hen hung up once more. Evelyn couldn't bear to hear Grace's beautiful voice and leave another pointless voicemail. She did not get an answer from the prior six, she wasn't going to answer this one.

Evelyn cried.

And she prayed, even though the wife knew praying didn't work.

It took thirty-three doors and a whole canteen of incredibly lukewarm coffee but Deputy Penny was able to locate Charles Raile's address by knocking on all doors and peeking through countless mailboxes in the vicinity of the bank.

He went to the front door and knocked. Standing a good thirty seconds, he began to hear his tummy rumble. David had not eaten much that day, not even dinner. But this really was not a moment to think of edibles. A teenage girl was missing, and he finally had a situation to work on. Not that he really wanted work, for the man was lazy but he was a good soldier, too, doing whatever tasks Ellis assigned him to. He took his assignments with good heart but he didn't really yearn for important duties such as this. He knocked again, and waited more, guessing correctly that he was not going to reach Raile at home. He turned on his flashlight and peeked through those door windows. He couldn't see anyone or anything. He walked around to the side of the house. Again, Penny glanced in the windows with his flashlight. Nothing out of the ordinary, a couch, a television, and a bookshelf.

Penny spoke into his walkie-talkie:

"He's not home, sheriff."

"Damn it. Ten-four."

"No Raile?" asked Vicki.

"No Raile."

Fearing the very worst, she stared through her window. Vicki didn't come all this way to be involved in Gabrielle Part-Two.

15.

IN THE MIDDLE OF THE NIGHT

It was now a tad after midnight Saturday/Sunday morning as the pastor made his rounds. The pastor was fortunate people were up at this time. Seth was equally fortunate that their curfew had been relinquished for everyone so they could search for Gracie.

His first stop was Tom Fenwick's shack, which was a little dump on the outskirts of Oostburg. The Fenwick family was the shadiest of what the sinless town had to offer. For many healthy generations, they had been "that family". They mowed their grass on Sundays, and they did not give a rat's behind who saw them. They did not care for coy appearances, and in return, Oostburg didn't care much for them. In Oostburg, they were rebels.

Thomas Fenwick worked at the lumber yard in Oostburg and had been there since he was a high school dropout so many years ago. He did attend church but did not quite get it. He didn't want to get it, either. Nonetheless, he made his path there about fifty percent of the time.

Rachel Fenwick was a stay-at-home-mom who was told by her parents—and many others—not to marry Tom, predicting that Tom wouldn't amount to anything decent. But Rachel married into the black sheep family of Oostburg anyway, and while they were not well off, they were not poor, either. Thomas had done okay for his wife and daughter, Michelle.

Staring at the walls, Michelle was understandably saddened that Gracie was gone especially since they had planned a secret party for this night. A party that she had to cancel. A handful of those males gathering were handsome boys that shy Michelle was hoping to chat with as she got over her anxiety.

The worst thing was not the canceled social. The worst thing was that she had no idea where her best gal friend was and here was Gracie's father—*pastor*—coming over at midnight to look for his daughter. Timid Michelle had nothing to give even if she spoke about the party. She wished a million wishes that her friend was hiding under her bed or in her closet, but Gracie wasn't.

Seth walked into their living room. The three Fenwicks were awake and dressed. Mom Fenwick was drinking a coffee.

The pastor could feel Fenwick's greasy fingers on his shoulder.

"Sorry to bother you so late."

"I'd be doing the same thing," said Rachel. "We're all praying... it's something little, like maybe her car and cell phone died, some... I am sorry. I feel stupid. You don't need to hear that. It's so difficult. You know..."

"Thank you. Evelyn, bless her heart, is trying to remain positive. But... I can't help but think... there is something very wrong. This is not like Gracie. She's always so... reliable. Gracie—" Seth let it hang in the air. Dad just wanted his baby to be here, at her friend's house, or playing a stupid prank on him.

"Michelle, is there anything you know of? Maybe a boyfriend?" asked Tom.

"Matt Zimmermann likes her," Michelle confirmed.

"Yes, I'm going to Matt's house next. Do you know if they were dating?" asked Seth.

"Not that I know of. Matt just liked her," said a sad Michelle.

"Isn't she in the school play?" asked Tom.

"Yeah. She has to come back before opening night. That's six days away! And we still have tech too," said Michelle.

"Aren't you her understudy?" Tom asked his girl.

"No, Matt is."

"You like Matt, right, Michelle?"

The embarrassed teenager dipped her head.

"Yes."

"Huh. I guess that gives you a little motive, baby girl!" Tom joked distastefully.

Seth looked at him. *What a prick.*

"I'll get going," said Seth.

Fenwick followed the pastor out. It was getting a little chillier. Tom blew on his hands.

"It's going to be okay, pastor. God wouldn't take such a beautiful young kid from this world. So pretty."

Seth looked at Tom and swallowed. Tom was beginning to creep him out, and for just one brief moment Seth wondered if Tom knew more than he was letting on. He quickly denied that possibility, realizing that Tom was a moron and if he did have anything to do with Gracie's disappearance, he would get an award for acting like an idiot these past twenty years. No, he was a bit too stupid for this.

Taking out a cigarette, Fenwick watched him drive off.

Seth kept driving. He knew not where he had been—it was late—he was exhausted but couldn't sleep. Roads were too dark, and Oostburg did not have traffic lights. There was really nothing he could do; at least not at 1AM. The only thing he could do was hallucinate.

Hallucinate and cry.

Gracie sat next to Seth just as she did the final time they rode in a car together, the Friday afternoon when he drove her to practice. In fact, Gracie was even wearing the same clothes. Her hair was the same. Everything was the same. She was safe in his car, and no one would ever lay a hand on her.

She was smiling, too. Very happy.

"Promise you'll protect me?" she asked her daddy.

Seth took his eyes off the street for a second to look at his happy daughter, who really wasn't there.

Seth replied:

"Does anyone think there still is not a reasonable doubt?"

Reality hit when Seth drove into a trio of silver garbage cans.

He got out to assess the damage. The bumper was a little bent, and two of the three cans were dented.

Starting to put the cans up, he heard a voice:

"You watch yourself, young man."

It was a very old male, a man in his seventies. A bit odd for him to be up this late.

"I'm sorry—let me help you with that—"

Seth helped the Old Man straighten up the garbage cans.

"No harm done."

"I've been looking—"

"You're the pastor of the missing girl. May I get you something, a soda pop?"

Seth waved his hand.

"No, that's alright. I just need to be going."

He swallowed. It had been twenty-four hours. That press was notified and the four cops were sprinting around. The church was on the search. It was... official. And scary. Oh so... scary. His precious little girl was really missing. This really was happening.

The Old Man picked up the last can.

"Remember pastor:

Forgiving someone who doesn't deserve it...
is the hardest thing in the world."

Seth's eyes widened. Seth knew a subtle hint when he heard one. All those years of preaching, he knew how to deliver hidden messages. However, he wasn't used to receiving them.

Seth stared at the Old Man.

Did this Old Man know something?

One more thing—who was this Old Man?

Seth nodded and got back in his car.

In the dark, Seth drove off trying to see through the tears.

"It's alright, daddy."

Seth stared at her for a tiny look; unsure if she were real. After a second, he noticed he was driving in the dead of night and looked at the street. Readjusting the wheel, he was safe to look at the passenger seat.

She was gone.

A few minutes later, he was safely back home.

The pastor had no direction. He was lost. Seth prayed but every second she did not come back made the prayers feel as if they were landing on deaf ears. Of all the severe prayers Seth had called out to the Heavens, this was the one that the Big Guy needed to come through on.

Walking up the stairs of his porch, he met Evelyn sitting there. Seth wondered why she hadn't gone out to search as well, but he was too tired to find out.

"Grace?" she asked.

Seth shook his head and walked past her.

Evelyn took one more look and followed him to the bedroom.

They zoned out from their last few hours of pain. They had no way to deal with it. They were not prepared for this. They were caged, not knowing how to get out.

It was Evelyn who broke the silence:

"Where did you go?"

"Fenwick. Nobody knows anything."

Evelyn paused, and then said quietly:

"She's out there. In this freezing cold..."

"Maybe she's... safe. Inside someone's home."

"Where are our savings, Seth?"

Damn it. This was not a time to ask about money.

Seth looked over to his bride. He didn't desire to answer that he had been gambling for a few years—alright, more than a few—and the savings were gone. She did not need to learn that and certainly didn't need to know that now. In defeat, Seth left his bedroom.

16.

IRON RUSTS IN THE RAIN

As the sun was fading on the Adams' marriage, the sun was rising in almost-frozen Oostburg. It was Sunday morning; a day and a half since Gracie was last seen.

A reporter was on the TV in Coralee's kitchen.

"If you have any information on her whereabouts, please contact the number at the bottom of the screen."

Vicki shut off the television as her Aunt Coralee entered dressed in full church attire. No missing young lady was going to stop her from praising Jesus.

Coralee looked at Vicki with a raised brow.

"Are you going to church like that?"

Vicki put down her steaming hot cup of coffee.

"Aunt Coralee, I'm not going to church—there's a missing kid out there."

"Exactly why we need to go to church. To pray."

Vicki shook her head.

"Prayer isn't going to help find that girl."

Coralee stashed some yams in her purse. They went along nicely with the apple that was already there.

"With this old body, I can't run around town—but I certainly can pray."

Vicki sighed, putting on her hat and mittens.

"And you need a ride."

Coralee smiled.

"Well, you can give me a ride to church while you look around."

Driving Miss Coralee to church, Oostburg's newest deputy made haste. She was determined to find that girl *this morning*. Vicki caught a glimpse of the town's character. Many citizens were around and about. For a town as tiny as Oostburg, where Sunday morning was to praise the Lord, Vicki was pleasantly surprised to see so many citizens walking around when normally they'd be in church worship. Vicki could see people chatting, obviously in distress. She imagined their conversations; probably all in the ballpark of "*I can't imagine if she were my child*" or "*Poor Pastor Seth*". She swallowed quickly as she thought of that pastor. Only two days ago he seemed to be so deceptive and now—she felt terribly sorry for the guy. Sure, Adams could still be shady but now there was a new layer to him: Pastor may have lost his eldest daughter forever. Vicki racked her brain at her own sad pessimism; she so desired to be optimistic but her past would not let her... not with Gabrielle Adjami's killer still on the run. She stopped driving and from her left eye, she caught a male taping a picture to a stoplight. This picture was Gracie with that cheesy grin and those earrings, one of which found its way to the Oostburg PD lost and found. The other earring... perhaps still with Gracie.

"My god," said Vicki under her breath.

Working his tie, Bob grinned at himself in Seth's office mirror.

Pastor Zimmermann had the brass balls to be there, and it was his morning. He was proud of today's message as Bob spent all week on it.

It was going to knock them—

"Go get them, Bobby. First sermon in ten months."

Bob stopped.

"And don't let any dead teen derail that."

The noose around Zimmermann's neck tightened...

"You're going to church?" she asked her husband incredulously. Evelyn was still in her pajamas this Sunday morning, waiting for her Grace's return.

"Yes."

Evelyn hopped off her bed and into the bathroom.

"Fine."

Seth could sense there was trouble brewing, and he didn't want to deal with it. However, he knew if he did not deal with it now, Seth would have more to deal with later.

"What?"

Evelyn hollered from behind the bathroom door.

"What do you mean "what"? You are really going to church?!"

Seth shook his head out of his wife's view.

"Many of her friends are there. Maybe someone saw her."

Evelyn flushed.

"They would have said something by now!"

Seth didn't want to start an argument now. Pastor needed silent solace and the only place he was going to get peace was by listening to the Holy Word. So he said what any husband does when he yearns to end an argument peacefully:

"I love you."

Seth left his wife and walked down the stairs. In the kitchen, sat his younger daughter killing a bowl of Fruit Loops, still not dressed in her Sunday best.

"You're not dressed for church either?"

Lainey didn't even look up.

Seth shook his head, grabbed a banana, and jilted. *Holy moly! What a bunch of fair-weather-Christians I am living with.* He then repented for judging the ladies in his life.

Sulky Seth drove over to the church, passing many Oostburgers along the way. A stop sign had a picture of Gracie sloppily taped to it. This was real. His daughter was missing, and there was not anything Seth could do about it. The only thing Seth could do was pray, and he did pray, parked at the stop sign until someone gently honked at him.

He continued his way to Oostburg Community Church and was there minutes later. Seth pulled up at the same time as Vicki.

"Pastor Seth?"

Seth walked over.

"Yes?"

"Why are you here?" asked Vicki.

Seth half-smiled.

"For strength. Answers. Anything?"

Vicki stared a moment before answering:

"No. I'm off to find her."

Maybe everyone else was just leaving it up to God or his will or prayer but she knew better. She knew she could not leave it up to the almighty Jesus, so she had to do something.

Coralee walked over from her ride, not wanting to eavesdrop.

"How's Evelyn, Lainey?" asked Coralee.

"I don't know." Seth helped Coralee upstairs. The pastor turned around. "I'll give her a ride home."

I don't know? thought Vicki. Seth was acting very strange for someone who may never see his daughter ever again. Maybe Oostburg was a bit too laid back for her.

Vicki nodded as she watched Pastor Adams help her aunt to church.

Seth and Coralee walked into the church and much to their chagrin, a couple of people were giving the pastor an unsupportive feeling. It was not a familiar greeting for Pastor Seth; he always felt his congregation was a very supportive one. Today, however, the room felt cold.

One woman mouthed to another:

"What's he doing here?"

Another man whispered to his wife:

"That's what you get for leaving a fourteen-year-old home alone!"

Hearing these comments and a few others, Seth held his tongue. His job was not to satisfy them; rather his job was to satisfy the God who created them. Adams knew deep down, that church is where he needed to be at this very moment. Lord's house. Church. The pastor knew this church was where he would receive the greatest strength and guidance for the trials that were to come.

Seth and Coralee walked down the center aisle and sat in the front row pew.

Seth stared down Bob Zimmermann and the stare was reciprocated.

Zimmermann took a sip of his water and began:

"Hello, Oostburg Community Church. As it was said last week. I'm going to give the sermon this morning as Pastor Seth and Evelyn... were out of town, umm, celebrating twenty years of marriage—"

"Wednesday," interrupted Seth.

Zimmermann paused; zoning through the air. He had never been interrupted before at the pulpit.

"Wednesday?"

"Wednesday is our twenty-year anniversary."

The congregation picked up on the poor vibe. This was not a normal service; half the little congregation was not there because they were out searching. The half that was present could not understand why the pastor would be there when his daughter had disappeared just the day before.

Zimmermann cleared his throat.

"Yes, Wednesday," said Zimmermann. Bob continued: "To open our worship, I'd like to begin by singing hymn number 602—"

Seth stood up.

"One second, Bob."

The congregation glanced around uncertain of what to do or what to say.

Pastor Seth went to the pulpit. Pastor Zimmermann begrudgingly stepped aside. He gave his superior a fake smile.

Seth took over:

"Has anyone seen my girl? You know... Gracie? The girl who sang a few songs for you about thirty-six hours ago...? You know she wrote one of those songs? I know because I listened to her practice them over and over again in her bedroom. Just wondering... anyone see her recently? You?"

Some of the congregation fidgeted in their seats; some others sat there frozen. Some people felt horrible for their shepherd; some felt awful for judging; others continued to judge him for being there.

"Nobody...? Hmm. Well someone knows where she is. *Somebody*."

Zimmermann took a step towards Seth.

"Seth, why don't you sit—"

Seth shook his head.

"No, Bob. I don't want to sit." Seth gave a small chuckle as he looked around. This was his congregation; and he felt as if they were stoning him for his choice. For sure, he could be out there overturning every rock and leaf but he needed something else—he needed... the reassurance of his Lord's grace... and oddly... for the first time in life... *he wasn't finding it.*

God—didn't seem there anymore...

"My wife was right. I shouldn't be here. There is nothing that this building or congregation… just… nothing."

A woman in the congregation broke down and cried. Seth heard her and looked at her, five rows in. He felt lost as he looked around his own church—the warmth was gone. He felt cold... and alone.

Then it hit him: he made a very big mistake. At a time like this, he should not be there. *Sometimes there are more important things than church; like, my Grace.* Seth came for solace and got hostility... *why was it so cold in here? Did I forget to pay for the heat this month?*

"Why are we here now? As a church body, shouldn't we be somewhere else?"

Zimmermann stepped closer to Seth.

"Where else would we be on a Sunday morning?"

Matt, who was listening in the last row of pews, swallowed his head.

Seth licked his lips.

"Where else would we be, hmm, I don't know, Bob." And Seth leaned forward, almost tipping over the pulpit as he screamed at his sheep:

"MAYBE WE SHOULD BE OUT LOOKING FOR GRACE!"

The congregation sat in stunned silence. Seth had never blatantly yelled at them before. The pastor began to see his grey sheep in a different light. And for the first time... he realized some people didn't care—even if they were sitting right in his church.

"Why aren't we out there?" Seth asked his sheep.

"The sheriff's department is doing everything—"

Seth blew up:

"The sheriff's department is a joke!"

Zimmermann attempted to get Seth off the stage.

"Seth, please sit down—"

Seth knocked away Zimmermann's arm.

"Don't touch me!"

The congregation was stoned; watching their two shepherds sheering it out—winner getting the flock.

Matt began to make his path down the center aisle when out of nowhere Big Mack beat him to it.

"Stop!" Big Mack boomed in his deep, bass voice. "I came to learn this morning, learn, and grow. That I did. I learned that I need to serve."

The flock stared at him. There was a fleeting silence before Big Mack preached from the pews.

"Please, stop this bickering! You are both grown, Christian men; you are leaders in this community." Big Mack looked around before continuing: "And please show love. He's right."

Both pastors looked at one another; each slightly embarrassed of their actions.

"Now is *not* the time to go to church," yelled Big Mack.

The silent congregation was confused... not go to church? This was Oostburg—where townsfolk met every Sunday morning to get their weekly dose of religion.

Big Mack looked around once more.

"Now is the time to BE the church!"

From the pulpit, Seth began to water up. Big Mack was right. Seth failed today. Failed as a pastor, a spouse, a father, and as a man. Big Mack walked over and Seth Adams disappeared in Big Mack's massive embrace.

Big Mack rallied the masses:

"Now, let's get out there!"

Big Mack left the church and lots of members of that congregation, men, women, and children followed.

Wesley got up and began to leave.

"Wesley, you're going?" Brooke asked.

He looked at her briefly.

"Of course," he said, leaving the woman behind.

"Okay, I will get a ride," Brooke said to herself dejectedly.

Instead of looking for his girl, Seth ended up in the men's room. The only real place where he could look himself in the ugly mirror and realize what a damn jerk he had been. That Bob pissed him off so much sometimes. He bent down to wash his face.

"I'm losing it," he spoke into the mirror.

The mirror did not disagree with him.

Rising, he could see his little princess stand behind him.

"It's okay, daddy."

He opened his mouth to tell her he loved her, but before he could speak his rival entered. Bob Zimmermann walked over to the sink, and in a moment of repentance, said:

"Sorry for your loss."

Pastor Seth could have been the better man right then and there but no, he did what any male of maturity would do: he flicked some water on Robert Zimmermann's crotch.

In the sheriff's car, Vicki hung up her cell.

"The credit card company. She charged eight bucks and seventy-seven cents at Pizza Ranch. Five days ago."

Vicki continued: "Not much to go on."

"Hopefully Big Mack can give us some answers."

They pulled into the church parking lot just as a few dutiful citizens were leaving to go and search. The officers got out of their vehicle and stopped fiery Big Mack as he and a couple of buddies descended the stairs of Oostburg Community Church.

"Big Mack," Ellis initiated the conversation.

She could discern a little tenseness in his tone. Vicki took note and stored it on the back burner of her little grey cells.

"Sheriff."

"May we have a word?"

"Sure. Did you find her?"

Vicki took off her sunglasses.

"No, we're hoping you could help," Vicki said.

"Anything."

"The earring you gave me yesterday, where did you find it?"

"It was Main and Ninth. Did you find the owner?"

She took out the newspaper clipping and handed it to Big Mack, who looked at it thoroughly.

"That's Gracie. Wearing the earring."

"Right. You found Gracie's earring on Main Street."

Ellis looked down at his feet.

"Anything else you can tell us?" he asked.

"It was just laying in the street. Nothing big; not covered. Like it was just dropped."

"Thanks," Vicki said.

"No problem. The congregation is searching today. We'll call if we find anything."

"Thanks."

And just like that, the big, black giant was off. The two quiet friends followed and the trio went off to find Gracie, along with more than a dozen other worship goers that breezy October morning.

Vicki watched Big Mack shrink, although it took a while.

"Seems like a real nice guy."

"He's not the worst guy in the world."

Vicki knew something was between Big Mack and the sheriff. Now was not the time to discover his past with Big Mack. They had bigger crosses to bear.

"Nice job. You really blew that," Matt said as he walked in to find his father furiously throwing a Bible down on his desk.

"Get out."

The teen took a step before scolding his old man:

"What's the matter with you? My friend is missing and all you can think about is your position in the church?"

Matt could view a photo of him on his desk; a photo that showed happier times with his folks. He knew his father was more than the asshole he had been acting like. Deep down, his dad was decent. He was just having a rough day; well, a rough decade.

Matt continued with one last jab at his old man:

"I bet you're rooting for her to not come back."

Matt left and shut the door. Zimmermann paused as he tried to keep his cool.

Then he threw the Bible at the door.

The man was an excellent chess player. His father taught him the cruel board; beginning to train his boy from the youthful age of six, a year before he left for good. The father told him: "You have to be able to make three moves in advance, and not only that, you must anticipate the opponent's moves as well."

The father taught his son well as the son won his high school's chess tournament and went on to the state championship, where the child was victorious again. The son liked chess and even though he did not play on that board any more, he still played the game.

He picked up the phone and dialed.

"Hello. I have a job for you and in exchange for my silence—silence about your actions on Friday night—you're going to do me a favor."

The man paused.

"You're going to kill Evelyn Adams."

Checkmate.

"Gracie is not coming back, is she?" Lainey asked as she slowly walked up to her mother.

The mother turned around and granted her youngest kid the hardest smack she ever received, for across her soft left cheek resided the red mark; resembling a huge glove.

In shock, Lainey stared at her mom. The youth had never been hit before, at least not physically.

"Don't you ever say that again! Grace will return, and everything will be normal again, you understand? It will be normal! You know what, Grace? It's my anniversary this week. That is normal. And I will celebrate and Grace will be here. Now, you go to your room, and do not come out until I come get you for dinner, understand?"

The child stared for a few short seconds and went upstairs, as her mother did not even realize she called her "Grace".

The mom thought of following her and apologizing. She was sorry she snapped, but she couldn't say "I'm sorry" right then. Evelyn needed to wait in that living room for when her precious Grace came triumphantly marching through the front door.

Wesley walked through Oostburg Community Church's parking lot and inadvertently met up with Seth, who had not as of yet made it out of the parking lot, paralyzed with fear.

"Hey."

Seth broke his trance.

"Oh, Wesley. You joining the search?"

"Yeah."

Wesley looked around the parking lot.

"Evelyn out looking?"

Seth shook his head.

"No. She's waiting for Gracie to come home."

Wesley licked his lips.

"That's good," Wesley said, continuing to look at the near-empty lot. "Did they find her car?"

"They haven't found anything."

He took three steps but stopped when he heard the sad voice of his pastor.

"You know what I'm... afraid of?"

Seth paused and swallowed.

"I am afraid of finding her."

Wesley stood there waiting for Seth to talk more, but he was done. Adams was lost in his own little world and it wasn't healthy for the pastor to do anything at that moment other than take a breather and let others do the walking.

Wesley walked away, leaving his buddy to confront the demons in his mind.

Coralee Mentink did not know what to do.

By this point, old Coralee forgot that Vicki had driven her to church this morning and she had also forgotten that her pastor agreed to drive her home after the service, which was not taking place.

Matt found her sitting in her normal pew.

"Hello, Mrs. Mentink."

Coralee looked up.

"Hello, Jim."

Matt gave a sad smile. Coralee Mentink was fading but he didn't think it was coming this fast. She should know his name. She even wiped his butt not fourteen years ago, a truth that she often teased him about.

"It's Matt."

Coralee smiled and winked.

"No, it's not, silly. Jimmy, we have been married forty-two years. I know your name."

Captain Jim Mentink was Coralee's husband who had passed away years ago in a fire.

The teen smiled and looked around. Seeing no one, he asked her:

"Why don't I take you home?"

Down on Main Street, Ellis and Vicki pulled up to the curb and got out. Main Street was where Vicki first greeted Big Mack, who had the talent of discovering the proverbial needle in the haystack; or in this case that tiny earring in the street. It was likely Gracie was on this street Friday night or Saturday morning. Where she was traveling to and in whose companionship she was in, was a bit trickier.

"Main and Nine. Anyone live here that knows her?" Vicki asked.

"Everyone knows everyone here. We'd have to knock on every door."

The team each put on latex gloves, hoping to find something of significance. It had now been almost forty hours since Lainey last saw her older sibling and there had not been one trace of her anywhere, other than that earring. Her car was absent; she had no large financial transactions with her credit card and her phone was off or dead or simply not being picked up.

Vicki looked at Ellis.

"Longer she's gone, the worse her chances are."

"I know," Ellis agreed.

They continued to walk down Main Street hoping to find anything.

"It's unlikely that she was kidnapped."

"I know."

"For one, people don't kidnap pastor's daughters. When kids get kidnapped, it is usually because there is some chance of financial gain. Pastors do not make much money usually. There has been no change in her account. No credit card action. This isn't financial."

Ellis connected the dots. "So you're saying it is personal?"

"And if she were kidnapped, why haven't they been contacted? Unless of course they were contacted and are simply not telling us—*that* would be a different case."

Ellis looked up and smiled. There were a dozen or so community members in his view searching and probably countless more all over.

"Gotta love a small town," the sheriff grinned at his deputy. "For sure a silver-lining."

Coming from a large city, Vicki was a little more pessimistic than her boss. Even though he had the lead and the authority, he was not cut out for this. The sheriff knew very little and Vicki predicted that she'd have to gently lead the investigation without stepping on toes. Although she figured that even if she did step on toes, Ellis might not mind or even notice. Ellis was the most laidback law enforcement boss she had ever worked with. He was very calm—either that or just did not care—but she guessed the former.

"It is risky. You know how many perpetrators dive into an investigation? It happens often."

"We need the eyes. Good or bad," stated Ellis.

Deputy Weathers glanced around. They were getting nowhere. Vicki hoped others were having better luck.

"She wasn't the type to run away?"

Ellis shook his head.

"No. She's very reliable."

Vicki put her head down.

"Damn it."

"What?"

"I used past tense."

The exhausted officers continued to patrol around Oostburg, interviewing residents without any luck. Gracie Adams, a beautiful and talented seventeen-year-old, full of promise and a blue sky future, had simply disappeared.

It was at that moment Ellis thought about eating; even proposing lunch with his deputy, who declined that offer. It was still early for her to take even a little break. Ellis, on the other hand, could hear his stomach grumbling, but there wasn't any way he was going to let her investigate without him. At least not now.

Ellis's phone rang, and he jumped on it.

"Hello?"

The voice on the other end was loud and clear:

"Hello, this is Frank Blanton from U.S. Cellular. I have that information you requested."

"Yeah, thanks, please give it to me," the sheriff responded. The sheriff looked over to his deputy. "It's the phone company."

The new deputy nodded and licked her lips. *Please let there be something here.*

Mr. Blanton went on:

"Gracie was texting an unknown number—a prepaid phone, we believe —from 9:02PM until 1:12AM on Friday evening into Saturday morning. There was a lengthy pause in the messages, probably she met up with whoever she was texting. The nature of the texts was indeed romantic; would you like me to read them to you?"

"Send them in an email, if you can," replied Ellis.

"Sure thing. Now, the texts weren't anything eye-opening, it just seems that Gracie Adams did indeed have a romantic relationship. The only interesting one was the last one."

"Go on."

"The last one stated: SEE YOU FRIDAY AT 12AM."

"What's so interesting about that?" asked Ellis.

"The interesting thing about this text is that it was sent at 1:12AM, that final text. She was indicating a different Friday."

Blanton cleared his throat.

"Gracie was intending to meet someone at midnight on a Friday in the future. Probably this Friday."

Ellis nodded.

Vicki whispered to Ellis:

"Ask if they traced the location of the phone."

"Did you trace the location of the phone?"

"We tried. No luck. Either the battery was taken out or the phone was destroyed."

Vicki overheard Blanton and shook her head.

"Thanks, Mr. Blanton. And please send an email with those other texts," Ellis spoke. "We don't care how innocent they look. Thank you."

Ellis hung up and relayed the chat to Vicki.

Vicki spoke:

"Probably she met this person she was texting. It also appears she texted this person after they went their separate paths. I am very interested in reading those texts. Vernacular is big in these types of cases."

"Vernac—what?"

"Vernacular. The way a person talks, their speech patterns. Vocabulary. Perhaps a phrase that someone has used will come through the text."

Throughout this Sunday afternoon, the gossip mill was running rampant. Oostburg, for the very first time, was put on a map. Unfortunately, it was not for reasons that they wanted to be on the map. By now, young Gracie was all around the internet, as everyone in America was on notice. Other police stations across the country had been notified. No one knew where the girl was. She had, for all intents and purposes... just vanished. She did not purchase one thing. She didn't take a dollar out of her account. She did not make any phone calls.

She was... gone.

Vicki and Ellis weren't the only citizens looking around. Many people continued to ask each other if they had seen anything.

Nobody saw or heard a thing.

Big Mack stood on the corner and digested all the madness around him. He picked up his cell phone and dialed.

"Hey, young lady. It's your uncle. Please call me when you can. I know you tend to take off every now and then, and you are an adult. I'm not worried. But I miss you. I love you. God loves you."

Brooke Demko wheeled up to the corner and glanced around. Oostburg was crowded for a tiny town of about a thousand or so and it appeared that everyone and their grandmother were on the street. She wondered if anything had happened; had they found Gracie? It didn't appear as if they did. She was worried. She was also stranded as her husband had taken their car to look around the town. It was incredible, the whole damn situation. People always think this will happen in other places to other unlucky someones—but no, this time fate or God or whatever you want to call it had selected little Oostburg, Wisconsin for the latest tragedy. It was Brooke's own church that it happened to. Brooke's home.

She turned her head and saw a flyer on the telephone pole. It was a photo of Gracie; her parents' phone numbers below her picture.

Something caught her attention. Brooke wheeled in closer to get a better look.

Taking the picture down to examine it better, her jaw dropped.

"Son of a bitch!"

Sheriff hoisted his deputy out of the dump. Vicki smelled and looked like crap but she didn't care—Vicki was determined to find this teen and close this case... not like her previous case. This wasn't going to happen in Oostburg, not under her watch.

"Let's keep going."

Ellis paused.

"I could use a drink; a burger too. You hungry?"

Vicki looked at him and did a great job of hiding her disgust. She was hungry too but she wasn't going to let it derail her.

"No, I'm good. Go eat."

Ellis breathed a sigh of relief.

"I'll be back in a little."

Quickly walking to the diner, Ellis passed by the church parking lot where his pal Seth was still sitting in his car. Odd. It had been about four hours since the church broke out to go look for Gracie and yet, her dad had not even left the starting line.

"I will have a chocolate shake," God spoke to the barista. He was on His hourly coffee break.

"Oh, sure. Can I get you anything to eat, perhaps a brownie?

God smiled. He loved brownies.

"Sure, what the hell," God stated as He salivated over the chocolate overdose.

God waited for his chocolate fix, and to His calm surprise, His buddy Satan walked through the door.

"Speak of the devil. How you been?"

"Business is booming. It's getting way too easy." Satan demurred.

"Satan, I am so sorry to hear this. Should I make life harder?"

"Oh, that would be appreciated."

"Can I get you something?" the barista asked the Devil.

"Sure, I'll have a steaming cup of coffee." Satan chuckled. "Hey God, shouldn't you be somewhere, helping someone?"

"Oh... I don't know. Let these little humans help themselves. Even I need a break once in a while. All these damn prayers. I am so tired. Do you know how many I had yesterday?"

"Of course I don't know—I'm not You."

"Five hundred billion, three hundred twenty-three million, forty-two thousand, seven hundred, and ten." God shook His head. "Look at some of them," God said as he whipped out His phone. "Cancer, pizza to be on time, a math test, cancer, divorce... look at this—pray that the Packers beat Dallas—"

"I hate Dallas," declared Satan.

"That's a lot of prayers to answer and I invented prayer."

"Sucks balls," Satan declared as the counter girl handed God and Satan their consumables.

God grinned. He devoured the smell of that fresh chocolate in His holy nostrils. "I bless you," God told the barista.

"Go to Hell!" Satan yelled at the barista as he sprinkled some of his steaming coffee on her.

Satan and God went to the corner table. The sight was beautiful out of the Glas Coffee House window, just about fifteen miles from where God was needed.

"So, anything new with you?" Satan asked his good rival.

"Oh... a teenage girl is missing 14.8 miles south of here. A tiny town called "Oostburg". Ever hear such a stupid name? Oostburg." God went on: "And the kid's mother is just about to get attacked too."

"Oh, that's nice." Satan slammed his beverage. It was hot as Hell, just the way he liked it. "So is momma going to get it?"

"Hmm..." thought God. "Satan, you want to place a bet?"

"Oh, I enjoy bets. Remember that time you offered your servant... what was his name... ah, yes—Job—just to prove his loyalty?" Satan chuckled.

"How could I forget? I'm God, remember!" God gave a hearty chuckle. "What an idiot! I let you crash his entire livelihood and he still praises Me. These stupid humans—some of them will never learn."

"He didn't. But some of them do come to my side."

"Some do, some do. And then they burn in Hell for that," The God shook his head.

"So the momma, she's going to be attacked?" asked Satan.

"Oh, yes, very soon."

"Will she survive?" asked Satan with all the curiosity of a child asking about sex.

"Oh, Satan. Have a little patience. After all, it is a virtue."

"I hate virtues."

Seth opened his eyes.

"Where did that thought come from...?" he asked himself.

17.

THE THIRD PERSON

Inside, the Adams' home was silent. Evelyn was in the living room wrapping gifts for her husband, and her daughter was in her room recuperating from her mother's smack.

Outside, this house was equally silent. Reporters had dissipated to various corners of the town searching for the latest juicy gossip. Other frostbit Oostburgers had also scattered and it was Evelyn and her young girl who remained waiting at home for beloved Grace to grace them with her presence again.

There was, however, one person who wasn't looking for Grace.

That person was looking for a different lady from the Adams family.

She was halfway done wrapping her husband's anniversary gifts. She had gotten Seth a watch; one that he subtly hinted at last father's day but they did not have the money. Evelyn also got him a nice, red button-down shirt and tickets to the Rick Raybine concert out in Sheboygan. Raybine was one of Seth's favorite bands.

With Evelyn in the living room and Lainey blasting rock music in her earbuds behind the closed door of her upstairs bedroom, a third person was safely roaming the backyard. The third person opened the unlocked back door to the kitchen and made their way easily into the home. Oostburgers, like many other small-town citizens, don't lock the doors to their homes or cars. One time, Seth left his car unlocked in the church parking lot. And to better that, Seth left the keys in the ignition and the car turned on, begging to be stolen. But alas, that car was still in the parking lot nine hours later when Seth had finished writing his sermon. Oostburg, for the most part, was a safe town.

The third person slowly made their way through to the kitchen. The third person, wearing a ski mask and a hood, tip-toed through the soon-to-be crime scene.

The third person exited the kitchen and into the connecting hallway between the kitchen and living room. From there, the third person could see the back of that robust blonde hair. Evelyn was about fifteen paces away and had no ideas of her impending death as she blindly continued to wrap her gifts.

The third person walked slowly towards the large, white couch. It would be a shame to drip her blood here but this third person really did not have any choice.

Evelyn was closer.

The third person had no choice because the third person did something horrible on Friday night into Saturday morning.

Evelyn was closer.

She picked up the tape and—

The third person grabbed her neck in a chokehold. The lady seized the culprit's arms and attempted to get out of the chokehold, but to no avail, the third person was stronger, and this wife was caught off-guard. Evelyn kicked and tried to scream but the wife couldn't make a sound. Her drink went flying all over the carpet. She mouthed "Lainey".

Evelyn continued to fight back but she was losing air and getting wobbly. She tried to bite her attacker, but could not get her jaws on the attacker's arm. The third person was overpowering her. *It... is not over... yet!!* Evelyn laboriously thought to herself. And she was able to twist her way close to the table and

...grab the scissors...

With all her strength she stabbed her attacker in the bicep.

Bleeding quite a river, this third person grabbed their puncture and screeched as they stumbled away. For a brief second, Evelyn thought about chasing her would-be killer, but she was too fragile at that very moment. She collapsed to the floor.

And Satan picked up the check.

After a few minutes, Evelyn regained the strength to pick up her cell. She dialed quickly.

Her husband picked up in seconds.

"Evelyn?"

"Seth! Seth—someone just tried to kill me!"

Seth started his car.

"What?"

"Come home now Seth!" Evelyn pleaded, attempting to get off the floor.

The frantic pastor put his car in drive and broke the speed limit as he had done many times before.

Seth could not believe what he had been doing the previous few hours, sulking. He scolded himself as he wanted to hold his wife:

I wasn't looking for Gracie... was not protecting my wife... I was sitting in my car doing nothing but... praying... All this time, I could have been looking for Gracie or protecting Evelyn. All of my life, I had been taught to pray in trials. What if it was for no reason? What if I have been serving a careless Lord... all this time?

Ellis and Vicki were walking down the street when they heard and eventually saw a car going at an ungodly speed. Vicki saw the ride and realized it was the same car she had followed two days ago—Seth's car.

She was pissed.

"Damn it, Ellis! That's Seth's car—again!" Vicki threw her limbs up at Ellis. "He was going about eighty miles an hour! Your pastor is a madman!"

Ellis opened his mouth to speak just as his phone rang.

Within seconds, Ellis was talking to that madman himself.

"Seth? We just saw you drive past us—anything?"

Vicki slapped her hip, ticked that Kirkbride was taking this so very lightly.

Over the phone, Seth could be heard:

"Get to my house—now!"

Within seconds, they were speeding down the route as fast as Seth.

The sheriff and his new deputy listened patiently as Evelyn retold her nightmare attack. Seth had his arm around Evelyn, and even Lainey seemed scared. Some person was attacking the tight-knit Christian family.

No one was safe.

"I was wrapping your presents, Seth. Your anniversary presents. And someone just... grabbed me, from behind, grabbed my throat and started choking me, and I couldn't scream... I couldn't scream, Seth..."

Pastor Adams held his wife a little tighter. Seth appeared five years older to Vicki. The man was slower. Vicki would swear on the Bible that he now had a little grey at the edge of his hairline. This pastor looked... defeated.

Evelyn took a sip of water.

"And I managed to get the scissors—and I stabbed him—"

Vicki perked up like several bulldogs hearing the dinner bell.

She took a step towards the would-be victim.

"You stabbed him?"

Evelyn grew tense.

"Yes, he was choking me!" Evelyn yelled at Vicki.

Vicki half-smiled, reassuring Evelyn.

"No, that's excellent. And you broke skin."

Evelyn looked at the scissors.

"Yes, my scissors have blood on them—"

Vicki snapped her fingers at her boss.

"Bag it."

Obediently, Ellis left the room to get a bag.

"Evelyn... the blood trail connects your couch to the driveway. Whoever attacked you, sped away after you stabbed them. Where on the body did you stab?"

"Here, right here," Evelyn said as she pointed to her left arm. "Upper left arm."

Vicki licked her lips. Finally! A taste. At last, there was a tiny something to go on other than a stupid earring and a vague text that, as of now, led nowhere.

"You stabbed the attacker and drew blood. There's a good chance someone is at a hospital, maybe right now getting stitched up. Sheriff!"

Ellis came back and placed the scissors gently in the bag. They did have a stain of blood on them. If the guilty person was in their system, it was going to be a short case.

"We need to call all hospitals within a thirty-mile radius to see if anyone checked in with a left-arm flesh wound."

Seth chimed in:

"There's three: St. Nick's and Memorial, both are north in Sheboygan. There's another one south in Grafton, but that's a lot further."

"You sure it was a male?" asked Ellis.

Evelyn closed her eyes to relive the nightmare:

"I never saw him. I only grabbed his arms... come to think of it, they weren't very big."

"Could it have been a woman?" asked Ellis.

Evelyn thought for a moment.

"It happened so quickly. I guess. I don't know."

"Call the hospitals," Vicki commanded.

Ellis began dialing.

Evelyn looked at her husband.

"Raile... Charles Raile did this! Raile said if I defied him... bad things would happen... Grace, and now this... tell me you found Grace?"

Vicki swallowed, staring at her for a moment, the same way she stared at Gabrielle's parents in New York when they asked the same question.

"Sorry. The only thing we found was an earring."

"Her earring?" asked Evelyn.

Vicki pulled out the picture of Gracie from their local newspaper. Evelyn grabbed it and stared at Grace. She looked and saw the little girl she carried for nine months. The photo was too much for her, and she gave the paper back to Vicki.

"Yes, I guess that's her earring. I never saw her wear it before that night. I—didn't really even notice it."

Vicki continued:

"We also got in touch with her phone company. She was texting an unknown number until a little after 1AM. Whoever she was texting, they were on close terms; very possibly romantic."

"She doesn't have a boyfriend, right, Seth?"

"As far as I know," Seth agreed.

"The only interesting thing from these cell phone messages was that she had plans to meet somebody Friday at midnight." Vicki continued: "Would you know anything about that?"

"No," stated both parents.

"Lainey?" asked Vicki.

"She never told me anything," Lainey said.

The pastor glanced out the window, praying to see his priceless Grace pull up the driveway, which reminded him to ask about her car.

"You didn't find her car?"

Vicki shook her head.

"Still looking."

Penny came in from the outside patrol.

"Penny—go search Raile's house again."

"Yes sir—I mean, miss."

"And stakeout Raile's home till he comes back and when he does bring him in for questioning."

Penny tipped his hat and left.

After the long, unsuccessful day, Deputy Weathers finally broke down and went home for an overdue bite at 7:30PM. Opening the door, she could see

Matt Zimmermann reading with her aunt. Matt seemed to be a good teen. Not many eighteen-year-olds would be helping out an old woman in the beginning stages of dementia on a Sunday night. If she were a bit younger—maybe twenty years younger—perhaps he would have caught her eye.

Coralee saw Vicki enter the room and smiled.

"Hi, Jessica!"

Vicki smiled through her inward tears. This silly disease was devouring her old aunt slowly, and there was nothing she could do about it.

"Thanks, Matt."

Matt handed the book to Coralee.

"Any word?"

"No."

Vicki's cell phone rang, and she picked it up.

It was Ellis.

"Yes, sheriff?"

"I called all three hospitals, Vicki. No one came in with a large wound on their left bicep."

Vicki took a deep breath. Again, nothing.

"Ok."

She hung up and grunted.

"Who typically has the ability to stitch?"

Matt paused for a second and said:

"A doctor. A nurse."

Vicki added:

"Maybe a woman."

18.

CHESS WITH RAILE

The sun had clocked down for this chilly night in Oostburg. It was eight o'clock, and normally this little town would be winding down for the work week ahead, but not tonight.

Many citizens—about fifty—assembled at the park for a candlelight prayer vigil for Gracie. Pastor held the prayer meeting while Evelyn decided to remain home. She was still hoping Grace would walk through the doors, and everything would be just fine. At times, denial can be a cruel bitch.

There was a beautiful photo of Gracie on an easel to the right of the pastor. It was blown up so that the searchers could view every detail of her face. Gracie's left eyebrow was slightly longer than her right. Gracie had symmetrical dimples which enhanced her bright smile tenfold. Her nose had a little button point at the tip, a trait inherited from her maternal grandmother. Gracie really was a beautiful young lady.

This crowd stood under the park canopy, each person with lit candles. The sun had set, so now it was going to be more difficult to continue their search. Look by light, pray by night.

Seth stood forward and began preaching.

Publicly, Pastor Seth kept his cool for his sheep and even though they disappointed him greatly today, he still loved them. His eyes caught Big Mack in the night nodding in agreement. Big Mack was a strong soldier who the pastor knew he could count on. Seth wanted to know Big Mack better. Maybe when this was all finished, they would go out for coffee.

"Thank you, my friends, for coming. Please... pray as you have never prayed before. I know my God is huge. He can do ALL things. Not some, not a few; BUT ALL. He can make this trial a testimony. And for the one out there who did this to her—God loves you, and He will forgive you. As will I."

Charles stayed in the distance, inconspicuous as ever. Raile watched with wonder as the pastor continued to praise Jesus even through this terrible juncture. It inspired him at the same time it stumped him. Raile always questioned the existence of God, and if God were real, then Raile questioned God's choices. He wished he could have that faith, even in times of strife.

The prayers continued for a couple of hours. Many citizens stayed around the entire time, while some left after about the half-hour. There was less that could be done in the dark, but even in the blackness some people were out searching. Nobody's phone rang because nothing had been located. It was a horrible feeling not knowing anything. Just staying there waiting for an ending that may or may not ever come.

Charles Raile traveled that half-mile back to his house on the southern side of Oostburg. The weather was decent but not so chilly that he needed his car. As the man walked, he saw a trio of young ladies with blinking flashlights. *Smart young girls.* Raile never took a girl when they were with another person. As he walked past them, he saw about a half block down there was an older man following them. Raile looked at the man and wasn't sure if he was competition or not. The man held a flashlight and called out to his daughter—at least presumably—"Don't get too far ahead of me," the man spoke. Oh, *yes.* This business would be harder now that Gracie was gone. Raile was probably going to have to go pack soon and move on to another town. That was Raile's method—steal a girl or two, sell them to the highest bidder, and then leave. He zig-zagged across the US and had been quite good at his trade, selling girls for almost twenty years. That sort of consistency was great on a resume.

Raile's mother was a hooker; his father left when he was little. He had no respect for his parents. Maybe if they were more responsible, Raile's world would have been much different. Alas, it is pointless to wonder about "what-ifs". Charles grew up learning that the woman was property to be bought, sold, or traded, and in some rare instances, killed.

"Yeah, Jesus. I doubt you'd ever forgive me," he said to himself.

Women were nothing but a meal ticket.

The town of Oostburg was going to see the last of Charles Raile soon.

Raile walked up to his front yard and saw a large officer waiting for him. Raile chuckled to himself.

Let the chess game commence.

Charles Raile sipped a can of soda as the sheriff pumped himself up for what possibly could be the most important interrogation of his career.

"My best friend's daughter has disappeared. There has been gossip that two hours before she was last seen you threatened her mother. Can you explain that?"

Raile grinned as he was clearly satisfied by this moment. Ellis was too inexperienced to see Raile in the driver's seat, just as Ellis had failed to realize his deputy had taken over this case. He did think it odd that she had declined to come to the interview.

He wanted—*needed*—her help.

"Should I get a lawyer?" Raile asked smugly.

Raile's grin caught Ellis a bit off-guard; ticked him off actually. Ellis didn't get mad frequently; then again, his pal's girl didn't go missing often, either.

"Her name is Gracie. She's seventeen and loves to sing. She has a ton of friends; great grades. Wonderful young lady. Responsible."

Raile leaned back and took another sip. He looked like Satan in the spotlight.

"Sounds lovely."

Ellis stared at the wolf.

"What's that supposed to mean?"

Raile smiled again, the arrogant bastard. The sheriff felt like punching the jerk, and he may have achieved it had it not been for Gracie Adams hanging in the corner.

She spoke:

"Forgive him, sheriff. He's a bad man."

Ellis stole a step towards Gracie but she quickly disappeared. The sheriff glanced at Raile, who had that same cocky smile. Apparently, he did not see Gracie.

"Evelyn Adams said you've been paying her to deliver stuff. She said she doesn't know why she is doing it but she believes it might be illegal."

Raile shook his head.

"Oh, I certainly don't have to answer that. We're here to talk about the girl, not my, um, relations with her mother."

Ellis continued:

"Where were you early this evening, say 5PM?"

Raile took out a folded piece of paper and handed it to the sheriff, who looked it over. "Judy's Place. I ate dinner. Here's my receipt."

Nothing out of the ordinary: steak, side of fries, and a coke. Time matched, too. Unless the receipt was stolen, he was where he said he was when Evelyn was attacked. The sheriff took note of the last four digits of the credit card.

Ellis felt defeated. He wished Vicki was there.

"Um... can I see your upper arm, the left one?"

Raile raised an eyebrow.

"Why? You have a thing for older men?"

Bastard. This wasn't a comedy club.

"I could get a warrant if you wanted to hang out for twenty-four hours."

The king was in check. No, he didn't want to wait twenty-four hours, plus he had nothing to hide with his arm, so he obliged.

"As you wish."

Raile took his shirt off. Nothing out of ordinary with his biceps. They were the usual size and shape for a slightly overweight male of about sixty. He smiled as he put his shirt back on.

Raile was curious.

"What was that for?"

"Evelyn Adams was attacked today. Almost died."

Raile sat up. For the very first time, he did not recognize the information. This interested him.

"*Almost?*"

"Yes almost. She was able to fend off the suspect by stabbing them in the upper part of the left arm."

The man was annoyed but he hid it well, hiding it behind his sarcastic Cheshire cat's grin.

"A resourceful young lady."

The wife sat with her husband passing a bottle of vodka back and forth.

"The man looked right at me. He said I would have to forgive..."

Evelyn took a swig.

Pastor stared out the window, hoping his daughter would be there.

But no, she wasn't.

"How can we..."

Suddenly, she appeared just as she did with Ellis minutes before, and just as Gracie did early Saturday to Vicki the night she disappeared.

Seth looked over at Evelyn to see if she saw what he saw, but she obviously didn't.

Gracie was haunting Seth.

"How can we forgive this monster?" Evelyn asked her husband.

As she vanished, Gracie spoke with meaning in her tone:

"*Through Eyes Of Grace.*"

Ellis continued to grill Raile:

"Friday night. I was in Chicago."

"What were you doing in Chicago?"

"I have my reasons."

"Seth and Evelyn were in Chicago."

"What a coincidence."

The sheriff did not like the smirk on the face of his opponent.

"Evelyn said she's been delivering some envelopes for you. She also has no idea what's in them. Could you tell me what was in the envelopes?"

Raile snorted.

"Huh, sheriff. You are talking to me for the sake of this youth, not my lifestyle. You keep badgering me; you are wasting your time when you could be out looking for the girl."

Raile had a point but Ellis didn't really care at the moment.

"Can you prove you were in Chicago?"

Charles Raile smiled and took out an envelope. He happily gave it to Ellis, who took it with hesitation.

Ellis guessed he was slowly being backed into the corner. His king was about to be ambushed.

Raile coughed.

"I think that may save your time, Kirkbride."

Ellis opened it.

"Speeding ticket. Date, time, and location." Raile licked his lips and continued:

"Nothing like the police to corroborate an alibi, huh?"

Checkmate.

Ellis wished his new deputy Vicki had been there. He was actually quite frustrated that he had to let the man go; perhaps if Vicki had been there things would be different. He acknowledged that she had more experience and at the time he was willing to let Vicki take charge if only that girl was found. The longer Gracie was gone meant the less chance she had of being discovered.

Ellis, along with everyone else, knew that.

Vicki wasn't present for good reasons. The deputy had her own way of thinking—if Charles Raile was roped up with his interrogation, then he could not be there to catch Vicki snooping around his home.

No, she did not have a warrant; but she no longer cared. Weathers followed the rules with Gabrielle and it got her nothing other than a pink slip and a one-way ticket to Hell, WI: Oostburg. Damn it, all that mattered was recovering the girl. If the kid were locked away in Raile's home, she would be worth finding even if Vicki lost her job or went to jail. Results were now the only thing that counted, damn the protocol.

With a crowbar, Vicki broke into Raile's house. No neighbors saw her, as far as she knew. Using her flashlight, Vicki was able to jimmy the window just enough so that she could loosen it.

Vicki looked around and entered.

Peering in with her flashlight, the deputy didn't see anything of significance.

She went into another room. Vicki kept telling herself that she did not break in; Raile's window was open, to begin with—if she was caught, Vicki would have to lie her way out of it.

Using the flashlight, she went into the next room and found a clump of hair. Weathers picked up the hair. It wasn't Gracie's color. Too dark.

Down through the hallway, there was a door. Vicki opened the door and behind it was a grey staircase. She slowly descended the stairs, full-knowing if he had the youth, and Vicki got caught, Raile wouldn't hesitate to dispose of her. She knew her decisions could quite well lead to her death, but right now she didn't care. Vicki just wanted Gracie. She only met Gracie once, but there was a bond. A bond taken back all the way to Gabrielle Adjami. Gabrielle is dead. Gracie is "missing".

There was a noise down in the basement...

Opening the door slowly, she saw massive piles of boxes sprawled about. So many boxes. It was as if the guy had just moved here and had not finished unpacking. She wanted to look through the boxes, but there wasn't time for that—Gracie certainly wasn't in a box that small.

Unless she was in many boxes...

She walked closer to the loud noise and screamed.

A large, orange cat jumped out from behind one of those piles, sniffing around.

Damn you, Garfield.

Vicki stopped to pet the feline, and after she was finished she turned around.

She was eye-to-eye with Charles Raile.

Pastor Seth sat in his living room staring at the television. It was now 1AM Monday; about fifty-two hours since Lainey last saw her older sister Gracie leave their home.

Seth had called Gracie's phone thirteen times and his wife had called her an additional forty-four, for a grand total of fifty-seven times. He left one voicemail on the third try. She left a message every three calls.

Under normal circumstances, his daughter would have responded.

She was gone.

Seth knew it. He just did not want to admit it to himself or anyone else. Certainly not Evelyn or Lainey. He needed to bring it together for them. The passengers can't see the pilot panic. Seth secretly prayed she was ignoring them; that maybe Gracie skipped town with some boyfriend. Maybe that secret boyfriend was treating her wonderfully, and they were safe and joyful. Then there was always the chance that his girl was pissed off at their family and simply ran away. Maybe.

Seth kept lying to himself to make this suffering go away, but it didn't.

The pastor sat there watching an old video of his girl's childhood; Seth and Gracie were dancing. She was about four in this video. Oh, how he missed swinging her in his arms.

"Who loves Gracie? More than anyone on the entire planet?" Seth asked in the video.

Little Gracie was wide-eyed and full of teeth.

"You do, daddy!"

Seth—in the video—ceased to swing her. He knelt to her eye level and looked her right in the eyes.

"I love you so much, Gracie. Your daddy is always gonna love and protect you."

Knowing she had her daddy's full heart, the young child smiled and said:

"I love you, daddy."

Seth stopped the video and moved on to the next one. He was not sure why he kept watching these videos, as each view was another sharp dagger stronger than the last one. He needed to feel the pain. Eventually, maybe it would go away, even if he did not want it to.

The next video was more recent. Gracie was around fourteen in this one. Only three years ago. Here Gracie was chasing after two smaller children, and the three of them were laughing quite a bit.

Gracie looked straight at the camera.

"Look, dad! They think they can catch me!"

Seth grinned and continued to feel another sharp dagger slice his chest.

In this video, the two children tackle Gracie, as they smiled and giggled and rolled around in the grass. In the background, Seth could see Lainey pouting across the yard. That stinker. Pastor wondered what Lainey was so pissed about, but then again, she was always pissed.

Seth closed his eyes and swore under his breath.

He did something that no father should ever do:

He wished it was Lainey who was gone...

He shook his head, not knowing where that thought had come from and not wanting it to return. Through the corner of his eye, Seth could see his wife walk in. She was in her sexy satin pajamas but looked terrible as if she had not slept in a week.

"You coming to bed?"

Pastor did not look at her. He was too ashamed of his previous evil thought regarding Lainey.

Where the hell did that come from?!

"In a minute," he replied.

Evelyn yawned and walked out, leaving her husband to paddle in his guilt.

He shut off the television and dropped the remote on the couch.

Seth walked upstairs and went into their bedroom. He could tell Evelyn was crying under the covers, so he moved in and snuggled next to her. Pastor took her left hand and squeezed it tightly, spooning his torso behind her.

His cell made a loud, awkward noise and he pulled it out of his pocket. Looking down at the message, Seth could notice that it was an Amber Alert.

Whenever Seth got an Amber Alert on his phone, it was his ritual to pray for the child and the family. He began to pray; getting three words in: "Dear Lord, please—"

It was three words in that he realized he was praying for *his* family. Seth looked down at Evelyn, who still under their blanket, was not moved by the awkward beep of his phone.

"We're going to find her," he said.

Evelyn sniffled.

"Please... Seth. Pray. When you pray, I feel like we can overcome anything."

Seth squeezed her hand again.

"Heavenly Father, please bring our Gracie back to us. We pray for Your power and mercy, that wherever our Gracie is, that she is... safe and healthy. I... please Lord. Hear our prayers. In Jesus Name, Amen."

Seth kissed the back of her head.

"Feel better?"

Evelyn closed her eyes.

"No."

Wesley Demko tramped into the back doorway of his kitchen and was startled when the light flicked on.

He despised when she did that, and sadly this was becoming more and more frequent of late.

"Where were you? It's 1AM."

"Out."

"You were out last night as well."

Brooke wheeled over to her husband, who hated the corner.

"Three nights in a row."

Wesley stumbled for a response.

"I..."

Brooke took a pregnancy test from the counter.

"It was negative again."

Wesley glanced at the test for a second and began to leave the kitchen.

"I'm going to work on my novel."

The author ascended the stairs but was stopped by the woman's piercing words:

"Stupid novel."

Wesley stopped. He returned down the two steps he climbed and turned to the bitch, looking at her like a scolded pup in bad need of a swat on the butt. However, Wesley restrained himself and went back up the stairs.

After Wesley exited, the woman looked down at her legs. She knew her husband was drifting away from their marriage. Brooke wished he spoke more. Her husband only wrote—if only she could read his min—then it hit her—*read*—

his book... she *could* read his mind. If she could read what he was writing, perhaps there would be a clue or something as to what was going on in his head.

Brooke wheeled herself to the staircase. The wife wiggled her way down off the chair and crawled up the seventeen stairs to the second floor. From their landing, it was a little crawl to his writing room, the man cave. In the hallway outside this man cave, another wheelchair was there for her. She crawled into the room to find her husband on the computer, but not writing as he said he was. He was playing solitaire instead.

She crawled in and hoisted her torso up the frame of the door. The wife could stand if she was leaning on something sturdy.

"You play solitaire when you're stressed."

Wesley wished the woman would go away.

"I'm stuck."

"In the game or the book or both?"

"Novel."

Brooke paused.

"Do you want me to help?"

"No," Wesley blurted out. He composed himself and continued: "I mean, no."

Brooke caught a glimpse of his left hand.

"Where's your ring?"

Wesley looked at his hand and closed his eyes.

"I'm having it polished."

Brooke wasn't buying it, but now past 1AM, she did not want to battle, so she left.

He turned his head—the woman was gone. Finally. He clicked the screen and his novel appeared before his eyes. The author stared at the screen and the following words stared back at him:

"And the two children, loved by God, perished."

He closed his eyes, picturing the story:

Two terrified children sat huddled in an upstairs bedroom slowly suffocating as the flames crept closer and closer. Scared and all alone—well, not really alone, as God was watching them suffer—the older girl hugged the younger one and tucked her under her wing. The fire had engulfed the stairs, and by this point, the only way out was jumping out of the second-story window. They could have thrown a mattress out the window to land on, but neither girl thought of it, and even if they had they might not have been strong enough after many minutes of inhaling the intoxicating smoke. The two girls were terrified, but they couldn't do anything. Other than watch and wait, for a promise that would never be fulfilled: God's promise to protect them.

Wesley continued to type the familiar prayer:

"Our Father, who art in heaven, Hallowed be thy Name."

The children spoke as the fire began to engulf their hallway.

"Thy Kingdom come. Thy will be done on Earth,"

The girls spoke as Wesley typed.

Wesley began to recite with the ill-fated girls:

"As it is in heaven.
Give us this day our daily bread.
And forgive us our trespasses, As we..."

Wesley swallowed. It's difficult to kill characters you love. He took a pause and continued to type.

"...forgive those that trespass against us.
And lead us not into temptation—"

Temptation.
The word sent him to look at his wedding photo.
Before everything happened.
Back when he and Brooke were happy.
The blaze continued to grow, eating the prayer and the chapter.
He talked at a whisper as he closed this horrific chapter... killing off these two precious children.

"But deliver us from evil. For thine is the kingdom,
The power, and the glory,
Forever and ever.
Amen."

Flustered, Wesley took a sip of cold water.
It was the first time he killed off a character.
Brooke bitched from the other room:
"Wesley, are you coming to bed?"
Wesley shook his head.
"I'm... writing."
The author paused while waiting for a response.
Thankfully, there was no response from that woman and he continued to type.

Wesley spoke again with the girls, who were close to the end.

"Deliver us from evil..."

God had another decision to make this evening, as brave Deputy Vicki Weathers was in the lion's den on her own initiative. The man looked at her, as she hoped to be "delivered from evil."

He smiled.

"Hello."

Vicki was not backing down, damned if it could be her last minutes on Earth.

"Where is she?"

"Where is who?"

This steamed Vicki.

"Gracie Adams, you sick bastard. Where is she?"

"I don't know who you're talking about."

"Gracie Adams. Pastor Seth's eldest daughter. Her mom was almost killed this evening."

"Oh yes... I just got back from chatting with your sheriff. Nice fella. He told me about the pastor's wife. It's bad luck for you since he already proved my innocence."

Raile moved closer as she backed away.

"Now. About you—why are you here?"

Vicki, in all her New York toughness, was afraid. She knew this was her fault. Deputy Vicki knew she was breaking the law even if she was doing it for the right reasons. She knew—well, guessed—that Charles Raile was quite capable of murder but Vicki had come this far and was not backing down.

"I assume you have a warrant."

"What is this?" asked Vicki, ignoring Charles and holding up the hairball.

Raile raised an eyebrow.

"I believe that is hair, miss. The warrant?"

Vicki backed into a pile of boxes. The deputy was cornered.

Charles was about to win his second chess game in less than two hours.

"You don't have a warrant, do you? Well... if I were a killer, I'd probably kill you right here. But since I have nothing to hide, I suggest you get the hell out of my basement."

The deputy slowly backed up the stairs and exited Raile's home.

A minute later Vicki was in her car, slamming the steering wheel. She whispered to herself:

"Damn it, Vicki!"

Weathers looked at the clump of hair in her hand. Turning her head, she could see her suspect peeking out the window and quickly shutting his curtain.

After seeing the cop drive off, Raile turned from the window and walked down the dark hallway into the living room, where the bookcase was, the bookcase Vicki walked right past.

Pushing the bookcase away, he opened the big door that led to the second, more interesting basement. Much more interesting than the spot Vicki investigated.

In the secret room, Raile looked around.

A cute little girl, approximately seven or eight, appeared. The kid was filthy, blonde, and had the cutest little button nose.

She spoke:

"I saw through the peephole. That girl was WAY too big for us, right Uncle Harry?"

Charles Raile looked at the little girl, and for the first time saw her and all females in a different light.

"Oh my god." Raile swallowed. "I can't do this anymore."

Pastor Seth headed for the quiet woods just a few miles outside of Oostburg.

It took Seth a few seconds but the dad found her—his princess, Gracie Adams was sitting in the woods and perfectly healthy, safe, and normal. She sat on a yellow blanket and was wearing a thin green dress, covered with a variety of flowers. Gracie had a dolly and a tea set, patiently waiting for her daddy to play house with her one last time.

"Daddy! You made it!" she beamed with excitement.

"Gracie? You're alive?"

"I've been waiting for you for a long time! What took you too long?"

Seth looked around.

It was just him and his princess.

Gracie curiously looked at him.

"Why did you do it?"

The dad half-smiled and turned his neck. He knelt to his baby.

"Do what?"

Gracie gave a pregnant pause and said:

"Why did you kill me, daddy?"

Seth quickly stood up and teetered. Dad stared at his girl and in an instant, she was no longer beautiful: Gracie was severely sliced up. Blood spilled from every pore of her skull and she was slowly lying down on her pretty, red-stained, yellow blanket.

Seth felt a hand grab his arm...

Pastor screamed as he could feel the cold hand on his arm. He sat up and she did the same.

"You ok?"

Seth looked over. His child was gone, replaced by her mother.

"I need water."

He got up and went to the bathroom, where the man splashed his face with warm water. He knelt to the streaming fountain of liquid and took a sip. Even warm, it was refreshing after the ominous nightmare he had.

The pastor stood up again and looked in the mirror to greet Gracie, staring at her father from behind. She was clean again, with no bloodstains.

Daddy stared back at her—and could only make out the song *Cinderella* by Steven Curtis Chapman. For the pastor and his precious girl, this song was their favorite to dance to.

> *"Cause all too soon,*
> *the clock will strike midnight,*
> *and she'll be gone..."*

She spoke:
"If you hadn't done what you did, I'd still be on Earth."
He screamed at the top of his lungs.
"NO!"
Pastor snatched the sink with all his strength as if he were trying to yank it from the plumbing.
Evelyn rushed in and hugged his shoulders. Gently massaging them, Evelyn was unsure of anything else that could be done.
"Who are you talking to?"

19.

MANIC MONDAY

An alarm clock rang loudly in the Demko bedroom. Groggily, Wesley s-lammed it back into silence. He raised his head and looked at the time. It was seven.

The woman wheeled over and kissed him on the lips.

"Morning."

Wesley hid back under the covers.

"I'm not feeling well."

"What time you work today?"

"I open at ten."

"So why is your alarm set for seven?"

He got out of bed.

"The kids need me."

Back in the Mentink kitchen, old Coralee was busy scrambling some toast on the stove. Coralee broke three eggs on the plate and with a fork, she began to swirl it around.

Vicki entered with a paper and saw this gibberish of dementia that was slowly scrambling her aunt's brain.

"Aunt Coralee!"

She walked over and stopped Aunt Coralee from her attempt at cooking.

Coralee, confused as ever, said:

"What? What is the problem? Do you want scrambled eggs as well?"

Vicki put down her paper on the table.

"I will do it."

"That's kind of you."

Coralee sat down as Vicki began to fix the issue. Coralee snuck a peek at *The Daily Sermon.*

"Oh! No!"

Vicki stopped what she was making and walked over to her aunt.

"What?"

Coralee pointed to the headline.

"Evelyn was attacked yesterday!"

Vicki took the paper.

"It's in the paper?"

Coralee looked up at her niece, who hovered about the paper.

"You knew?"

Vicki drove with a feeling of confidence. They were going to find Gracie Adams today, and yes, she was going to be healthy, alive, and joyous. That Amber Alert had been sent forth, and Deputy Weathers was waiting for more information.

Going right to her chair, Vicki checked her phone messages. One caller had come in about a woman that was found alive in Minnesota, but it wasn't Gracie.

"Yes, thank you... and if you could please let me know ASAP, that'd be greatly appreciated. Thank you."

Vicki hung up.

Momma looked over.

"Any luck?"

"No."

Ellis entered, less casual than normal, carrying a few pieces of paper.

"Got Gracie's text messages. I read them over. Blanton was right; not much to go on."

He handed the pages to Vicki, who scanned them.

"Not much. He does text like a boyfriend. Well, here is something: Our boyfriend has a weekend job."

"Matt is a janitor at Jesus Take The Wheel. He works weekends."

"Right."

"But it doesn't make sense. Why would Gracie and Matt keep it a secret? Seth is practically rooting for them to get together."

"What about Bob?"

"I love that movie."

"Knock it off—does Bob Zimmermann approve of Gracie?"

"No, he hates her dad."

"Well, that explains the need for secrecy."

Ellis and Vicki sat down with Penny and Momma for a team meeting.

Weathers took the opportunity to gently scold the station. Protocol in Oostburg was not as serious as the protocol in New York City.

She was going to change that.

"And not to be rude, but be careful with what you tell the reporters. We don't want the public knowing everything."

"Why not?" asked Penny.

Wow. I have officially entered the sticks.

"Cause now our attacker knows as much as we do. Always stay two steps ahead by not revealing."

Ellis stepped in:

"Well said. Alright deputies, here is where we are. I talked with Charles Raile last night. Man had an alibi for Friday night; in fact, he was in Chicago just like the Adams'."

Vicki butted in:

"Weird coincidence. Continue."

Ellis did.

"So if she were kidnapped, either he did not do it or maybe he paid someone. His alibi that Sunday evening checked out as well; so again, he did not attack Evelyn Adams himself—"

Vicki interrupted:

"He is not the type of guy who would get his hands messy. Raile calls the shots but he has people working for him."

"Yeah," Ellis agreed. "We do know that Evelyn was working for him, but she did not know what Raile was up to. All she did was hand envelopes to some guys."

"What's in the envelopes?" asked Penny.

"She didn't know," Ellis answered.

"Five to one Evelyn was delivering cash," offered Vicki.

"Probably she's the middle man," Ellis said.

Vicki offered her theory:

"She threatens Raile, either to quit on him or to blow his covers. Raile gets the urge to play hardball. He kidnaps the teen—or more likely someone under Raile kidnaps her. Then he gets the middleman to kill Evelyn as well."

"We should get his call records," Ellis said.

Evelyn picked up the phone and dialed.

After a few tense seconds, Raile answered.

"Hello?"

The lady paused, knowing she was rolling the dice even calling him.

"It's Evelyn—"

He stopped her, as he was furious.

"You know never to call this number! Usual place. High noon."

Charles quickly hung up. Raile walked over to his table and from the drawer pulled out a small pistol.

On the other end of the call, she took one little breath. She knew he may kill her. The meeting place was very secluded but at this point, she only really had one more thing to lose—

Lainey entered the kitchen with her blue knapsack bulging. It was the first day of school since Grace left.

"Do I have to go to school today?"

"Yes."

"Why? Are you so busy you can't watch me?"

"Lainey, shut up."

Lainey started to walk out but Evelyn quickly ran over and hugged her.

Going down to Lainey's eye level, Evelyn spoke:

"I'm sorry. Please, forgive me. It's... a bad time right now. I'm so... scared."

Lainey half-smiled, trying to reconcile.

"I'll take my bike."

Evelyn smiled back. Maybe there was hope for this worn-out family after all.

"No, I'm driving you."

It took them approximately five minutes to get to school. As they drove down the streets, the two did not speak. They were too busy watching townsfolk search and chat. Deep down Evelyn knew it was hopeless, but it was still nice to see some people at least trying. Oostburg had been covered.

She wasn't here.

Evelyn stopped the car outside of Oostburg Middle School and young Lainey got out.

"Have a good day, Lainey."

Lainey gave a half-smile and walked away.

Evelyn took a breath and sat there watching her kid shrink away. Adjusting her mirror slightly, she let out a small scream when she saw an old man in their back seat.

He spoke:

"Why don't you tell that girl you love her?"

Evelyn looked out the window to try to see Lainey but she was already in the building. Evelyn looked back to talk to the old man but he was gone.

Evelyn began to drive away just as Ellis and that new deputy walked up to her window.

"Hello Mrs. Adams—" said the new deputy.

Evelyn stopped the car.

Evelyn cut to the point. "Any news?"

"No," Vicki said, shaking her head.

"Then get back looking!" she rudely yelled at the two officers, driving away at a rather quick speed.

Taking the scenic path to school, Matt Zimmermann exhaled on his hands. It was ten to nine, and he was an hour late already. By this time some worried teacher was probably calling his father; especially in light of what had happened over the weekend. He wondered how the school would react, and he wondered how many, if any, of her friends would be playing hooky today to search. The teen stood there at the border of Oostburg looking into the backwoods. He did not want to find Gracie Adams in the forest... and yet, that tiny voice in his head told him that he should walk into the woods. A small grumble in his stomach, a feeling of nausea, like that kind of nausea you feel right before you go on stage to perfor—*oh crap!*—he thought. Matt remembered about the tech practice that was happening after school for their High School's play *Twelve Angry Men*, that Gracie was playing the lead. He was the understudy for Gracie, the lone juror who initially defends the kid on trial. Now, Matt was worried since he really didn't know any of Gracie's lines, especially not any of those large paragraphs. He was content playing the clerk, who came on to the scene a few times with some evidence. The clerk had about ten lines, and he was fine with that. But now, if she did not return by Friday, he was going to have a lot more lines. He had not really picked up the script since he learned his lines so quickly. *Why should I memorize Gracie's lines when she was so reliable?* he reasoned. Maybe that's why Gracie went away—stage frights? No, that didn't really fit. Crap... he better get studying. He started to walk away from the forest and slowly wondered to himself—he wondered if anyone checked there yet...

A little after nine and Wesley remained in bed.

He remembered a time, not too long past, when he, Brooke, and three other pairs were having a Bible study at the home of Seth and Evelyn. The Zimmermanns—before Bob's wife died—were there as well as a fourth couple— the O'Connells. What were their names... Cheryl and...

Wesley remembered before the Bible Study. And the Bible Study. And the terrible nightmare that happened during that Bible Study.

"Wesley," a female voice spoke.

Wesley laid there trembling.

The voice spoke again.

"Wesley."

The man returned from this horrendous daydream to notice the woman tapping his shoulder. He looked at her, and for a brief moment, remembered how pretty she was, even in the wheelchair.

"It's 9AM. You have work in an hour."

Demko nuzzled his head in the pillow like a quiet child feigning illness to get out of a math test.

"I'm not feeling well."

"What's the matter?"

"Just not feeling well."

"Then call in sick."

Brooke began to wheel away and turned around.

"I'm going for breakfast. You want?"

Wesley swallowed for a quick moment, trying to decipher if he was more hungry or tired.

"No."

The woman left and after taking a few seconds, he got out of bed to start the day. Walking to the bathroom, he felt very dizzy. He couldn't remember why. He didn't think he had many drinks the previous night. Now in the bathroom, he splashed water on his face and grimaced in pain. He was still groggy and couldn't see much. He was able to pick up his phone and dial his boss, Krissy, who was a much younger lady that he despised.

"Hey, Krissy. Sorry, but I am not going to make it to work today. I got chills. I think I'm coming down with something. Ok."

He hung up and grimaced again.

Pastor Seth sat at his desk clearing his brain.

The past weekend was supposed to be free of worry and trouble, spending time and having sex with his Evelyn. Remembering the past and looking forward to the future. He never imagined this. Seth never imagined his God would not answer his prayers. He never thought God would... turn a deaf ear to Seth Adams, a pastor of so many years, Seth who served the Lord for pretty much his entire life...

For the first time in his forty-five years, Jesus wasn't there...

Seth picked up a family photo. They were at Times Square in the heart of New York City. It was a spur-of-the-moment trip. Driving there and back, the family had a nice time bonding in the car. They enjoyed seeing the scenery and being tourists. The sun was shining nice that Tuesday in August. Seth couldn't figure out why he remembered that detail. It was a Tuesday though. Oh, who the hell cares... where is Gracie!?

The pastor started to break down as he picked up this photo. He saw for the first time Lainey wasn't smiling. The little brat. Always ruining family pictures. Lainey didn't want to go, he recalled because she didn't want to sit in the car for twenty hours. They drove straight through to save money on two hotels.

He picked up the other photo. This was one of Gracie alone holding a balloon. This photo was from her friend's seventh birthday party and she had come home with that huge balloon after winning a round of silly musical chairs. Anyway, as soon as they got to the front porch, that balloon popped, and out came a copious amount of tears from Gracie. The child would not stop weeping for about a half-hour; her entire life all over because the silly, insignificant balloon popped. Seth tried to calm and console his oldest kid but to no avail. He told her that balloons were meant to die, meant to explode. They only lasted for the moment; in our lives and then, they were gone. A vapor in the wind; a flower quickly fading. Don't get too attached, he told his little princess...

There was a knock at the door and that was Pastor Bob Zimmermann in all his humility.

"May I intrude?"

Seth gestured to the chair opposite him.

"Be my guest."

Zimmermann sat.

"Look, I was a jerk yesterday."

Seth stole one breath. He appreciated the apology but was not in the mood to have a heart-to-heart with Bob Zimmermann, a man he only barely "tolerated".

"You weren't the only one."

Zimmermann opened up.

"I lost Lisa, not too long ago. I thought it was the end of this world as well. It's cliché, but a piece of me died that evening. I still miss her."

That struck a chord.

"All due respect, Gracie's still alive."

Zimmermann knew he opened his mouth a bit too much.

"She is."

Even though both knew in large likelihood, Gracie wasn't.

"Forgiveness granted."

"Right back at you. Any word?"

"No. Nothing."

Seth shook his head.

"It doesn't make sense," added Bob. "Has anybody—contacted you for money?"

Seth lowered his eyes. He did not want to look at Zimmermann when he was seconds from crying. Pastor Seth kept looking at that picture. New York City. A lifetime ago...

"No."

Pastor Seth was poor and all of Oostburg knew it. Their cars were crap, a 1997 and a 2000. They could not afford to replace either ride so they were running them in the ground.

"So whoever has her is making it personal."

Seth zoned out at that picture again. Gracie was—*is*, is, damn it— gorgeous.

"Gracie didn't have an enemy in the world."

"But do you?"

Seth looked at his rival.

"God loves me," Seth said.

Evelyn Adams knew Charles Raile took her daughter and she was hell-bent on doing whatever it took to make sure Grace was safe and alive.

At the end of the day, Raile was a businessman. The only thing that made Raile dance was money, and she was going to do whatever it took to get her baby back.

Evelyn marched straight through the bank right up to Margie, the same lady who helped her on Friday. What a difference three days make.

Margie knew what happened and gave the same puppy-dog face that everyone else had. Evelyn didn't want sympathy. She wanted her daughter back.

"Evelyn—I'm—"

"I'm closing all my accounts, and I want all my money."

"Evel—"

"Now."

Still feeling a tad bit fuzzy, Wesley Demko tried to type. He had a story to write but like most writers, there was a blockage.

"The fire. The fire was... come on adjective..."

"Hot, like your wife?" she proffered.

Why won't that woman leave me alone? Bitch always sneaking up on me.

Then he remembered he was with her, and it was her job to be a pain in the ass once in a while.

"Hot is too obvious."

"The solution is often right in front of you."

Wesley ignored it and changed the subject.

"No work today?" he asked.

"Day off."

Damn. Now he wished he went to work.

"You should watch the news. Gracie's all over the channels. They are going to check the woods next."

Wesley stared at his screen. The man clicked save and got up.

"Where are you going?"

He left the room as she hollered:

"Remember you have Malachi at 3PM."

Big Mack and two of his friends, Larry Burkes and Sam Preston, had been journeying about the woods of Oostburg's outskirts for quite some time. In fact, they took vacation hours from their sanitation work for the search.

The three males had been there for hours and had gotten nowhere. Stomping around the forest, the trio of seekers were aimlessly wandering about, like Moses in the desert, looking for that needle in the haystack. And to make things worse, cell reception was sporadic and bare, to say the least.

Big Mack had great eyes. They were big and brown, like his physical stature. At six-foot-six, he was like a huge, cuddly teddy bear. The cold did not stop him. His muscles were in great shape. Shivering by his side, Larry and Sam looked like tiny pets compared to Big Mack. The great thing about Big Mack is that he did not let these physical attributes get the best of him. The man didn't think he was better than anyone and he treated everyone as equals. He was a true Christian man.

Back to Big Mack's eyes—not only were they large and dark, but they were also twenty-twenty. And the big twenty-twenties saw something about a quarter of a mile away.

Big Mack tried to dial his cell but to no avail. The woods sucked when it came to the reception.

Help wasn't coming, to his little haystack in the woods.

"Guys. Do you see that?" he asked his partners.

"No," they both said.

"Follow me," Big Mack said.

It was 10AM and around seventy people crammed in Oostburg's Town Hall meeting room to discuss the unfortunate situation.

A few reporters were interviewing Ellis Kirkbride and his deputy.

A young reporter, a cute blonde by the name of Kimberly Jumes, was especially pesky.

"Can you tell us anything?"

Ellis sat forward and took the question.

"Right now, we have searched every square inch of Oostburg. It is unlikely she is here. The department is doing everything in our control to cover ground, follow leads. We will find her."

Miss Jumes asked quite rudely:

"Do you think she is dead?"

There was a little murmur from the crowd.

Kirkbride licked his lips and swallowed his swear words:

"Miss—"

Vicki stopped Ellis. It was going to take all her strength and tact to be "polite".

"That's a really tactless thing to say, don't you think?"

Miss Jumes did not back down:

"I'm paid to get to the truth—"

Vicki gave being polite a try, but after two long seconds, she was done.

"Truth is you're a bitch."

The majority of polite Oostburgers don't cuss, so coming from an official was very shocking to the crowd. A photographer, the same person who took Gracie's last photo, took a photo of Vicki at the panel.

Others followed with their cell phones, hoping to get a good-old-fashioned catfight.

Miss Jumes was used to this. What she didn't know is that Deputy Vicki was used to arguing as well.

"Well, I'll be sure to get that on television—"

Vicki slammed her hands on the table.

"Unbelievable—"

Ellis took her left hand to calm her down.

"Deputy—I'll take it from here."

Miss Jumes smiled.

"Are you saying she is not in Oostburg?"

"It's unlikely she is in Oostburg. An Amber Alert has been sent across the country. If Gracie is seen, we will be contacted. We have every police station in this nation looking for her," Ellis explained.

Someone spoke out—an old guy:

"Have you checked Grover's Creek?"

There was quick agreement amongst the Oostburgers that whatever Grover's Creek was would be a great place to check into. Vicki, however, was clearly in the dark.

She leaned into Ellis.

"Grover's Creek?" she asked.

Ellis leaned back to her.

"It's a creek just outside of town," Ellis paused before continuing: "In the woods."

Vicki's eyes bulged out of their sockets.

"The woods?"

20.

GROVER'S CREEK

Ellis drove Vicki to the outer edge of Oostburg.

"I can't believe you didn't mention a forest."

"It's on the outskirts of town. Not really our borders. It's eight miles of nothing."

"I don't give a damn! We should've been searching in there sooner!"

"It was on my list of places to check. Last resort," Ellis poorly attempted to justify.

"We were last resort yesterday!"

Vicki looked out the window and could see nothing but trees and dry bushes.

Open space for miles and miles.

They got out of the car.

Oh my god, thought Vicki. This was going to steal their clock to explore. They better get a helicopter.

"There's our sticks, Vicks. Eight square miles of her."

Vicki and Ellis began their hike into the woods...

They weren't the only people making their path in the woods.

Around an hour later, after the deputies arrived, Charles Raile pulled up. Raile had his gun in the glove compartment and was about to pull it out when he caught the sheriff's car twelve feet away from his own.

"Cops," he muttered to himself.

He put away his gun.

Charles made his entrance into Grover's Creek and slowly walked to his meeting spot with Evelyn. The unlikely pair had met a couple of times here before, so he knew the path to the obscure bridge over the creek.

It took about forty-five minutes to get where the man was going. As he approached the bridge, Raile could see Evelyn standing on it. Interestingly enough, Evelyn had driven there. *Ambitious*. It was quite risky driving in the woods, cause the ground was full of dirt, rocks, sticks, pebbles, pinecones, and all sorts of other items that could pop your tires or kill your transmission, so Cody had told him.

It briefly occurred to Raile that perhaps she was baiting him into a trap, maybe even to kill him, but he was prepared, even without the gun. Raile was not a man to be messed with, as his trusty pocket knife was close within reach if necessary.

Raile did not like to kill people. Blood made him ill, and he did not want to be responsible for someone's death. It was only in rare cases he would kill someone, or rather have them killed. It only happened four times in his career.

He met Evelyn at a bar, a couple of years ago. He frequently went to bars to catch people doing dumb things, and then he would blackmail them into doing what he wanted.

This is what happened to Evelyn:

Evelyn had been at the bar quite a while. Noticeably intoxicated, Raile walked over and could smell the gin on her hair. One thing led to another; they had spectacular sex—as he recalls, she was plastered so she did not know if he was lying or bragging—and he owned her ever since. In fact, it was because of his moment with Evelyn that he made Oostburg his next landing spot. The refuge he was currently staying at, arranged by his subordinate, Cody, had that slick bookcase secret passage, so it was perfect for business. He kidnapped the black girl on Friday. Cody transported the kid to her new home, so Raile was going to be leaving town soon. He had made his mark and now had the finances necessary to live for some time. He got paid quite aptly per kid, the younger the better. The black girl was almost a little too old.

He couldn't do this anymore. The pastor's speech in the park—it was the first time he heard the victim. If what the pastor said was true, that he could be forgiven, maybe it wasn't too late.

The little girl. His niece needed a better childhood. Not hopping from town to town unknowingly helping her devious uncle.

But he didn't want to get caught, either.

He walked up to the pastor's wife, who did not appear to have any weapon other than a suitcase.

"Yes?" Raile asked her. Evelyn looked around. They were alone.

"Take the suitcase." She gave him the suitcase but he didn't look in it. He continued to stare at Evelyn and be on his guard just in case she attacked him with a knife or something. "I don't care what you have done—just give me my daughter back."

"Evelyn—"

She pushed the suitcase at Raile's torso.

"Take the suitcase—there's our life savings—it's not much—four thousand dollars. Please…"

He looked around. Still no actual cops, just the car.

"I don't know where your daughter is."

Fearing the suitcase may be bugged, Raile walked away. A lousy four thousand bucks were not worth communion in a shot glass to him. He turned around and heard her scream:

"I quit!"

Raile took two steps towards Evelyn. He grabbed her tight ass and gently breathed in her ears. The pastor's wife smelled good, unlike the stench of alcohol from their last close encounter. She was quite pretty for a pastor's wife.

"You can't or the husband sees the video," Raile whispered in her ear. Then he kissed her on the neck.

Evelyn wished she never met Charles Raile. He owned her, she knew it. If only she could make him disappear…

She saw him starting to shrink as the distance grew. Quickly glancing at the ground, she found a large stone with a jagged edge. Evelyn picked it up and briefly thought of murdering the evil wolf, ending her blackmail… she didn't want to live in his shadow forever… but what if he was lying… what if he *did* know where Grace was… she would never know…

She was trapped.

"Oh my God…"

Looking around, she saw the rock in her hand and dropped it.

She was about to murder someone…

Evelyn couldn't believe who she had become…

She got in her ride as quickly as her legs took her. Starting the ignition, she poured a bucket of tears. What had this life become?! She had no idea what she would do next. Her precious girl was gone, the man she thought was responsible wasn't budging, she couldn't murder him, and there was nothing she could do about it!

As she drove through the forest, Evelyn thought she caught a glimpse of two people but she was driving so quickly she couldn't tell if they were people or mirages. She may have been going insane as well, and she was aware of that…

But it wasn't a mirage, it was Ellis Kirkbride and Vicki Weathers finishing the first hour of their tedious search. Even though the woman was driving quite fast, Vicki was able to recognize it as the car they stopped by earlier that day at the school.

"Wasn't that Evelyn?" asked Vicki.

Ellis watched Evelyn speed off.

"What the hell is she doing here?"

At the outer edge of the woods, the pastor's wife noticed she had one voicemail. Thinking and hoping it was Grace, she pulled over to the side of the road and quickly listened to her phone.

It was about her daughter...

Wesley Demko entered the welcome offices of Dr. Benjamin Malachi, professional head-shrinker and in Wesley's humble opinion, basket brain himself. So the good bible says, Dr. Malachi once lost it over a bag of hot dog buns at Walmart. He claimed he only needed seven buns and so he removed one bun from the package and left it on the shelf insisting that he was only paying for seven buns. He reasoned that since hot dogs come in packages of seven, the buns should also. Malachi went to court over this issue, and the doc was placed on some medication, so the rumor goes. But that was a long time ago and now Malachi was back to normal.

The receptionist, Sarah Smiley—as if she could be anything but a receptionist with a name like Smiley—looked up and saw Wesley. Happy as hell, she said:

"Well, hello, Mr. Demko. Nice to see you."

Wesley looked down. He felt out of place being at the office of a quack who may or may not be crazier than him if the rumors were true.

"I have a three o'clock," he said to Sarah.

Sarah gave an even bigger smile, pushing the ears off her head.

She looked at the clock across the room and continued:

"Ah... Mr. Demko... you are quite early."

Two hours and forty-five minutes early, to be exact. Ever hear the joke about the man who didn't want to go home because his woman was there?

"Yeah, um—I like your magazines."

Well, that was a stupid lie, Wesley thought to himself. *It's not a sperm bank.*

The receptionist nodded and smiled.

"Feel free to help yourself."

Wesley half-smiled and walked over to the chairs. He plopped down next to an older gent and picked up a magazine. This older gent slapped himself, at random, every ten seconds or so. He also twitched a lot.

Wesley hated being there.

The slap-happy older guy slapped his cheeks a couple of times and looked over to Wesley as if to say, "What you in for?"

"I'm not crazy," Wesley replied, even though the older guy never spoke.

A few minutes later, she steam-rolled past a group of snotty, pimply tee-nagers on her way to the principal's office of Oostburg Middle.

The wife stomped up to the desk of the school secretary and asked for the principal, Russ Hoffmann.

The secretary smiled but Evelyn could tell it was fake.

"Hello, Evelyn."

Principal Hoffmann entered from his big office and invited Evelyn to come into his office.

Evelyn sat down next to Lainey and began the meeting.

"How are you, Mrs. Adams?"

"How do you think I am? I don't have time for small talk that's for sure. What is it?" she rudely replied. After she completed berating the principal, she noticed a picture on his wall. It was an old picture from four years ago when Grace and the Hoffmann girl were in middle school. It was that eighth grade trip to Chicago, and in the background, they could see Wrigley Field.

"Mrs. Adams, we cannot have this kind of aggression from our students," the principal added, breaking the wife's train of thought on the picture. "Now, the school's policy is a one-week suspension for any assault."

"Grace," Evelyn said, still looking at the picture.

"I'm Lainey."

Evelyn shook her head.

"Of course you are."

Desperate for attention, Lainey said to her mother:

"Tracy started it. She said that Gracie wasn't coming back."

That broke Evelyn out of the trance and she turned to Lainey. Now grinning, Evelyn spoke to Mr. Hoffmann:

"We'll take the suspension."

She got up and took the picture off the wall. After one second of realizing her mother wasn't waiting for her, Lainey got up and left.

The forest did not get any smaller for Vicki and Ellis. There was a helicopter coming in from Milwaukee to search the place but they were still at least fifteen minutes away.

"Eight square miles, huh?" asked Vicki.

"Yup."

"That's a lot of ground for three cops."

"Penny's quick for a fat guy."

Ellis hopped over a large log. He turned around to offer his hand to Vicki but she was already mid-air. Ellis smiled.

Down the path, they came across another very large log. They knelt and looked—nothing.

Vicki sighed. She was getting tired. Ellis could hear his stomach barking at him again.

Keep looking. Keep looking.

"Favorite movie?" Ellis asked to lighten the mood.

Vicki was not sure she should engage in small talk at a time like this but she did.

"*Silence of the Lambs.*"

Vicki wanted the small talk to end but he kept going:

"*All Dogs Go To Heaven.*"

This made her giggle. Vicki saw him as a child trapped in a man's body... a nice body, for that matter... *oh stop and focus*, she thought to herself. But she really couldn't help but laugh.

"What?" Ellis asked.

Vicki smiled as she continued to look.

"Kind of an unmanly answer."

Ellis went on:

"Maybe I'm an unmanly type of guy."

Vicki smiled again.

"Goober."

Ellis gave her a wink.

"Promoted from jackass?"

Vicki thought of a great comeback but decided to swallow it. This really wasn't the time to be fooling around.

"We should be more focused. Let's go," she said.

Vicki walked a little faster.

They continued to troop for about an hour, not talking or finding anything either. Ellis contacted Penny a couple of times to no avail.

He was glad the walkie worked even if the cell phone didn't.

"We really need more deputies. If this were New York City, there would be like a thousand people covering this area," Vicki complained.

"Probably don't want to find her out here."

"That is true."

At that moment, Vicki squinted her eyes.

She could see three people in the distance—hoping one of them to be Gracie, Vicki jogged towards them, with Ellis slowly following. They were running towards them, so Ellis and Vicki picked up the pace.

"There are people over there. Waving to us."

"It's Big Mack," Ellis clarified.

The five met seconds later.

"Follow us," Big Mack stated.

It took them another forty-five minutes to get where Big Mack was leading them, and in that time the sheriff had ordered Deputy Penny back to the station to await further instructions.

As they walked further, Vicki could hear her heart beating faster and faster. It was not due to the excess exercise but rather it was the tension. She really did not want to find Gracie here. Finding the youth here would probably mean she was dead.

Big Mack led them to a deep segment of the forest, and they walked up to a car. It was a little four-door Toyota, blue and a bit wore out.

A small blue car in the middle of the woods. Nothing around the car for miles.

Walking up to it, Vicki knew without the sheriff telling her. She knew it would turn out to be Gracie's car.

Ellis took over, putting his gloves on.

"Ok, stand back."

Ellis opened the car door.

Vicki turned to Big Mack and his friends and in that brief moment, Vicki did not want to see Gracie.

"None of you touched this vehicle, correct?" Vicki asked the trio of men.

Big Mack put his head down and turned to his friends.

"Um—well yes. I opened the door," Big Mack said.

Vicki shook her head. *Awesome... now your fingerprints are on the car, dumb-ass.* He found her earring and now his fingerprints are on her car.

"It's her car," Ellis spoke as he looked in the car.

"Well. That's not something you see in a teenager's car."

Vicki peered in to find a half-empty champagne bottle.

Wesley Demko looked at the receptionist to his right. Miss Smiley was playing a ravaging contest of solitaire. Wesley liked solitaire too even though he rarely was victorious. It was the challenge of the match that enticed him to sit there for hours during bouts of writer's block. Actually, he played more solitaire than he wrote. Miss Smiley needed the five of hearts.

Wesley flipped through a *People* magazine. The latest gossip, ads, celebrities getting married, divorced... remarried again and pregnant, cheating... cheating... Cheating. What a horrendous thing to do to this partner you apparently loved. *Brooke*. As he flipped the page to see what celebrities had his birthday in October, a useless Bible pamphlet fell on the floor next to his size eight shoe.

He snickered as he remembered the night:

"Hi, Wesley. This is Seth. Hey... sorry to call but Gracie is not going to be able to come tonight—she came down with a nasty virus."

"Oh, that's too bad. Thanks for letting us know."

"Sorry for the short notice."

"No problem. We'll just stay home tonight."

"Oh, that's not necessary, Wesley. Kids will be in bed, right?"

"Yeah, they'll be in bed."

"Then just come over. God will watch over them," Seth promised.

"Ok. We'll figure it out. Thanks."

Wesley hung up. Brooke walked over to him.

"Who was it?" she asked.

"Seth. Gracie is sick and can't come over."

"That's alright. I'll just stay home."

Had they stayed home that evening, things would have been... much different. Maybe Wesley would still be drinking the Kool-Aid...

The little male shook his head as he leaned over and picked up the Bible track.

He looked at the receptionist again; she had started a new match. Wesley closed his eyes as he continued to remember that horrible night:

It was the Adams' turn to host the Bible Study. Evelyn made a good quiche. Wesley and Brooke sat on the love seat, across from Bob Zimmermann and his frail wife, Lisa. Next to them sat a new couple that they had met in church a few times, those O'Connells—Mike and Cheryl.

Seth began the study as the last bits of quiche were finished, as well as the final bit of typical conversations. Women—mostly—lovingly complaining about their mates; men talking over the latest games in the world of sports.

"I'd like to welcome Michael and Cheryl to our meeting— happy to meet you—hopefully we'll be seeing more of you at O.C.C."

"Hello," spoke the O'Connells.

The group returned a cheerful "Hello." *New blood.*

Wesley loved the Kool-Aid back then. Nowadays the sour taste made him bitter.

Michael O'Connell spoke up.

"Just, uh—to come out of the closet—sort of speak—I'm... not a religious guy, it confuses me, but I am willing to talk about it and discuss."

Cheryl smiled at her husband and gently touched his knee.

"And I am very thankful for that. Mike doesn't object to me going to church, and once in a while—"

"Christmas and Easter," Michael jokingly interrupted, getting all smiles from the group.

Michael added:

"And when the Packers have a big game!"

The minor laughing continued from the group.

At least Michael, if he was telling the truth, of course, was willing to talk about. So many hardheads were difficult nuts to crack for Christians.

Bob's wife, Lisa, touched her head as she chimed in:

"Hello, I'm Lisa—and as you can see I have cancer. And I get it—there are some moments where I just want to lay down and pass away, but I know that the Lord isn't finished with me yet."

Bob, in nicer, more positive times, squeezed her hand.

Wesley spoke. He was good at speaking back then, before... before God decided to destroy him.

"And no matter what happens… God is bigger than any circumstance. He is in control; he is the almighty, the Alpha and Omega. God is going to take care of you."

Brooke smiled and nudged closer to Wesley.

She spoke:

"Mr. Demko?"

Why would she call him that?

Wesley shook his head and realized he wasn't at the Bible Study.

He was in stupid Dr. Malachi's office.

"Take care of you..." he sarcastically chuckled.

"Mr. Demko?" Brooke said again.

Wesley looked up.

The receptionist, confused as to what Wesley was conversing about with himself, continued:

"Dr. Malachi will see you now."

21.

DR. BEN MALACHI'S
HOUSE OF TORTURE

After using the men's room, Wesley sauntered over to Dr. Benjamin Malachi's office. Malachi was a handsome man, one you would immediately trust just by glancing at him. He had a cleft jaw, a toothy smile, and piercing blue eyes. At one point Wesley suggested he become a model, to which the great doctor laughed and said: "I think this is where I can do the most good". He was about forty, although he could pass for thirty, had a happy wife and a plethora of kids. Wesley couldn't remember their names—the wife or the kids—but he knew the doctor had a family.

Wesley slithered in to see his therapist pouring a cup of coffee. Malachi did not notice Wesley at first, and in that brief moment, Wesley felt like stealing his life. It was not fair to Wesley how some people had everything while others scrounge for nickels. The doctor was happy. Wesley wanted that. He wanted to be happy again but god would not allow it. The good old scripture verse came to his mind:

> *"What then, shall we say in response to these things?*
> *If god is for us, who can be against us?"*

This used to be Wesley's favorite verse in all of scripture because it made him feel confident—he could attempt any challenge, and if god were on his side, he would be successful.

Then, after the tragedy, it became his least favorite verse... in fact, he *hated* it. After the tragedy, Wesley realized god *wasn't* on his side—which made him see the honest scripture in a different light—the *opposite* light—what if the opposite were true? If god is against us, then who cares what we do? Or what we think? If good god is against us, nothing matters—because *we're screwed anyway.*

He hated the doctor. His doctor had everything and obviously, god was "for him". In that brief moment, Wesley felt rage—he felt... ready to murder...

Dr. Benjamin Malachi turned around.

"Wesley! Wesley, buddy. Glad to see you! It's been a while."

He was so damn friendly.

"Have a seat."

The tiny man walked over and sat in his usual spot, with his back to the clock. He knew, or he figured he knew, that this clock placement in conjunction with the chair was most strategic. Malachi wanted entire control of the conversation, even the time and pace of it.

The sneaky, intelligent bastard.

"So... how has my Wesley been?" Malachi asked as he sat down. "Oh pardon—you want some coffee?"

"No. I had three cups already today."

"Wow—that is a lot. Staying up late writing your novel?"

He knew Wesley all too well.

"Yeah, trying to."

"I admire you, Wesley. Writing a book is not simple. My book took me months to finish and even then it wasn't done. Editing, publishing, etc. Keep plugging away."

Wesley glanced down. He had everything... and Wesley had... a nagging woman and a crappy video store job. Malachi was well over six feet; Wesley barely passed five. Damn it all, Wesley hated him. He wished he could kill Malachi, and he would have... if it wasn't for the fact that people would miss him. Wesley shook his head as if to get the evil thoughts out.

"How's the marriage?" continued Dr. Malachi.

Wesley paused.

"Like most marriages, it sucks." Wesley chuckled. "And how's yours, doc?"

Wesley liked turning the questions away from himself.

"Mine is going well. Thank you for asking. Why does your marriage suck?"

Wesley licked his lips.

"I guess it doesn't entirely suck. I mean, the sex is still good. She may be paralyzed, but the woman still has it. But anyway, marriages aren't only about sex."

"No, it's not—"

Wesley interrupted.

"It's about support. Supporting each other's dreams."

"She doesn't support your dreams?"

Wesley took a breath. The session was beginning to feel like another rerun.

"No, she doesn't."

Malachi was relentless:

"Do you support her dreams?"

Wesley avoided eye contact with the good doc. The answer was very painful for him to utter.

"I... all she wants is babies. I can't..."

Wesley glanced out the window. Damn it, he wanted out. Why in the hell did he come here? It had been a while, and he had run out of excuses. It was very difficult to avoid Brooke for long. Eventually, she would have nagged him enough that he had to come in to see the apt doctor. If only he could leave that woman—but he couldn't do that, not in her unstable condition. Leaving a paralyzed woman? Boy, he would be ostracized by the novel community. He wouldn't sell one book.

Malachi paused to let Wesley digest his thoughts and emotions.

Wesley continued to bitch:

"You know there's a height requirement to donate sperm?"

"Excuse me?"

"Five foot eight..." Wesley shook his head. "You know how fucking offensive and discriminatory that is?" Wesley swallowed. "I wonder what black people would do if they only accepted white sperm?" Wesley smiled at the doctor. "You get it? White sperm, cause sperm is white. See what I did there?"

"Oh, I see what you did there." Malachi shifted his seat. "You're particularly aggressive today."

"Can't even donate sperm. That's how "little" the world thinks of short people. Maybe we should just be eradicated. The entire damn short race."

"Well, being short is not a race—"

"Oh, but it is. It's a fucking marathon."

Malachi cleared his throat in apparent discomfort.

"How's your relationship with Jesus?" the doctor asked.

Wesley looked up at the ceiling as if silly Jesus were Spiderman hanging around the room eavesdropping.

"Oh, I believe in God. Very much so. I believe that this Heavenly God almighty created the Heavens and the Earth all by speaking it."

Malachi gave a small smile.

"That's good."

Wesley continued:

"Yes, doctor. I believe it all. I also believe that this Almighty Creator who can build something from nothing can also cure cancer. Just by—"

Wesley snapped his fingers.

"That's all he has to do. Now tell me, doc—why doesn't he?"

Wesley loved it when these so-called Christians could not come up with the right answer. Granted he only opened up to Seth, once.

"Umm..." was all Malachi could muster up before Wesley plowed him over.

"And don't give that "everything happens for a reason" shit. Yes, the reason is god crapped on you because he felt like it. Or maybe the lord was too busy answering someone's prayers for their football team to win or some mundane trivial thing like that. Oh yes, I believe in god. I do believe in him. And he sucks."

Malachi was getting uncomfortable. He was a therapist, not a real pastor, and even though Malachi confessed to being a follower of Jesus, he was not very good when people attacked his faith.

"Well, I'm not here to be God's lawyer—"

Wesley quickly stepped in.

"That's a shame, cause he needs one."

The little man continued:

"I believe in the lord. I just don't like him." The man paused to gather his thoughts. "Let me tell you a tale, doc. I... "had" a friend. You see, he prayed a long while for a wife and kids. And he waited. He had some genetic issues. So he stayed away from smoking and drinking and that sort of thing. And he married a woman who did the same. So they plan everything and do everything in their power to keep their children away from the poor genes. They avoid bad things, they pray, etc. All that good stuff. First kid, what do you know? She comes out with the same issues as the dad. Second kid has different issues; he's sick as a dog and can't catch a break or even his breath. Asthma; allergic to his own skin and can't bite hardly anything but gluten-free ice cubes. They quit having children but this friend is super bitter. Then surprise! Along comes kid three. But here's the damn catch: this time, he *does not* pray. Not one damn prayer. He does it on purpose, too. And lord almighty—guess what? Kid three is healthy; perfect. Ten fingers and ten toes. So daddy is super depressed cause all these years he thought his prayers meant something... and yet they meant... *nothing*. He prayed his soul out for kids one and two, who were unhealthy, and he didn't pray at all for kid three, who was healthy. You see—now here is the lesson so pay attention, doc—if prayer mattered, kid one and two would be healthy and kid three would be dead. That's the kicker. Guy was depressed because he realized he had wasted thirty-five years of his life, praying to a god who really didn't care. He served; went to church, prayed and witnessed—only to see that it was meaningless—as it says in scripture, correct?"

"Well, in Ecclesiastes—"

"I know the scriptures, doc. And he got depressed because he wasted his life, it made him go crazy, and so what's he do?"

Wesley paused waiting for the doctor to respond.

"He took his life," the doctor guessed.

Wesley stared off.

"He took his life."

"He was a friend of yours?"

Wesley looked out the window.

"Cut himself. While his family was at church."

The doctor paused.

"Have you ever thought of taking your life, Wesley?"

Wesley half-smiled.

"Every damn day."

The doctor nodded.

"You know, Wesley, there's medicine—"

"I can't." Wesley looked at a picture on the doctor's mantle. The picture contained: the doctor, his attractive wife, and their four happy children. "I need to finish the novel first."

Wesley stared and stared. He wanted to cry... but he couldn't. He didn't have it in him anymore.

"It's not fair. Just not fair."

"Life isn't fair, Wesley."

Wesley and his therapist were silent for a few seconds, digesting the philosophy.

Wesley broke the silence.

"Everyone should get one hundred years."

"How's that?"

"One hundred years. You are born on a certain day, and you perish exactly one hundred years later to that date. If a woman is born on April 17, 1999, then she should pass away on April 17, 2099. Everyone would—know their expiration date. No one would die... young." He paused; a bit teary. "That would be fair."

"That would be nice."

"Yes. And fair."

"You are very keen on "fairness.""

"Yes."

"And all this connects to the last three years, correct?"

"I don't want to talk about the last three years."

The doctor re-shuffled his position.

"You've heard Gracie Adams is missing, right?"

"Yes."

Malachi paused before asking:

"You didn't have anything to do with that, did you?"

That mild accusation made Wesley shutter. It was quite a leap for the good doctor to make. Wesley paused, turned around, and looked at the clock: 3:30.

"Oh look, we're out of time."

"I might make an exception."

"But that would be *unfair* to your next victim; I mean, patient."

Wesley winced and shook his head.

"You ok?"

Wesley looked down.

"Yeah, I'm fine."

Dr. Malachi stood up and walked over to Wesley.

"Are you sure? Let me check that out—"

Wesley raised his hand.

"No, I'm fine. I gotta get going anyway."

The doctor continued: "You need Jesus."

Wesley smiled. An evil smile.

"If this Jesus *can't* save my babies from a fire, or *won't* save my babies from a fire, I don't want him."

Wesley got up and left.

Feeling dizzy and nauseous as he drove, he thought of the lengthy conversation and how it went so south. How dare Ben Malachi tell him he needed Jesus or god or whatever the hell it wanted to call itself these days.

Wesley needed god three years ago, not today.

Today was too late.

Wesley's kids died in the fire. A fire that happened at random.

While he was at that bible study; praising Jesus.

Jesus stabbed him in the neck.

He was mad at god.

And he had every right to be.

22.

THE NEXT CHAPTER

Matt Zimmermann walked into his house with his school bag to find his father reading the newspaper. It was a rough Monday, rougher than a normal Monday. One of his closest companions was missing, and he didn't know where she was, not even a clue. He tried many times throughout the day to phone or text, but no avail. The beautiful girl next door was gone without a trace.

Bob Zimmermann looked up from his paper.

"Where you been?"

He could have lied and said he was at play rehearsal but with her missing, the rehearsal was canceled. If she did not return, the role would slide on Matt and if that were the case, he had a ton of studying to do. He was secretly hoping Mr. Schultz, the drama teacher and the director, would cancel the play or at least postpone it till Gracie came back.

Instead, Matt told his father the truth. Something he rarely did these days.

"Out looking for Gracie."

Zimmermann folded his newspaper in defeat. "Can't scold a boy for searching for his friend. Evelyn was in the paper. She was attacked yesterday. After church."

"Attacked?"

Zimmermann got up and walked to their kitchen to make supper, a turkey sandwich.

"Yes. Someone tried to kill her."

Matt followed his dad. He was hungry too. He grabbed a butter knife from the drawer and inadvertently pointed it at his father.

"Who would want to kill Mrs. Adams?"

For a brief moment, Matt thought the worst:

Wouldn't it be interesting if Gracie attacked her mother...?

Ellis took out his walkie.

"Penny, we are in the forest, about three miles out. We found her car, but no Gracie. Ten-four."

Big Mack shook his head. There, right in front of them, was Gracie's car. She was not there but there was evidence that something awful happened. How bad was yet to be determined. But there was something bad to report.

"Weathers, call the Adams'—"

"No."

Ellis looked at her, figuring he misheard.

"Huh?"

Vicki looked at him and for the first time, she showed her boss fear and sadness.

"Not right now." Turning to the sanitation worker, she asked:

"Big Mack, have you told anyone?"

Big Mack looked down at her.

"No, Mme. We went looking for you."

Nobody knew about the car other than the five standing there. And of course, perhaps, one other person.

"Call forensics—we need this car dusted."

Ellis looked at his phone and in this particular location, he did have one bar of juice left. Ellis dialed and was connected to the right people. He tried his best to give their coordinates and hoped that they would be able to get there in a timely fashion. The sun was grouchy and close to bedtime.

Ellis pulled Vicki aside.

"Vicki, if her car is out here..."

Vicki pled.

"Please, Ellis. Just wait."

Visibly upset, she stepped away. Ellis looked up at the sky for a moment and decided to follow her. She had no idea where she was, and he didn't need her to get lost either. He followed her for a minute before opening his mouth.

"You okay?"

Vicki stared.

"Yeah, I know it sucks. I know Gracie. It's breaking my heart, and now we've found her car. I mean, how in the hell am I going to tell my best friend that his daughter's car is miles into the forest?"

"I just... want her to be alive."

Ellis patted her shoulder.

"We haven't found her. Maybe she got high-jacked and kidnapped."

Vicki looked out onto the horizon. The sun was pretty today.

Ellis glanced about and took a short breath. It was going to be a long night, perhaps very long if forensics couldn't find them.

Vicki turned to him—suddenly remembering something:

"Did you leave civilians alone at the crime scene?"

Ellis looked over.

"Um—"

Vicki stormed past him.

Returning to the car, Vicki put her game face back on.

"When did you find this car?"

"A couple of hours ago, Mme," responded Big Mack.

"How come you didn't call?"

"We tried. Our cell phones don't get reception out here."

Ellis chimed in:

"He's right. Even if someone found Gracie, they might not be able to tell anyone. Cell phone reception is spotty out here. Anyone who has lived in Oostburg for any length would know that."

Vicki checked her phone. It was dead.

"Maybe he knew that as well."

"He?"

"He. The person who dragged her out here."

"Little bit of a jump."

"No, it's not. I'm done waiting."

Ellis smiled and turned to the three men who found the car.

"Thank you, gentlemen. You might as well leave, while we figure out the next steps."

There was no point in keeping them any longer. The guys told what they knew, which was not a lot. Ellis and Vicki were appreciative. They were one step closer to finding what happened to Gracie Adams. The car was their first big clue.

"Praying for you," said Big Mack.

Vicki inwardly chuckled, as if to say: "big deal".

"Thanks," said Ellis.

Big Mack offered his hand and Ellis took it. The three buds began their journey back through Grover's Creek. The sheriff eyed Big Mack as he walked away with Sam and Larry.

Vicki picked up on an awkward vibe between the two.

"You two friends?"

Ellis paused.

"Friends is a... no, not really."

Avoiding a conversation, Ellis went to his walkie. It was working fine.

"Penny, call the Sheboygan PD and tell them to have their forensics unit come over to where we are, about three miles in. Ten-four.

Penny responded:

"Yes, sheriff. Ten-four."

Vicki picked up the conversation where they left off:

"I'd like to hear the story sometime."

Ellis and Vicki turned around and looked at the car.

"Gracie... who did this?" Ellis asked himself.

Vicki blew on her hands.

"Damn, it's so cold here."

Ellis chuckled.

"You should see February."

Waiting for forensics could take forever, and they did not want to wait any longer. If something ghastly did indeed happen to Gracie, they wanted to be the first ones to know. They walked around the car but did not notice anything out of the ordinary, at least not from the outside. The body of the car was great, no scratches. License plate checked out; registration was within the requirements. There was no busted glass, no flat tires. Nothing.

The only thing odd about the car was the location.

He opened the car door again but this time he peeked in deeper.

"A champagne bottle. She's not old enough to drink." He gently moved the bottle to peak at the label. "Cellar Dweller, Extra Dry Champagne." Ellis grinned. "It's a nine-dollar booze that you can get anywhere. I saw this just the other night at Piggly-Wiggly."

"Champagne usually means a celebration or a party of some sorts," added Vicki. "What were you celebrating, Gracie?"

"And who were you celebrating with?" Ellis chimed in.

"People don't celebrate by themselves."

Ellis looked at her.

"This is going to shock everyone in town that she had a bottle of champagne in her car. I still don't believe it myself... and I'm seeing it. Maybe the person she was with..."

"Forced this on her," added Vicki.

Ellis licked his lips and moved on to the back seat, gently maneuvering his large torso to not disrupt anything. Ellis peered in the back seat with his flashlight and came across something abnormal.

Ellis closed his eyes as he came out of the car. Passing off the flashlight to his inferior, he said:

"Take a look."

Vicki took the flashlight and peeked in the back seat. Her figure was not as big so it was easier to move.

"Damn it."

She came out, upset at what she had found.

"Would now be a good time to call the parents?" asked Ellis.

Evelyn Adams picked up the phone.

"Seth?"

Seth was in his office at church, close to being done for the day and ready to get back home and prayerfully hear some good news.

"Evelyn. Any word?"

"Nothing on Grace. But our other kid was suspended from school."

Seth shook his head.

"For what?"

"She punched another girl. The girl was insulting Grace."

Lainey peeked into the kitchen unobserved. She could hear the conversation, even Seth's voice on the other end.

"We don't have time for Lainey right now."

This comment made the youth furious and it increased her frequent suspicions that her parents didn't give a damn about her.

"Just tell her we'll deal with her later. I'm leaving in a little, and I'm going to look around town again."

Seth waited but Evelyn did not respond. She held a few tears inside instead.

"We're going to get her back, Evelyn."

A loud buzzing sound crept into Evelyn's phone, and she lifted the phone from her ear to check it.

"Ok. It's Brooke. I'm going to take this call."

Evelyn switched to Brooke.

"Brooke?"

Brooke was watching television and heard the reporter make a plea for help:

"—you have any information, or see anyone with a bloody left arm, please contact the authorities."

Brooke shut off the television.

"Hey. Just calling to see how you're doing? Any update?"

"No. Well, none on Grace. But a little on me."

Brooke picked up the newspaper to glance at it again.

"I know—I just read the paper and saw it on the news."

"It's on the news?" asked Evelyn, a little taken back.

"You haven't read the paper?"

Evelyn looked in her refrigerator.

"I've been tied up today, Brooke."

"Sorry. It says you defended yourself and stabbed the guy?"

"Yeah."

"Good for you. Did they catch him?"

"Not that I know of. Not sure it was a "him" anyway."

Brooke's ears perked up.

"Oh?"

"Yeah, I'm not sure. I grabbed the arms. They just didn't feel... manly."

Brooke sat back in her chair.

"So, it was a woman?"

"Maybe. Whoever it is, they have a nice cut on their left arm."

"Girl power," Brooke talked into the phone.

Wesley stormed past the woman.

"Wesley?"

Brooke wheeled to the stairs with the cell phone between her head and her shoulder.

"Evelyn, can I call you back?"

Brooke clicked her cell phone and glanced up the staircase. After crawling up the wooden mound, she could hear Wesley behind the bathroom door making some odd sounds.

She knocked.

"Wesley?"

Wesley shook his head. He did not desire to see the woman.

Actually, he never did but especially not now.

"Go away!"

Brooke persisted:

"What's the matter? You throwing up?"

"Go away, Brooke!"

She tried to nudge her way in but Wesley was sitting there by the door.

The spouses sat at the opposite side of the door pushing back and forth. Both weighed the same—about one-thirty—but with Wesley woozy, he was going to lose this battle. After a few cold seconds, Brooke was in the bathroom watching her husband bleed on their burgundy rug.

"What the hell is this, Wesley?!"

Wesley grimaced in pain trying to thread a needle through a wound in his left bicep.

Wesley made a poor attempt to downplay it.

"It's nothing—"

Brooke gave him a stupefied look.

"It's nothing? Wesley... you're bleeding all over! You need to go to the hospital!"

Wesley attempted to get up but didn't get very high.

"No! I can't!"

"Why not?"

She remembered Evelyn's words:

"Whoever it is, they have a nice cut on their left arm."

At that moment, Brooke knew.

She read the article.

She saw the television reporter.

Brooke's face changed—she understood fully.

But why in the hell would her husband attack Evelyn? There was no bad blood. They were friendly and heartfelt at church and other events. Brooke never knew of anything that would make her husband yearn to kill Evelyn. It made no sense to her! Why would he do this!?

Brooke paused for a calm moment, briefly terrified as she crawled closer to him. Wesley was her husband and she was going to take care of him. She was a nurse and knew how to stitch people up. She did it often at the nursing home. Those elderly fell quite a bit and she was able to sew them back together again. This injury of Wesley's was in her wheelhouse.

But why?

That was the nagging question. Perhaps, it was some other reason. Maybe he fell on a knife... what the hell! Wesley Allen Demko! What are you thinking?! Brooke married an idiot, she knew it for quite some time but this was the clincher. Why would he attack her—and in broad daylight! She married a complete jackass!

She did not want to believe it. That her husband was an attempted murderer...

The wife needed to make a wise decision and fast. Either she was going to turn him over to Ellis or not. She could let him bleed to death; after all, he was a terrible husband. *He had been a terrible husband for the last few years now. It would serve him right; to die on their burgundy rug, slobbering all over this bathroom, with her sitting there next to him, with all the ability on the planet to stitch Humpty Dumpty together again. All she would have to do is... nothing. Nothing and she would get rid of Wesley Demko forever... let the man bleed out. "Oh, I'm sorry Sheriff Kirkbride, I had the television up loud, if he called, I didn't hear... I'm paralyzed; I couldn't get there in time!*

Yes, murder could be quite simple when all it takes is—

But stop that, she thought to herself. *You made a promise to love this man, this pathetic, stupid, little male and you were going to love him till death do you part and if you don't do anything now, that death part was going to come sooner rather than later!*

Damn it, Wesley! Why the hell did you attack Evelyn?!

"I'll help you," she said.

Pastor Adams packed his desk and headed home. He knew they needed milk but he couldn't even muster the strength to go to the local store. He was dead tired, physically, and emotionally drained. It was only 5PM but it may as well been midnight.

Gracie, please come back. That's all he could think of. There was nothing he could do; he knew that. He had no contacts. He had no inside tips. She just vanished. Vanished into thin air. He hoped she was okay, perhaps she secretly disliked her father and she ran off with some nice boy who would treat her right.

Please come home, Gracie. I'll treat you better. I'll be a better father...

On his way home, he drove past Grover's Creek. He stopped—why he didn't know at the time—but Seth did and he looked into the woods from his car. He was quite the distance but could see a Buick pull up to the edge of the forest. A man got out of the ride, looking very serious and officious. Seth did not know what was happening. He swallowed some air. Weird for a man to be walking into the woods... especially now when the sun would be going down probably in an hour or so. What was he doing? Seth could follow the man. He could. Part of him did not want to know for he was frightened... that if he did find his Grace, she would be gone. Deep down inside, the pastor realized he was a damn coward. He couldn't handle the fact that she was gone. With her missing, there was still hope. Hope that she was safe and alive and perhaps playing a sick and cruel prank on them all. But that was not Gracie. She wasn't a trickster. That's the worst part—this was not like her at all. She was the good daughter. Lainey, yes... he could see Lainey pulling something like this, running away and coming back sometime later when the scores were settled. But Gracie, no. Gracie was responsible. She was...

The man carried some bags, three to be exact, out of his car.

Seth was scared. Why would anyone go into the forest?

He didn't want to know, so he drove home.

The Demkos spent their evening on the bathroom floor as the woman sewed up her husband. Wesley had a little whisky to numb the stitching but he was in some pain.

The report was direct—as was Evelyn—whoever attacked her was stabbed in the left bicep. The likelihood of Wesley getting stabbed in some other manner was minuscule.

"Wesley, what happened?" Brooke asked.

Wesley paused.

"I was attacked."

Brooke smelled bullshit.

"What?"

Wesley attempted to stand but could not get four inches above the ground.

"Just kill me now. I have nothing to live for anyway."

Brooke paused as she looked at her husband; offended by his cold, callous statement. *Nothing to live for? What in the hell did that mean? You don't have a wife to take care of? You don't have a wife who wants to take care of you? How dare he make that comment!*

"You're right. You don't have a wife who loves you. Six inches to the right would have done the job."

Brooke looked him in the eyes just to make sure the idiot knew where she stood.

"You're a moron," Brooke said as she jabbed him harder.

Wesley barked a terrible squeal as he quickly stood back up, this time standing successfully.

Without even thanking her, Wesley stepped over the woman and opened the door.

The wife sat there blankly in defeat as his legs swung above her head.

She spoke:

"I hope your book burns."

Almost out the door, Wesley Demko stopped in his tracks.

He stayed upright for a full three seconds before turning around, kneeling to her level, and smacking her right across the face.

He looked in her eyes and said:

"Don't ever say that."

Wesley got up and left.

Brooke looked at him as he shrunk into his lair.

Who did she marry?

The sun was not too far away from going to sleep for the night so things needed to be finished quickly and with precision. Finding Gracie's car was the first serious break in the case and they could not blow this clue.

John Walker, the intelligent man known for his expertise, entered Grover's Creek. With his gangly legs, he was able to locate Ellis and Vicki within an hour. He had two assistants with him.

A bottle of champagne in the car of a teenager might seem typical nowadays, but it is certainly not legal. Even if Gracie were found, she would probably be in a heap of trouble. In a town like little Oostburg, there is no way she would have been able to purchase the alcohol on her own with everyone knowing her. And with that being known, there was for sure someone else involved. Gracie also did not look twenty-one, so she would have been carded wherever she—if she—bought the champagne. This was clear to Vicki and Ellis from the get-go.

Walker arrived and quickly shook hands with Ellis and Vicki.

It was difficult for them to sit and wait. Wisely choosing not to contact Seth or Evelyn, they wanted more information before unloading a bomb on them—so they stood and waited, not touching anything more.

Walker was not one to beat around the bush. He knew time was of the essence, having read about the case himself. Missing children cases were always the worst.

He put on his gloves and began his thorough search. He leaned and found the bottle. In the back seat, there was a little bloodstain. The blood was not big enough to indicate major injury—with that amount no one would die—but there was a loss of blood in the back seat. The bottle was bagged. The car was dusted, the blood was collected, and Walker was efficient. Nothing else major was found in the ride other than an empty package of skittles. Ellis mentioned that Gracie liked skittles so it did not appear to be a major segment of evidence, but the bag was collected as well.

Walker's assistant from the Sheboygan Police Department, Benjamin Collins, took photos: the back seat, front seat, the position of the seats, the location of the vehicle, the blood, the bottle. Nothing was moved, at least not by them. Everything was prepared carefully. Another hungry officer walked away with the pieces of evidence.

It was going to be a long night of studying for all involved.

By 6PM, the sunlight in Grover's Creek was starting to fade. The dogs were on their way, and the car was about to be towed.

Vicki sighed.

"Gracie meets someone; they have a romantic encounter... and then what...?"

"We'll know within a day the blood type and if there are any fingerprints on the bottle. Do you know her blood type?" Walker asked.

"Not off the top of my head," declared Ellis.

Vicki gave her theory:

"Girl meets someone, and they drive off together..." Looking over in the opposite direction, she could see a tow truck slowly maneuvering through the rough terrain. The lights were beaming, like New York City. A lot was like New York City now, unfortunately. The bright lights, the cameras. The action.

Walker spoke:

"Once we get that car into the station we can begin to put together the puzzle."

The tow truck made their way slowly to the site wanting to disturb as little as possible. The driver and his assistant chained up Gracie's car to the tow in no time. Getting back in the truck, the two gentlemen began to pull the little ride, and seconds later Vicki and the gentlemen were privy to an odd cracking sound...

Quickly, Vicki yelled at the driver:

"Turn it off! Now!"

The driver obliged and all was quiet again.

"Didn't sound like a stick."

Vicki got on the ground and crawled under the car.

She dug at some of the leaves under the back driver's side tire.

After a few seconds of digging, Vicki Weathers gently tugged that obstruction in the foliage:

An arm, still attached to its owner...

23.

I'LL DANCE WITH CINDERELLA

Back at the Adams' house, not many blocks from where Vicki, Ellis, and the rest of the search committee were in Grover's Creek, stood Seth Adams. He danced with his eldest daughter, Gracie. No, she wasn't there physically, of course, but she was there in his mind; and at this stage of the game, this very hour, that was enough, for somehow, Pastor Adams knew something was wrong. Very... wrong. He knew something was going to happen soon, and he knew it wasn't going to be good.

Call it *"father's* intuition".

He stood there dancing with the memory of Gracie every small step of the way. Within seconds, she turned from a six-and-a-half-pound little baby into his one-hundred-and-twenty pound little baby. He remembered teaching this girl to ride a bike, shoot a basketball, smack a baseball, and the last thing he taught her— how to drive. He glanced out the window and peeked at where her car would be parked. He wished he never taught her how to drive or even balance a bike. Pastor wished he had homeschooled like he thought he should—maybe she would still be around if only he protected her more. Keep her trapped in her bedroom until she was twenty, thirty, sixty-five. Bubble wrap Christianity: hide under your bed till the Lord comes. He knew deep down that he could protect her; perhaps even better than God could.

No longer singing, Gracie stopped dancing with him as well. Young Gracie backed up slightly and looked deep in his eyes as if to say good-bye for the final time. Pastor gazed back, knowing it was the last dance. Knowing that dream was about to stop, the dream that would soon turn into a vivid, very real, nightmare.

Through eyes of haze, Seth looked at his baby girl in confusion, hoping to trick his conscience into thinking that stopping was going to bring her back to reality.

"Why did you stop, Grace?" was all Pastor Seth Adams could muster up to his little girl.

Gracie took another step back and spoke:

"Daddy. The dance is over."

And she disappeared the moment the phone rang.

Grover's Creek was the hot spot to be on this dry Monday night in October. The Sheboygan Police Department had brought in the mutts in an attempt to sniff out any clues that might be lurking around the forest.

The Oostburg Department was swarming as well, all four in uniform were thankful to have the Sheboyganites at their call. The large forest would never be covered by just four Oostburgers.

Deputy Vicki remembered something that was once told to her about the deceased. Something about passing love and receiving the same love, searching and finding, living, and dying. How the deceased now came to a full circle. It was her therapist who told her that.

She could not believe that in the middle of Wisconsin, the middle of nowhere, she would be reliving the very same nightmare.

She never legally caught Gabrielle's killer even though she knew who did it. Her mind raced in opposite directions—one of raw fear, where she wanted to sprint away and never look at evil again; the other part of the brain wanted to run toward the fear—toward the pain, shake it, and bury it in the dirt— bury it right next to—

"Gracie," Ellis said as he removed the leaves from the top of her face. An attractive face, bloated in death, missing one earring. She was topless, wearing only a bra. The blood-stained shirt was wrapped around her head.

Vicki shook her head.

"Even the weather is on his side. If it were a tad warmer, we may have smelt her body hours ago."

Ellis stared at Gracie. The sheriff had been there three days after she was born. In fact, he helped Seth and Evelyn leave the hospital. He saw her three days after she was born and was now here to see her three days—maybe—after she died.

Gracie's eyes were closed forever. All this time, Gracie had been buried in the forest, under her damn car. Last seen a little after 9PM Friday by her sister Lainey, it was now about seventy-two hours later. For approximately seventy-two hours—at least, probably, as they did not know for sure when she died—she had been lying in this forest, under her very own car, buried under leaves. Vicki looked at her. The kid was at peace, regardless of the deep incise on her left temple. Stained blood, she was obviously hit with something solid, across the left side of her face—which would indicate a right-handed assailant.

Seeing a hundred cops running around, Vicki screamed as she waved to the other cops:

"Secure the area! Let no one enter the perimeter!"

For the most part, Gracie was uncovered. Her thin legs were still under the foliage as forensics went through the gory details. Vicki was able to locate her purse, which was buried under her head, serving as a pillow.

The newest deputy in Oostburg opened the purse and plowed through the contents. As Vicki was digging, she overheard Ellis and John Walker chatting:

"Oostburg hasn't had a murder in like, fifteen years," Ellis said casually.

"Not suicide... that's for sure. Can't kill yourself and then bury your body neatly under a pile of leaves," Walker deduced. "And then park your car over your body."

Ellis knelt to get a better look. Not a gent to weep, he was almost sobbing.

"Some stranger preying on teenage girls..."

Vicki finished digging through Gracie's purse. She pulled out her credit card and some cash.

"Random strangers don't murder and leave money and a credit card." Vicki surmised. "She very likely knew her assailant. Her arms were sprawled out. Whoever buried her, he didn't care." Vicki took the cell phone battery and the phone out of her purse. "Cell phone didn't have the battery in it—no wonder the phone company couldn't trace the location."

Ellis looked at Gracie's eyes. At that moment, he was very glad to have Vicki Weathers on his team.

As he gently grinned at his more experienced inferior, a massive amount of ruckus came from about fifty yards away. Seconds later, Ellis could realize it was Seth and Evelyn, sprinting as fast as their forty-something-year-old physiques would handle them. Ellis suddenly lost his breath. He felt the sorrow that Seth, his friend, would feel. Ellis did not have children and could only guess how this was going to clear out. He couldn't breathe as he watched his friend helplessly run through the forest, thirty, twenty, ten yards away with his frantic bride following seconds behind. Running to greet their daughter, there was nothing Seth could do to fix this, and there was nothing Ellis could say to make it any better. Seth and Evelyn Adams knew what they were running to. He could only walk up to Seth, meet him about five yards from his deceased daughter, and give him a hug.

"Lord Christ help them," Walker mumbled under his breath as Vicki quickly covered up their daughter.

Seth pounded Ellis's chest as he yelled his friend's name.

"Ellis! Ellis! Ellis!" Seth screeched over and over again as his friend blocked him. Seth being six inches shorter and a hundred pounds lighter had no chance of advancing.

"I need to see her!" Seth screamed into his friend.

"It's best not to—"

"Ellis, don't make me punch you—let me go!"

Ellis paused for a second and in that second made the decision to let Seth see his daughter one last time. Vicki looked at him disapprovingly but it was too late.

Seth and Evelyn saw their precious daughter two final moments and screamed.

The reporters were vultures that evening; not caring about anyone but themselves—who had the best angle, who had the wisest information. None of them gave a damn what really happened; they didn't care about a slice of truth. They wanted the gossip.

From the entrance of Grover's Creek, blonde Kimberly Jumes was in front of the camera not two hours after Gracie had been found.

"We are live from Oostburg, Wisconsin... where seventeen-year-old Gracie Adams was reported missing Saturday morning. Sadly, after a very extensive search, young Gracie was found tonight in the woods, lying under a pile of leaves, beneath her car."

Many viewers watched this display of fake sympathy news, including the Demkos. As they saw Kimberly Jumes take the first bite of juicy gossip, Wesley looked down at a photo of him, Brooke, and two kids—the same two kids that he was writing about. Wesley's eyes glistened.

It did not go unnoticed by Brooke.

Evelyn was on the television now.

"Grace was my baby! How... could someone do this... oh my god... a precious per... what has this world come to... I don't know why—I—"

Brooke turned her head to Wesley.

He knew what he had done.

On the television, Seth put his arm around his wife as they sadly walked away.

Miss Jumes continued:

"After a day of prayer vigils, a candlelight walk around her high school, all the prayers that went up, were not answered in the way they were looking for."

Ellis and Vicki were also watching the news from his office.

On the news, Miss Jumes asked Vicki:

"Deputy Weathers, any ideas?"

Ellis popped a red skittle in his mouth.

Vicki answered professionally. Unfortunately, she had been in this sad position before.

"We are not ruling anything out at this point. We have launched a full-out investigation."

Miss Jumes concluded:

"Oostburg, Wisconsin. The tight-knit, little Christian community with a population of about a thousand, brought into the spotlights under the most unfortunate of circumstances. Live from Oostburg, I'm—"

Ellis turned off the television.

Vicki stood up.

"You mind if I... take an hour or so?"

Vicki stormed through the restroom door. Her cheeks were damp from the few water drops that managed to slip past the goalie. She punched a bathroom stall door and turned around to face the mirror. Seeing herself for the first time in hours, she noticed some grey hairs on the left side of her head. She quickly attempted to rip them out but realizing the task was nearly impossible, she just pounded the sink instead.

"That is for you, god! I hope you are enjoying the turmoil you're causing everyone!"

She began to cry some more as Momma entered with a newspaper.

Vicki quickly turned her head to see her. She was too embarrassed that she lost her tears, which she rarely did, but she did not want lax Momma to get the wrong impression of her; for it was still early in her Oostburg tenure.

"You ok?"

Vicki wiped away her tears and nodded.

"I know it's terrible, Miss Weathers. I've known that young child since birth. Very sad when the children die, it's just not fair. That's what I tell God."

Vicki gave a small, sarcastic chuckle.

"You know what I tell him?" replied Vicki.

"What do you tell Him, sweetheart?"

Vicki paused for a slight moment.

"If I said what I truly feel, you'd close the book on me."

Vicki stomped out, missing the concern on Momma's face and a second later bumped into her boss, Ellis.

This startled Vicki.

"Ah! You scared the shit out of me."

Ellis smiled.

"Let me buy you a drink."

Fifteen minutes later, the pair arrived at Jesus Take The Wheel, the same bar that Vicki trailed Pastor Seth on the Friday she arrived. Apparently, it was the bar that people went to when they didn't really prefer to be noticed. It was just far enough for a few secretive Oostburgers not to be present but not so far as to kill a tank of gas.

Ellis ordered them each a beer, and the beverages came in a timely fashion. Vicki didn't speak much on the drive down. She was still slightly embarrassed from the bathroom meltdown that he obviously overheard. The drink felt great. A nice, cold beverage sliding down the gullet really helps when you want to forget the world. And Vicki wanted to forget. She wanted to forget she ever met Gabrielle Adjami or Gracie Adams, two teenagers that would haunt her forever. Even if she did find the killer, it would not matter. This would be lodged in her skull till she passed. She... hated god for that. She hated god for not protecting these girls. She hated god because she had to clean up his bungle. Yes, the killers are to blame. But if we are made in *his* image...

"So what's going on?" Ellis asked the daydreaming Vicki, who then spilled a little of her beer. Vicki took a swig to avoid that question. She really did not want to speak to him but she felt obligated after he almost caught her attempting to damage company property.

Ellis pursued:

"Tell me. This case has really rocked you."

Vicki took another swig.

Ellis paused for a moment and continued:

"I'm the one who should be freaking out. You're from New York City. You should be used to this."

Vicki finally opened up:

"And that's the trouble. I'm not used to this. That's why I left. To help Aunt Coralee, too, but I thought... life would be easier here."

Ellis smiled.

"Sorry, we didn't meet your expectations."

All of sudden, her words spilled; passing the downward flow of booze.

"My last case was exactly like this. Missing teen. Found dead."

A waitress tramped over asking about nuts, and a few minutes later the p-eanuts were there. Ellis cracked the shells, slowly devouring their souls.

"Two years of searching. Solved the damn case. I just... couldn't prove it. I took a leave of absence... but—"

"Yeah. I know."

Vicki looked up.

"You know."

Yes, of course, Ellis knew. Vicki was stupid to think he would not.

"I would not have brought you on without the background check."

Ellis took a swig.

"Man said you were great, you just lost your cool at the end."

Vicki shook her head.

"He just thought a change would do you good."

Vicki could not help but wonder about Gags. Maybe she should give him a call. He wouldn't believe the garbage she was in now. Ironic, you sprint halfway across the country just to end up in the same place.

Life sucks.

"The girl in New York... she looked just like Gracie."

A bulb lit up across Vicki's mind—why she did not know—but Vicki felt the urge to ask a stupid question.

"Wait a minute—when was Oostburg's last murder?"

"Fifteen years, I think."

Vicki paused. She didn't want to ask but she had to:

"And how long have you been sheriff?"

"Twelve."

Damn it. It was his only murder. She was under the authority of a rookie. This sheriff may have been almost the same age physically—late thirties maybe—but mentally he was a rookie saving cats from trees. He never had a murder... which meant he never *solved* a murder! As tired as Vicki was, she now realized she would have to essentially take over this case but make Ellis feel as if he was leading.

Damn it.

Ellis looked around. There was a pool table in the backroom that was beckoning his name. It was incredibly late but at this point, neither of them cared. It was going to be an all-nighter anyway.

The champagne bottle.

The smaller bloodstain in the back seat of the car; that was not the same size as the larger bloodstain on her head.

The purse with all her money and credit card remaining.

The phone battery detached from her cell phone.

The body under the car.

Like the balls on the pool table, all these clues needed a pocket to be put in.

After a solid fifty minutes, Ellis realized he had met his match. Vicki was a pool shark and while Ellis was not terrible, he was getting his ass kicked by a woman. This was rather emasculating.

Ellis lined up to make a difficult shot, and Vicki just laughed at him. The crowd had dissipated somewhat so it could have been worse.

By now, Vicki was a little buzzed to the point where she was more liberal with her words.

"I went to Raile's basement," she proudly admitted.

Ellis stopped mid-shot to decipher whether his new deputy had committed a crime.

"How did you get in there?" the sheriff asked, full-knowing that it was highly unlikely Vicki had obtained a search warrant.

"I busted in—well actually, not busted in. The window was opened, and I went through the door... I mean, window. Yeah, window. Window was open cause I opened it with a crowbar!"

Ellis stood there.

"You went to Raile's basement? When did you do that?"

"Oh, I don't know. Last week."

"You haven't even been in Oostburg a week."

"Oh. Well then maybe I don't remember."

It was last night but she couldn't remember that.

"Boy, you suck at holding your liquor."

Vicki continued:

"You are missing the point. He did not report me to the authorities which means he has something to hide."

"I am the authority," Ellis reminded her.

"Just make your shot," Vicki laughed as she smacked his ass.

Ellis looked down and smiled. He was not nearly as buzzed as Vicki was, thankful of his two hundred and sixteen-pound body.

He continued:

"So, now you feel by solving Gracie's murder... you'll solve this case and the New York one?"

Vicki laughed.

"But it's ridiculous, right? They can't be connected." She walked over to Ellis and grabbed his neck. Ellis was surprised at the move but at the same time was enjoying the goofing off. She got in his cheek and whispered: "Tell me I'm crazy."

"Oh, you're crazy," Ellis confirmed.

Vicki smiled and gently nuzzled her head on his broad chest.

"Shut up," she said, right before kissing his neck. Ellis paused, not sure of where to go. After about a second, he returned the kiss and walked her to his car, leaving the pool game unfinished.

Ellis burst through the door of his home, kissing his tall deputy vigorously as they attempted not to step on his dog, Conrad. Conrad had seen this a few times, his master bringing home a female to wrestle. It did not happen often but this wasn't the first moment, either. Being an agent of the law has a lot of stress that needs unwinding, and when you don't have a wife, you need to find substitutes now and then.

In comparison, this wasn't like Vicki at all. The stress of Gabrielle, finding Gracie, the seven or seventeen grown-up beverages, and the point that she hadn't had sex in seven or seventeen years overcame her. She didn't care right then and there. Even in her drunkenness, she knew she would regret it when the sun rose... taking that walk of shame, but at the moment... it didn't matter. She needed to relieve herself of the tension. The sex was good.

At about three in the morning, the two laid on his bed looking up at the ceiling; her thoughts playing ping-pong on a football field. She was already beginning to regret the sex. This damn move and all of a sudden she was a whore, like one of those one-night stand girls—actually, she deciphered, she was worse—she wasn't even on an actual date. She was a woman just chilling with her boss—

HER BOSS—the thought glared through her mind. Ellis was talking about something—she wasn't really paying attention—although it was strange that he was talking at all—most men after sex just need to fall asleep—anyway he was talking—and the word boss came about her and then she came to think of Gagliano. Ugh... Old Gags in New York. Gags was a father figure... but was quite out of shape and overweight. She then thought about having a screw with him and that made her gag a little—ha! Gags! That's where he got his name from—and oh my god...

"And my mother died—"

Oh my god... he was still talking! How in Hell's Kitchen do I get away? She thought. They were going to have to meet each other again, Gracie's killer needed to be brought to justice.

She certainly put herself in a tight squeeze...

Vicki closed her eyes briefly and remembered the car. Gracie's car.

She sat up.

"Tight squeeze!" she said out loud.

"Huh?" Ellis questioned.

"Tight squeeze!"

Vicki sat up quickly; getting out of bed to dress. "Get your damn clothes on."

24.

TIGHT SQUEEZE

About fifteen minutes later, they were in the holding place where Gracie's car was being worked over in great detail. Andrew Goldstein of forensics allowed them to enter when they showed their badges. The car had not been adjusted much, other than the maroon blood sample had been cleaned away to be analyzed.

"And you haven't touched the driver's seat?" Vicki asked.

"No, not an inch."

Vicki opened the driver's seat door to check out the seat.

"How tall was Gracie?" she asked Ellis.

"Gracie was five-foot-seven," he spoke before officially checking the file. "No, five-six."

"Let me see the photo of the car interior."

Ellis took the picture out and handed it to Vicki. The two looked at the photo. Deputy Vicki knew what she was looking for. Ellis stood as he watched his inferior teach him how to solve a murder.

Vicki scrutinized the driver's seat, from head to toe. Attempting to sit in the seat, she realized quickly that she wasn't going to fit.

"Mommy long legs isn't fitting in that seat."

Ellis began to catch on.

"How tall are you?" he asked.

"Five-six."

"Same as Gracie."

"The driver's seat is pushed up very close to the steering wheel. Now, why would someone five-six put their seat that close to the steering wheel?" Vicki asked hypothetically. She smiled as she licked her lips; answering her own question like a college professor:

"She wasn't the last person to drive her car."

Ellis nodded.

"We're looking at a five-foot-four driver."

Seth Adams sat on his sofa. He wanted to wait for the sun to rise and only had a couple more hours to go. Seth was tired but there wasn't any way he was going to miss it. A few hours ago, he lost his baby girl forever. The sun rising was, he argued, his Gracie saying hello to him. There wasn't anything he could do anymore. The pastor couldn't pray for her safety. He couldn't pray that she would come home. She was gone. He sobbed when he realized how little he had done to assist in that police investigation. He still had not told the police everything, but at this time... who the hell cared? Gracie was gone. Even if they found who was responsible, it wouldn't matter. Nothing mattered anymore. Nothing. Why didn't the lord protect Gracie? A whole seventy-two hours where she was gone and being prayed over by thousands of people. And yet, god, in his infinite wisdom and mercy, chose to sit back and do nothing. Allow this horrible nightmare to become a reality. Why? To—test his faith? Wasn't his years of service proof enough of faith? Apparently not. The greedy heavenly father wanted more. He wanted the blood of Seth's little girl. And he got it. God always gets what he desires. Pastor tried to console himself with the thought that Gracie was safe in Heaven; Seth tried real hard to wonder positively. She was now in Heaven, worshipping that same lord that could have prevented her pain and suffering. No. It just did not add up anymore. Nothing added up anymore. He turned and glanced at his bookshelf, overflowing with Christian literature, devotions, and Bible commentaries. What were they for? Nothing. A decoration in his house, a decoration in his heart and mind. It just didn't matter. Nothing mattered. He could have prayed a million prayers and it wouldn't have mattered. God's will was accomplished. For what purpose? Seth didn't know. He may never know. God took her... god stole her from Seth and will never give her back. And by god, what was Gracie thinking in her final moments? Was she scared? Did she suffer much? Did she even know her killer? So many questions went through Seth's brain. He looked over to the other couch to see his wife, lying there motionless; wide awake in shock. Perhaps she was having the same thoughts he was. But he knew that didn't matter either. Seeing her lying there still reminded him of Adam and Eve. Adam and Eve had the perfect garden, the perfect life, and then all of a sudden... things weren't perfect. Things were painful and hard. Suffering was born. Adam and Eve had a choice; they stole one piece of fruit and because they did all mankind had to suffer. *Why did they steal that damn piece of fruit?* And why weren't they stronger? Their punishment, and now Seth's, was to suffer—for all eternity. They stole one piece of fruit and because of that Seth's daughter was brutally murdered. It's their fault. Adam and Eve. They did it... then he remembered scripture and how god is the author of all things, and god is all-knowing and all-powerful... and then, for the very first time, humanity wasn't to blame... this was *god's* fault. He is the one who killed their Gracie. *God was to blame...*

Why didn't god stop them from eating the fruit? Why did he create the temptation in the first place? Why did god create hatred, greed, and envy? Was free will really love? If God is the author of everything, then *he must be the author of sin as well.*

Yes, Pastor Seth saw his god very differently now...

Physically, Evelyn was ten feet from her husband but mentally she was a million miles. She couldn't move or think and she didn't want to.

The clock struck five but Evelyn did not move. She did not bat an eye. She had to tinkle but it didn't matter. Who cared anymore, even if she wet the couch? She'd just clean it later but it didn't matter. What was the purpose of all this hurting and suffering? She did not have the strength anymore.

She stayed there, awake, urinating on the couch.

Down the road, Vicki made her way back home in a brief attempt to get an hour of sleep. As she walked up the porch, Vicki could smell the coffee steaming up from the mug in her aunt's hands.

"You're home pretty late," Coralee observed.

"Yes... Ellis and I have been running all over town," Vicki said. Which was mostly true, minus the hour-long sex break.

"I heard about Gracie," Coralee said. "Any clues?"

"Yes, some, but sorry I can't fill you in on them."

"Oh, now I see." Coralee got up and went into the home; seemingly ticked that Vicki would not share the clues.

Vicki yawned in confusion. She did not have the time or energy to deal with her dementia-ridden aunt right now.

She needed a catnap.

Vicki set her alarm for an hour and in ninety minutes she was up. A quick shower, a short drive to the local coffee shop for an extra-large mocha with ten pounds of sugar, and she was ready to go.

Hoping today would be the day they found Gracie's killer, she dug into her paperwork. She glanced over to the sheriff's door and noticed he was not yet in. She could not bear to see him after the night they had, but it was inevitable that they would speak. Maybe, he was so drunk that he wouldn't remember. Unfortunately, Vicki remembered everything.

Not that the wrestle was poor; on the contrary, it was quite good, although Vicki wasn't sure if it was good because Ellis was good in bed or if it was good because Vicki hadn't done it in so long. Much like if you are craving Chinese, and hadn't had it in years, then maybe any old Chinese restaurant would do.

A few minutes of daydreaming was followed by the sheriff tramping through the door. Odd that he didn't have a coffee, Vicki thought.

"Morning, Weathers," he said casually.

"Morning, Sheriff," replied Vicki, still unsure if he remembered. The last thing she wanted was awkwardness.

"Hey, you remember Matt Zimmermann?" he asked.

"Sure, he helped take care of Aunt Coralee the other night."

"Okay, on Friday night, I saw Matt jogging past my house, late at night. Past curfew."

"You send him home?"

"Um, no I didn't. I'm sort of lax on that rule."

Idiot.

"Anyway, I want us to get to his house before he goes to school."

By seven in the morning, Vicki and Ellis were at the porch of the Zimmermanns. It was bright and sunny and unusually comfy for October in Oostburg. They walked up the four steps, and Ellis knocked on Pastor Bob Zimmermann's door.

"The coroner called this morning. Three tidbits: Gracie passed sometime between 1AM and 4AM Saturday."

"Sounds about right. The last text came at 1:12AM. Unless she was already dead, and someone else sent the text."

"Second, that champagne bottle had two sets of fingerprints: Gracie and an "unknown"."

"And the third piece of information?"

"The night she died, she also lost her virginity."

And on "virginity", handsome Matt Zimmermann opened the door.

Matt led the officers into the living room, where they discovered his father biting into a slightly burnt piece of bagel. The high school senior was stuffing last-minute homework into his book-bag. With Gracie now officially gone, he was going to have to cram sixty-something pages of dialogue. Matt regretted the moment he accepted the role of Gracie's backup. Gracie rarely called in ill and so he never even began learning the role. Now he and his not-so-great memory had four days till opening night. The boy was hoping under the circumstances they would cancel the play, but so far, no luck.

"We were real good friends, sheriff. She was pretty," Matt declared, still fairly nervous of the chat.

"Yes, she was," Vicki said, finally succumbing to past tense. She pulled out papers.

"Care to read these over?"

Matt glanced at the papers, reading Gracie's text messages.

"Do they look familiar?"

"No."

"These are messages that Gracie sent to somebody, a boyfriend, probably."

"Not me." Matt took out his cell phone and showed his message history with Gracie. "Here are all my texts with Gracie."

Vicki and Ellis looked them over.

"You don't have another phone?" Vicki asked.

"No."

Ellis continued:

"Where were you Friday night?"

"I don't remember," Matt said untruthfully.

"Matt... it's Tuesday morning. Friday night was not that long ago and you're too young to drink. What did you do on Friday night?"

Matt looked at his father, perhaps for a spot of spiritual wisdom or an alibi.

His dad obliged.

"He was with me. We went bowling."

Vicki smiled. She knew a lie when she heard one.

"Did you go bowling, Matt?" she asked.

Bob looked at the female deputy disapprovingly.

"Lady, I am a deacon at the church."

Vicki turned to Ellis. After a little pause, the deputy continued her pressing:

"Matt, sheriff tells me you went jogging past his house on Friday night. The night Gracie... disappeared. Care to explain?"

Matt swallowed for a second and then answered, noticing the sweat drop from his brow into his eye.

"I jog at night."

"Sheriff says you were alone."

"Yes, I was alone." Matt looked at Ellis, who looked at Vicki. "I jog alone sometimes, after bowling. I didn't go anywhere in particular, I didn't do anything special."

He looked at his chess opponents.

"Honest."

Ellis looked at Vicki, silently nodding for approval.

"Thanks for your time," the sheriff told the Zimmermanns.

As the sheriff began to leave, Vicki shook her head, which Pastor Bob Zimmermann duly noted. Bob stared her down as if to play a round of chicken, in which Vicki backed off and left the premises with Ellis.

After hearing the front door close, Zimmermann turned to his son, infuriated.

"Where were you?"

Matt huffed past his father, apparently playing hooky today.

Ellis put the key in the ignition and turned on his car. Quickly, Vicki got in, slightly annoyed. This was a lead, perhaps not a huge one and it appeared her superior was just letting it go.

"We're not going to get anywhere if you don't press the suspects. But that's none of my business."

"They're not involved."

Ellis started to drive.

"How do you know? Maybe she rejected him, he went bat-crap psycho and killed her," Vicki suggested.

Ellis turned left and headed for the station.

"Because I've lived here more than two days. They're good people. Bob's a deacon; the kid's an honor student. His mom died last year from cancer."

"The way you work we'll have it narrowed down to no suspects real soon."

Seth stood in the shower, an hour after calling the church office to let them know he wouldn't be in today, as the pastor had quite a bit of thinking to do and maybe, if he was capable, planning his daughter's memorial.

He stood there, not bathing, not showering, just letting the hot, steamy water drip down his naked body. He saw the soap but chose not to use it. What the hell for? He might not go anywhere today anyway. And Seth had just lost his daughter, so it really didn't matter if Seth smelled good or not. Showering was not going to bring her back.

What was the purpose anymore? He looked up and saw past the ceiling and into that sky, in an attempt to reach his heavenly father who had abandoned him in his greatest hour.

Why, god, why?

Why... why... why...

Didn't she have more work on this Earth? Seth couldn't fathom any reason why god would take her other than god's own selfishness.

Why was Gracie not spared? It's not as if he were some modern man in Noah's time, who did not believe and therefore drowned in sorrow. He wasn't Noah's friends who laughed at him when he was building that huge boat.

Seth was Noah!

How could god abandon Seth? Seth, like Noah, had witnessed to his friends, telling his friends that judgment would come someday soon.

Little did Seth know judgment did come, but towards himself.

God was punishing Seth.

The water continued to drip down his face like some Chinese water torture, but it didn't matter. There was nothing that could torture him worse anymore.

His Grace was gone.

Evelyn slept in this morning. The pastor's wife did not desire to get up as she knew the tasks that she had lined up for the day.

She had to plan her daughter's memorial.

It was a memorial and not a funeral. The coroner did not want to release her body, as it was still an unsolved case.

Kids are supposed to plan their parents' memorials, not the other way around. Nonetheless, this was what she had to do today, whether she wanted to or not, Grace deserved a proper memorial. No, correction—she didn't deserve a proper memorial—she deserved a proper life.

Evelyn plucked up the phone to call the local funeral parlor. She closed her eyes and leaned against the counter, light-headed and dizzy. She wished she had siblings who would do this for her, but there was no one, at least not on her side of the family.

The funeral director, Dan Schumakker, was very courteous. Being a small-town, Oostburg was juicy for gossip, and so when Evelyn picked up the phone, she should not have been surprised to find that the memorial had already been set up—and paid for.

"Huh?" Evelyn questioned.

"That is correct, Mrs. Adams. All set up and paid for. Gracie's... memorial is tomorrow, Wednesday morning. Burial..." He paused. "I mean—will be when the authorities permit."

"I'm sorry—I don't get it."

"The person who called said they were calling on your behalf. I... assumed you had told him to set it up."

"I didn't."

"Oh, I'm terribly sorry... umm. Mrs. Adams, do you still want the arrangements?"

Evelyn paused. Who would have done this? Who would have done this without telling her? Surely Seth would not have done this. This was not a surprise party.

"Umm. Yes, that's fine." Evelyn didn't really want to set this up anyway. She was thankful and perturbed all at the same time.

"Okay, well we are all set. We will begin the gathering at ten in the morning and we'll commence the service at eleven. Pastor Zimmermann has agreed to do the service."

"Was he the one who set it up?"

"No, Mrs. Adams."

"Then who?"

"He just said: a friend."

"A man?"

"Yes, a man."

Evelyn stayed silent.

"I'm sorry for your, uh, loss, Mrs. Adams. We'll see you tomorrow at ten."

The memorial was all set forth, no questions asked, no bill to be paid. An anonymous donor, a generous donor... or a crazy person...

In Oostburg, she was no longer sure of her surroundings...

Matt Zimmermann paced back and forth in his bedroom. He was on page seven of sixty-five. It was going to be a long day for him; a long night. For the first time since Gracie went missing—he felt sorry for himself. He had a lot of studying to do. *"Why'd she have to die?"*

He looked in the mirror. He was a little like his dad after all.

Other Oostburg fathers were feeling the effects of Gracie's premature departure. Pastor Adams opened up his secret alcohol cabinet. The one bottle that he purchased was nowhere to be found. "Where is it?" he said to himself.

"Evelyn. Do you know where the bottle of champagne is?"

Deputy Weathers went home for lunch this Tuesday. No progress had been made and she needed a breather. She walked in to find her old Aunt Coralee panting and crying. Vicki immediately marched over to her aunt, who was shaking in Vicki's muscular arms.

"What's the matter?" Vicki asked.

"It was an accident!" Coralee sobbed. "An accident!"

Vicki stepped back to look at her aunt, who was wearing a t-shirt and her underwear.

"An accident?" Vicki asked. She took another glance at her underwear and noticing it was dry, asked again. "You had an accident?"

Coralee looked down at herself and felt her private area. Coralee smiled.

"I guess I didn't have an accident today..."

Dr. Ben Malachi got himself a coffee. He did not know what to do, just hearing the news that a female was attacked on Sunday. The female, Evelyn Adams, was fine due to being fit enough to fend off her attacker with a pair of scissors. *A remarkable lady*, he thought.

There were bigger issues though, as Ben Malachi sucked a cigarette. He rarely smoked; only when he was incredibly stressed and this was one of those moments. The news mentioned that the attacker would have a nice wound on their left arm and would be seeking medical attention. It crossed his brain when he was sitting with Wesley Demko that he was bleeding from his left arm towards the end of their discussion. Ben did not know if Evelyn and Wesley had ill feelings toward each one another. Everything fit together. That patient was unstable. Dr. Malachi knew that. Wesley had the bloody left arm. The question was "why". Why would Wesley do that?

The other question was—what would the humble doctor do with this information? Doctor-patient confidentiality trumped any psychiatric treatment. Should he speak with the sheriff? What if Wesley was innocent? Suffice to say, Malachi did not sleep well the previous night. His mind playing ping-pong and he could not keep up with the game. If Wesley was innocent, Malachi's practice would probably get shut down. Or if Wesley was guilty, and he was the missing piece, then perhaps Malachi would be praised—but even then, who would tell their darkest cold thoughts to a therapist who would scamper to the sheriff if the secrets got too dark? Either path, guilty or not, if Malachi spoke it would probably mean the end of his practice.

Malachi lit another cigarette. It was ten o'clock. He rarely called in, but he did today, canceling all his patients. With his mind in a tizzy, there was no way he would be any good to the five gentlemen he would be seeing today. He had a decision to make: turn in a probable attempted murderer and possibly finish his practice, or keep quiet, say nothing and perhaps more people die, perhaps Evelyn.

Ben looked through the phone book, scrolled down the page of last names, and dialed.

"Hello, this is Dr. Ben Malachi. Could we meet and talk?"

Sheriff Kirkbride and his new deputy entered Walker's office. The forensics expert had more results to share.

The autopsy confirmed the obvious: Gracie Adams died from a blunt force trauma to the head.

Not too much was learned: The bottle of champagne had two sets of fingerprints: the deceased and another set that wasn't in their system. That bloodstain was also of the deceased. The blood type was Gracie's, B positive. The blood on the back seat of the car wasn't enough to kill anyone so she was not killed in her car. The gash on the left temple of her skull indicated a right-handed assailant but that did not help much since most of the world is right-handed. She wasn't killed in her car, most likely.

She did have semen in her vagina, which was sent to the lab for testing. Everything downstairs was consistent with a consensual sexual encounter. Gracie was not molested based on the evidence, or at the very least she did not fight off her attacker, or her attackers. By the look of things, Gracie lost her virginity in the car, indicated by the small bloodstain. Other than the glaring slice on her head, she looked at peace with the world.

Walker did notice other fingerprints on the passenger's door, three sets of fingerprints, indicating that the teenage girl had some friends with her that did not wear gloves. One set of fingerprints—Gracie's—were on the driver's seat belt buckle. Three were on the passenger's side seat belt buckle. Big Mack's fingerprints—the sanitation employee submitted to a test as well—were on the driver's door but nowhere else. Two sets were in the back, Gracie and the unknown.

"No match, I presume?" asked Vicki.

"No matches, other than the sanitation worker and Gracie." Walker continued. "Whoever was in the kid's car is not in our system and has no criminal record. We're looking at a rookie."

"A rookie who doesn't wear gloves to kill a girl?" asked Ellis.

"Maybe the guy had no intention of killing her," added Vicki. "It appears that this was not premeditated but rather an act of passion."

Sheriff Kirkbride breathed in all of these thoughts and could not make anything stick together. Gracie had sex, she threatened to tell on the assailant, and so she was silenced? That's the only thing that made sense to Ellis.

"Two sets of fingerprints," Vicki said. "The best bet is to bring the family in to get fingerprinted."

"Vicki—they just lost their daughter."

"Yes. And I'm not losing this case. Bring them in."

"We did find the blood type on the scissors Evelyn attacked with. Blood is O positive," added Walker.

"Well, there's a start," Vicki said.

Ellis offered his hand to John Walker.

"Thanks for all your hard work, John."

"It takes a village," explained Walker.

A village... Vicki wondered...

"Hello, Dr. Malachi."

"Hello, Mrs. Demko."

"Please come in."

"Thank you," Malachi responded as the doctor stepped in the Demko hallway. Brooke gently shut the door and locked it.

"Can I get you anything, coffee, water?"

"Um, no, thank you. I don't want to take up a ton of your time."

"I see. So what brings you here, Dr. Malachi? Is my husband, umm, making progress?" Brooke smiled. "I'm sorry... I forgot. Doctor-patient confidentiality."

Malachi absently looked around. Not sure what he was looking for, he continued:

"Yes, there is that."

"It's a shame he didn't sign that waiver. Sad that a spouse feels the need to keep his close secrets from his wife," Brooke sarcastically smiled, trying to get Dr. Malachi to show his cards. "But you know. You know more than I do."

Malachi nodded.

"Perhaps I do, Mrs. Demko."

"Please, call me Brooke."

"Brooke."

"Come, have a seat."

"Well, I will," Malachi stated as he sat in Wesley's large grandfather chair. The doctor took off his fedora and placed it on his knee. Brooke noticed the good doctor was balding.

"So, what brings you here?"

"Brooke," Malachi sighed, unsure of what to say next. "Um... I—I don't know how to say this... but are you aware of a nasty mark on your husband's left arm? It's a pretty deep scar. Is there anything you know of?"

The wife stared for a moment, debating which side of the fork she should turn.

"I've never seen any mark, Dr. Malachi."

"He has this red scrape on his arm, someone obviously stabbed him and he was... avoiding my questions when I asked him if I could help."

"Well, maybe he doesn't like people prying into his life." Brooke paused.

"Sorry, doctor. That sounded rude. My apologies."

"We're all a little on edge right now." Malachi continued to look around, not seeing anything of significance.

"Well, the real reason why I am asking about the mark is that I read in the newspaper that Evelyn Adams was attacked Sunday afternoon and—oh, I'm sorry—did you hear of it?"

"Yes, I did. Go on."

"Anyway, umm. Evelyn is alright but she did attack her assailant and apparently stabbed her attacker in the arm. Wesley's shirt was a little red in the same area. And of course, I got a little concerned."

"Concerned?"

"Well, yes, Brooke. Actually, quite frightened... I don't know if Wesley did anything, and it is certainly circumstantial. I've... well..."

"You've...?"

"I've debated telling the sheriff."

"Sheriff Kirkbride?"

"Yes. I don't know what to do, and I was hoping you would be able to help me make my decision."

Brooke looked at him, quite unsure if he was threatening her with a blackmail request. *What the hell?* Why would a doctor need more wealth from a poor couple who are already in debt—and then it hit her. Maybe he didn't want money; maybe he wanted something a little more... personal...

Brooke looked at her husband's therapist in a different light. He was a married man with kids... but this certainly wouldn't be the first time a married man cheated on his spouse. She knew that firsthand. She was looking for a signal of what Malachi was hinting at. Ben was a very good poker player.

"What are you... talking about, Benjamin?"

"I'm talking about life and death, Brooke. I am not sure... but I think Wesley may be involved."

Brooke had three options:

She could pay him off.

She could blow him off.

She could... bump him off.

"I understand that." She wheeled over to him and took his hat off his knee and placed it on the table. "But... how do you want me to help with your decision?" She looked at him deep in both eyes. Wesley was at the video store... at least for a few hours.

Touching his knee, she asked:

"What do you want me to do for you?"

Ellis placed a call to Seth.

"Hey, bud. It's Ellis."

"Anything new?"

The sheriff looked over to his deputy, who nodded in approval for him to continue. Even though he was in charge, she was.

Ellis coughed.

"Hey, we were wondering if you, Evelyn, and Lainey could come down to the police station."

"Did you find something?"

"Well, yes we did. Could you come down?"

Within fifteen minutes, the remaining members of the Adams family were there, still not sure what was going on.

"Ellis. What did you find?" Seth immediately asked.

"Come into my office."

"Lainey stay here," Evelyn ordered.

Momma smiled at the little girl and offered her a piece of candy. Lainey rolled her eyes and watched her parents enter the sheriff's office, shutting her out again.

Inside Ellis's office, the two showed Seth and Evelyn the bottle of champagne that was found in Gracie's car.

"This was in her car, Seth," Ellis explained.

"There it is," Seth said.

"What do you mean?" Vicki asked.

"My bottle. I've been looking for it the last couple of days."

"This is *yours*?"

"Yeah, I bought it for Gracie's graduation. It was in my cabinet. Up until recently. You found it in her car?"

"In Gracie's car," Ellis said.

"Gracie's car? But she can't drink."

"You are right, she can't," Ellis agreed. "Toxicology reports came back—Gracie had some alcohol in her system."

"What?"

"Sorry, Pastor Adams. She wasn't drunk, but she had at least one, maybe two," added Vicki.

Seth shook his head.

"I never should have brought this into the house. Oh my God, It's all my fault."

Vicki noticed that Seth's spouse did not console him, so she took the opportunity:

"Don't beat yourself up, Pastor Adams. Kids... experiment."

The pastor looked down at the ground, submerged in guilt.

"Is there anything else?"

"Uh, yes. We're going to ask that you and Evelyn and even Lainey, submit to a fingerprint—"

"You want our fingerprints?" asked Evelyn incredulously.

"If you don't mind."

Vicki looked at Ellis. *If you don't mind? No, you are the sheriff, and if you want their fingerprints then they must submit. If they don't have anything to hide, they wouldn't be resistant!*

"Yes, sure, of course," Seth agreed.

"Even Lainey," Ellis said.

"Why?"

"Just precaution. We did find a couple of sets of fingerprints in the car," added Ellis.

"Well... my fingerprints will be there. I taught her how to drive recently," Seth confessed. "I sat in the passenger's seat."

Vicki predicted he would say something like that and even if Seth were lying, it was a believable lie.

"Mine are probably there as well," added the wife.

The three Adams family members submitted to the tests.

In a couple of hours, Ellis and Vicki had their answers:

Seth's fingerprints were all over the passenger's side and the bottle.

Evelyn's fingerprints were all over the passenger's side but not the bottle.

Lainey's fingerprints were not there at all.

With Seth and Evelyn being a match, that accounted for two of the three fingerprints on the passenger's side and the unknown in the back remained unknown...

Wesley Demko entered his humble abode late on this Tuesday afternoon. A quiet place, which he enjoyed. Finally, some peace and solitude that he could create. He walked into the kitchen to check the calendar—Brooke worked this evening. Perfect. He picked up the phone and ordered a pizza. Walking into the living room, he found a familiar fedora. Yes, familiar, but he could not place why it was familiar. Picking it up, he peered into the hat to see if there were a name or initials on it, which there wasn't.

The hat was not his own. Putting down the hat, he switched on the television to catch the news. On it, he heard that Grace's memorial was tomorrow. *Very quick*, he thought.

He wondered how Seth and Evelyn organized it so quickly...

Almost like they knew ahead of time...

Wesley walked up the stairs. He had a solid twenty minutes before the pizza would arrive, so he took a leak and got to work on his novel. It was so nice not having that nagging woman blabbering in his ear.

He opened his document and began to stare at the computer. He had the quiet, but not the ideas.

The kids needed him...

The daddy looked over to the picture frame of his family. He and Brooke. Nicole and Angie. Their children.

Their deceased children.

The two kids he was writing about were...

Wesley was not at home that evening. He did not know exactly what happened or how it started, how... long they suffered. The firefighters never figured out how it started. All of his thoughts were guesses; sad predictions.

The babysitter that night called in sick but being devout Christians, Wesley and Brooke trusted the Lord to watch their kids while they attended a Bible study.

The Bible study was hosted by Pastor Seth Adams at his house.

The sick babysitter was Gracie.

That was the day Wesley began to hate God.

That was the day Wesley began to hate Seth.

That was the day Wesley began to hate Gracie.

That was the day Wesley began to plot

his revenge...

25.

A TIME FOR EVERYTHING

Seth straightened his tie for no other reason than habit. Who the hell cared if his tie was straight? Gracie sure didn't care and that is who this day was about. Staring at himself in their mirror, Seth didn't know what would come out of his mouth today. Maybe scared of what might come out of his mouth.

Evelyn walked behind him—strange, he didn't notice the woman was there—and got a comb out of her drawer. Robotically, the wife combed her hair, not speaking to her grieving husband. There were no words for her either.

Seth walked downstairs and saw his other teen sitting on the sofa all ready to go. She wasn't dressed in a typical black get-up, but in a purple outfit that was far too short for a thirteen-year-old, in Seth's humble opinion. Pastor briefly considered challenging the child on this act of rebellion but decided against it. This wasn't the day to fight. This was a day of mourning. Remembering the scripture: "A time for everything" in the book of Ecclesiastes, Lainey would win this battle.

Lainey got up and followed her father out the door. Silently, the two sat in the car waiting for Evelyn, who arrived three minutes later in tears.

Seth took his wife's hand. Evelyn turned around to Lainey. No one smiled or spoke, just looked, as if to steal one final glance at the notebook before taking a test. Seth started the car and began the short drive to church. On the way, Seth thought of all the things he would normally be doing today; a normal Wednesday in October. Finishing his sermon. Visiting the nursing home two miles into the country. Beginning to prepare for the Tuesday Bible study.

Yeah. All those normal things went to the wayside now that Gracie was gone.

Matt Zimmermann paced around his bedroom. The show must go on, he had been told. All this time he could have been working his lines—even before Gracie disappeared—but he trusted Gracie to be there and he did not learn any speeches until after she was gone. Of the sixty-five page script, he had a line on about fifty-five of them, and he was up to page seventeen. He was screwed.

He left his room to catch his dad for a ride. Dad was not home.

Big Mack poured some orange juice and stepped onto his porch.

He was praying to see his niece walk up the steps and return to his life. He wasn't normally worried about her disappearing, since she left and returned four times already; plus she was nineteen, not really a child anymore. However, with Gracie Adams gone, this time his niece's disappearance was a little more concerning. The sanitation employee wondered if his niece had anything to do with Gracie. She had a temper and not many friends. Big Mack hoped Ivy would return.

He was beginning to worry...

Big Mack walked into her room and to his surprise, found a tiny, crumpled piece of paper on her nightstand...

Ivy's kidnapper, Charles Raile, had been up all night. He watched the news and read the newspaper. He saw that pastor bleed his heart out all over the news; he saw the wife, Evelyn, cry copious tears over what had transpired the last few days. There was something else that quickly happened—in Raile's heart.

For the first time in his life, he felt guilty.

He picked up the phone.

"Hello. I would like to speak to a pastor."

Brooke wheeled to the kitchen to grab an apple for a late morning brunch. Her husband Wesley was there, eating a small bowl of Fruit Loops.

"Hey, there was a hat in the living room yesterday—I don't think it's mine—do you know whose hat it is?"

The wife couldn't think of any reason why there would be a hat in the living room.

"No, why?"

Then she remembered.

"How do I look?" asked Aunt Coralee.

"Like an old woman," Vicki responded.

"Well, that's not a very nice response."

"You are going to a funeral, not the senior citizen's prom."

"You don't need to be butty."

"The word is cheeky, Coralee." Vicki corrected. "Let's go to this damn funeral."

Sitting in his office, Robert Zimmermann could hear the condolences and sobs of the congregation. He leaned back in his chair and for a brief moment felt angry that this hardship could very well benefit him. If Seth was so distraught he left the church, Robert would certainly be promoted to Senior Pastor, something that should have happened too many years ago.

He was so jealous of Seth...

Things were lining up nicely for Bob Zimmermann. The congregation must have seen Seth's outburst on Sunday as a sign that he couldn't handle tough circumstances.

Gracie's death was going to benefit him quite nicely.

Oostburg Community Church was crammed to the bounds for the first time this somber Wednesday morning.

Seth sat in the front row not wanting to say anything or speak to anyone. He saw his Evelyn standing by the casket. Gracie was not in the casket, nor was this an official funeral. Ellis said they could not release the body since the crime wasn't solved. This day was only a memorial service. Evelyn stood there and was crying, but she was social and accepting of her friend's words of encouragement. Seth didn't understand having a damn funeral when they couldn't even bury his daughter, due to Gracie being "evidence". He hated the fact that she was "evidence". She wasn't evidence. She was his daughter. Seth didn't want any of that. He wanted to do battle with god.

Looking up at that Last Supper painting—that he helped hang—he couldn't help but wonder what good it all did. He remembered the sermon of that lady cop—what was her name now?—and how she cursed the god... hated him. He couldn't help but wonder if all these many years perhaps, just perhaps, he was wrong. Maybe everything he knew about the lord was false. Maybe god didn't love. Maybe god was everything the critics of him said he was—or maybe, just maybe—

... he was never there at all...

He listened to his mind hum over and over again his favorite song of all time, *Cinderella* by Steven Curtis Chapman. Mr. Chapman is a Christian singer who wrote the song several months before his adopted little girl was run over in a horrible car accident. In an interview, Chapman said that the child was eager to meet God; was curious to see him. At the time, Seth was inspired by the singer and his attitude; the way he handled this horrific tragedy. Yes, it was admirable. The singer kept praising the Lord in the storm and he was... at peace.

Seth wondered if he could follow in this singer's footsteps. They now had this in common—they both lost their little girl.

How can a loving father let his children suffer so much...

The doubting pastor needed to know everything, and Seth needed answers from the sheriff and god now. At this point, he knew very little. He knew his little Gracie was hit on the head with something: a bat, a tool, a rock. Something hard enough to crack—god damn it—her skull. The killer must have been pretty strong as well...

Why was he pondering this?! This was not the moment to be playing Sherlock Holmes. As it says in Ecclesiastes 3:4: "A time to weep and a time to mourn." Seth needed to get all those feelings and thoughts away from his head, for Gracie, but also for himself. He needed to punch the pause button and remember...

The last dance—the last daddy-daughter dance. He remembered that night as if it were this morning, even though February was eight months ago. The pastor had a nice chat with her, sitting down at the table resting from an hour of dancing. Daddy and Gracie sat and watched other fathers and daughters doing the limbo. Seth remembered the girl's eyes and how beautiful and big they were. She was so pretty...

"Was".

He remembered this conversation, as he was listening intently. It was funny because he was so tired that night. He had a rough day at the office mentoring a teenager that went to Gracie's high school—what was his name?— and he was drained. The kid was angry cause he couldn't date someone. Very angry. But still, the pastor went to the dance. He felt like backing out... but somehow, he knew he had to go.

God knew too. God knew it would be the last dance.

Seth talked to Gracie, listening hard through the loud music, and asked her what she thought her future held. The youth indicated how she wanted to travel, spreading the gospel to many different areas. She did want a husband and three children to join her on the journey. He taught his daughter that the only purpose for living was to serve God, witness, and be faithful. Through good times and bad.

But that was not part of his plan. His plan was to have Gracie Adams beat to death and left under her car. His plan was to abandon her in her last moments as some sick bastard stole her young life. His plan was to sit back and watch this monster destroy his precious Gracie. God sat back and watched... *he was there*. God is always with you... God was there... God was there to watch... he watched her suffer... God watched her suffer...

That's all Seth could think about...

The pastor began to question things... stuff that all his life he thought to be true, now became questionable... did god love him? Did he love her? Did god love her when he watched her get beat to death?

Seth didn't notice, but the sanctuary had filled up. People lined the back row. Elderly, teenagers. Gracie had touched such a wide variety of so many lives. Seth didn't notice because he was too focused on that picture standing beside the casket. It was her headshot. Gracie had this friend who was a beginning photographer, and so Gracie was her first model. She was beautiful; a young Grace Kelly.

Grace Kelly. She died young and beautiful as well.

The photo was a sharp contrast to her current state. In this photo she was perfect; in the woods, she was pale and still. Bloated. She looked like a doll version of Gracie.

It was time to say good-bye.

Evelyn kissed the photo of Gracie. Bob Zimmermann gave her a full-on hug that lasted far too long in Seth's opinion. Evelyn came and sat next to Seth. Seth glanced over and saw Lainey sitting next to him—he had no idea how long she had been sitting there.

Bob Zimmermann began:

"Thank you all for coming. As the head deacon of this church, I'm heartbroken to begin this memorial. All of us loved Gracie. Her spirit; her optimism. All of us wanted to possess her grace, her generous soul. She was wise beyond her years. I did not know her as well as some so my speech will be brief. In times like this, our thoughts turn to the book of Job."

Seth lost his tears.

"Job's friends told him that he must have done something wrong to deserve this fate. And yet it was the Almighty at work in Job's life. I know; that hurts to hear. But God has a plan for this travesty. In this plan, all of us must learn to forgive the one who did this, to our very beloved Gracie Adams."

Seth zoned in and out throughout the rest of Zimmermann's speech, catching words here and there. A lot of those words made Seth feel like punching Bob in the baby-maker, but he wasn't really sure if it was the words of Bob or Seth's attitude. He glanced up and Evelyn was speaking. He had no idea how she got there.

"Most women say that the greatest suffering is to give birth to a child. I... know that's not true. The greatest pain is to bury one." A few minutes of his woman rambling and she was back, sitting next to him. He turned to her and she stared at him for seconds. He had no idea she was signaling him to be a man; stand up and say good-bye to his daughter.

He walked up to the pulpit. The final time he preached at that fundraiser, the last evening of happiness. The final night—presumably—of her short life. If only they didn't head to Chicago... it was his idea... she would be alive...

He looked out in the crowd, gathered his thoughts, and focused.

"I am trying really hard to... forgive... you."

Pastor caught eyes with a man in the back of the church.

Raile, knowing he was being eyed, looked around to avoid eye contact with Seth.

Seth continued:

"I know you are here. I just... know it. I don't know why you did it. But I know whoever did it is paying their respects right now."

Raile swallowed.

Vicki sat next to Aunt Coralee, towards the back, and fumed.

Pastor Seth was holding it pretty well together, she concluded, but it didn't matter. The deed was done.

She turned around and caught Raile standing in the back.

Raile returned the gaze and spoke:

"I did it, Deputy Weathers. I needed leverage against her folks."

Vicki's jaw dropped and she looked around to see the reactions of everyone in the sanctuary. To her cold surprise, they had not heard his confession. In fact, they were still focused on Seth's monologue.

Matt Zimmermann turned around from three pews in front of her and stared at her pupils.

"She rejected my love," he declared.

Again seeking confirmation from the crowd—and again not getting—she began to panic. She attempted to ignore them all and focus on the raised platform.

Holding the pulpit tightly, Bob Zimmermann zoomed in on Vicki and spoke:

"I wanted this."

Feeling dizzy now, she swallowed and closed her eyes hoping it would go away. She felt nauseous and almost threw up in her lap.

Opening both eyes, she saw Gracie sit up in that empty coffin—a bloody mess—the same train wreck that she was before they pulled Gracie out of her temporary grave.

"Please, grant grace to the one who did this," the deceased youth spoke.

Now fearing the worst, that everybody in the sanctuary was going to confess, she wanted to get the hell out of there. But when she tried to escape, Aunt Coralee grabbed her hand and looked at her.

"I did it, niece—but I don't remember!"

Vicki's eyes widened. She was not going to escape.

From the front pew, Evelyn stood up and turned around.

"She was fat and ate too much of our food!"

Her daughter, sitting next to her, followed:

"I wanted the bigger bedroom!"

The short guy stood next:

"She rented a movie two months ago and didn't return it!"

The paralyzed woman next to the short guy stood:

"I needed her ovaries!"

Even her boss got into it:

"I prey on young ladies and once I get what I want, I hit them on the head with a rock."

For some reason, that one hit home and she threw up a little, not letting it trickle out of her mouth.

Vicki hoped it would go away if she focused on the actual funeral at hand.

Then, the pastor himself looked at her.

"I did it, Deputy Weathers. *And you know why...*"

Vicki stood up and screamed.

"STOP IT!"

Turning their necks slowly, everyone and their grandmother stared at Vicki. She didn't even realize she was standing until Coralee tugged at her skirt. She slowly sat back down and the service was over minutes later.

Many congregants mingled around the lot. The weather was cool but it was actually pretty nice for an October in Wisconsin.

Seth began to doubt the argument: "it was not the end, but rather it was the beginning". And it hurt; it hurt like hell to begin to doubt the god that he called father for essentially all his life. The daddy he shared with many people throughout his life.

The father that let him down.

He peered over to Evelyn, who was being hugged by a couple of other ladies in the congregation. He could tell she was bawling. It was the worst day of their lives, and there was not a damn thing they could do about it. They couldn't pray. Prayer wouldn't take away the pain. He knew prayer wouldn't bring her back. It was over.

Seth turned to see Bob Zimmermann coming over.

"Crap," Seth mumbled under his breath. He really didn't desire to talk to this asshole right now.

Bob sat down next to Seth.

"If you need to, um... take a leave of absence, no one will think less of you."

Seth turned to stare at him. *Was Bob—trying to take my position? What a jerk.*

"It's perfectly understandable. I'm here for you, Seth. We're all here for you if you ever want to talk. I care about you."

Seth was not sure if Bob was lying or being genuine so he decided to take Bob on his word.

Walking away from Bob, Seth bumped into Vicki. Like a signal from god, a weight off Seth's shoulders needed to be removed. Seth needed to get these addictions off his chest, for the sole purpose of discovering what happened to Gracie.

"Officer Weathers—can we talk?"

As Seth gave her a small piece of paper, and his wife caught a little glimpse of this interaction, seeing Vicki look around and put it in her cleavage. Even through her crying, she knew there was something elusive going on. *What was that all about?* she thought to herself. *He's passing her secret messages at Grace's funeral!?*

The two walked their separate ways. Seth wandered off while Vicki found her Aunt Coralee.

"Why are we here?" her aunt asked her.

It wasn't a good day.

"Why are we here?" Vicki sarcastically chuckled and then answering her own question:

"Cause Jesus is on a never-ending coffee break. It doesn't protect anyone—it doesn't heal—it couldn't care less!"

"God is here—"

Vicki found it funny that even on her bad days Aunt Coralee could still praise the almighty jerk. Maybe you needed to be sick to do that.

"Big crap! If Jesus is not going to help, who the hell cares if it's out here?"

Coralee swallowed. She briefly remembered why she was there.

"You can't save them all, my dear. There is evil is everywhere. You can't run from it."

Vicki shook her head.

"I guess god can't run from it either!"

"Veronica—"

"My name is Victoria!" Vicki yelled and stormed off.

Walking about for just a few minutes, she ended up in the almost-empty parking lot. A few cars remained, but behind the side of the pastor's car, there was a little smoke coming from it off in the distance.

Worried that it may be a bomb, she hustled.

The little sister, huddled behind the pastor's car, was smoking a cigarette. Vicki scolded her.

"You shouldn't smoke. Smoking will kill you."

"Well, something will kill me... it might as well be these cancer sticks," the sassy teenager replied.

Vicki smiled as she realized the smart-ass little girl was right. Vicki grabbed the cigarette from Lainey, inhaled, and stomped the cancer stick out with her heel.

"I'm... sorry, Lainey."

"It's ok. Lots of people smoke. You caught me fair and square."

Vicki raised an eyebrow.

"About your sister. I'm sorry about your sister."

"God has a plan."

Vicki hated that reasoning but she wasn't going to start a battle with the little girl who just lost her big sister.

"I promise you. I will find out who did this."

"I hope you don't."

Vicki paused and looked at her.

"Why would you say that?"

"Sometimes, the dead need to bury their secrets. You keep digging and you may find that people aren't who they really are."

Lainey paused to gather her thoughts.

"Town like this. Nobody is perfect. Everyone has secrets."

Vicki knelt to the intelligent little girl.

"Do you know something?"

Lainey briefly paused.

"No. And that's what scares me. People are... different. Once you.... find out who they really are."

"Who's different?"

At the empty casket, Brooke struggled to wheel herself to Evelyn. With the fire killing her own children, Brooke knew exactly what Evelyn was going through.

"Hey. If you need anything..."

The ladies sat there silent for an awkward minute. Brooke touched Evelyn's hand, gently squeezing it. Brooke started to leave but got her wheel caught on a chair. Evelyn sat there motionless, oblivious to her friend's problem.

"Evelyn..."

Evelyn was silent for an uncomfortable amount of time.

"Yes?"

Brooke's eyes began to get glassy.

"Can we talk sometime? Alone, in private?"

Evelyn nodded.

"Sure. Give me a couple of days, and I'll call you."

"Yes, that sounds good. Love you, Evelyn."

Brooke hugged her and attempted to get her wheel detached. Evelyn noticed her circumstance and stood up to fix the problem. As she stood, Charles Raile stood in her view.

Evelyn's eyes grew with rage.

"What are you doing here?!"

"Offering my condolences."

Brooke watched her friend get in the face of this older gentleman and yell—she had never seen this side of her before.

"Get out!"

"Please, Evelyn. Hear me—"

Raile took out an envelope.

"I cannot believe you would show up here trying to get me to do a job—"

"No job—this is for you."

"I don't want it—"

"Please, take it."

Brooke noticed the pastor running out of nowhere, furious like he was going to kill this old man.

"Is that him?" Seth furiously asked his wife.

Seth pushed the old man, knocking him into an empty chair. He grabbed Raile by the collar and was about to open his mouth when he saw about ten of his friends watching him. Seth released him but it was too late; the reputation was already damaged.

Seth looked over behind Raile and saw the Old Man.

The Old Man spoke:

"That's not forgiveness, Pastor Adams."

"Not now, old man!" Seth yelled angrily.

Evelyn took a couple of steps towards her husband.

"Who are you talking to?"

"The old man over there! He's the one—"

Seth, Evelyn, and Brooke glanced around, as did the other seven or eight witnesses to the attack.

There was no Old Man.

Raile stood up and dusted himself off. He handed the envelope off to Evelyn and walked away. Seth took the envelope and opened it.

Astonished, Seth read the piece of paper—a check.

"A check for twelve thousand dollars," he told his wife.

Not believing, Evelyn looked at the check. It was real. Raile had given them quite a bit of money, and they did not have a clue as to why. Was this his way of confessing? And if so, why would he feel sorry? Why would he repent? What's different now?

"Gracie's dead?!"

Seth and Evelyn turned to see who made this insensitive remark.

It was Coralee Mentink, having a very bad moment.

26.

WHO IS DANIEL WATSON?

Ellis sat with Seth and Evelyn to discuss updates.

"The cell phone records indicate that Gracie had been texting someone with an unknown number, a pre-paid cell, for many months. We went back and read every text message. In one message, dated way back on the first of March was the name "Daniel Watson". Ring any bells?"

Seth and Evelyn looked at each other.

"Never heard of him."

"Classmate?" asked Ellis.

Two minutes later, Evelyn was digging through her daughter's last yearbook.

Stopping at Grace's junior year photos from that year, she saw an old photo fall out of the book. It was a photo of both her daughters at the Oostburg movie night a few months ago. June, she thought. She never saw the photo before, but looked at the photo now, Grace all smiles and Lainey with a sassy look on her face. *Why can't Lainey ever take a good photo*, Evelyn thought. Studying the photograph, she saw there were some words written on the back. She turned it over and read:

Lord, take care of my sister.

Evelyn choked a little at this, full-knowing that Grace cared for her little sister. It wasn't a public parade for attention; it was even in her private thoughts. How was Evelyn going to get through this terrible hurdle?

She searched through the pages, seeking the secretive teen "Daniel Watson", the last person to text her daughter.

Mr. Watson was nowhere to be found.

"See you Friday at 12AM is what the text said."

Seth shook his head.

"There's no way she would be out that late. I just don't understand..."

Ellis leaned in.

"It may be time to admit you might not have known Gracie as much as you think you did. "Daniel Watson" and Gracie had a date planned at midnight next Friday, which is tomorrow."

"No. This isn't her. Not Gracie."

"The coroner's report came back on Tuesday. I didn't want to say anything till after the funeral. She wasn't a virgin."

Seth stared at the floor. Not his baby girl. They had "the talk"—no sex before marriage. Seth knew he had planted that seed of knowledge firmly in Gracie's moral compass. He knew she would never do that...

"She had sex the night she died," added Ellis.

As horrible as the thought was, Seth spoke it anyway.

"It must have been forced."

Ellis shook his head.

"No sign of force."

Seth's phone buzzed and a text appeared. He read the message and hoping that Ellis wasn't spying, Seth got up to finish reading the text in private.

Evelyn returned, passing by Seth as he left to go to the kitchen.

"No Daniel Watson."

Speeding per usual, the pastor got to Jesus Take The Wheel in fifteen minutes. The sheriff's department had bigger fish to fry—like catching Gracie's murderer—in addition to Evelyn's attacker.

He looked around for a short moment and spotted Vicki in a corner booth. As he walked over, he continued to nervously look around to make sure no one from his congregation was there.

"Thanks for meeting me."

Vicki sipped her drink.

"Something to say?"

"I haven't been completely honest."

"I guessed that much."

The waitress marched up to them with two menus, but Seth absently brushed her off. He took a double stare as the waitress looked a little like Gracie. She really didn't but the pastor was beginning to lose it.

Seth poured his guts out.

"I—I owe a lot of money. Twelve thousand dollars for... gambling debts. I bet on a lot of things. Sports, a horse in Kentucky... how quick a drop of rain can

trickle down a windowpane. It's fun. More than fun. The thrill of winning the pot...
even the thrill of potential defeat is exhilarating. I win, I lose. Well, I lose more
than I win. I can't stop pulling that trigger. And now... I'm so in debt that I'm
holding church fundraisers to save my butt."

Vicki shook her head.

"Talk about the shepherd sending his sheep to the shears. This is why I d-
on't believe, by the way. Go on."

"We're all sinners, Officer Weathers."

"But not all of us are hypocrites, Pastor Adams."

Seth put his head down.

Touché.

"Why didn't you tell us that night?" Vicki pursued.

"Two reasons. That evening I heard Gracie's voice—I mean for the first
time—she told me it wouldn't be worth mentioning."

Vicki stared at him.

"Never a good idea. What's the second reason?"

"Uh. Ellis bet me five hundred dollars that I couldn't quit gambling."

Vicki's jaw dropped.

"Betting a gambler that he would stop gambling?"

She picked up her jaw and continued:

"I checked your bank account. It appears that every time you lose money,
your wife puts some back in. Coincidence?"

Seth had no idea this was going on. Was this deputy trying to say his wife
was the bookie? It made no sense! Why would she even do that?

"She does mail runs for Charles Raile. Every time she gets a gig, it is
right after you have lost big. Who is your bookie?"

What other information was Seth in the dark about?

Seth responded:

"I don't know." Seth shook his head. "Wait a minute... I'm not in debt
twelve thousand dollars!"

"Excuse me?"

"Charles Raile just gave us a check for twelve grand."

With very few trails to pursue, and things being dead ends, Ellis and
Vicki decided to try on Matt Zimmermann. For one, the young man had a rumored
crush on Gracie. Two, he was out later that night jogging, as seen by Ellis. Third,

Matt received her role in the play, *Twelve Angry Men*. The text from "Daniel Watson" went nowhere. Potentially, it was a code name but there were not many clues—at least none that Ellis could notice—to indicate who Daniel really was. Daniel Watson was not in the yearbook, nor was he a friend of Gracie's on Facebook.

Charles Raile was still the choice suspect, even if he was Seth's secret bookie, but either he had covered his tracks incredibly well, or he was in fact innocent.

So, the officers turned to their second-best suspect, high school senior Matt Zimmermann.

Ellis picked up Vicki and they spied on the Zimmermann house from across the street. They took Vicki's car because it was less noticeable.

"He gave Seth twelve thousand dollars? Ha. Raile hired someone to kidnap Gracie. Whoever he hired did this to her," deduced Ellis.

Inside, they could see Pastor Zimmermann on the phone. They could not decipher what he was saying.

After a trio of hours sitting there, the sun had gone to bed and Vicki was beginning to feel the yawns herself. Perhaps this was not the best night to go out. After all, not many teenagers go out on Thursday. Vicki thought it as soon as it popped in her head—the word "Thursday". Tomorrow would be a week that young Gracie disappeared, and despite having some borderline clues, they really had gotten nowhere. Tomorrow, Friday, would also be when that coy "Daniel" would be meeting Gracie at midnight. If only they knew where they were meeting, perhaps that would give them an angle.

By 9PM, the cops had gotten quite friendly, discussing everything from their personal lives to their taste in music to their taste in a mate. Interestingly, their sexual encounter was not discussed; Vicki was hoping Ellis forgot and Ellis was hoping the same. He did not want to be tied down. Likewise, she didn't want the reputation of being a "slut".

The conversation took a turn towards the cause and Vicki recalled the chat she had with young Lainey after the funeral.

"And the girl said: "Everyone has secrets". She seemed so sure."

"She's probably right."

Vicki playfully smiled.

"Oh yeah? What's your closet look like? String of girls hiding in your basement?"

Ellis kept looking at the Zimmermann window.

"You wish."

Vicki laughed and was about to say something before Ellis began:

"High School football. I was the starting quarterback... all four years. Anyway, senior year we were quite good. We made it to conference finals. That final game, the championship, this guy comes up to me—dad of the other team's quarterback—anyways—he comes up to me and asks if I wanted to make a little money. Fifteen grand to throw that damn game. Fifteen grand... well, it's a lot of money to a teenager. So I did. And in that fourth quarter, threw an interception. Cost us the game. No one ever knew."

"Why you do it?" she asked.

Ellis stared at the window, although he wasn't looking at it.

"Mom needed a kidney."

Ellis licked his lips.

"Died next year anyway."

Vicki saw him in a different light.

"You know who the other quarterback was?"

"Michael Jordan?"

Ellis looked at her to see if she was being dumb.

She smiled.

"Big Mack."

Seth walked into the bedroom to find his woman sitting up in bed. Just sitting. Not reading or writing. Or even playing on her cell phone or watching television. Just sitting.

"Where were you?"

Seth ignored this question. After meeting Vicki at Jesus Take The Wheel, he went for a joyride to clear his brain. Seth took off all his clothes and changed into his pajamas. The pastor had no desire to speak to the woman as if perhaps Gracie were the glue that was holding them together.

She continued:

"We are supposed to be a team, you know?! I can't help you if you don't talk—"

Just shut the hell up, he thought.

But she didn't:

"We lost a child! All you can think about is yourself! Maybe your wife could use your ears—"

And that was it.

As if she were the only one who lost a child?! He did not want to deal with her or his torment. He didn't want to tell her that he was to blame for Gracie's death—yes, *he* was to blame—Gracie had said this in the vision. He had no idea how much he was involved, but in some way or form, Pastor Seth Adams was to blame for his seventeen-year-old healthy princess dying under a car in the woods. He couldn't look at his woman, knowing this. Knowing that he had single-handedly stolen this daughter. Damn it all—if he only knew what Gracie meant by "*You killed me.*" Seth couldn't take it anymore. Forcefully, he propelled his dirty clothes in the hamper.

"Damn it, Evelyn! I loved her too! She is not only your daughter! She is *our* daughter! And I want her back!"

Seth threw the entire hamper and flipped it over.

"I'll kill whoever took my Grace!"

For the first time in their marriage, he frightened her...

Ellis tapped Vicki, who had fallen asleep leaning on her window.

Waking up quickly, she saw the kid leave his house and get in his car.

"Here we go," stated Ellis.

It was almost midnight by the time Matt Zimmermann was caught breaking curfew again.

However, this time, Sheriff Kirkbride would not be as lenient.

Ellis and Vicki trailed the good teen all the way to Milwaukee—a solid forty-five-minute drive, at midnight, on a school night. *Finally,* Ellis thought, *they were going to get a decent break in this case. What the hell could he be doing at this time of night?*

The pair got out at exit 76 and drove a couple of right turns before driving two miles. Matt pulled up to a small, hole-in-the-wall place called The Petri Dish, which from the outside looked very stylish and well maintained.

"Is this where Matt goes?" asked Vicki.

"He certainly didn't jog here last week," joked Ellis.

The sheriff and his deputy spied Matt as he walked up to the bar.

A large, black bouncer of about thirty-five hugged him tightly. The bouncer also slapped Matt on the ass.

"A bar on a Thursday," Ellis stated.

"And he's not twenty-one," Vicki added.

They got out and walked up to the door.

"Ladies first," insisted Ellis.

"Why, so you can check out my ass?"

Ellis smiled.

"I've already seen it," Ellis playfully said.

Damn, he remembered.

She smiled back. It appeared that the duo had become friends and even their random act of sex didn't ruin it. Both were content.

The big bouncer stopped Vicki.

"You sure you want to enter?"

Vicki smiled.

"Are you trying to say that I don't look twenty-one? Thanks for the compliment."

"Please, white girl, don't flatter yourself. You're old enough to be my mother."

Ellis chuckled, much to the chagrin of Vicki, who elbowed her boss in the gut. After giving him a cold stare, Ellis whipped out his badge.

"Props, cool."

"Ellis Kirkbride. Sheriff. Oostburg Police Department."

"Oostburg. Sounds made up."

"It's not."

"Whatever."

Ellis and Vicki entered The Petri Dish.

"Matt must have a fake ID for him to get in here," Ellis said.

"Or he has friends in high places," Vicki added.

Ellis and Vicki glanced around. They were minutes behind Matt but there was a mound of people blocking the view, dancing and partying at the top of their lungs. Vicki noticed that she was the only woman there and was getting quite a few odd looks. And the men varied in their colors, shapes, and ages.

A real... petri dish.

Except for women.

Ellis went back to the bouncer's comment.

"Props? What the hell is he talking about?"

Vicki smiled.

"I think you'll realize soon."

A man in his fifties eyed Ellis. Gent was mostly bald and graying behind the ears. Ellis gave him a weird look.

Ellis hoped they would find some clue in this bar that would link them to Gracie.

Vicki, on the other hand, knew this was going to be another dead-end. She could have told Ellis, but she was enjoying his reactions too much.

The two cops walked past a table of men playing strip poker. Four of them had clothes left to lose; the fifth player was completely naked except for one strategically placed sock. The fifth guy did not seem to mind and neither did the others.

"Well, I've never seen strip poker played without women," Ellis offered.

The men laughed as another one lost his undies.

The dynamic duo continued to search; Ellis mesmerized and disgusted all at the same time. On the other hand, Vicki was having much fun, seeing his various degrees of shock.

This may have been her favorite Wisconsin moment to date.

Another man smiled at Ellis.

"Why are they smiling at me? You're much hotter."

What an idiot, Vicki thought.

"Why are there so many flamingos?" Ellis asked.

The two continued to pummel through the blockage of male.

"*It's Raining Men*", the homosexual national anthem, blasted all over the sound system.

"And where are the chicks?"

A third man, a black one, came up to Ellis.

"Can I buy you a drink?"

Ellis gave the male a "what the hell are you doing look" and took a couple of more steps.

And there, in a secluded corner of The Petri Dish, sat teen Matt Zimmermann, swapping germs with a young male.

Ellis coughed but no one heard him.

"Oostburg PD," Vicki screamed as loud as she could. This startled Matt, who quickly attempted to hide his erection.

Matt paused and then had a change of heart. "I'm going to have to come out sometime. That closet isn't going to hold me forever."

Matt smiled.

"I dare you to tell my dad. It will ruin him."

Vicki gestured to Matt.

"All right. Let's go, coat rack."

The three left The Petri Dish and headed north up to Oostburg. Ellis gave the bartenders a warning to check those IDs better. Matt Zimmermann had a great false ID, from a friend in Sheboygan, a piece of information that was duly noted.

Ellis and Vicki drove, following Matt again.

"Maybe Gracie found out, and he killed her. Maybe Matt didn't want to disappoint dad the deacon," Ellis hypothesized.

Vicki smiled.

"I don't think he'd care if dad found out."

Ellis shook his head.

"Ok, so Gracie didn't have sex with Matt. And that brings us back to Raile and his man. Who is he?"

27.

IT DIDN'T MATTER ANYMORE

Seth got up this Friday morning not knowing what to do. Like many pastors, Fridays were his Sabbath. Working Sunday, pastors usually took Mondays or Fridays as their Sabbath, their "day off". Seth was a Friday pastor. He always enjoyed working his tail off Monday through Thursday, having two solid days off, and then preaching Sunday morning. It worked for him and his family.

He considered taking a short leave of absence, or even completely stepping down. Both options seemed appealing at the current moment. At the very least, he had till Monday morning to decide.

It was early, seven to be exact. The ladies were still asleep, and Seth was able to have his alone time with god. But, it was... different now. Gracie was gone. His alone time was no longer praising, but rather questioning. He had begun to feel as the female cop did, he had noticed days before. It was sickening that one tragedy—albeit a huge one—would make him doubt and question his faith of so many years.

Was he really that weak?

Or maybe he never believed at all...

Seth grabbed his Bible off the bookshelf to do some business with god. He wanted desperately to go back on the path of God when life was perfect; Gracie was here, taking far too much time in the bathroom.

God, he missed her.

Why did god take her? He could see her every morning from heaven. Why did he need her there? His perf—

Was she perfect?

She had sex. Underage, pre-marital sex. He taught her better than that, didn't he? He couldn't believe it, but Ellis said so.

Damn it... it doesn't matter. As if being a virgin would bring her back to life... oh, maybe it would...

She blamed him. According to her, Seth Adams was the culprit. But how could that be? He was in Chicago Friday night. There is no way Seth could've done anything. Unless he sped to Oostburg in the middle of the night, murdered her while he slept, and then drove all the way back? Why would he do that? Could he have done that? People sleepwalk all the time—could you sleep *kill*?

Good god—she said I was to blame...

I do not remember anything, he thought. *Did I kill my Grace? Why would I do that?*

He needed his Bible and opened to Genesis, where it all began.

Adam and Eve sat around naked, chilling out, eating whatever they wanted—except for that one tree. They stole that simple piece of fruit and now all mankind had to suffer and die.

From a pastor's perspective, it all made sense; it was fair. Adam and Eve sinned and therefore they needed to be punished.

But now, it was not fair anymore. What, god? You couldn't forgive your two children for stealing a piece of fruit? Why did you create the fruit in the first place? Why didn't you create your kids to be stronger? No, Adam and Eve did not look guilty anymore.

Seth began to jot down his thoughts:

Did God create a perfect world?

It may be hard to fathom that the Almighty Father would build great beauty in such a small amount of time. In six days, God created the sun, the stars, the moon, the waters, the planets, the animals, and the humans.

There was beauty all around. The plants were pleasing to the eye. The water was cool and clean. The sun was warm.

The male was created first, so the book says, and the Lord named him Adam. The book doesn't tell what the man looked like, only that the man was created in God's image. One can pontificate that the man was smart and handsome, but we really do not know. Adam was the firstborn of the Almighty Father, and Adam was loved, so the book says.

But Adam, the man, was lonely. And so the Father created a sister, a partner, a lover. The man decided that she would be called Eve, the mother of all beings.

She was beautiful. She was naked, as was the man, and they both felt no shame. The two frolicked in their beautiful space without a care in the world. They loved the Father, and in return the Father loved them, so the book says.

They were happy day-in and day-out. They hung and took care of the garden with no worry in the world. The two praised their Father and the Father was pleased, so the book says.

Everything was perfect.

But was it?

No. Life was not perfect, because God created a talking snake waiting to devour them.

In perfection, there would be no temptation.
In perfection, there would be no talking snake to tempt them.
In perfection, there would be strength to counter the temptation.
No, it was not perfect.
A perfect father created an imperfect world.
Why?
That's the toughest question men and women of all walks have been asking since the onset of time.

Did humanity betray God—
or did God betray humanity?

So, when a father places such temptation in his children's space without giving those children the strength to resist, who is to blame? And when the father punishes them for not having the strength that he could have given them, well, some would call that unfair.

If a father placed an opened jar of poison on his family's dining room table, and then stood behind their curtains as his children devoured this poison, he would not be praised for granting them free will.

He would be incarcerated for negligence.

Two naked people stole one piece of fruit, and so all mankind was damned to Hades. Man had to work; woman had to give birth, so the book says.

The father could have easily given them the strength to resist.
The father could have easily not created the tree or the fruit or the snake.
The father could have easily been more forgiving.
No.
The children never had a chance.

They were set up to fail...

He skimmed ahead to Noah—he was obedient and all... but the lord decided he was going to send rain to drown everybody else for their transgressions. What once were lessons of love and obedience turned into an allegory of hatred and massacre. God drowned his children—yes *HIS* children for disobeying. Under this new theology, Seth and every other parent had the right to kill their kids if they talked back, sassed, or any other act of rebellion. God no longer loved; he tortured. And he killed—he drowned his disobedient children. He gave humanity free will and then killed them for using it. That's not unconditional love; actually, it's the opposite.

He flipped a third time...

Lot's wife—turned into a pillar of salt for "looking back"... Wow, God, you can't forgive shit!

Seth studied those scriptures for more than thirty years. And for the first time saw them in a completely different light...

They were terrifying...

He asked himself—does it matter? Does it even matter at all? His years of service and obedience—why?

He skimmed Isaiah 64:6:

> *"All of us have become like one who is unclean,*
> *and all our righteous acts are like filthy rags;*
> *we all shrivel up like a leaf,*
> *and like the wind our sins sweep us away."*

So our good deeds are like filthy rags? So... god, if you are not going to appreciate our efforts, why serve you?

What was it for? So, God, you're going to kill my daughter anyway, then why serve you in the first place? Did I waste my life?

Did it matter what my resume looked like? Did it ever matter that I prayed, served, witnessed, and was mostly obedient? All of these years... I could have been partying, drinking, or anything...

No, nothing mattered anymore... obedience be damned! I'm going to live a little before I die, he thought to himself.

And he did.

He didn't have any alcohol in the house, the only bottle they had was being saved for Gracie's graduation. *She was drinking with...?* The bars were not open this early. Sure, the pastor could go to any convenience store and pick some up, but he decided he didn't want to even leave the living room... he just wanted to do the wrong thing, or maybe, maybe it wasn't wrong... maybe it was just... a different way of living...

The pastor began to play with himself. "*It Didn't Matter Anymore*", would be the current chapter of the section of his autobiography. After he finished, he cleaned himself up and went out in the backyard. The weather was still decent, a little chilly. The man thought of his next step.

Seth looked around at his backyard. He walked to the front, side-stepping a big rock that always made him trip—but to his surprise, the rock wasn't there. *No matter*, he thought. Nothing mattered anymore.

Now he sounded like Wesley...

Seth took out his cell phone and dialed. The pastor had his voicemail message all planned, but to his great surprise Bob Zimmermann picked up his office phone.

"Seth?"

"Uh, yes... Bob. Surprised to see you're there this early..."

"Well, someone has to be here."

Dick.

"How can I help you, Seth?"

"Well, I, uh, decided to take your suggestion."

"Oh?"

"I am going to take that leave of absence you recommended."

Seth could picture Bob's wide grin over the phone.

"Really?"

"Yeah. I got a lot of business to do with god."

"I understand..." Bob paused to pat himself silently on the back. "And, how long you thinking?" Bob asked as he valiantly flipped through his calendar.

"Oh, I don't know, really. A month, a year. Play it day-by-day is my new motto."

"That sounds great." Bob was already outlining the next fifty-two sermons. He was finally in command of the ship.

The Interim Senior Pastor Robert Zimmermann continued:

"You take as long as you need, friend. Remember, the congregation supports you and your family in this time of great difficulty."

He did know the right things to say, but Seth knew Bob was lying, or at least did not mean it.

"Ok, Bob. Take care. I may come on Sunday, I may not."

"You do what you need to do. Call me if you need anything."

"Bye, Bob."

"Bye, Seth. And take care."

And they hung up.

Seth could now relate to Wesley since they both lost a child. *"Perhaps he could mentor me!"* the former pastor thought to himself. He laughed as he thought this. Wesley was a crazy little bastard—Wesley was a real bastard—he never met his father. Oh... Seth could not remember the last time he used such strong language. Again, it didn't matter that he used coarse language anymore. God took his girl. No... nothing mattered anymore. Wesley felt that way too. Poor Wesley. Trapped in his stupid damn story. He couldn't mentor a fish on the mainland to jump back in the ocean.

But somehow Seth knew today...

He needed Wesley...

Midnight Friday had come and gone, with Vicki and Ellis not quite really knowing who or where Gracie was going to meet.

"12AM..." Vicki said to herself. It was interesting that there wasn't a location in the text, nothing but a time. Obviously, whoever Gracie was meeting, that someone knew the location. Gracie received the text early Saturday morning, so it wasn't meant for the Friday she was last seen.

And who was this "Daniel"? There was no Daniel in the yearbook or even in the school. There was not one Daniel Watson in the entire phone book, either. Only one Watson, a Michael Watson, who was called and had no idea who Daniel Watson was.

And the light switch turned on.

Vicki remembered the newspaper this morning, how Big Mack had received a reward for all his hours volunteering. "Big Mack" was a nickname for McKenzie. Vicki grabbed the newspaper off Penny's desk and stared at it. *McKenzie—Watson.* Big Mack was McKenzie Watson—same last name as the inconspicuous Daniel.

The one who found her earring...

The one who found her car...

Ellis and Vicki turned to one another; both incredulous that they did not make the connection before.

"Ellis? Big Mack Watson!" Vicki exclaimed.

"I never knew his last name; he was always just Big Mack."

Within minutes, they were pounding on Big Mack's door. He was not home, so they guessed he would be on his route.

After one call to the department of sanitation, they were able to locate Big Mack halfway through his route.

"Big Mack Watson?" asked Ellis.

"Yes?"

"May we have a word?"

"Sure, any progress?"

"Your last name is Watson, correct?"

"Yeah."

Vicki stepped in.

"The night Gracie disappeared, she received phone messages from a Daniel Watson." She paused. "Do you know a Daniel Watson?"

"Well, my niece—her name is Danielle Watson."

Ellis was bewildered.

"I thought your niece's name was Ivy?" he asked.

"Danielle is her first name. But she went by her middle name Ivy because she liked it better."

Vicki was equally confused.

"Evelyn Adams checked the yearbook—your niece wasn't in it."

"No, for safety reasons I don't allow for her to do that sort of thing."

"Why?"

Big Mack frowned.

"Ivy's dad, my brother Andre, abused her. I tried to keep her as safe as possible. That's why I didn't allow her to get in the yearbook. Also why we're not in the phone book. Andre doesn't know where his daughter is and I'd like to keep it that way."

"Where is she now?"

"Ivy's gone."

"Gone?" Ellis and Vicki asked at the same time.

"Gone. She left a few days ago."

"You never reported her missing?" asked Vicki.

"She left a note. She's alright."

"May we see that note?"

Ten minutes later, the three were in the young lady's bedroom, reading the letter.

Uncle Mack,
I've decided to leave town.
Please know I always appreciate everything
you done for me.
Ivy

"She's nineteen, Ellis. An adult. She can leave if she wants to."

Vicki took over.

"Did she know Gracie?"

"Everyone knew Gracie."

"Did she like Gracie?"

"She was... jealous of her."

"In what way?"

"Every way. She wants to be just like Gracie, but Ivy is stubborn; she'd never admit it."

"Jealous."

"Yes, Mme. Jealousy can be very dangerous."

Danielle Ivy Watson was taken the same day as Gracie. Charles Raile enticed her into a free ride that Friday afternoon; shoving her into the elusive passageway. There the girl remained, for a couple of days, before Charles Raile had his lackey, Cody, drive Ivy to her new owner. Raile made a pretty penny off Ivy since this particular client in Missouri enjoyed "dark meat".

After chatting with Ivy for a long stretch, they crossed into the eastern part of Iowa when it dawned on him—this wasn't the life he wanted. The man knew what he was doing was wrong; and so one moment, as they were staying in a motel in Davenport, Cody made a change.

"I can't do this anymore," he explained to the older teenager. By that point, Ivy had given up all hope of ever having a dream again; she was so despondent that she knew this life would be that of a sex-slave until she was beaten to death or until she got too elderly to be of any use. Ivy, that fighter, had given up. Locked away in a closet for a few days can destroy someone mentally.

Cody took her by the hands and told her she would not be sold. He would buy her freedom and take her somewhere cut off from Charles Raile and Mr. Horn-Dog Missouri. He told her to write the note, and they placed it in her room on their way out west.

Instead of heading southwest to Nixa, Missouri, he decided to head northwest. Cody had a cousin in Duluth, Minnesota. As they were driving, they rested along the way. It was at this rest joint that Cody decided:

"I am going to kill Charles Raile."

It was the only thing to do.

Stealing Ivy from Raile's clutches was not going to protect those other young ladies from the exact fate that Ivy would have succumbed to had it not been for his valiant save. No, the evil must be punished. He had dodged the law once or twice in the south but skated out of it. Raile had sold thirty-three girls into sex slavery in the last nine years all across America. Eleven of those girls Cody worked on.

Until now...

Ivy was different. Like those others, she kicked and screamed but eventually gave up. The difference was that when she gave up, it pulled at Cody's heart. If Ivy wasn't going to wrangle for Ivy then who would?

Cody. Cody would.

They made the journey back to Oostburg. It was dangerous cause it was still daylight this Friday, one week after Ivy and Gracie disappeared.

Cody pulled up to Raile's home. The young crook had a revolver in the glove compartment, a gun that he never used. This would be his very first shot.

Ivy looked at him and touched his hand. She was not sure anymore; killing would be just as criminal as selling women. They would be wrong as well, but if Raile were killed, then he couldn't be punished for his crimes.

The two sat there for a while, unsure of what to do.

Cody and Ivy made their decision.

Quietly, Cody walked into Raile's home. From the distance, he saw the old bastard sitting in his recliner, watching the Andy Griffith rerun.

Cody received the shock of his life when he saw another gentleman, standing over Raile.

The other man had a gun, too.

Raile sat in his chair, his conscience more at peace than ever.

He paid and arranged for the memorial, he even had an appointment to sit down with Pastor Zimmermann on Sunday after the service. Charles Raile was planning on turning a new leaf.

Charles Raile had always wished for a life like that, a childhood where he could be Opie and go fishing with his dad.

He never had that...

Ivy heard the shot and closed both eyes. Cody saved her, or maybe there was some Lord higher being, or whatever. Whatever it was, she was fine. She wasn't even raped. She remembered how Gracie used to tell her all about how the God was so good. Was it possible Gracie was right all this time?

Ivy picked up her cell and dialed. Getting his voicemail, she was about to speak when all of a sudden Big Mack dialed in. She stopped leaving the message and picked up her uncle.

"Hi, Uncle?"

"Hey, Ivy! How are you?"

"I'm fine, Uncle Mack. Just fine."

"Where are you?"

She paused. She didn't want to say where she was, waiting for her sort-of boyfriend to finish killing her abductor.

"Iowa. My... friend and I are here. I left you a note."

Big Mack was so relieved to hear his niece's voice that it didn't matter she was leaving.

Ellis indicated he wanted to speak with her and Mack handed him the phone.

"Hello, Ivy. This is Sheriff Kirkbride."

Crap! How did he know already?!

"Yes, sheriff?"

"I just wanted to confirm that your name is Danielle Ivy Watson."

"Yeah, so?"

"Did you text Gracie saying you would meet her at 12AM Friday?"

"No, G and I weren't friends... I don't even think she knew my number."

Vicki chimed in.

"Did she know your first name?"

"Um—yes, I did tell her Ivy was not my real name."

And at that moment, Cody ran back into the car and began to drive off.

He whispered: "Who is it?"

"The sheriff," she whispered back.

Cody's ice-cold blue eyes bulged with fear. He sped a little.

"Look, I'm off now."

"You never texted Gracie?" Vicki hammered once more.

"Never," Ivy said as she clicked the phone.

Cody and Ivy were on their path to happily ever after, Bonnie and Clyde style.

Vicki sighed. Another dead end.

"The text message records say Gracie texted Daniel Watson," she said.

Ellis took out the phone records, and Big Mack looked at them. "It looks like Gracie was dating Daniel Watson," Big Mack said. The cops, bewildered again that there were two names so closely matched. Could it be a coincidence...?

"Crap. Nothing again," Vicki stated in frustration.

"So, what is the thought, if you don't mind me asking?"

The sheriff glanced at his deputy, who shook her head no.

Ellis divulged anyway:

"It seems as if our prime suspect paid someone to take Gracie, but we have no proof anywhere."

"And you suspect this guy, his partner or whatever, kidnapped and killed Gracie?"

"Off the record, yes."

There was a brief pause before Big Mack changed the subject:

"Are you going tonight?"

"Where?" asked Ellis.

"Are you going to 12 A.M.?"

Slowly, Vicki and Ellis looked at each other—12AM?

"What are you talking about—*going to* 12AM?" asked Vicki.

"12AM, midnight?" asked Ellis.

"No, no, not midnight!" Big Mack chuckled. "The high school play, *Twelve Angry Men*—12 A.M.?"

"12 A.M.— the play, of course!" Vicki said out loud.

"My God..." Ellis licked his lips. "Gracie was meeting Daniel Watson at the play tonight! Not midnight!"

"Which mea—thank you very much, Big Mack—you cracked a clue for us," stated Vicki.

Vicki and Ellis hurried back to their car and sighed some relief.

"We have to go to that play tonight," confirmed Vicki.

"Damn it," said Ellis. "I hate plays."

28.

A COUPLE OF LUNCHES

Seth made good on his objective to take Wesley out for lunch this Friday afternoon. He read the papers, farted around on the internet, ran a couple of errands, and showered. So, some pizza was in order. He earned it.

The pastor drove up the fifteen miles from Oostburg to Sheboygan's northern side, where Wesley was employed at the local video store. It's funny, Seth thought, because he never actually called to see if his pal was working. It was quite possible today was his day off.

But it was not and Wesley was standing at the cash register bored as hell.

"Wesley, give me a second," Seth spoke to him.

"Sure."

Seth walked around the video store for a good ten minutes. He was indecisive in his selections today, but once he saw the movie, *Thy Neighbor*, Seth knew what he wanted. *Thy Neighbor* was an independent, Christian thriller about a minister bothered by a creepy and potentially dangerous neighbor. The premise of the film was how do you serve God—and man, for that matter—when the one you are trying to help could be out to harm you? Somehow, it hit home and he wanted to check it out. In addition, he picked up a chick-flick for his wife. He did not know what he grabbed but it had Sandra Bullock on the cover; and what man doesn't like Sandra Bullock?

Seth walked to the counter and laid the DVDs down.

"Hey, Wesley."

"Seth."

Wesley was not incredibly pleased to see Seth. Besides the humble Dr. Malachi, Seth was his other mentor. Come to think of it, he had not seen Ben since the appointment on Monday. The shrink had a bad habit of keeping in touch with his patients.

Wesley began to check the videos out of the system.

"*Thy Neighbor.*"

"You've seen it?"

"The guy who played the neighbor is overrated."

Seth ignored the critique. He was not really here to rent movies.

"How you doing? I've been worried about you."

Damn, Wesley thought. *He wants to chat.*

"You've been worried about me?" Wesley thought it surprising that a man who just lost his daughter would even care about his friend. Seth really was a good person, but Wesley had no desire for conversation.

"I am still a pastor," Seth told him, even though he did not feel like a pastor anymore. At the current moment, the switch was turned off.

"Aren't you on break?"

Seth handed him a credit card.

"Yes, I'm taking a few weeks off to get my brain back."

Wesley looked at Seth intently:

It will never be back, Wesley thought to himself.

"Can you do lunch?" Seth asked.

Wesley's boss, Krissy, overheard the conversation.

"Go for it. Take your half," she said.

Wesley rolled his eyes, not sure if Seth caught them rolling.

Seth and Wesley walked the forty-second journey over to the pizzeria, which almost shared a parking lot with the video store.

The place was crowded; with many North High teens devouring pizza before their next class. Seth and Wesley actually had to wait for a table, something that seldom happened. Usually, Wesley went, got a couple of slices, and headed back to his car. He hated being in crowds. He preferred the hypocrites in his novel to the hypocrites in the actual world.

Minutes later, the two men were able to bag a table in the corner by the window, perfect for a cozy chat.

They shared a pie, half just cheese for Wesley and the other half pepperoni for Seth. Each man ordered a soda.

Seth remembered it was he who initiated the lunch meeting back on Friday, last week before Gracie disappeared. Seth asked Wesley to lunch to help work on his depression. Now that the two men had a bit more in common, the tables had turned, and now Seth just might get some counseling from Wesley.

"So it's been a while. How you doing?" Seth asked.

Wesley took a bite. The pizza was nice and hot.

"Umm... the same. Same questions... not many answers. Yeah... not much different."

Seth gave an understanding simper. It was a shame that he now had the same questions. Wesley's kids died in a fire. Had Seth not encouraged him to be at the Bible Study, Wesley would have been home. He would have died for his kids.

All these signals added up to a bigger picture: where is god when you need him the most? And the other big question: If god was not going to be there when you need him the most—the real question remains... do you sincerely need him?

Seth was pissed to hell that he now had to tackle these new, hard questions. He could have wrestled them decades ago before he had spent the first half of his life serving.

Depressed, Seth slurped his drink.

"Yeah, I understand. More now than I did before."

There was an awkward pause as the men ate their pizza.

Brooke wheeled herself the mile through Oostburg to the Adams' residence, where she was able to hoist herself up the four stairs of the porch and text Evelyn.

She texted her: "I'm here."

Evelyn got the message, befuddled. Brooke never called to say she was coming over. Normally, Evelyn wouldn't care. She was a social butterfly. But now...

Evelyn opened the front door to find Brooke sitting on the porch. As Brooke crawled inside, Evelyn retrieved her friend's wheelchair.

Seth no longer felt like having a deep meaningful conversation; yearning for the small talk that would calm him down.

Seth knew how to get Wesley to loosen up. It was the one thing he seemed to care about these days.

"How's the story coming?"

Wesley perked up. He enjoyed thinking about his novel, but he did not enjoy talking about it.

"My novel is about seventy pages in."

He lied.

Evelyn was smearing mayonnaise on the turkey sandwich for Brooke, who was emptying her heart.

"Are you sure?"

Brooke blew her nose.

"Yes, I believe so."

She looked at Evelyn; not fathoming why her husband would assault Evelyn. She chuckled. Her husband was such a jackass. Only Wesley would attempt to kill someone and fail. That is how she knew he didn't murder Gracie. If he did kill her, she would be alive today.

Evelyn finished making Brooke's sandwich and began to make her own.

"But I don't get it. I thought you both were... doing ok," Evelyn lied. She knew they were struggling, but she didn't want to hurt Brooke any more than Wesley was hurting her.

Brooke took a bite. The wife was pretty sure he was cheating. She was also pretty sure Wesley tried to kill the woman who just made her a sandwich. There were only three people in Oostburg who knew what Wesley had done: Wesley, herself, and Dr. Ben Malachi. And Brooke made the hard choice to see that Malachi kept quiet.

"No. No, Evelyn. We are just used to playing pretend... I believe everyone pretends. Some people are just better at it than others."

That hurt Evelyn.

"It's about aliens?"

"Yeah. Big, brown ones that bite your neck, and then you turn into them," Wesley lied. He was getting quite experienced at lying, based on all the lies he had told the woman. At times, Wesley enjoyed lying. One time he did it for no reason other than to "practice". He once told the woman he went to McDonald's when he really went to Burger King; just to see if he could get away with it. He did.

Wesley was quite the sick bastard. Having your almighty lord kill your babies can do that to a man.

"How's Brooke doing?"

Damn. He went there.

"She's fine."

Brooke bawled. Her husband was: a liar—definitely, a cheat— probably, an attempted murderer—highly likely and a killer—maybe.

"He never... tries anything anymore. He is not interested in sex. Maybe cause I can't get pregnant again; maybe cause of the accident. He really wanted kids."

She wanted more; he could not muster up the strength. He felt trapped—he did not want more children, but she did. Wesley just wanted to curl up and die, not make love. They were in different places yet trapped in the same cage.

"Still... that's no reason to have an affair. Have you confronted him?"

Brooke shook her head.

"No, I haven't. I'm afraid..."

"Of what?"

Brooke paused.

"Wesley."

"Why doesn't he do that?" Wesley asked in between nibbles. He was almost done with his side of the pie.

"Why...?"

Wesley wiped his mouth on his sleeve.

"Why doesn't he give us what we want?"

Seth sat back.

"Well, usually because He has something better for us. If God had given me the first girl I ever prayed about, I would have never married Evelyn. God turned down my prayers for that first girlfriend so that He could say yes to my prayers for Evelyn."

Wesley spoke nonchalantly:

"Maybe I shouldn't have prayed for Brooke."

Seth was taken back by that comment.

How can you say that about your wife?

"He doesn't love me anymore. Maybe he never did," Brooke deduced.

"You did marry quickly."

They dated for six months and were engaged for another five. Within the year, they were married.

"We both wanted kids; had lots in common. Never knew that I would have trouble getting pregnant again. I didn't have any problems getting pregnant before. That's probably why he's seeing another woman... so he can finally have his baby."

What Brooke didn't know is that her husband really did not desire any more babies. He had two; they passed, and with their death died his desire for children. Actually, his desire for life died; his desire for Jesus died and his desire for his marriage died as well. All Wesley had was his novel. He was going to finish and make his exit.

"I'm so sorry, Brooke."

Brooke kept going. She gave a subtle hint:

"Probably someone younger. Who can walk."

Evelyn didn't get it.

"You should always pray for your wife. That's what Jesus calls us to do."

"What if you married the wrong person?" Wesley challenged.

Never hearing that argument, Seth licked his lips. Oostburg had a very low divorce rate. In his many years of preaching, Seth had married thirty-six couples; Wesley and Brooke being one of them.

Not one divorce.

"I'm not sure that's possible."

Wesley pushed harder.

"You make a mistake; pick someone who is not a good match. That's what I did."

Seth sat back; bothered by the conversation.

"Thanks for the lunch and vent, Evelyn. I'll try to be more encouraging. Maybe I'll win my husband back."

She was willing to battle for her relationship, do anything—Dr. Ben Malachi—even if Wesley had given up. Even if he was an ass, a liar, and a cheat. She was a "death-till-they-part" type of wife.

"That's the spirit," encouraged Evelyn.

She began to worry about her own marriage. Seth did have a secret meeting with that lady deputy. She still did not grill him over that.

"Any news on Gracie?"

"Raile hired someone to take her. God, what a world we live in…"

286

Evelyn paused.

"That someone would take money to destroy a family."

"Times have been tight nowadays. Thanks for buying lunch, Seth," Wesley said, holding his wallet.

"Yeah, us too. Please, let's do this again," Seth spoke; not very certain he was being truthful.

Wesley offered his handshake but Seth hugged him instead.

With a twinge of guilt, Wesley returned the hug.

Pulling apart, Wesley looked deep in his eyes, something that was not common for Wesley—eye contact—as well as sincerity.

"Sorry about Grace."

Light switch.

Seth nodded.

"Huh... never heard anyone call her Grace before."

Seth paused.

"Other than Evelyn."

Seth was confused. *Why did Wesley call her Grace...?*

He left not knowing the answer...

Wesley put his wallet away. Sticking out was a small, hard piece of red paper. Sobbing, he pulled it out of his wallet.

It was a ticket to 12 A.M...

29.

A DATE AT 12 A.M.

Vicki told Ellis they had to watch the play this evening. He knew he had to, even though he did not like theater at all. Almost as bad as going to church—even worse when the actors were bad. And a high school play? Ellis had not seen one quality high school play production in his life. Still, he agreed they may see someone that may have been planning to meet Gracie, and it was in their best interests—albeit a long shot—that they search the auditorium.

Ellis sat in his office waiting for the play to start. He ordered Chinese from the local China Buffet and began plucking the food. Penny and Momma were off at the current moment.

He sat there thinking about how life had changed in Oostburg this last week. Ever since... *Vicki* came to town.

What do I know about her? he thought to himself. This chick could be some insane psychopath who escaped from the asylum, a female who got her kicks from killing teenage girls. Maybe that Gagliano lied as well.

It was true... Ellis really knew *nothing* about her...

Vicki decided that she wanted to be fresh for the performance, so she went home to shower in peace and quiet. Coralee was asleep down the hall and she had twenty minutes where she could just stand and think.

She stood in the shower enjoying the hot drizzles of liquid descending her naked body.

Many thoughts rattled her mind:

Who was Raile's right-hand man?
Who was meeting Gracie at the play tonight?
Who killed Gracie Adams?

The Oostburg High School Auditorium was packed this Friday night. Parents, faculty, and students crowded the walls as the school got ready for their town's rendition of *Twelve Angry Men.*

Vicki was amongst the crowd, waiting for Ellis to arrive. Since it was packed, the seats were quite far from the stage, but the auditorium was designed so that there really was not a bad seat in the theater. It wasn't Broadway—not that Vicki attended Broadway much—but it was nice for a small-town like Oostburg. Vicki found herself to be oddly impressed by the setup, another sure sign that she had lowered her standards.

She looked around for anything; anyone. Vicki had no idea who she was meeting or if she was going to see anyone. She was going on a poor hunch. It was very likely that the person she was meeting wouldn't even be there, considering Gracie was not alive and everyone knew it. It was also possible that whoever sent the text message did not kill Gracie.

But still, it was a lead worth pursuing.

"Where the hell is he?" she said to herself.

She went to the ladies' room before the show started. The program claimed it was an hour and a half, and the school opted for a short intermission.

Since it was printed the day before she had disappeared, Gracie's black and white photo was still in the program. Matt Zimmermann was listed as the clerk and her understudy in the program.

Nothing was out of the ordinary. The new deputy didn't see anyone who appeared suspicious. Vicki purposely wore her uniform to see if she could get a reaction out of someone; anyone.

No... something was out of order. Missing. Vicki felt someone was missing...

She looked around and it hit her.

Matt's father, Bob Zimmermann.

He was missing.

Vicki checked at her watch. The performance hadn't started and it was running late. Ellis was still not there.

Where was the trusty sheriff?

He had received a call not too long ago. A nosey mailman had seen through the window of a house—a body lying on the floor. Ellis drove a bit faster than usual, and in that, failed to inform his deputies.

The ambulance came, and even though Charles Raile was shot in the shoulder, incredibly close to the heart, he was still breathing.

Raile was admitted and in critical condition.

Ellis met him in the room and spoke to him briefly:

"Any idea who did this to you?"

Raile breathed laboriously:

"Pastor..."

"Pastor Seth shot you?"

Oh my god—he did it... Seth took revenge...

"Charles! Did Seth shoot you?"

And he fell asleep.

Seth and Evelyn were home eating their dinner of tension. They did not chew much, they simply swallowed. Each of them didn't even know what they were eating. There was very little discussion; as if the pair sat with a stranger. Twenty years of marriage, and at the first sign of tragedy, it was a bad sign that maybe they weren't as strong as they thought...

Evelyn broke the silence with meaningless chatter:

"Packers play Dallas on Sunday."

There was an awkward pause.

A few minutes later, after another bout of silence, Seth realized Lainey wasn't even there.

"Lainey at a friend's?"

Evelyn had absent-mindedly forgotten her other daughter as well.

"She's having dinner at the Candleberry's. Can you pick her up at eight?"

Seth didn't even answer but changed the subject:

"Had lunch with Wesley today."

Evelyn perked up:

"I had a surprise lunch visit with Brooke today."

Seth took a bite of his meal.

"Funny."

"Yeah, funny."

"He seems to be doing well. Seventy pages into an alien story."

Evelyn was sick of Wesley. He was hurting Brooke.

She took a sip of her wine.

"Brooke thinks Wesley is having an affair."

"Really? That's not the vibe I got."

Evelyn chuckled.

"Well, you're a man. Men are stupid."

Seth took a hit. He was about to attack back with a snarky remark when lucky for Evelyn, the phone rang.

Seth went to go get it.

"Seth, it's Ellis."

"Any news?"

"I need you to come to St. Nick's."

Seth sped up I-43 and made it there in roughly seventeen minutes. The pastor found Ellis in the hallway outside the room. Having no idea what happened, his primary thought was Gracie, even though she was dead. He then thought of Lainey, his living daughter.

Ellis walked up to him.

"Seth—"

"Ellis? What's going on?"

Ellis held Seth's shoulders.

"Seth, sorry I didn't give you any detail. If I did, you wouldn't have come."

Seth looked at Ellis and followed him into the room.

Inside the room was Charles Raile, the choice suspect in Gracie's disappearance and murder. The only suspect, really.

"Seth..." the body spoke.

Seth looked at the man, pausing for thought. This was the man who threatened his wife by speaking: *"we wouldn't want anything horrible to happen"*. Even though there was no proof, it was the only possible cruel outcome for Gracie. Evelyn went against Raile, and in return, he unleashed his lackey to harm and kill Gracie. Raile proved he was in Chicago based on the speeding ticket so they assumed he didn't physically do it but he had someone hurt her. That someone was out there.

The demon who hurt Seth the most was now seeking his help and in that tiny moment, Seth had to decide whether he was going to follow his heavenly father or his flesh.

He saw Charles Raile lying there, breathing slowly, and hooked to the monitors. A nurse was by his side checking his pulse.

Seth could have easily pushed a pillow on him, once Ellis and the nurse left.

He made his choice and attempted to leave.

Ellis blocked him at the doorway. Even though Ellis wasn't really a believer, he knew the rulebook and played by most of the rules.

He also knew his friend, Pastor Seth, down the crooked road would severely regret not doing anything at this moment.

"Seth—"

Seth was livid with his friend.

"How could you bring me here?!"

Ellis justified his decision:

"If I told you, you never would have come."

"Damn right!"

Seth took a step out the door. Ellis stopped him easily.

"Look, Seth, I may not have the faith you have, but if your faith is real, then you need to be here. He asked for you."

Seth fumed. He wanted to punch Ellis but he knew the outcome might not be to his advantage.

"I got the call an hour ago. He was shot. He's probably not going to make it."

Seth could not look at the sheriff.

"He killed my daughter!"

Ellis concurred.

"Probably. If I were in your shoes, I'd let the bastard cook. But I'm not the preacher."

Seth remembered the Old Man's advice:

"Remember pastor,
forgiving someone who doesn't deserve it...
is the hardest thing in the world."

A small, muffled sound was heard in the distance:

"Pastor... ?"

The nurse tried to encourage Raile not to speak, but he was being as stubborn in death as he was in life. He was stubborn in his wickedness and stubborn in his repentance.

Seth slowly walked over.

Raile breathed heavily.

"... need... talk."

Raile coughed.

"...didn't... any... you... God... forgive..."

Seth stormed out.

As he walked out, Raile pled in broken English one last time:

"Sex... traf... you..."

Ellis caught up with Seth in the hallway.

"Seth!"

From Raile's room, Seth and Ellis could hear Raile's monitor make a noise—a flatline. The nurse who had attended to Raile ran out of the room screaming:

"All available doctors to room 206!"

Four doctors ran to the room, passing Seth and Ellis.

Seth was defeated, and he knew it.

"You might regret that," Ellis gently rubbed in.

While Ellis was following Seth back to Oostburg, Vicki was at intermission of *Twelve Angry Men*.

Vicki learned there was a bad seat in the house—hers—for it was facing that stage. The show sucked. Oostburg was not known for its actors and unfortunately for Matt, he had the beast's share of the work on short notice. He tried his best, but he just had way too many lines. There was no acting, it was all: "Oh crap, let me get the right words". That was a big issue, considering he had all the large important parts, especially in regards to the evidence. It was clear that he had most of his speeches on a notepad lying on the table. He attempted to trick the audience by flipping through the pad in character but the audience knew what was going on. This audience was forgiving. Speaking of the audience... *Where was Bob Zimmermann? Where was Ellis?* Vicki thought. Vicki did not have any inclination of what was going on and she was a huge fan of the Henry Fonda movie. The play was so awful she wished the whole jury would receive the death penalty.

She checked her voicemail. Nothing. *What the hell?* He's supposed to be here. He said he didn't like plays, and he ditched her. He didn't even have the decency to text. Vicki laughed. She sounded like a whiny girlfriend. But for real—*where in Hell's Kitchen is he?*

As she turned around to look for him—she saw someone else. That odd little man from church—Wesley—with a bag of skittles—and he was wearing... a tuxedo?

Vicki approached him and re-introduced herself.

"Hi, not sure you remember me—"

Wesley interrupted.

"I remember you—you're the chick Ellis is dicking. Skittle?"

Vicki's jaw dropped.

"Excuse me?"

"You're looking around for someone, and since you've only been here a week, the one person you really know is... Ellis. And you're not looking for someone casual, like say, your aunt, no, your body language is tense, you're frustrated he is not here. He stood you up—and you're pissed off because you already gave him your body."

What.

"Did he tell you we had sex?"

"No. You did."

Popping a green skittle in his mouth, Wesley walked away, heading back to his seat for the second act. In that little moment, Vicki felt something she did not expect—she felt fear. This little, insignificant male, who was barely five feet tall and one hundred pounds... terrified her.

Vicki turned around, breathing heavily. He was right but still... why was he wearing a tuxedo to a silly high school play?"

"Wesley!" she yelled across the lobby.

He turned around.

"Why are you wearing a tuxedo?"

He paused.

"I support the arts."

He walked away, and Vicki stared him down.

"Lying bastard," she said to herself.

Seth and Ellis picked up burgers on the path back home.

Ellis checked his voicemail and saw that Vicki had called him two times—once leaving a message and once hanging up.

"Damn it. I forgot the play tonight."

"*Twelve Angry Men*?"

"Yes. We found out that whoever texted Gracie did not mean twelve midnight, but meant the play, *Twelve Angry Men*... or in code, 12 A.M. She was meeting someone at the play or after the play."

Seth sat back.

Ellis took a bite.

"Good news for you though—Raile said you didn't shoot him."

Seth's phone buzzed. It was Evelyn.

"Seth! Get Lainey and come home now!"

The men picked up the girl from her friend's and were back home in thirty minutes.

Evelyn stood in the living room, a little book in hand.

She was furious and asked Lainey:

"Lainey, what's this? I found it under your bed!"

Lainey looked at the sheriff and spoke:

"She said I might die if I read that..."

It was Gracie's unknown diary...

30.

THE DIARY OF GRACIE ADAMS

"Well... the plot thickens," Ellis said as he flipped through the pages.

Evelyn spoke in a muffled whisper, not able to truly believe what she was saying.

"Grace was... Daniel Watson is a married man."

Ellis continued to flip through the pages.

Evelyn turned to Lainey as Seth sat in the corner motionless.

"Lainey, if you had told us this sooner—"

Ellis defended the young girl:

"Evelyn, with all due respect, Lainey was scared."

Then turning to Lainey:

"She saved your life, Lainey. She was a hero."

Lainey sadly smiled.

"I don't know if Charles Raile is married," Evelyn wondered.

"Raile wasn't married," Ellis clarified.

"Wasn't?"

From his own little corner of the world, Seth said:

"Charles Raile is dead."

Ellis nodded at Lainey. Evelyn picked up on the hint.

"Lainey, why don't we get you ready for bed?"

Evelyn and Lainey started to walk upstairs. Lainey walked up, but Evelyn lingered back. Ellis noticed Evelyn was still there.

"Raile's last words were: "sex—traf—you." Ellis paused. "He may have sold Gracie. Whoever bought her..."

The stuffy air slugged Evelyn in the stomach. She stood silenced; stunned. What the hell happened to her little child in her final hours? She looked down and walked upstairs.

Seth sat, motionless. He could not take any more. One more surprise and it would probably push him off his pulpit.

Ellis continued to flip pages.

"Where are you, married man?"

After a few seconds, Ellis sat up.

"Hello. Our married man is an *author*."

Sitting up, Seth whispered to himself:
"Wesley..."

Vicki picked up her cell.

"Where the hell were you? I just endured the most miserable play and you were supposed to be there to make it easier to swallow!"

Ellis briefly grinned. He was glad he missed the stupid play.

"Get your ass to the station."

"Why?"

"I'm picking up Wesley Demko."

"Ah. So you figured it out, too."

"What?"

"He was here. At the play—get this—dressed in a tuxedo."

"Who the hell wears a tuxedo to a stupid high school show?"

"The kind of man who is obsessed with a girl."

Wesley entered his home and was startled by the woman.

"Where were you?" Brooke asked.

"Out."

"Where?"

"I went to the bar."

"In a tux?"

Shaking his head, Wesley looked at his attire. He knew he overdid it.

Brooke continued:

"The bar? You haven't drunk in years."

Wesley paused. He knew he lost this argument. *The damn... tux.*

"I needed to clear my head."

"In a tux."

"In a tux."

"Did you drink?"

"I had a root beer."

"That's all?"

"That's all."

Yes, that was all. That was all she could take before she finally exploded:

"Bullshit! You're cheating on me! I am not stupid, Wesley! You're out every night, even though you're only scheduled till—"

As Brooke yelled at him, she slowly hoisted herself up to assault Wesley's chest with her fists. He restrained her after a couple of hits and forced her back in the wheelchair.

"Brooke—"

"Who is she?"

"Brooke—I'm..."

Brooke continued to scream.

"I have a right to know! You are my husband! How dare you violate that trust?!"

Wesley put his head down. He took a couple of steps upstairs.

"We'll talk about this tomorrow."

Brooke grabbed his tuxedo jacket as he took a step.

"No, we're talking about this right now. Who is she?"

"I'm going to—"

Brooke yelled at the top of her lungs:

"Who is she? I demand to know!"

"She's... not in the picture anymore."

Brooke's mouth dropped and she buried it with her hands. A few tears ran down her cheek. Without Wesley saying it, he said it. Brooke's worst fear was confirmed. She knew all along that the seventeen-year-old child was "spending time" with her thirty-six-year-old husband.

"You gave her my fucking earrings!"

With emphasis, he repeated himself:

"She's not in the picture."

"Oh, my word. Wesley... no."

And she knew.

Her husband attempted to murder Evelyn Adams.

Her husband murdered Gracie Adams.

She screamed:

"You killed her! You beat her to death and threw her under a car! And because she was—"

Wesley yelled back:

"We'll talk about it tomorrow!"

But Brooke could not wait anymore. Suspecting all these days, she had a right to know. Brooke defended Wesley even though he attempted to kill Evelyn. She defended Wesley to the point where she even slept with his therapist just to keep him quiet. She did all these damn things for their marriage, only to find he killed a teenage girl. She could barely forgive everything else, but when it boiled down to it, Wesley killed a teenage girl. Brooke could no longer defend her husband.

"You were with Gracie... weren't you, Wesley? The night Gracie disappeared you came home with bloody fingers!"

He didn't talk, and so the time came for Brooke to reveal that he wasn't the only deceptive one in the marriage—

She stood up...

"Brooke?"

On her way up the stairs, she retrieved the vase on the table and lifted it over her head. Stomping towards her, Wesley grabbed the glass and plucked it from her—throwing it and destroying it into a hundred fragments. Then, the man pushed the woman down the three steps—Brooke falling to the ground.

"Look at us! What a couple of liars we are! Maybe we do belong together! The woman who fakes paralysis with the man who... well it doesn't matter anymore. All that matters is finishing my novel," Wesley chuckled, walking up the stairs.

Brooke sat on the floor, weeping. Hearing a sound, she turned her head.

It was Gracie.

"Once, when I was bathing you, you... flinched. I didn't have the heart to tell him. That was your job; to tell him that you were faking. I should have."

And she was gone.

"Damn you, Wesley! Damn you... I tried so—"

There was a knock on the door, and Brooke screamed.

Beyond the door, a voice spoke:

"Brooke—it's me, Ellis. Please, open up. I need to talk to you." Ellis paused. "And Wesley."

Brooke took a second to compose herself.

"One second."

Brooke didn't want to see the sheriff like this. She was hurt and confused. Her husband never admitted to seeing the kid. Or killing her. Maybe he was a good person—maybe—oh god... she had no clue anymore...

Brooke took a few seconds to wipe her tears. Sitting on the floor she opened the door.

Ellis stood there.

"May I come in?"

Brooke scooted her way out of the door, permitting Ellis to nudge his way in.

Ellis saw Brooke sitting there and immediately thought the worst.

"Hey, you okay? Did you fall? What's with all the glass?"

"Yeah, I'm fine. Vase just fell."

"It doesn't look like it just fell."

Being a gentleman, Ellis hoisted Brooke up by her armpits. He gently placed her back in her chair.

"I heard you crying."

Brooke swallowed.

"I'm fine."

Ellis looked around.

"Is Wesley home?"

Upstairs, Wesley admired the tuxedo in the mirror. It was quite a nice tuxedo. Even nicer was that he purchased it for ten dollars at the Sheboygan Theater Company's garage sale. Ten bucks, what a steal. Not a lot of men could fit in the tux, which explained the heavy discount, so score one for the short guy.

Hearing Ellis's voice made Wesley know that the end was close. He stood at the top of the stairs, just out of sight of the sheriff, and pondered what his next move would be.

Wesley remembered contemplating the razor in his bathroom earlier in the week. He could easily run to the bathroom and end it now. It was over. Ellis was here to take him. Maybe for what he did to Grace, maybe for what he did to Evelyn, but he knew the end was coming.

Wesley contemplated coming clean, but there was no point. He just wanted out. All he needed to do was finish his novel.

And worst of all... he knew he would never finish that novel now. His tale would never be read; *their* tale would never be read. He wanted so badly to complete it... for his kids. But it wasn't going to happen, and that made him look forward to the edge of the razor ever-so-more.

"Can I speak to him?" Ellis asked downstairs.

Please, Brooke. Think of something...

"Wesley!"

Wesley stayed silent, hoping Ellis would take that as a hint that perhaps he was gone or asleep or... stupid Wesley. He knew he was in a lose-lose situation.

Die now, and never finish the novel. Or, perhaps die later, after a few months or years in jail, and maybe, just maybe, finish his novel. He did not mind dying after the novel was completed; in fact, that was his plan... his plan until... Grace came into his life.

Brooke had three seconds or so to muster up the courage to defend Wesley. She had done so much for him: married him, given him two loving children; lied for him; hell, she even slept with his therapist for him. And yes, he was a liar and a cheat but damn it he was her liar and her cheat and she was going to help him and support him no matter what—even if it meant supporting his work—

And it hit her.

His work.

His work. That's the one thing she never supported. She never supported his dream of becoming a writer. She downplayed it as fantasy, his dream. She never took him seriously... and she knew, right then and there, the reason she lost him.

She didn't support his dreams... she hindered them...

She knew the advice: wives support your husbands; be their cheerleader. The wife knew husbands rarely admitted it, but they needed that cheerleader. She failed. She was not his cheerleader. Gracie. The young girl. She... was his cheerleader.

Brooke made one final attempt to save her husband. The only thing left to do...

Brooke had to kill Ellis...

—the sharp glass all over the floor—

—she picked up the biggest shard of glass and—

—there he was. Wesley Demko coming down the stairs.

Ellis gave a warm, inviting smile in his attempt to lure the sick snake into the cage.

"Hey, buddy. Can we talk for a bit?"

Wesley stood still, seven steps above Ellis.

"My husband has been going through some depression," Brooke tried to steer the boat into another lake, grabbing Ellis's hand after tossing the would-be murder weapon.

"I was wondering if I could see your novel," Ellis said, ever-so-gently.

"I haven't even read it. Not sure it really exists," Brooke divulged.

Ellis kept his eyes on Wesley.

"Oh, I'm pretty sure it exists. Well, buddy?"

Wesley stared back.

"No."

Ellis paused.

"Wesley, we can do this the hard way or we can do this the simple way. The hard way would buy you a few hours, but will not be helpful at all."

Wesley closed his eyes. It wasn't fair. God took his children. He took Grace. And now god was going to take him, too. God never loved the little man; because he let his kids die in that damn fire.

If only he wasn't a Christian...

If only he stayed home that night...

If only Grace weren't ill...

If only...

"Now how about that novel?"

Game over.

31.

INTERROGATION

Vicki Weathers met Ellis Kirkbride and Wesley Demko at the police station in ten minutes.

Guiding Wesley along the drafty hallway, the three walked past an incarcerated drunk.

He spoke just as wobbly as he stood.

"I seen pastor's daughter's car that night. She drivin' it!"

"Knock it off, Homeless Jay," Ellis said.

Homeless Jay laughed hysterically as the three continued the walk back, where the interrogation room awaited them.

Ellis made him and Vicki some coffee. They both knew it was going to be a long night. Even if Demko confessed to whatever he had done, it would be many sleepless nights for the two of them.

At the end of the day, they really didn't know what Demko did. The tuxedo at the play. The mention of a writer in her diary. Maybe it was a different author. It was certainly possible they were only dating. Maybe they didn't sleep together. Maybe they did sleep together, but he did not kill her.

Or maybe Wesley Demko was as evil as they thought he might be...

They were about to find out...

Ellis took notes with a pad and pen.

Vicki began.

"You realize why we are here, correct, Wesley?"

"I am aware."

"Okay. The two things that snatch our attention most are what she wrote in her diary. She wrote she was seeing a married author."

"She wrote that."

303

"Yes. And when I meet you at the auditorium, dressed in a tuxedo, it leads to certain thoughts."

"Did she ever say the name of her married friend?"

"No," Ellis confirmed.

"So, basically, you have nothing."

"We have enough to bring you in to question," stated Vicki.

"That's all we want to do, Wesley, is talk," Ellis added.

Wesley looked at them. "But she never mentioned a name?"

"No," Vicki said.

The sheriff and his deputy knew they really did not have proof of any kind. If Wesley did something, the proof was going to have to start with him. Vicki knew bringing up the kids would leave him vulnerable.

"We understand Gracie babysat for you a few times?"

Wesley's eyes began to glisten.

"Yes. Yes, she did."

"Forgive me. I am new to Oostburg, Wesley. Would you mind telling me what happened the night your kids... passed away."

Vicki could see the little man shrink more and more.

"It happened on a Tuesd... Tuesday... My wife, Brooke, and I were going to a Bible study, at Pastor Seth's house. I got a call from Seth. Grace was sick and couldn't babysit. So alright. Grace was ill... so we decided to leave the kids home alone. It's Oostburg. Nothin... bad ever happens here. But, yes. There's a first time for everything. We went to Seth's. I even saw Grace there, wished her well. And by the end of that damn Bible study..." Wesley swallowed. "They were gone..."

Wesley broke down.

Vicki felt bad for him, even if he was a murdering pedophile.

"They never had a chance..." Wesley dabbed his nose on his sleeve before Ellis got him a box of tissues.

"My kids never had a chance... we still don't know what happened. Or how it started. We know they were in the bedroom... under the bed... I left my babies to die... God didn't keep them safe... he failed me... he failed them..." Wesley swallowed. "It isn't fair..."

Ellis felt horrible but Vicki knew Wesley was very close to the breaking point. He just needed one more push.

"How close were you to Gracie?"

"Grace."

"Huh?"

"Her name is Grace."

"Is?"

"It is Grace."

"Wesley. How did you feel about Grace?"

Wesley paused.

"She is a good woman."

"Well, legally she was a girl."

"Woman."

Gotcha! You sick, stupid bastard.

"Did you ever want to harm her, for letting your kids down?"

Wesley paused.

"Yes, I wanted to hurt her."

Ellis sat back in awe and watched his deputy take over.

"Did you kill her?" she asked.

Wesley shook his head.

"No."

Vicki took a deep breath. He was lying. She knew it. It had to be him. He blamed her for his kids' deaths, and so he killed her. All they needed now was the confession.

"Were you having an affair with her?"

Wesley stared off into space.

"Affair... is a strong word."

Damn you.

"Well then what would you call it?"

Wesley searched for the right word.

"A... friendship..."

"A friendship with a teenage girl?"

Ellis stepped in, playing good cop.

"Wesley. We have been friends for twenty-nine years. You are in a heap of trouble, especially if you don't answer."

Vicki re-took the steering wheel. Charles Raile was no longer the prime suspect.

"We have reason to believe that a man was trafficking Gracie."

Wesley's eyes got large.

"What?!"

"Did you pay to have sex with her?" Vicki asked.

Ellis coughed and shook his head. Vicki could tell he wasn't very comfortable with this line of questioning. He spoke:

"I need a water," Ellis said as he left the room.

Vicki looked at Wesley in disgust before following Ellis.

In the hallway, Vicki slammed the door shut.

"What?" she asked.

"I'm just… not ready for this. He's my friend."

"Ellis, with all due respect, you are too close to Wesley. At this time, it doesn't matter that he is your friend. Now get your ass in the game."

Vicki left Ellis to stand in defeat. He knew she was correct, but Lord he hoped she was wrong. Ellis loved Wesley, like a brother. He loved Seth, too. This was tearing him apart.

He did something he rarely did.

He prayed.

Ellis prayed for strength and guidance. He prayed for God to take this cup from him. It was worth a prayer. God did not take the cup from Jesus, but maybe, just maybe, he would answer his prayer. Sheriff Ellis Kirkbride. An all-around decent guy, defender of kittens in trees. Just maybe God would answer his prayer.

Seth and Evelyn stared in their kitchen, unable to ponder. Gracie never mentioned a name. Was that man Wesley? And how far did it go? Was it simply random meet-ups in her car? Or was it much worse? Did they... have sex?

Evelyn spoke:

"If Wesley did it, you will have to forgive him."

Seth stared off.

"So will you."

Evelyn thought: *I'm not the pastor. I don't have to forgive one damn person. You do.*

"Can you?" she asked her husband.

He silently recalled his sermon the night she disappeared:

"So what do you do? When someone hurts you so bad? Makes you cry at night wondering why God—why God did You—let this happen? Most of us know that our Lord can do anything. The Almighty. He can change hearts; change lives."

He closed his eyes and continued to remember:

"Can end pain and suffering. But sometimes He doesn't. Sometimes, He lets us go through that pain; that suffering so we can see Him on the other side. How do you rise up during moments of hurt? Do you punch and scream? Do you turn to God for that very first time? Or do you delete it all and start fresh? Do you... ask for forgiveness? Do you continue to question Lord Almighty? Or do you repent? Do you *forgive*? Heavenly Father, heal the wounds. Let us praise You in the storm. We pray for those out here who are listening to Your word, oh Lord. May we hear You—may we have eyes to view. May we see the world—

　　　—through eyes of grace."

A voice spoke out:
"You can't put grace in a box."
Incredulously, they both saw her.
It was Gracie.

"Wesley, we know a shorter somebody drove her car. You're not the tallest crayon in the box," belittled Vicki.
"I didn't drive her car."
"You didn't drive her car. Hmm. Alright, here's where the problem lies: The driver's seat is adjusted so close to the steering wheel that it is impossible for a five-foot-six *girl* to fit. We know, because I am five-six, and I couldn't fit in the seat. So... in conclusion, a shorter person drove her car that night. Someone... shorter than five-six." She paused, staring at him. He was either a damn good performer, or the man was genuine. He did not appear to have a clue what she was talking about.
She continued:
"How tall are you Wesley?"
"Five-three."
"Five-three," Vicki repeated.
"But I didn't drive her car. I've never driven her car."
Wesley paused and spoke with meaning:
"I was never in the driver's seat."
"No? Then who was? Who drove her car?"
"She did. Grace did. She always drove."
Ellis and Vicki looked at each other.

Ellis stepped in:

"It's a hard pill to swallow, Wes. A teenage girl's diary is very similar to a married man's novel. Her diary says: *"He is writing a book about our love"*. Your book happens to be about a married man... who is in love with a teenage girl. Can you explain that?"

"Was she sold?"

"Your book, Wesley." Vicki pressed.

"Was she sold?!"

Vicki shook her head.

"Gracie was texting "Daniel Watson"—Wesley Demko—same initials—backwards."

"That was her idea, to rename me Daniel Watson... since that Watson girl was in the witness prote—was she sold?!"

"You were going to see her at *Twelve Angry Men*?"

"Yes, we supported each other's achievements. Now damn it answer my question! Was she sold?!"

"We don't know."

"Wesley. Please explain," demanded Ellis.

"I can't."

"Do you know a man named Charles Raile?"

"No."

"Where were you this afternoon?"

"This afternoon?"

"Yes, this afternoon," Vicki pushed.

"I had pizza with Seth... finished work at the video store and went home for a shower. Then I went to see the play."

"You went straight home?"

Wesley looked at the two of them.

Vicki smirked but Ellis stepped in before she could bite.

"Wesley, please... make me understand. If you don't speak, people are going to think the worst," Ellis reasoned.

"If I *do* speak, people are going to think the worst."

Ellis continued:

"Seth is your best friend. You married his sister."

Vicki stared—an unbecoming stare—

Gracie and Wesley... Seth and Brooke are—*brother and sister*?

"Wait... what? You're Gracie's... uncle?" she asked incredulously.

Wesley took too long to respond:

"Not by blood."

Vicki swung her arm at the air. This was over.

Wesley rubbed his left arm, triggering Vicki's thought. Since she moved here, seven days ago, there had been three attacks: Gracie's murder, Evelyn's attempted murder, and the Charles Raile shooting. She was so focused on Gracie that she forgot the other two.

"How's your arm?"

"I'm done."

"Lift up your sleeve."

"No."

"There's a small red stain there. Blood perhaps? From where Evelyn Adams stabbed you? Where were you Sunday afternoon?"

Wesley did not speak.

"Wesley..." Ellis tried to encourage him to talk, and it worked.

"You don't know what it's like to not have your wife support you. And then along comes this woman—"

Vicki interrupted with the correct demographic.

"*Girl.*"

Wesley stared her down.

"*Woman...* and she thinks you are the best guy in the world. And it makes you feel... special. For the first time in my stupid, little life I felt special. Brooke didn't want me to succeed. She just wanted me to give her babies. And I couldn't even do that correctly. I work in a video store. My life is going nowhere. But I did have love. I never hurt her. I never laid a hand on her."

Vicki laughed callously.

"Really? You took her virginity without using your hands?"

Vicki stormed out of the interrogation room in need of the coffee break. Ellis followed her seconds later.

"He did it, sheriff."

"I've known him a long time, Vicki and—"

"Yes! And that is the problem. See... here's what happened: They go out for a date. Gracie is driving to begin with. His fingerprints are on the passenger side—I bet you he is the unknown fingerprints, and they will be found there once we get the warrant—they fool around in the back seat. That's the little amount of blood, Wesley taking the girl's virginity. And because there are no signs of force, we assume that either it was A. consensual or B. she did not fight him and just let it happen. After they're done fooling around, she threatens to tell, and so he kills her. Then he drives her car, adjusting the driver seat, buries her in the forest, parks the car and walks back home." She paused to watch Ellis digest the accusation. "His mistake is forgetting to re-adjust the driver's seat back to her height."

"How come there are no extra prints on the driver's side?"

"After he dicks her, he puts on the gloves. I tell you his prints are on the passenger's side and the back seat—the unknown prints Walker found—but after he commits the murder, he is more careful."

"Damn."

"Sorry, Ellis. Check the DNA—bet you it's his DNA, his semen."

Vicki added:

"Evelyn Adams said she stabbed her attacker on the left arm. This guy has a pain in his left arm... he was rubbing it and grimacing. Plus, he has no alibi for the Raile shooting this afternoon—says that he was going home to Oostburg from the video store—so he said he went home to shower—after he shot Raile, he needed a shower."

"Why did he attack Evelyn?" Ellis asked.

"Wesley hates the family for hosting a Bible Study while his kids died. He probably plans to kill the whole family."

The reaction on Ellis's face made Vicki turn around.

Seth shut the door.

"How much did you hear?"

"Enough," Seth said as Evelyn sat down in Vicki's chair.

Seth stared into space.

"How do you forgive someone who did that?"

"I don't know. I'm not the pastor. Never believed in all that completely, anyway," Ellis said.

Seth paused and then asked:

"Can I see him?"

Ellis shook his head.

"I don't think that's wise."

"Are you speaking as the sheriff or my friend?"

Ellis paused.

"Sheriff."

"How about as my friend?"

"Don't tell the sheriff."

Ellis and Seth took the short stride to interrogation. While this may be a highly irregular procedure, Ellis was going to bend it for his friend.

Seth looked at his friend and grabbed on tight. Ellis thought the hug was a little longer than comfortable. With this embrace over, Ellis patted his friend on the shoulder and had no idea that his holster was empty.

32.

SETH CONFRONTS HIS DAUGHTER'S "FRIEND"

They entered to find Wesley sitting, staring at the sheriff's red pen. One could almost feel bad for the guy had it not been for the fact that they knew what he did. In Seth and Ellis's eyes, he was a pedophile and a murderer.

But in Grace's eyes...

"Three minutes," Ellis told Seth as he closed the door.

Outside the interrogation room, Ellis took two steps before being greeted by Gracie, who startled him.

Ellis looked around to see if anyone else saw them. *Was he losing it?* he asked himself.

Gracie spoke:

"Why are you doing this?"

Seth sat down.

At first, he didn't know what to say. Seth looked at this piranha who killed his beloved daughter. There was no longer a doubt in his mind. Wesley Demko was the married author she... he could not bring himself to even think that thought. Wesley was family, for Christ's sake!

Wesley stared back... genuinely sorry for what he had done. Plans had... not gone according to what he had hoped for. He wanted to kidnap her from the family. His feelings—his heart—god—whatever you want to call it—changed him. When god took his two girls, he wanted nothing to do with god. He wanted to ignore him until he got an idea—the idea to punish god for not protecting his girls. To punish Seth for holding the bible study and for preaching god's love when god obviously didn't care about anyone. Wesley wanted to punish Grace for getting a virus and not being there. Yes, he wanted to punish... but then something happened, a major something that changed his heart...

He began to care for Grace, his niece, his wife's brother's girl.

He fell in love with her.

And she was already in love with him...

Seth broke the silence:

"Funny... how we were having lunch like, eight hours ago and here we are. In here. I read your story—Brooke shared some of it. It's nothing about an alien invasion. It's about a married man invading a teenage girl."

"Seth—"

"Did you have sex with my daughter?"

Wesley paused.

"Yes."

Seth pounded on the table. He stood up, took a breath, and punched Wesley square in the jaw. Wesley didn't move. He knew it was coming and was willing to take his punishment.

"Damn it, Wesley! She was seventeen! She was your niece!"

"Yeah, and in the Bible, we would have been married with four kids by now."

Seth screamed at the height of his lungs:

"Don't you dare justify!" Seth huffed. "Gracie... threatened to tell Brooke and you killed her!"

Wesley stared off, remembering the night...

The May-December lovers sat in her car. Grace was in the driver's seat, having picked up her partner an hour before. They were parked off a road in Kiel, a nearby town, one of their many hideouts.

Wesley and Grace had been meeting secretly for ten months. Always about an hour away from home, they were able to sneak off whenever they felt. They did not sneak away too often. They found other reasons to be together; "randomly" met up: shopping, pretending to see one another: "Oh hi, Uncle Wesley! Didn't know you'd be here... of all the places!" Wink wink. "Stolen Moments" is what they called their encounters. She rented movies frequently.

To be perfectly frank, it was Grace who started this whole thing, the friendship, and the inappropriate relationship. Her uncle had fully intended to be her friend, lull her into security, and then kill her to punish everyone for the tragedy. Somewhere along the line, he developed feelings for her. It was her big heart; her kindness. Her patience with him. Her cheering him on. Grace tried to teach him to forgive the world and God. She tried to teach him to see the world through eyes of grace and to love and forgive anyone who wronged him. And so, because of good Grace's teaching, he wanted to forgive God... he wanted to forgive Seth for encouraging him to leave his kids home alone.

But he wasn't ready.

His wife thought his dreams were a joke. The relationship was not great to begin with and the catastrophe that killed their children also consumed their marriage. Brooke didn't want him to waste his hours with the stupid book; after all, how many people actually get published?

"Negative again?"

Wesley nodded.

"I don't even want another one anyway... at least, not, um..." He clammed up.

Grace touched his hand.

"There are other ways."

"Yeah, I can adopt—"

She interrupted him.

"I want to carry our baby." She smiled. "In six months, April 17, I will be eighteen. Mom and dad can't tell me what to do then. Just six short months. We can do whatever we want. No more sneaking around. It's not much longer now."

Gently, she grabbed his hand.

"Divorce her. You're not happy anyway," Grace said so simply.

Wesley couldn't divorce the woman. The witch was paralyzed—so he thought—and he would look terrible. As much as he loved Grace, he knew they could not go much further. This romance... their partnership would never be anything more than a sneaking around affair. He felt terrible because he knew it would never work out, no matter how much they wanted it to. He knew eventually he would let her down and break her heart.

"You're beautiful. You're smart. You could date any—"

To shut him up, and to persuade him otherwise, Gracie leaned in to kiss his lips.

As much as he loved her, he knew it was wrong. Maybe it was time; time to show her the love he had felt for her... by letting her go. The tears flowed inward knowing he would have to say good-bye to her this night. He loved her too much to let her go around in life sneaking. She was worth so much more. She deserved to be paraded around by some man's side, not hidden in a car only to be let out to play with once in a while. Grace was too amazing for him, he knew it.

For the first time in a long while, he yearned to do the right thing. Grace had taught him what was right in the world and now... she was going to get her heart broken because of it.

"... maybe we shouldn't be doing this..."

"Doing what? We're not doing anything."

Wesley shook his head.

"Just meeting you in secret—"

She didn't let him finish.

"I'll never forget the moment I fell in love with you."

Lovingly, he looked her deep in both eyes. He had heard the story before. It was a good story.

"I did not see the car. But you did. You always see things. But, I do see... you. I see the special quality that you have... the gift of your word. The tenderness of your tone. You care. You care for me... not because you have to, like, my parents. You care... because you choose to care."

"Grace—"

She smiled.

"I love how you are the only one who calls me "Grace". It makes me feel … so grown up."

He took her hands. She was always in the driver's seat, even when he thought he was. She smiled.

"And I was in your arms; my arms around your neck."

Lovingly, Gracie gently hugged his neck. They genuinely cared for one another. There were no ulterior motives. Just pure love.

"I looked in your eyes and saw warmth. Warmth, Wesley."

Wesley looked at the teenager. Conflicted, he sat there, the only passenger in her story.

"The day before that party, I saw *Cinderella* and I prayed for a prince."

Gracie smiled.

"The next day you saved me."

She leaned in and without kissing she spoke on his lips: "You are my prince. I remember how you carried me in your arms. I was... loved and protected. My knight in shining armor. Eleven-year-old Grace had found her prince."

Now seventeen, she was ready to claim him.

"That day, you placed me back in my father's arms, and I saw Aunt Brooke kiss you... and I knew... jealousy. At the age of eleven, I knew exactly what jealousy was. She had you."

Wrapped in each other's embrace, they were the oddly matched two. The teen caressed his cheek.

In return, Wesley melted.

"And that day is here. I knew, on that day I found my prince. That's why I love you, Wesley Allen Demko. You, and you alone, saved me from getting hit by that car. Possibly could have died yourself. And what does the Bible say?"

She responded to her own question:

"*No greater love than he who gives his life for his friend.*"

Grace continued.

"You love me, too. Because you were willing to lay down your life for me."

"Grace—"

Grace put her finger to his lips.

"Shh. Don't say anything. Just listen..."

He gave in.

He kissed her finger; took her by the hand and squeezed, secretly symbolizing that he was going to be there for her, now and forever. How he was going to do it, he hadn't a clue, but he was hers.

Grace looked at his fingers and kissed them. As her luscious lips met his silver ring, she pulled away from it.

There was one more thing to do:

Gently, she took off his wedding symbol and tossed it beneath his feet.

Wesley veered out the window... perhaps searching for a sign that he was making the right choice...

"Wesley. Look at me."

He couldn't move, unsure of what to do. He did not love his wife, but he didn't want to hurt her either.

Grace turned his head to make eye contact with her prince.

"What happened in the Bible? When Sarah could not have a baby? She gave Abraham the servant girl." Grace paused to nail in the point: "Who helps Aunt Brooke? Who bathes her?"

"You do."

"I do."

Wesley looked at her. It all made sense now.

"You're—"

Grace nodded and beautifully smiled.

"I'm your servant girl."

Staring at one another for what felt like years, Wesley knew this would be the moment he would give in to temptations. For the first time, he kissed her and kept kissing her, and it was over.

Grace won.

Completely listening and incredibly horrified, Seth stared at the man who took his daughter's virginity. He did not know what to believe. The pastor didn't know if this man was lying, half-lying, or telling the truth.

Seth watched that DVD over and over again, of the point where his Gracie had almost been killed by a car. In the DVD, a young man saved her... Seth's sister's husband... Wesley. Wesley saved her that day and ever since that day, Wesley, not her dad, was Gracie's prince charming. It didn't matter that he was much too old. It didn't matter that he was her uncle. It didn't matter that he was married.

Wesley was Gracie's prince.

Gracie wasn't perfect after all...

It was then that he remembered he had Ellis's pistol...

"Sheriff... I don't agree with... the way you run things here," Vicki said.

Ellis took a slurp of his coffee. It was already a late night.

"It's not New York City, Vicki."

"That doesn't matter. A crime is a crime; and procedures are procedures. It doesn't matter where—"

Vicki noticed Ellis's holster was empty.

"Where's your gun?"

The officers burst in and found Seth pointing the gun at Wesley.

Vicki began to sweet-talk him.

"Pastor, this wouldn't look good on your resume."

"He took my baby."

"Did he confess?"

"He raped my Grace!"

"It was consensual," corrected Wesley.

"Gracie was underage, Wesley. You raped a teen, and you're going to jail," corrected Vicki. Turning to Seth, she added: "Or, would you like to take his place, pastor? Wesley made his bed. If you kill him, guess who gets to sleep in his bed?"

Ellis stepped in.

"Seth. Friend. Please, give me my gun." Ellis took cautious steps towards the gun-swinging pastor. "We got him. It's over."

"It... will never be over," Seth said through the gnashing of his teeth.

"You're right, Pastor Adams," Vicki confirmed. "It won't ever be. He took your Grace. Even if you kill him now nothing will change that. He's not worth it. As the sheriff said, we got him. Let us do our job."

"Please, Seth. I don't want to arrest you as well," Ellis said.

Seth slowly put down the gun, and Ellis took it from him.

Now safe, Wesley spoke:

"I hated you—and Grace and God. I hated the three of you because you all had a part in me losing my girls. And I did plan on killing her to punish all of you—*but I didn't*. I didn't because I grew to care for her. I wanted her to have the dreams that my kids would never have. And believe me, Seth—I didn't kill your daughter. *I love her*."

The trio stared at Wesley, not knowing what to say. Seth began to leave, but before he left he was stopped by a small, genuine voice:

"I saved *your* daughter." Wesley swallowed before continuing: "Why didn't god save *mine*?"

Seth stood still for a brief moment, closing both eyes. He had no answer and even if he did he may not have wanted to share it. The pastor walked out on his brother-in-law, slamming the door for good. Ellis and Vicki paused to digest the question. Ellis left, leaving Vicki to look at Wesley a little longer. She left confused and disgusted.

The door shut. All alone, Wesley looked down at the table. He had done everything he could. She was gone from this world, and probably he would soon follow her into that unknown destiny of the next quest. They were surely going to arrest him for rape and murder, and there probably wouldn't be a jury in the world who would let him off. Wesley knew very well his life was over. He looked up and saw her. Grace... in a wedding dress he had never seen before.

She walked over and took his hand...

This made him happy...

She picked up the pen and held it out to him...

He looked in her eyes...

Green was his favorite color...

In the hallway outside the interrogation room, the three stood in silence to gather their thoughts. This hallway was quite cold... colder than it was twenty minutes ago.

"We're going to pretend that didn't happen," Ellis stated.

"Sheriff—"

"It never happened."

Vicki opened her mouth to speak. No words came out.

Seth entered the lobby to find his wife staring into space.

"He's sick," Seth said.

Ellis and Vicki followed. Vicki, for once, was speechless. Unsure if she should remain under Ellis's authority, she questioned whether she should be in Oostburg at all. Seth stole his gun, and he wasn't going to do anything about it. Vicki wondered what else Ellis was covering up.

The front door opened and Brooke entered; the room engulfed in awkward silence. Now that Vicki knew the relationships in Oostburg, she could imagine what Thanksgiving dinner would be like next month.

Brooke's husband was in a "relationship" with... her brother's... daughter—ah yes, pass the greens. Vicki would love to sit at that holiday table.

Seth and Evelyn stared at Brooke. Vicki was not sure if they were judging her or if they were sympathetic.

Brooke spoke first:

"I had no idea."

Without looking at her, Evelyn said:

"You knew he was having an affair."

Brooke looked down.

"But I didn't know with who," she spoke truthfully.

Seth couldn't grasp her statement.

"How could you not know?"

Brooke spoke quietly:

"How could you?"

Ellis gave an inappropriate chuckle.

"Small-town like this. Usually, people know each other's secrets."

Brooke looked away at her chair, having a very difficult time suppressing her triumphs. She had been faking her paralysis for months, and only Gracie knew, and she never said a word. Now Wesley knew too.

"Did he kill Grace?" Evelyn asked.

Vicki stepped forward.

"He confessed to statutory. It explains—" She paused; momentarily remembering that she was talking to the victim's drained parents. Vicki continued: "The blood in the back seat. That's …where they had sex."

"Did he rape her?" Evelyn continued her investigation.

"Yes and no. It was consensual rape. In case of rape... there are usually other... kinds of bruising. It appears Gracie's date—meeting was... consensual."

"Why? I—I just don't understand why she would be... romantically interested. He is a rather pathetic man," Evelyn said.

Brooke snickered.

"Sorry, Brooke."

"You're right. He is," Brooke agreed.

"Remember her eleventh birthday and Gracie was almost hit by that car?" Seth asked his wife, who nodded. "That is when she began to have feelings for him. He saved her life."

Vicki spoke up:

"It's still rape. Gracie was a minor, and legally she doesn't have the right to consent. She was seventeen, and here in Wisconsin, you have to be eighteen. If they would have waited till April... they would have been in the clear. Statutory gets him many—"

And before Vicki could finish, there was a noisy clatter from the interrogation room. The five adults looked around briefly to check that they all heard the same sound.

33.

HAPPY REUNION

Ellis and Vicki were the first to arrive, followed a second later by Seth.

Bursting through the door, the trio saw that the chair was empty, the chair they had left Wesley in. In fact, the chair was on the floor, turned over. The chair was lying right next to Wesley; who was shaking, convulsing, and struggling to breathe; swimming in a large, maroon river of wetness.

His struggles to breathe likely had something to do with the pen; which was protruding out of his neck, a pen that Sheriff Ellis had so carelessly left on the table.

Vicki ran out to grab her cell and bumped into Evelyn and Brooke, who were seconds behind the first group of three. Falling to the floor, Brooke briefly gave witness to her secret—but lucky for Brooke, no one was paying attention. Evelyn turned around and grabbed her tight to block her vantage point.

It didn't matter, as Brooke screamed, seeing what had transpired. Even though Wesley was a terrible husband, a liar, a cheat... she loved the man. She felt sorry for him, but she loved him.

Ellis walked over to pick up a note that was on the floor towards Wesley's side. There was some blood on the corner of the note.

Ellis read the note:

"If my best friends weren't going to believe me,
how would 12 A. M.?"

Seth, who thought justice had been served, stood in silence.

The paramedics came rather quickly, but they were not in time for Wesley Allen Demko. He passed away in the ambulance, on his way to the hospital.

The case closed for Gracie Adams and Wesley Demko.

Ellis and Vicki began the tedious task of paperwork, wrapping up the file. It was reported that Wesley Demko had killed Gracie Adams. They met late that night, had sex in the car, and presumably got into an argument—over what... maybe she was going to break up with him after the sex?—and so he killed her. He drove her body into the woods, parked her car over her body, and walked home. Even though they couldn't officially prove it, and he never technically confessed, Ellis was very ready to close this case.

Vicki was a little less than enthused.

"You okay?" Ellis asked.

Vicki stared as if this puzzle were missing one last piece, even though the pieces were all placed together.

"Umm... no, not really."

Ellis walked over to her desk.

"You should be. We caught the guy. You're a—"

"Don't you think it's odd that even in death, he didn't confess?" Vicki paused. "I just... feel like we missed something."

"He confessed in his note: "No one would believe me".

Vicki shook her head.

"Or maybe he meant: *No one would believe that I simply loved her and only had sex with her.*"

Exhausted, Vicki leaned back in her chair. "Two hours ago, I was... so positive. In my experience, Ellis, when someone kills themself, they lay everything out on the table. They tie up every loose end with laces and ribbon and everything pretty. They *confess*." Vicki paused. "I just think there's a piece missing. It's—"

Ellis looked up at Vicki.

"It's time to go home, Vicki."

And Vicki did just that.

Glued to the seat in her car, the supreme thought in her mind:
Why didn't he confess?

The left side of her brain was playing ping-pong with the right.

She was upset; very upset.

Parking her car outside the house, she sat in silence. This first week in Oostburg had been rough—and here Vicki thought she was leaving the hustle and bustle of New York City to the stillness and tranquility of the midwest. It was her aunt who told her *she couldn't run from the devil*. How right Coralee was. For that is exactly why Vicki had come to this small-town; to out-run Satan. But like God, Satan is everywhere, a knock-out battle with Jesus every painful step of the way.

And it seemed as though Satan were winning.

A week into her new job, and she was not sure if she was going to remain. Vicki wasn't sure if she could work for Sheriff Ellis Kirkbride any longer. Ellis let Seth go; completely without any consequence. Seth was a thief, but now also had assault with a firearm on his resume. The pastor stole the sheriff's gun for Christ's sake and almost killed that disgusting man. Seth should be in jail, but this noisy evening Seth was sleeping at home, completely off the hook. This was not how Vicki would have run the department.

She thought about running away, again. But then what would happen to her aunt? Cousin Jessica was in Green Bay, maybe she would take sick Coralee, but Jessica's house was small and she had kids. It wouldn't be fair to Jessica. No, Aunt Coralee would probably end up in some nursing home the rest of her days, which probably wouldn't be many.

Her thoughts went back to Wesley. That sick bastard admitting to everything except the murder. He said he loved her, dated her, and slept with her. He said he walked home after they fornicated. He had no great alibi. Why didn't he just confess to everything? She felt queasy as if she were going to vomit. Her last two cases racked her mind, spirit, and stomach. Gabrielle Adjami was never solved—at least not proved, in her opinion—the killer got away. Here, the apparent killer was brought to justice and duly executed—by himself. But still, in her opinion, both cases were not closed.

If Wesley were innocent, who else could've done it? There was not a financial gain from Gracie's death. If it were a random stranger that attacked her, why didn't he take her cash? Did Charles Raile hire someone to take her? And if so, who was that person? Raile was not talking either...

Vicki shook her head. According to Ellis, the case was closed.

She felt uneasy.

Wesley Demko did not kill Gracie Adams...

Walking into her house, the first thing Vicki saw was her screaming aunt, swinging a shovel in the air...

34.

BURYING THE EVIDENCE?

Aunt Coralee screamed like a banshee:

"Who are you? What are you doing in my home?!"

Oh my god.

"Aunt Coralee? What's going on?"

Aunt Coralee snapped back into—her—reality, and began to bawl.

"I don't know! I don't know. I can't remember. I can't... remember anything anymore... did I kill her?"

Vicki's jaw dropped but she could not produce any sound. All of a sudden, it made sense although she couldn't believe it. The deputy left her aunt alone that evening, to go visit her cousin up in Green Bay.

"Aunt Coralee, I don't know... why would you? I was only gone for a couple of hours—"

Coralee covered her mouth in fear.

"Good Lord. I killed her! I—I—I thought she was an intruder and I... oh. I picked this up and killed her! *I had an accident!*"

I had an accident...

That punched Vicki in the stomach. Aunt Coralee said that she had an accident some days ago, but she was completely dry. Was *this* the wet accident, the horrendous accident, she was talking about?

Coralee sat down, in a full-blown panic. She did remember... Gracie came in—she was happy about something—and Coralee did not know—she could not remember who Gracie was—and thinking Gracie was going to rob her, she defended herself with the shovel.

It all came back to Coralee.

She killed Gracie Adams.

"Please. Please don't say anything..."

Vicki stood there, unsure of what to do...

Quickly, Vicki ran into the bathroom to splash her face with cold water, drowning her face. Crying, she looked in the mirror and screamed in fear, vomiting in the sink.

Gracie was right behind her...

The dead teenager spoke:

"You're going to let her get away?"

Staring in this mirror—that was reflecting her ideology—was she going to turn into her boss? Ellis let Seth off by covering up and here Vicki was faced with the same situation—actually, this was a lot worse. If she tells Ellis, Coralee goes away—for good. Sure, she would plead insanity—and definitely get by with a lesser murder charge—but that would still mean a lengthy hospital stay, and at her age, probably life.

Or does she swallow the knowledge? Wesley was dead. There was not one good reason for proving his innocence or clearing his name. His name was mud anyway after his confession.

There was no harm in this very little, insignificant, white lie.

But it was the moral of it. Deputy Vicki Weathers lived by a certain code of ethics. And yes, she broke into Raile's home, but that was a much smaller transgression. This was covering up murder.

Switching her jumbled thoughts to Gabrielle Adjami—the case that intensified her insane bitterness—she concurred that perhaps something similar happened in the Gabrielle case... was Gags or someone under him covering as well? Where did the corruption start? Where did it end?

And for the first moment since her mother's death, Victoria Weathers bawled.

She did not know what to do...

Getting home pretty late, they sat in the living room not knowing what to say, how to feel, or what to do—they just existed.

It was over. The killer was caught; Gracie was laid to rest. This chapter was finally over; but a next chapter, with unending pain, would never go away. Being a pastor and his wife, they knew that.

The entire Earth would continue... but Seth and Evelyn would not.

Oostburg, Wisconsin, America, Earth, time all moved on. Except for Seth and Evelyn Adams. They sat there.

"What now?" Evelyn asked.

They sat for another minute before Seth spoke:

"I'm thinking about quitting my job."

Evelyn was silent.

"How would you feel about that?"

"I think it would be fine. Just fine."

"Yeah. I think I'm going to quit."

"What would you do?"

"I don't know."

"We don't have much money saved up."

"No, we don't." Seth paused and went on: "Maybe try working at Pizza Ranch?"

"They have good food."

"Yes, they do."

"We still have Lainey."

"Huh?"

"Lainey, our other daughter," Evelyn reminded her husband.

"Oh yes. I forgot about her."

At that moment, they looked at each other.

They forgot about her.

All this time, these eight days, Lainey, Gracie's younger sister, had been pushed to the shaft. She was on the back burner and completely out of the picture. To be honest... Seth and Evelyn did that frequently but now that Gracie was gone, they no longer had a reason. Being out of the picture was what Lainey desired, in fact, it was Lainey who pressed her parents away to begin with, but now with Gracie gone, this couldn't happen any longer.

"We need to reach her," Seth said.

"Does she want to be reached?"

Seth got up.

"Come."

"Now?"

"Yes, now."

"She's sleeping."

"Evelyn... Gracie is gone. Who knows how much longer we will have Lainey? Can we really trust god anymore to protect our daughter? He failed our first one."

Seth and Evelyn went upstairs and opened Lainey's door.

To their surprise, their little girl was lying on her bed fully awake. They wondered if she heard anything of the conversation that transpired downstairs.

"Laincy?" Seth asked.

"Yes?"

"How are you?"

"I'm... fine."

"Lainey, tomorrow... could we eat out for breakfast...? The three of us?"

"Sure."

The folks stayed there for an uncomfortable amount of time before the father took over.

"I love you, Lainey."

"Thank you."

"I love you too, Lainey. We're going to get through this," Evelyn added.

"Lainey. Your... Uncle Wesley... killed Gracie," Seth said.

Lainey sat in silence.

"Hey, Lainey."

"Yes?"

"What do you want to be when you grow up?"

Lainey was quiet. The thirteen-year-old digested the question, and her eyes began to get moist. She finally replied:

"Loved."

In the doorway, Seth and Evelyn looked at each other and immediately walked over to Lainey, knelt, and hugged her.

For the first time, the family of three mourned together.

Vicki couldn't sleep this Friday night/Saturday morning. She laid in her bed thinking of what could have been; what is true; and what may be yet to come.

There was a phrase that kept swimming in her brain, she could not get it out; nor could she make sense of it. A phrase she recently heard:

It takes a village...

She sat up.

Walking downstairs at three in the morning, she could see her old aunt in the rocking chair. Aunt Coralee was stroking a kitty, yet there was no cat on her lap.

Vicki stopped at the archway of the door, waiting for her aunt to acknowledge her.

"You could not have done this alone."

Coralee kept staring at the wall.

"You don't drive. There is no way you could have dragged her body all the way into the forest and buried her. You had to have help."

Coralee cried.

"I don't know! I don't remember anything!"

She walked over and knelt by her dementia-ridden auntie. Gently touching her hand, Vicki felt horrible probing the older woman, a blood relative that she loved for facts that she couldn't remember.

"Think—who helped you?"

"I don't know!"

"Someone *had* to help you! There is no way you did this alone! You had to—*someone* helped you cover up! Aunt Coralee... who do you rely on when you need help?"

"You! I go to you, Vicki!"

"Yes... but I wasn't here that evening. I was visiting Jessica in Green Bay. Before I moved here, who drove you to the grocery store? Who helped you around *before* I came to Oostburg?"

Vicki closed her eyes.

She knew the answer...

Eight minutes later, she was on his porch slamming on the door. The dog barked a good two minutes before the man appeared, almost naked.

"Vicki, it's four in the morning... you, uh, hungry?"

He chuckled at his not-so-subtle hint at a sexual escapade.

"You helped my aunt. You covered up for her."

Ellis rubbed his eyes.

"Covered up? For what?"

Vicki couldn't believe she was having this conversation, with this man, at this time of the morning.

"My aunt has dementia and forgets her name at the drop of the Bible. She saw Gracie that evening, thought she was an intruder, killed her with a shovel, and then got scared and called you."

"Are you kidding me?"

"She said you are the one who drives her around town."

"I have driven her quite a few times."

"Right, so naturally *you* would be the one she would call when she needed a ride."

"Are you out of your mind?"

"She killed her—thinking Gracie was an intruder. But you helped her bury—no, correction—you didn't *help* her bury—you did it all by yourself. That is why you wanted to avoid the forest because you *knew* she was there!"

"Vicki, Vicki, Vic—"

"No cop would be that dumb. You were lax on this case because you knew the more I dug, the more likely the crime would be brought to your door."

Ellis shook his head.

"Is that what you believe?"

"Yes, that is what happened."

Ellis yawned.

"So what's next?"

Vicki stopped. What would happen next? The deputy knew the truth, and again and again the truth—the truth—

The truth is that her aunt was a killer...

And the local sheriff helped cover it up...

Vicki swallowed, unsure of what she wanted the outcome to be.

"I want you to confess to Seth and Evelyn, Ellis. Now. We'll take it from there," she spoke bravely, unsure if she was bluffing or not.

"There is nothing to confess, Vicki. I didn't do anything."

"Consider yourself warned," Vicki pressed.

Ellis spoke:

"Where's your proof?"

Vicki looked in his eyes.

"Fine. I'm giving you five hours to figure it out. 9AM, Ellis. If you don't do the right thing, I am turning you and Aunt Coralee over to the authorities."

Vicki turned around and took two steps before she heard him say:

"I am the authority."

Damn it.

And she went home.

When she got home, she slammed the door. Stomping past the living room, she saw her aunt still stroking the imaginary cat. She loved her aunt. She... couldn't... she couldn't turn her in.

And that meant she couldn't turn Ellis in, either.

She sent him a text:

"I quit."

The funeral for rapist Wesley Demko did not last long. It was a little affair, and after all that press coverage of him molesting and killing Gracie Adams, only two mourners showed up: Pastor Bob Zimmermann, who was presiding, and Wesley's widow, Brooke.

As he desired, Wesley was cremated. Tiny ashes were scattered all over Lake Michigan as Zimmermann and Brooke took a little dinghy out on the water. Brooke no longer needed help walking; both legs miraculously healed three days after her husband's death.

Robert Zimmermann had begun to discover what a faulty preacher he previously had been. Now that he was in charge of the church, he felt a closer calling to God and felt a stronger desire to do the right thing, even if it were difficult. From this horrific tragedy, Bob had become a better person. He felt terrible for the way he had treated Seth and his family these past years, Brooke included. His apologies and sincerities were happily accepted.

As they got a mile in, Brooke dumped his ashes into the lake. She got a second container, which contained another set of ashes:

Wesley's unfinished novel.

"You sure you want to do that?" Bob asked.

"Yes. I don't even want to know what he wrote about."

"You do know a little?"

"A little. Enough, really."

And the ashes of *Through Eyes Of Grace* were dumped in the blue lake, right above the ashes of Wesley Demko, never to be seen again.

Life continued. Every day got easier and harder for Seth and Evelyn Adams. They bonded more with Lainey; got to know their daughter. In addition to being "loved", she wanted to learn how to fix and ride a motorcycle, cure cancer, play softball in high school. It was not easy, getting to know Lainey. This was the little girl who hid in her room so frequently. She didn't want to be a part of the family at all it seemed until Gracie was gone. Nonetheless, things were improving. Lainey was personable. She had an intelligent sense of humor. Seth and Evelyn couldn't help but wonder why she wasn't this way before; why she shut them out all these years...

Seth sat with Ellis having a beer in Jesus Take The Wheel.

"I couldn't forgive anyone. Not Raile; Wesley. It has been a week since Wesley... all I can feel is *good for you, jackass*. What kind of a pastor am I?"

"It's understandable—"

Seth cut him off.

"It's justifying. He wants us to always forgive, even when it hurts the most."

"Don't be—"

"I resigned. Lainey's baptism on Sunday is my last day."

The front door opened.

Seth could see his sister, Brooke. A small smile came on his face as she walked over to the men. He was happy—a coy solace—that she was able to toss the wheels.

The bartender, a slim, black-haired lesbian in her late twenties, immediately took an attraction to Brooke.

"What will it be, sexy?"

The compliment caught Brooke off-guard. She had never been hit on by a woman before.

"Vodka on the rocks."

"You got it."

While the bartender made the drink, Brooke, Seth, and Ellis stared out of their own cages.

"Put it on my tab," Seth said.

The bartender made the drink and handed it to Brooke, who slurped it with concealed enjoyment.

"Getting the hang of walking again?" Seth asked his sister.

Brooke was getting used to walking in public.

"Yeah. Three days after Wesley died, I felt my legs again."

She was also getting used to lying.

"How you holding up otherwise?"

"Umm, just buried my husband, who was sleeping with my niece. Not sure if I am sad, angry, or in denial."

Brooke looked into her vodka on the rocks. She had made a serious mistake. She was in love with Wesley, but at the end of the day, he was a pedophile and a killer.

Raising her glass, she added:

"Well. Here's to whatever the Good Lord has next for us."

The three clinked their glasses to their respective futures.

35.

A COFFEE AND A ROAD TRIP

For Seth, he knew the future to a degree. The next chapter of his life would be mending the bond with his youn—*only* daughter, Lainey. He missed out on so much, mainly because Lainey was locked in her room, but also he felt terrible that he had praised Gracie to the point where Lainey felt left out.

Saturday, the day before Lainey's baptism, Seth took his daughter to Perkins in Sheboygan. This was his favorite place to dine, as he and four others had a men's group the second Saturday of the month. Seth decided to step out of this group to focus more on his daughter.

"Maybe you can be Ellis's partner," Seth grinned as he said that.

Ellis told him Vicki resigned.

"Ha. Maybe."

"You're a very smart young lady, Lainey. I'm sorry we didn't tell you more often."

"It's okay. I wasn't... the easiest daughter to deal with."

"No, you weren't," Seth smiled. "Sorry."

"I'm sorry too."

The waitress walked over and handed them menus.

"Can I get you anything to start?"

"I'll take a coffee, black," Seth ordered.

"Me too," Lainey followed.

Seth smiled at his daughter.

"I will get that right away," the waitress said before she walked away.

The daughter stepped up to the plate and asked a special question that made Seth's heart melt:

"Will you go to the daddy-daughter-dance with me?"

"Absolutely."

Wishing he had two dates that evening in February, Seth was delighted Lainey finally wanted to attend—not that he asked many times—he only asked once and was turned down harshly so he never asked again.

"I love you, Lainey."

"I know you do," Lainey paused. "Now."

"Yes, now."

"But will you tomorrow?"

"Of course, why wouldn't I?"

Lainey paused to clarify.

"I'm getting baptized. Is this still okay?"

"It's your choice. You are an adult." Seth smiled. "Almost."

"Maybe forgiveness... isn't such a bad thing."

Seth sat back.

"Some things are not forgivable."

She packed all of her belongings, as well as her aunt's.

Vicki called her friend in Virginia Beach who used to be a cop in the NYPD. Her friend, Dana, relocated to Virginia Beach after her husband received a job offer. Vicki called Dana and she agreed to house them for a little. It meant she'd have to live with two little brats as well, but at this point, killers can't be choosers.

The tiny car was packed as Vicki and Coralee began their journey southeast to Virginia Beach.

Vicki felt ashamed. She was ashamed she was running from the law. She was ashamed she knew the truth. Gracie's killer was none other than her Aunt Coralee, a good lady with a bad bout of dementia. She thought about turning her in but did not want to send Aunt Coralee to the mental hospital. She knew how horrible they treated people sometimes, and she didn't want that fate for her aunt, especially since old Aunt Coralee was probably not going to live much longer anyway.

Was it the right decision? Perhaps. It was the mercy way to go.

Driving through Milwaukee, south on I-43, Vicki took in the buildings. Milwaukee was nothing in comparison to New York City, but it still had a big city feel. Half a million citizens are nothing to sneeze at.

It was in Milwaukee that she remembered Gabrielle Adjami. How her killer got away. Vicki was not fully aware of how the killer got away—but the monster was free. Free to murder and rape and do whatever else it wanted.

Vicki wiped her cheek as she had been leaking tears for some time. Deep down, she knew this was wrong... this was running. Something Vicki was not trained to do, even if she had done it two weeks prior.

And then there was Kirkbride. The law in Oostburg. And even though his intentions were kind-hearted, he was at the end of the day quite deceitful and really could not be trusted. He was an accessory to the fact—how could he be in charge of Oostburg?

Vicki knew she could run a better place. Maybe she should turn in her aunt, and Ellis, and then simply take over the sheriff's mantle. Then she can sleep till noon and read the paper and...

Vicki took the following exit off the highway and pulled into the gas station. They had only gone about sixty miles or so, but Vicki felt the need to gas up. If Vicki was going to turn in the dynamic duo, she needed to do it now. They had not wasted much gas or time. She certainly did not want to travel all the way to Virginia Beach and then have the change of heart. No, the change of heart needed to occur here.

As Vicki was gassing the car, she saw a female teenager walk into the station. About Gracie's age. An older fellow, hopefully her father, was filling up as the girl went into the store.

Vicki looked at the man, who caught her looking, and he smiled at her.

"Nice day, huh?"

"I suppose," Vicki responded.

The man paused before saying:

"You alright? You look deep in thought."

"Yes, I guess I am."

"You lost?"

"I'm not… sure anymore."

"Huh?"

The girl came back with a diet soda and some dollars in her hand. She gave the bills to the man and got back in the car.

"She your daughter?"

"Yes, miss. My daughter, Stephanie. We are driving down to the hospital to visit my wife. She's been in ICU for six days now. Car accident."

"Sorry."

"Yeah, me too. To be honest, this young lady and my wife, they're all I have." The man tapped the hood of his ride. "Well, we best be off. Best of luck to you."

And they were gone. Vicki hoped the wife was going to make it.

The word "honest" floated in her mind... went down her gullet and sat like a boulder in her gut.

She wasn't being honest.

Running isn't honesty.

Vicki sighed a difficult breath. She knew what she had to do.

"Hypocrite," she whispered.

And then she remembered that time in the bar when she had a drink with Pastor Adams. She had used that very word to accuse him:

"We're all sinners, Officer Weathers."
"But not all of us are hypocrites, Pastor Adams."

She couldn't be a hypocrite. Not former Deputy Victoria Weathers.

Even if that meant turning in her dear aunt. Even if it meant she would be sent to the mental institution, fed crappy garbage, and abused daily. Even if it cost Ellis Kirkbride his badge and gun. She needed to be honest and stand up for what she believed in.

Looking in the driver's side window, Vicki turned to Aunt Coralee in the car.

The old lady spoke:

"We have to tell pastor what I did."

36.

THE SECOND BOY

Sunday morning began the subsequent chapter in the life of Lainey Adams. The girl sat on the stage in front of about seventy witnesses waiting to hear her life switch to Jesus. Pastor Zimmermann sat next to her as the two watched her father give a short introduction.

Yawning at the pulpit stood Seth Adams. He had a horrendous, dark nightmare the night prior, which awakened him at 1AM, and afterward, he was unable to go back to sleep. Holding onto the sides of the pulpit as he had done many times before, Seth felt the difference this moment and knowing it would be his last time, held on a little tighter. He grabbed on as if this life jacket were being chucked into the ocean never to be used again. Seth became his own man and decided he was not going to use the almighty father as a crutch anymore. He gave his life to Jesus many years past, and on this day he was taking it back. He was tired. He was tired of the praying, the devotions, the Bible study, the hours. He was burnt out.

And it was god who burnt him out.

Had god answered the most important, fragile prayer of his world: "*please keep my precious daughter safe*"—things would be different. The truth is: if god couldn't answer that one prayer, then he was not worth it. If god's not going to help you in your greatest moment of need, the question remains... do you really need him? Four years of seminary, many years of service—it was all for nothing. God did not care about him or his family. He remembered a part of scripture that he used to cling to. Deuteronomy 31:6:

> *"Be strong and courageous.*
> *Do not be afraid or terrified because of them,*
> *for the LORD your God goes with you;*
> *He will never leave you nor forsake you."*

He clung to it—past tense—but it was not gospel. Sometimes god does forget you. Sometimes, god does forsake you. Even Jesus asked: "*My God, my God, why have you forsaken me?*" And because of that, the pastor was afraid.

It was all a lie.

Jesus was forsaken.

Job was forsaken.

Pastor Seth Isaiah Adams was forsaken.

Looking out toward the first row, he could see his beautiful wife Evelyn. Feeling incredibly guilty, knowing he sacrificed precious time with her, he knew he would rectify that. This female, Evelyn, was going to get his best, not god. Seth Adams was going to be a new man.

"As you know, this is our last Sunday here."

Zimmermann smiled and nodded.

"This evil tragedy has taught our family many things. Mainly, how unprepared we are for life, and our faith. We say we're Christians, but at the end of the day, when our faith is put to the test, we typically screw up. Yes, god is there to forgive us. Even when you cannot forgive those that trespass against you."

Seth swallowed a little before continuing:

"Pastor Zimmermann will bring this church to that next height—if you f-ollow his path. Not Pastor Bob's, but god's. Let god himself lead you. You know what Gracie would say? Love. Love each other."

He still knew the right words, even though they were now empty.

In the back of the sanctuary, Seth could see his beautiful Gracie clinging hands with that—rapist. Stopping his vomit, he stared at them for an uncomfortable amount of seconds; enough seconds for this worried congregation to feel awkward. A few people turned around to see what he was staring at, but only he could see the disgusting couple.

Seth went on:

"Love one another. My Gracie was... so forgiving. Gracie is back there... forgiving the man who did this to her."

Evelyn looked around, giving an awkward smile to the lady next to her.

"Gracie was as perfect as humanly possible. She was too great for this world. Too good for me." Seth paused and looked up at the ceiling. "Maybe that's why you took her."

The congregation started to become uncomfortable as if Seth were an embarrassing, drunk uncle at a family reunion. They were hoping Seth was finished.

Bob Zimmermann stood up and took the pulpit. He shook Seth's hand and Seth knew it was his last moment preaching. Bob hugged him tight; a genuine hug. The manager was going to the bullpen to let the closer get the final three outs.

Seth slowly walked down the small steps and sat next to his wife, gently grabbing her hand.

Bob gestured to the girl, and she went up to the pulpit, standing on a short stool to accommodate her five-foot-nothing frame.

"My name is Lainey Adams. I'm thirteen-years-old and I've decided to accept Jesus as my personal Savior."

The sheep applauded.

"Being a Christian... means accepting that you do bad stuff and that... the Lord will forgive you. It means that people aren't perfect. Nobody. Not even pastors are perfect."

Looking around, Seth smiled confusingly. Out in the distance, he could see that female deputy sitting next to Coralee. Seth was under the impression she left town. *What was she doing here?*

"Sometimes pastors make mistakes too. And that makes me feel much better because if pastors can make mistakes, we shouldn't be so mad at ourselves. We should forgive everyone. Even yourself. Sometimes, even I do naughty things. Like that time I drove down the street after dad had taught me how to drive—even though I couldn't reach the pedals."

A couple of "oohs" and "aahs" were heard from this entertaining tale of a pastor illegally teaching his underage daughter how to drive.

"He told me to put a big book under my butt—wear Gracie's heels—I remember dad told me not to tell mom. Never let others see—"

Vicki stood up; then the sheriff did as well. The remainder of the congregation sat there in confusion, looking to their neighbors for answers.

Victoriously, Vicki walked down the center aisle in silence. Aunt Coralee sheepishly followed.

"Pastor Seth, I'm so sorry to do this. And I know you hate Wesley Demko. You have every reason to."

Vicki paused.

"But he did *not* kill your daughter."

The sheep glanced around, stupid as ever.

Evelyn covered her mouth. Seth walked down the aisle, meeting the deputy half-way, where Ellis was standing.

"What?" Seth asked.

"You need proof, Vicki," Ellis said.

"What's going on, Ellis?" Seth asked.

Simultaneously, Vicki and Ellis stepped closer to Seth, as if the pastor were a fumbled football in the last minutes of the Super Bowl.

"She's about to tell you something that is completely not true, Seth," Ellis pleaded.

"Pastor Adams, Wesley did not kill your Grace."

"Yes, he did."

"With all due respect, we were wrong. I know... because..."

Ellis stepped in.

"Seth. Vicki has this silly idea that Coralee killed Gracie, and I drove the car into the woods and buried Gracie."

"What?"

"It's crazy. She thinks her aunt did it."

"I thought my aunt, Coralee Mentink, killed Gracie."

Seth, along with everyone in the congregation, stared down at the old lady, not fully believing the words he heard.

Ellis added:

"Coralee thought Gracie was an intruder and she defended herself. It was a complete accident. That's what Vicki thinks."

"Yes, but—"

Evelyn stood up and spoke:

"Coralee, is that true?"

Coralee nodded.

"I don't remember doing it, but I did it. She came to my house. I didn't know who she was—I thought she was coming to rob me—I swear!"

"Everyone just stop!" Vicki yelled.

Coralee was bawling.

"It was an accident, Pastor Adams—please, I'm so sorry! I didn't know!"

Seth turned to his friend.

"Coralee? Ellis? You?" asked Seth. "Is this true? Did you bury my daughter?"

"No! I didn't do anything to Gracie, you have to believe me," Ellis pleaded.

"Ellis?" Evelyn asked for clarity.

Vicki yelled:

"Would everyone just shut the hell up?! That's what I *thought.* I was mistaken. Up until about two minutes ago. But I do know who killed Gracie."

"Who?" Seth and Evelyn asked at the same time.

"I'm sorry. It was Lainey. It was your daughter, Lainey," Vicki said.

Slowly, Seth and Evelyn turned around to stare at their daughter, both shaking their heads in disbelief.

"No..." both said in different tones.

"She can't even—" Evelyn said; and then quickly covered her mouth, as the mom remembered that Lainey just stated not four minutes ago that Seth taught her how to drive.

Vicki went on:

"Ellis, do you remember the drunk and what he told us at the station?"

Ellis looked at Lainey, hoping for a sign.

"I remember the drunk."

"And you remember what he said?" asked Vicki.

"Yes, I remember what he said."

"I seen pastor's daughter's car that night.
She drivin' it!"

"He said: "*pastor's daughter*". And we assumed he meant Gracie since it was her car. But he didn't mean Gracie—he saw *Lainey*."

There was silence for a moment.

"She was driving the car. Lainey said Seth taught her how to drive—how tall are you, Lainey?"

"Five-feet," Seth admitted.

Ellis nodded.

"We are looking for a shorter driver."

"Mrs. Mentink is also short," added Lainey.

"But my aunt can't drive," Vicki said.

Lainey defended herself:

"Ok, I lied—a little. I did see Gracie come back. She came back and she was gloating about her silly boyfriend. I told her to stop because I didn't want to hear it and she left. She left to talk with her friend—the piano teacher!"

Lainey. Coralee. Ellis.

Seth and Evelyn stood there, unsure of whose story to buy. Ellis and Coralee were friends of the family, having been over thirty years. Lainey was...

Seth then remembered the nightmare he had the previous night:

Two teenagers, one about seventeen, the other somewhat younger... say thirteen, were walking through the woods. They were going to make a sacrifice. One boy was bringing the best thing he had to offer... while the other boy was bringing the leftovers.

"He's not going to be pleased by what you are offering," said the more generous teenager.

"I don't care. He's not getting the best. You are stupid to offer Him the best of your stash."

"It's not the best."

"It's not?"

"It's everything."

The two walked a little further and placed their offerings on the table. The first child set his on fire, which lit up a huge inferno. Smoke billowing left and right, the first kid knew that Father would be pleased with what he had offered. The first boy stepped back and calmly gestured to the other, "your turn".

The second boy stepped forward and knelt, almost knowing his offering wasn't going to succeed. He didn't want to give his best. The father didn't care or love him anyway, so why bother?

He lit the match; and nothing happened. He lit a second time, and again the same result. A third match was sacrificed to no avail.

"Screw this," he lamented.

"Hey, you can't disrespect Him like that!"

This made the other furious.

"You've always been His favorite!"

And the older picked up a stone and swung at the other, splitting the cranium; knocking him dead.

They were siblings...

Seth walked over to his little girl. Evelyn reached out to him; a reach that was shrugged off.

"No..." Evelyn sobbed, staring at her younger daughter.

Through eyes of tears, he knelt and looked her in the face.

"It was an accident, right Lainey? An accident?"

Lainey swallowed... and the swallow told Evelyn all she needed to know.

Evelyn collapsed; full-knowing her younger daughter killed her elder.

Seth continued to ease the blow:

"It was an accident, hun. Yes. An... accident. A horr—horrible... accident. Right, Lainey? And you got scared..."

Lainey looked at her parents. After a few seconds, she spoke:

"Damn it, dad."

Seth's eyes bulged.

"It wasn't an accident."

37.

THE PUZZLE COMES APART

Gracie entered the Adams' kitchen in a whirl of promise and hope. The world and future were theirs; she knew it. She had her man, she was certain he would leave his wife now and it appeared that the good Jesus had ordained it.

The beloved teen queen danced for a few seconds before seeing her younger sister sitting on a stool at the island. Sitting there, doing nothing but staring.

"You're supposed to be in bed," Lainey retorted.

Gracie smiled and walked towards the refrigerator, opening it for a water.

"Where were you?" Lainey asked.

Gracie opened her water and took a short sip.

"I was out."

Lainey pressed.

"Of course you were out."

"Don't worry—"

Lainey cut her off.

"It's so unfair that you get whatever you want. I don't even have a cell phone. I can't do anything, go anywhere."

"Lainey, you're thirteen. When you're seventeen you will have—"

"Who were you with? Uncle Wesley again?"

Gracie smiled.

"His name is Wesley. Wesley Allen Demko. Isn't it wonderful? I am getting close, Lainey. Close to all my dreams coming true."

Gracie took her sister by her little hands. Lainey flinched, perfectly disgusted by her sister's fantasies and hopes. Maybe she was the good daughter, after all.

Gracie looked her cold sister straight in the eyes, and in perfectly clear diction, told Lainey:

"I'm going to have his baby."

"What?"

Gracie smiled and went to the cabinet, taking out a large bowl.

The blue bowl fit perfectly under Gracie's dress, right below her breasts.

"His baby, Lainey! I'm going to have his baby! And I will be *the* Virgin Mary. Except, I won't be a virgin."

Gracie and everyone else thought awkward Lainey was the messed up one. Turns out Gracie was—

"Crazy! What about Aunt Brooke?"

Gracie gave an innocent sigh as she put away the bowl.

"I feel bad for her; I really do. But she will find someone else. Perhaps someone who doesn't want a kid. It's not proper for her to keep him when she can't give him what he needs."

Gracie patted her little sister on the head; a demeaning thing to do to a child who thinks they are an adult.

"Lainey, someday you'll understand. You will have happiness. But you need patience. You don't need to get so angry. One day you will get everything you ever wanted... just like me."

Gracie kissed Lainey on the top of the head.

And the older made her final exit, leaving Lainey in the kitchen, boiling like a pot of water.

Gracie sat on the grass, kneeling by her mother's flower bed. Smiling from ear-to-ear, she gazed upon the stars. "What a beautiful night," she said to herself as she plucked a daisy from the flower bed. Deflowering its petals one by one, she whispered: "he loves me; he loves me not" back and forth till the final pedal—a love me!—remained. Everything was perfect for Gracie. The two were going to run away after graduation—only a few short months now and they wouldn't have to sneak around in secret. How nice that would be, living as a couple out in the open. Of course, they would have to leave Oostburg, but that was a tiny price to pay. Oostburg was nice, but really, there was nothing going on here. Gracie wanted to head west, see the ocean. She loved the thought of California. She loved supporting her future husband's writing—maybe he could even write a movie one day. And she would be by his side, smiling and cheering him on every step of the path. That is all men really want. They want a cheerleader. Someone who is going to appreciate their efforts, clap when they put the toilet seat down. Brooke was not doing this for Wesley—she was doing the opposite really, and that killed the marriage. She knew why she almost died when she was eleven, as God says "everything happens for a reason." Well... that near-fatal car accident led to her finding the love of her life. Gracie was going to marry this man—this guy who was way too old for her numerically but probably even younger than her mentally—she was going to marry the man who saved—

OWWWW...

...Eleven...

Fatal...

Almost... accident... flower...

She suddenly felt so dizzy... so woozy... oh man headache...

She looked up...

Lainey... there, huge rock... rock had odd red stain...

Can't think... Wesley...

Her sister raised the rock again...

And Gracie Adams lowered her shades for the last time...

Good thing for Lainey, her father taught her poker at a young age. It was really the only thing they did together.

She knew how to play poker.

She knew how to cover her hand.

She was going to get away with this...

Putting on gloves, she began her cover: Grabbing Gracie's keys and heels, she drove the car back to the entrance of the yard, where she was able to load her sister—Gracie was not a large girl, only six inches taller and not much heavier—into the back seat of the car. Lainey took Gracie's top off and wrapped it around her sister's head.

She went back into the house and got some rags. Rushing back outside, she cleaned up the blood splatters on the ground. She sprayed a hose on the grass, washing away any evidence.

For a thirteen-year-old, she was an excellent driver and probably would have passed a road test.

Driving the short path into Grover's Creek, she brought Gracie to a region she felt was deep enough. Nobody really went into these woods, at least not till November when there was some hunting going on.

Pulling Gracie out of the back seat, Lainey placed her on the dry ground. Her purse was used as a pillow, and Lainey could see her sister's phone in it. Tempted to steal the phone, she decided not to and instead removed the battery from the phone, leaving both in the purse. Looking at her sister, she was somewhat remorseful for what she had done. Lainey didn't want this, but she could not live in her shadow any more. She proceeded to bury her sister, covering her limp frame with hundreds of leaves.

As a final touch, Lainey parked Gracie's car over her corpse as a headstone.

There was not much more to do.

At five-feet nothing, plus the three-inch heels, the younger sister needed the seat closer to the steering wheel. In her haste, she forgot to re-adjust the seat, accidentally framing her Uncle Wesley.

She found Wesley's ring and an earring on the floor. She could have left the ring on the floor, incriminating her uncle, but her Aunt Brooke had been through enough. With Gracie out of the picture, Aunt Brooke could get her husband back, even if he was a jerk.

Lainey then trudged the three miles back home, launching Wesley's ring and earring—which took an unfortunate bounce and missed the sewer—put away Gracie's heels, went to bed, and didn't have a nightmare.

Seth remembered the old photograph on his desk—that photo of Gracie all alone holding the balloon. The birthday party... Natasha Lowe's seventh birthday party and she had come back home with this huge balloon after winning a game of musical chairs. Anyway, as soon as they hit the front porch, that balloon popped, the balloon popped...

He remembered now. It was Lainey who popped the balloon.

Lainey popped it then and she popped it now...

Gracie would not stop crying for about a half-hour, her life all over because this stupid, insignificant balloon popped. He told her that balloons were meant to die, meant to deflate. They only lasted a moment in our lives, and then... they were gone. A vapor in the wind, a flower quickly fading. Don't get too attached, he told his little princess...

Don't get too attached...

Seth could not understand what she was saying. This was the little girl who turned down any sentiment, friendships, those daddy-daughter dances—everything... Lainey did not want to be a part of his family and so Seth and Evelyn left her be.

If only they had been more willing to look past the scars...

"How could you? How could you lie all this time?" Seth asked.

"You taught me if I can lie about the small stuff... it makes the big lies easier."

Seth knew what she meant—those poker teachings—the only earnest thing Lainey did with her daddy—that and teaching her how to... drive. Seth tried to bond with his... he couldn't even think "his daughter"... but she needed more—she needed to feel loved. Like her depressed Uncle Wesley, she needed a cheerleader, too.

Ellis licked his lips.

"Weren't you the one who called it in?"

Lainey smiled.

"As soon as I called it in you crossed me off as a suspect."

Ellis stared her down; full-knowing he had been out-smarted by a kid.

She continued—one more horrific nugget:

"The ball. I threw it in the street on purpose."

The video. The day when Gracie almost died.

Quietly, Seth spoke:

"Gracie was right. It is my fault."

He paused to gather himself.

"I taught you how to lie."

Seth paused again.

"And drive."

38.

FRESH STARTS?

Placing her box of luxuries down, Vicki stuck her hand out to shake Ellis's. The case was solved and Vicki was satisfied they discovered the truth and things were as settled as could be.

Her work was finished.

She did not want to work for Ellis Kirkbride. The sheriff's insistence that Seth Adams not be charged for stealing his gun and the assault on Wesley, while noble in action, was wrong.

And speaking of wrongs, it took Vicki herself far too long to turn in her Aunt Coralee. While Vicki learned the pastor was a hypocrite, she learned something about herself, too: she was just as much a hypocrite as he was. Vicki should have turned in her old aunt the moment she suspected something. Failing to do that simple task, it was time for her to go.

They shook hands.

"Thank you for your dedication to this case," the sheriff said. "If it wasn't for you..."

"You need to believe in yourself more."

"Maybe. You sure about leaving?"

"Yeah. I'm a city girl."

Vicki didn't want to say she couldn't fully trust him.

"Well... maybe God had some purpose for you here after all."

Vicki raised an eyebrow.

"God? Giving God credit?"

Ellis smirked.

"Stranger things have happened."

Vicki agreed with her former superior. She looked over to smiling Coralee, who sat in her old chair. Yes, stranger things have happened... who would have thought the tough cop from the Big Apple would end up in frigid Wisconsin? Who would have thought that she would figure out a case very similar to the one she didn't secure in New York City?

God thought—cause God knew. That Lord knew Vicki needed to be here to solve it. Vicki was needed in Oostburg, for this moment of their lives.

And the Old Man stood in front of Vicki, blocking the exit out of Oostburg.

Vicki stared, unable to understand who this Old Man was—although deep down inside she knew she was speaking to the big man himself.

He spoke to her:

"You ready to talk to me now?"

Seth was not ready, either.

Looking through the small window of his daughter's door, he could see his little snake strapped to a large hospital bed. She looked lost; not in any place of mind. Just staring. *What had they done to her? What drugs was she on?*

Evelyn walked up behind him to get a glimpse.

"My god... Seth. What are we going to do?"

"I can't do this."

Seth took a couple of steps away from the door.

"I can't. You do whatever you need to do. I can't."

"Can't what—you can't even talk to her?"

"I can't look at her knowing that she was the last thing Gracie saw."

Evelyn licked her lips and looked at Lainey.

"She is our *daughter*. We are going to love her. Is that understood?"

"I have nothing left."

"Nothing? What am I? *You are her father!* We are going to remain a family—"

Seth chuckled.

"A family..."

"Yes, a family! Grace is gone, and I am not losing Lainey either!"

She began to enter but Seth grabbed her wrist.

"No, we're not."

"Excuse me?"

"I can't love this one. I can't forgive—"

"Absolutely not. Let go of me right now."

"We'll start over. Move south. Anything."

"I can't lose her."

"I can't face her."

The two puzzle pieces no longer fit.

Inside the little room, Lainey was calm and ready to tell her story to her therapist, Dr. Ben Malachi.

"I was reading the Bible. The good book with a gazillion phrases and metaphors. Contradictory statements, sodomy, and gonorrhea."

"That's Gomorrah," the doctor corrected the girl.

"I was being sarcastic."

Dr. Malachi gave a small smile.

"I was reading Romans Nine. And I kept reading... I had even memorized it because it was so fitting; so true of my life. And all of a sudden—this—*LIFE*—all made: sense. It all made sense. No wonder my life sucks. God... hated me from the beginning."

She went on to recite:

"Not only that, but Rebekah's children were conceived at the same time by our father Isaac. Yet, before the twins were born or had done anything good or bad—in order that God's purpose in election might stand: not by works but by him who calls—she was told,

"The older will serve the younger."
Just as it is written:

"Jacob I loved, but Esau I hated."

She had the whole thing memorized:

"What then shall we say? Is God unjust?
Not at all! For He says to Moses,
"I will have mercy on whom I have mercy, and I will have compassion on whom I have compassion." It does not, therefore, depend on human desire or effort, but on God's mercy. For Scripture says to Pharaoh: "I raised you up for this very purpose, that I might display My power in you and that My name might be proclaimed in all the earth." Therefore God has mercy on whom He wants to have mercy, and He hardens whom He wants to harden. One of you will say to Me: "Then why does God still blame us? For who is able to resist His will?" But who are you, a human being, to talk back to God? "Shall what is formed say to the one who formed it, 'Why did You make me like this?'" Does not the potter have the right to make out of the same lump of clay some pottery for special purposes and some for common use?"

"I don't want to be common." Lainey swallowed. "I... want to be—loved. I want someone to tell me I am special and not just hide behind Gracie's wing the rest of my life. I am so sick of hearing: *"Gracie this; Gracie that."*

She paused.

"Even in the Bible. God hates some people. God hates me. He loves Gracie and he hates me..."

Dr. Malachi sat in silence. This little girl, cute, but absolutely terrifying, with her flame hair and blue windows, frightened him.

The little girl leaned into Malachi's right ear and very gently whispered:

"I don't want to be Esau..."

And she whispered it again.

And again.

And again.

39.

BROKEN HALO

The Adams' family home was quiet these days.

Seth and Ellis sat on the porch downing beers, lamenting what had transpired the past month. Almost turning into November, the winds were beginning to change color. Interesting scary Halloween decorations were popping around left and right. Seth normally enjoyed Halloween, being a pastor on the slight liberal side; he did not conform to some denominations that felt Halloween was Satan's playground. He did not love Satan or worship him, but Seth could appreciate the playfulness of Halloween. He did not think it was a major crime for kids to parade around in cute costumes begging for snacks. He usually decorated a little himself, but being home alone these days he didn't bother. He didn't even buy candy. Nothing mattered anymore. Life for Seth was... over.

Or maybe just on pause.

"Left Tuesday night; packed her stuff. Haven't seen or heard from her since."

Ellis took a swig.

"Well, she'll come around in a few days, I'm sure."

The two pals sat there looking at the sun setting on another day. It was really pretty.

"So, are you looking for another deputy, now that Vicki is—where is she?"

"Virginia. I'm looking but have no leads."

"Well, nothing ever happens—"

Seth stopped himself.

He could never say that again.

The men paused for a couple of minutes as they watched a bird eat the garbage Seth put out that evening. Normally, Seth would've taken on the bird, but tonight he didn't care. After all, birds need to eat too. God made them with the same needs as humans. Who is Seth to stop what the god ordained? Should Seth pray that the bird would go away? No, surely not. If god wasn't going to bring his daughter back, then surely he wasn't going to take away the bird. At this point, Seth didn't care if the damn bird ate him as well.

Ellis continued the conversation:

"Pretty surprising Raile survived. Two minutes of flat-lining and the doctors were able to bring him back. Doctors, you know? They can do anything."

Seth disagreed:

"If god did his job, we wouldn't need doctors."

Ellis bit his nail for a few seconds and then continued:

"Now we got the guy for life. He confessed everything. Even the phony speeding ticket—"

"Kids aren't supposed to get cancer." Seth looked up. "God didn't get that memo."

"Seth—"

"I'm to blame. Who taught her all those sneaky little things? Me. Who taught her that it was okay to tell harmless white lies as long as they didn't hurt anyone? Me. I taught her how to drive. At the same time as Gracie. Funny, I always thought Lainey was the better driver."

"Seth—"

Staring at the mess the bird made:

"How can I forgive myself?"

Ellis attempted to get his friend back on track:

"We figured out what Raile's last words meant."

Ellis swallowed before delivering the last blow:

"Sex-trafficking-your". He was trying to say "your wife". She was delivering for Raile's sex-trafficking operations. Delivering the money for Raile."

Seth didn't budge.

"It appears that Gracie was not involved with that at all. Because of her... death, countless girls will be spared from that life. And Evelyn won't be charged. She had no idea. I haven't told her, and I do not have any plans to. Always a silver lining, huh?"

Seth ignored the silver lining:

"Why did god take Gracie so young?"

The sheriff turned to his friend. He needed the correct advice to say. He prayed for the right words.

"I bet... Gracie is up there wondering:"

Ellis paused, hoping for the right answer.

"Why does God let wonderful people live so long?"

Seth turned to his bud. Silently, he nodded.

40.

THROUGH EYES OF GRACE

Former Pastor Seth Adams sat in his car, which was parked by the shore of Lake Michigan.

He didn't sleep the night before, or the one before that, or even the one before that. In fact, he couldn't remember the last time he slept; living on fast food and coffee for a while now. Evelyn was gone, and not that he couldn't cook for himself, he just had no... motivation. He wasn't sure he wanted to live anyway. Enjoying his new facial hair; it made him wonder if he should have had a beard all this time.

He also wondered what people were doing. Besides Ellis, he had not spoken to many others since the confession. Through Ellis, Seth knew Evelyn was seeing Lainey on a regular basis. He assumed Evelyn was staying with Brooke, but he really didn't know. It was odd to not speak with your wife for a few days. They had never gone without conversing for this long before, even when they were fighting.

Peering in the great lake, he began to recite his final sermon:

"So what do you do? When someone hurts you so bad? Makes you cry at night wondering why God—why God did You—let this happen? Most of us know t-hat our Lord can do anything. The Almighty. He can change hearts; change lives."

It was at this point that he stopped preaching, and Gracie's soft voice took over. She spoke:

"Can end pain and suffering. But sometimes He doesn't. Sometimes, He lets us go through that pain; that suffering so we can see Him on the other side. How do you rise up during moments of hurt? Do you punch and scream? Do you turn to God for that very first time? Or do you delete it all and start fresh? Do you... ask for forgiveness? Do you continue to question Lord Almighty? Or do you repent? Do you forgive? Heavenly Father, heal the wounds. Let us praise You in the storm. We pray for those out here who are listening to Your word, oh Lord. May we hear You—may we have eyes to view. May we see the world—

—through eyes of grace."

The little girl he mentored all these years was now mentoring him from the beyond. He missed her so much and there wasn't a damn thing he could do about it. He could sit there in his car till his last breath was spent and that wasn't going to change anything. She was gone. Or, he could fly across that bridge and attempt to move on to the next chapter in his life. He could remain with Evelyn. He could forgive Lainey.

He turned to the passenger's seat, hoping to get one more look at his precious daughter, but he didn't.

In her seat was the old man Seth had been bantering with the past three weeks.

"I can't see my Grace anymore. She's beginning to fade."

"That's good. It means you're healing."

Seth shook his head.

"I don't want to heal. I don't want it to be the end."

The old man peered through the windshield, peacefully seeing over the new horizon.

"Who says it's the end?"

Seth grabbed the wheel tightly, perhaps trying hard not to strike the old man sitting in the seat that should have been occupied by young Gracie.

"Who says it's the end?! My Grace is dead. I can't forgive. I can't… preach. Or serve. I can't—"

The old man interrupted.

"Seth—*Pastor* Seth, if I may—a few weeks ago you preached a wonderful sermon. Do you remember what you preached on?"

"Forgiveness."

"Forgiveness. The very night that Grace Adams left this sad, terrible world and went to the simple peacefulness of Heaven. Does that concept no longer exist? Do the acts committed by Charles Raile, Wesley Demko, Lainey and even yourself overpower the—"

"I miss her so much."

"Yes. I know, my son."

"You're… Him, aren't You?"

"I am."

"Then… why?"

"Pastor Seth, do you realize how many girls were saved because of Grace's death?"

Seth didn't answer.

"Because Grace passed away, Charles Raile was captured and repented. Had he not repented, forty-eight other young girls would have been sold into sexual slavery. *Forty-eight*. That is a lot of girls saved."

"A silver lining."

"In a sense, yes."

"Ellis said that."

"And he's not even a Christian—yet." The old man continued: "And not to mention the change in Robert Zimmermann and Charles Raile—both men are seeking my advice these days—your best friend, Ellis. He talked to me for the first time in years. Your precious Grace led to all this healing."

Seth paused to digest.

"Pastor, do you know what Grace is doing right now? She's smiling. A forever of no more fears or suffering. She is safe and sound. Protected from the poor tortures of this life."

"You were there."

"Yes, I was."

"You watched her die, you son of a bitch! You watched her die!"

"I gave humanity free will."

"I don't want to hear that!"

Seth Adams stared into the sunrise. Tears fell down his cheeks as he closed his eyes. He could not understand how god could let him down. He was hurt and seeking. His heavenly father abandoned him.

He hurt so badly. His father hurt him and he did not know why.

As he wrote in his diary:

Did God let humanity down?

God's sort of like the sun, we need it in our lives for warmth and care, but you do not want to sit on it or get too close, either. You'll get burned.

Job got burned. He got too close to God, and God sacrificed him to Satan. Yes, perhaps you can argue that God gave him a new wife, shelter, and children. One might say that was God's very small, indirect apology for screwing Job over. It takes a humble man or being in this case, to say "I'm sorry."

Not once in the Bible does God say: "I'm sorry."

He continued to write:

You can't blame humanity when a person dies during an earthquake, a tornado, hurricane, or flood. When someone expires because of icy or snowy conditions, you can't blame humanity when it storms. When someone dies from a heart attack because they shoveled the snow, you can't blame humanity for the snow. When someone dies because of an icy route, due to the snow, you can't blame humanity.

No, you can't blame humanity for everything.

Childhood cancer? Check. Stillborn babies? Yup, those are on god. Spend twenty years building a home just to see god blow a hurricane and destroy your hard work?

If God wants acclaim for the miracles, it is only perfectly equal that he takes the blame for the tragedies.

If god wants humanity to be held accountable, then he needs to be held to the same standards that he holds us to. And you know what... he needs to be held to a higher standard, because, you know, he's god.

But God doesn't make mistakes, Christians argue.

Why was baby Hitler created?

To fulfill His plan? What a terrible, God-awful plan. God could have easily not created baby Adolf. God knew the horrendous torments that man would pound on society. He could have spared that torment for millions of people worldwide. He knew what that little baby was capable of; he knew how successful Hitler would be.

You still think God doesn't make mistakes?

Had Wesley been home that night—instead of a Bible study—he would have saved his daughters. Wesley savored his children. But he and Brooke were praising the god when the almighty protector was failing to protect. While they were sacrificing time to their Jesus, he was sacrificing their children. Maybe Wesley wasn't so crazy after all.

Seth remembered the final time he saw her, how he was rushing his wife out of the house, too excited for the getaway that he did not have time to really say good-bye to his daughter. Seth didn't know—it would be the last time...

God knew. He knows everything.

He remembered the waitress, Kelsey, who he prayed over in Chicago. She needed to forgive her father for the abuse he caused her. The rough beatings; the hiding of her medication. He hid the medication for a few hours, she said. All that time he could have helped her and he chose... not to.

Her father hid the medication... god can cure cancer by simply snapping his fingers. He chooses not to. Like Kelsey's father, god is hiding cures for cancer, diabetes, AIDS, viruses, everything. We don't have to live in sickness and suffering. God created an impossible test for humanity. He created us to fail and then he punished us for failing the impossible test he created.

That's a tough pill to swallow.

Don't give thanks to god for the umbrella.

Instead, ask god why he created the storm.

He just did not understand anymore.

Seth got out of his car and knelt on the sand below. He raised his head to the Heavens and he fought god and cursed god and praised god and loved god all in one conglomerate of feelings.

And Seth did something incredibly difficult:

He forgave God.

Yes, Seth forgave God.

Seth returned to his car and sat.

"I don't understand, why, when I needed you the most, you would leave me."

"Son, every storm ends with a beautiful rainbow," the old man reasoned.

Seth pondered that and to be honest, it bothered him dearly.

He didn't want a beautiful, colorful streak in the sky that would vacate in a matter of minutes.

He wanted his Grace back.

And even though he forgave the old man, he couldn't trust the god anymore.

"It's time to move on to the next chapter, my son."

Seth agreed.

He kicked the old man out of his car and took the wheel.

Standing outside, the old man said: "I love you, my son."

Automatically, Seth recalled the line from *Twelve Angry Men*... the line Gracie couldn't get:

Does anyone think there still is not a reasonable doubt?

He had nothing.

He lost... his wife and his daughters, his mission; his job, his congregation.

He lost his faith, hope, and love.

And the only thing that remained was doubt.

A reasonable doubt.

41.

THE BEGINNING

Seth left his car and walked down the beach towards the lake,

leaving behind one set of footprints in the sand.

I would like to thank my friends for helping me with the editing process over the last few years. The insights and advice I have received from you have been monumental in the development of this story.

Vicky Almgren
Toots Habermann
Pastor Elizabeth Jaeger
Miranda Lorenz
Julie Lyon
Sandra Mahuta
Dr. Russ Petersen
Coralee Sandee
Phil Sofia
Danielle Staggs
Tracy Wolff

Thank you,
Dave

To my wife Stephanie,
my daughter Brooke,
my sons Seth and Ellis,
my mother Karin, my father Richard,
my brother Erik and my sister Kari:
I love you.

Kris 'Krissy K' Morse is a contemporary nature artist residing in Cascade, Wisconsin. Kris is a mother to Jacob, Kelsey and Connor and wife to her best friend, Bob. Kris is a self-taught designer and her fine art acrylic paintings, pet portraits and murals can be found throughout North America. For more information on this artist, visit:
www.krissykmorse.com or www.instagram.com/krissykdesign

Made in the USA
Monee, IL
06 February 2021